Two women—each fighting a passionate struggle to hold on to her virtue . . .

Two stories—of wicked scandals, heartbreaking betrayals, and the healing power of love . . .

One book—from "one of the romance genre's greatest storytellers" (*Romantic Times*) . . .

Edith Layton

For the first time in one volume:

The Disdainful Marquis
and
The Abandoned Bride

The
Disdainful Marquis

AND

The
Abandoned Bride

Edith Layton

A SIGNET BOOK

SIGNET
Published by New American Library, a division of
Penguin Putnam Inc., 375 Hudson Street,
New York, New York 10014, U.S.A.
Penguin Books Ltd, 80 Strand,
London WC2R 0RL, England
Penguin Books Australia Ltd, Ringwood,
Victoria, Australia
Penguin Books Canada Ltd, 10 Alcorn Avenue,
Toronto, Ontario, Canada M4V 3B2
Penguin Books (N.Z.) Ltd, 182–190 Wairau Road,
Auckland 10, New Zealand

Penguin Books Ltd, Registered Offices:
Harmondsworth, Middlesex, England

Published by Signet, an imprint of New American Library,
a division of Penguin Putnam Inc.
The Disdainful Marquis was originally published by Signet in September 1983,
copyright © Edith Layton, 1983.
The Abandoned Bride was originally published by Signet in May 1985, copyright © Edith Felber, 1985.

First Signet Printing (Double Edition), June 2002
10 9 8 7 6 5 4 3 2 1

A NOTE FROM THE AUTHOR

Gentle Readers, just a word about these two books Signet has put in one volume:

The Disdainful Marquis was written because I couldn't get one of the characters in *The Duke's Wager* out of my mind. I got many letters from readers who couldn't forget him either. They wondered about Sinjun, the Marquis of Bessacarr, and what became of him, even though he was a callow fellow in that book. I thought about it and decided that time and experience could make him into the man he should have been in *The Duke's Wager*.

The second book was inspired by a conversation I had with my editor, Hilary Ross. We were talking about subjects that had never been used in a Regency romance. Thus: *The Abandoned Bride*, a book that conquered a taboo, pleasing us both very much. We hope you agree!

So much for triumphs. Sadly, I have to admit that I am fallible. (Well, sometimes.) But yes! I can be wrong and beg your pardon for it. You see, there are some misuses of titles in both these books. And so I hope that if you can absolve Sinjun of mistakes made in his ignorance and see that he can grow into an altogether worthy person, you'll give me the same chance and forgive my earlier errors too.

With all best wishes, and wishing you happy reading,

Sincerely,
Edith Layton

The
Disdainful Marquis

*For three particular graces:
Dottie, Gillian and Renée.*

Chapter 1

The pavements were gray, the houses were gray, the very air was gray with cold October fog. Although it was a damp mizzly dank day in London, the fog did have its capricious moments. Here and there it lifted its skirts, or blew in little skirlish puffs to create small pockets of translucence so that anyone who had to be abroad on such a wretched afternoon had at least some small chance of finding their direction. But they had to be quick about it and gain their bearings to head in the right direction before the fickle mists encompassed them completely again. It was altogether a dreadful day for a stranger to be traversing the city, with the fog being so coy and whimsical.

The inhabitants of the city were used to the weather's vagaries, in much the same way that they might be used to an eccentric aunt's changes of mood. Those who had to be up and about traveled the streets with an air of grim tolerance, and they called comments to each other about how she was a right terror again today. But those who could afford to, avoided the outdoors entirely. And so the fog, most democratically covering the city's length from its most palatial houses to its most wretched stews, ironically only served to point out the undemocratic distribution of wealth and class. The poor groped about the town because they had to, the rich stayed snug at home because they chose to, and the only other travelers were the adventurers.

The occupants of the hired coach that picked its way through the mist-shrouded streets did not feel like adventurers. The rotund gentleman who kept tapping his neat little well-shod foot against the floorboards and consulting his gold watch and emitting periodic stifled sighs felt put upon, and his every ill-concealed gesture of impatience showed it. He was cold; the damp had crept through the floorboards and the ill-fitting windows of the coach into his very bones. He was bored, traveling through the gray city with nothing but gray vapor showing outside the windows. And he was hungry; his watch clearly showed teatime, just as his stomach had been telling him for the last hour. Yet every time his companion glanced at him, he tucked the watch back into his pocket, put on a brave smile of sweet forbearance, and pretended to gaze out the milky windows with active interest.

"Poor Arthur," his companion thought guiltily as she watched him once again check his timepiece and heard another little muffled sigh. She smiled brightly at him and wished again that she felt half so bright as she pretended. In truth, if he felt cold and weary and his every motion showed that he thought himself on a fool's errand, then she felt colder and wearier because the whole day had been a crashing disappointment. Added to that, she knew she was the fool who had sent him on the errand. But he only suffered boredom and hunger. She was enduring the pangs of crushing defeat.

It had seemed so reasonable, Catherine remembered, when she had been back at home, carefully penning all the letters to the London employment bureaus, stating her qualifications and expectations of a position. It had seemed so correct a course to take, seeking some kind of genteel position in Britain's greatest city, so as not to be any further burden upon Arthur or her stepsister now that they were expecting an addition to their family. For despite all their protests to the contrary, she knew that it was not right that they should support not only a new marriage and the coming of a new baby, but also an unwed stepsister as well. And a stepsister who, she felt, could well be able to support herself if only she were not a resident of a little country town. But London! She had been sure she would be able to find a place for herself there. But she hadn't. And now the coach was taking her to her last interview, her last chance to find a post. For she knew Arthur would never again take her to the City, and never allow her to go by herself. It was propriety and duty that had forced him to come so far with her; if she failed, he would be careful not to say "I told you so" more than a dozen times to her, for he was basically a kind man, but he would never be persuaded to leave Kendal on such a mission again.

She glanced down again at the small pasteboard card she held tightly in her little gray glove. "Introducing Miss Catherine

Robins," it stated in flourishing script, "to see Her Grace the Duchess of Crewe in reference to a position on Her Grace's staff." It was signed, with another discrete flourish, "The Misses Parkinson, Employment Counselors." It was the last card she had. The other six lay, crumpled and used, deep in her reticule, mute testimony to her failures in the past two days.

Yesterday, on Catherine's very first call, Mrs. Oliphant had taken her card, taken one look at her, and screeched, "Oh no, my dear, you'll never do. Reely, you won't do at all. Why, just take a look at Mum, just have a look. Why, I can't even lift her when she's a mind to be propped up for tea in bed. How can a slip of a lass like you do it?"

And, in truth, Mrs. Oliphant's mama had just lain there deep in her bed like a beached whale and grinned up in concurrence with her daughter. "Aye," she had puffed, "my arm's just the size of your waist, luv," and she had wheezed with laughter at the look on Catherine's face when she lifted said member and waved it about.

"But," Catherine had gone on gamely, "the agency said you required a lady's companion, not a nurse."

"Nurse!" Mrs. Oliphant replied, affronted. "Mum don't need a nurse. She's sharp as a tack just as she always was, but a lady's companion don't just sip tea and tattle. No, we need someone to shift her, now and again. Get her up out of bed when the weather suits. Dress her and lead her about now that she's not too sure on her feet. No, my dear, you'll never do."

"You don't weigh up, lass," the older woman had cackled, from her bed. "That's all. You'll do when you gain a few stone."

Catherine hadn't "done" for Miss Coleman either. That aged spinster had given Catherine a few sharp looks and then had said in her crackling voice, "Not suitable. Sorry, Miss Robins, but you're too young to have one thing in common with me, and I do like to while away the evenings in friendly chatter."

She had been "too young" for Mrs. Webster's great-aunt, and "too inexperienced" for Sir Stephen's mother-in-law. "Not what we're looking for," Mrs. Bartlett had said succinctly, and Lady Brewer hadn't even given a reason—she had just sighed and said in her fadeaway voice, "Oh, not at all suitable." And Mrs. White had just given her one gimlet-eyed look and snapped, "Not in this house, my girl. Not with three young sons on the premises. We want an older female to companion my aunt."

Catherine sat erect and listened to the horses' muffled tread. This call was her last, she had left it for last because she had felt that a duchess would be far harder to suit than any mere Mrs. Whites or Mrs. Oliphants. In fact, she had thought not to dare try for the position of a duchess's companion. But now she had to—it was her last chance. If she failed at that, it would be back to Kendal, back to Jane and Arthur's little house, there to wait for their children to arrive, to be a dependent till she dwindled to nothing more than a dependent devoted auntie. For she had no finances and no parents, and her birth placed her too high for Kendal's sheep farmers to aspire to, and her dowry too low for anyone higher. Most of Arthur's merchant friends were married and even the vicar had a large and hopeful family. No, the duchess was her last chance, she thought, as she sat up straighter and thought frantically of how she could present herself so that she could at last "suit," and wondered why she had so far failed so ignobly.

The coachman could have told her. But she was a lady, so he didn't dare be so cheeky. But when she had loomed up out of the fog to step into his coach, he had, for one moment waxed poetical and thought that in her muted cherry pelisse she had looked like a little robin redbreast come to cheer up London on a dark winter's day. In that moment's lapse of fog, her well-spaced sapphire eyes had twinkled up at him, and he had drunk in her fresh white complexion and noted, with approval, one saucy nose, two delightfully red lips, and a cluster of ebony curls beneath her gray bonnet. He had warmed for one moment, just looking at her.

Her brother-in-law could have told her. All the fellows he knew had tweaked him, from the moment he had married Jane, about the two dashing-looking females he now housed. Jane was well-enough-looking, they had teased, but to have another smashing-looking female under his wing as well was the outside of enough. He had laughed with them, for they meant no harm, but it did give a fellow a sense of well-being to come home to two delightful young women, to be stared at when he prome-naded with them, one on either arm, to be waited on after dinner by two attentive and lovely young women. Not that he thought of his sister-in-law in that way, no, that would be most improper. But it was rather a treat to have her around. He would be glad when this job-hunting nonsense was over and she came back to Kendal with him and they could go on just as before, the three of them. As for ever telling Catherine that she was a stunner, that was a thing that just wasn't done. While Jane might tell him that Catherine took no account of her looks at all, that was too much to ask a fellow to believe.

But of all the reasons for her failure in obtaining a position that Catherine tortured herself with, her looks were not brought into account at all. She thought raven tresses were commonplace, and bright blue eyes unexceptional, and her complexion ordinary, and her overall appearance unfortunate. She conceded she was not ill favored, but that was all. For Mama had been a pale and stately blonde, and her half-sister, Jane, had also the fair hair and light hazel eyes that were Catherine's only standard of true feminine beauty. Papa, she remembered from far back in the dim recesses of memory of childhood, had been dark haired and blue eyed. That was well enough for a male, but it was Mama who had been beautiful and feminine and sought after. And Jane, who seemed from her five years' seniority over Catherine to be the most beautiful of females. Catherine thought of many reasons for her failure as the coach proceeded through the streets of London, things that ranged from wearing the wrong sort of gloves to not speaking clearly or standing straight enough, but never once did the thought of simply being too young and too alarmingly lovely enter her mind. No one, after all, had told her so. Except for Mama and Jane, and they were just being kind. And a few scalawags in the streets over the years, and they were just being rowdy.

"This is the last call," Catherine said to Arthur, as she saw him lift the watch out of his pocket again.

"We'll finish up early then," he said, "and go back to the hotel for some tea. Then we'll leave straight away in the morning, and it won't be long before we're all snug at home again."

Catherine winced.

"There is the possibility that this time I might succeed, Arthur." Only a hint of reproachfulness was in her voice, and Arthur missed it altogether.

"Oh, aye. Of course there's that possibility, but it is unlikely. As I said before, some young gently born females have to go out and toil for their livelihoods, and some do get positions. But only after much privation. And then that is only when they are willing to sacrifice some of their, ah, expectations. They get harder, my dear, and they get more worldly-wise. It's just as well that you discovered this for yourself. Now I think it wasn't such a bad idea, this trip. Once you're done with all that air-dreaming, you'll be happier. As you should be, with a devoted sister, and myself of course, to look after you. You will understand how fortunate you really are, and be content to settle down with us.''

"I know I am fortunate in you and Jane," Catherine said as she had said so many times before, "and you do know how grateful I am, but Arthur, can't you see, I just wanted to do something for myself and not be only a burden?''

"Burden? Nonsense," Arthur said, warming to his favorite theme and crossing his hands around his stomach, which Catherine knew was calling for sustenance. She had noticed that Arthur, plump to begin with, was adding to his substance at a pace to almost equal that of Jane, who expected their baby in the spring.

"As if family could ever be a burden. When I met your sister, I knew of your closeness and never did I expect anything other than your coming to live with us when we wed. I made that clear to Jane at the outset. I have often wished for a large family—it was one of the sorrows of my life that I was an only child. Family is the backbone of the nation.''

Arthur went on, as he had done so often in the past on the virtues of family, while Catherine looked out the window again, seeing the city slowly pass by, trying to make out the shadowy figures that flitted by on the pavements, and hoping that some wildly wonderful thing would come to pass. Perhaps she might turn out to be the image of dowager duchess's long-lost sister, or perhaps the dowager had a little dog who would rush to her and the dowager would cry, "If FiFi likes you, the matter is settled. You must come to work at once.'' Or perhaps the dowager would be a sweet little old woman who would offer her tea and say, "I know just how difficult this must be for you. I have been looking for some pleasant young woman to keep me company,'' or then again she might say . . .

"We're here, miss," the coachman called.

Catherine felt her hands turn to ice. And her heart began a faster beat.

"Arthur. I won't be long. But if I'm delayed, there's no need for you to sit here freezing in the coach. Why don't you go back to the hotel, and I'll take another hackney back and meet you when I'm done.''

"Nonsense," Arthur said staunchly, with an air of seeing things through, as she knew he would. "I'll wait right here.

Can't have a young female on the loose alone in London. I'll wait right here. After all, it's your last call.''

Catherine shivered at his words and stepped out to the pavement and stared at the imposing entrance of the house before her. The fog had lifted for a moment, making the entrance of gleaming white steps dramatically clear. Catherine swallowed, only to find she had nothing to swallow, and began to walk toward the steps with much the same gait of someone preparing to mount a gallows. Her gaze was so fixed on the door above the street level, the door with the beautiful fanlight glasswork, the door that might either open onto a new future for her, or onto the end to her hopes of independence, that she almost collided with a pair of gentlemen who emerged suddenly from out of a bank of fog.

"My pardons, miss," said the closer of the two gentlemen, and after a look at her face, he went on more fulsomely, "a hundred pardons. It's this confounded fog. One moment the way is clear, the next I've almost run you down. Are you all right?"

As he had not even brushed against her, Catherine could only reply distractedly, "Why yes, quite all right."

But the gentleman, dressed, Catherine noted absently, in the first stare of fashion, only stood and gazed at her, bemused.

A deeper voice intruded.

"Cyril, the lady is fine. I suggest we move on so that she can reach her destination."

Catherine peered up to the speaker, who was so very tall that the fog, in a show of frivolity, shrouded his face as it might a mountain peak. He was dressed in unobtrusive grays that further blended with the day.

"But, Sinjun," the other gentleman protested, "I might have done her an injury. Or frightened her, looming up like that, out of the fog. Are you sure you're unharmed, miss?"

"Quite sure," Catherine answered, suspicious of the gentleman's inclinations to linger, and wondering if Arthur was watching this incident through the coach window. He might get it into his head that she was being molested and spring from the coach and make a scene, and if the duchess heard the altercation, her interview would be over before it began.

Seeking to end the conversation promptly, and yet not be rude, for these gentlemen might be friends of the duchess, Catherine asked the taller of the two, whom she could not see so well, rather than the shorter, who was staring at her in the most improper fashion, "Is this the Duchess of Crewe's address? In the fog," she temporized, "I cannot be sure."

"Oh yes," the taller gentleman answered in an amused tone, "to be sure it is. Never fear, you have come to the right place."

There was that in his voice, that undercurrent of sarcasm, that made Catherine look at him again. The mist, bored with veiling his face, drifted away, and she found herself looking into a pair of icy gray eyes that seemed as if they still held the depths of the fog in them. He was very handsome, Catherine thought with alarm, lowering her eyes from his frank stare, and very insolent.

As she turned to mount the steps, she heard him say again with amused cynicism, "You have come to exactly the right place, I believe."

"Good day," Catherine said firmly, sure that in some strange way she was being insulted and knowing one did not bandy words with strange men, friends of the duchess or not. She went up the stairs, lifted the door knocker, and rapped more firmly than she would have wanted to, in an effort to escape the two men's attention. But when she turned to look down again at he street, she could only see their shapes receding in the distance.

The butler who took her card almost took her breath away with it. He was old, and large, and impeccable. He looked at her with no expression and yet made her feel as though she were standing in her nightdress. "Yes," he said after he glanced at her card, "come this way." Without further comment he led her into the largest hall she had ever seen. It was floored with marble, and lined with spindly chairs. And each chair held a woman, sitting erect, each with a reticule, and a packet of letters on each lap.

"Oh," Catherine sighed to herself, her spirits sinking further than she had thought possible, for it seemed that every unemployed lady's companion in the kingdom was there waiting to be interviewed, before her.

By the time the clock at the end of the hall had discreetly chimed four times, Catherine had gotten sufficient control of herself to observe the other females in the hall. She had a moment's fleeting thought for Arthur, sitting chilled in the carriage outside, waiting, but she could no more have left than she could have asked the butler to dance. She was here now, she reasoned, and she would see it to the end.

There were twenty-three other females in the hall. Each one studiously ignored the other. Some stared into space. Some busied themselves with bits of needlework and some were browsing through small volumes that they had brought with them. They were representative, Catherine thought with sorrow, of the entire spectrum of women companions. There were some who were elderly and looked like timorous spinsters. Some were motherly-looking women, large in their persons and almost dowdily dressed. One or two were elegant-looking middle-aged females, who looked as though they themselves might be advertising for companions. There was one huge muscular woman who might have easily belonged behind a barrow, hawking turnips. Catherine wondered if she might drop a hint about the elderly Mrs. Oliphant's search for a companion, for that woman looked as though she might be able to turn both her and her daughter in bed without a thought. But the women all sat silently, and she could no more speak to the female beside her than she could have whispered in church. None of the women looked happy, and all, she thought, wondering if there were some truth to Arthur's lectures, looked downtrodden in some fashion. Worst of all was the realization that she alone was under middle age.

Miss Parkinson, Catherine thought frantically, would not have sent her if she felt she would have no chance. It was true that she had looked at Catherine and whispered, "Oh, dear. You are not at all what I expected from your letters." But when Catherine had explained her mission, and convinced her that she had nursed her own late mother through her final illness, Miss Parkinson had said, filling out the cards, "Might as well have a try at it. But," she had cautioned, "a lady's companion is not an easy life, child."

Looking at her fellow applicants, Catherine could well believe that. They all seemed resigned to their waiting, to their very lives.

After the butler had admitted two more prospective companions and seated them, he reappeared.

"The duchess," he intoned, "is ready to begin her interviews." And he motioned for the woman closest to a door at the end of the hall to come with him. She was a spry wiry woman with spectacles. With ill-concealed eagerness, she closed the book she was reading and sprang up to follow him. After a few minutes, in which Catherine had only time to smooth out two of her gloved fingers, the little woman reappeared. She seemed confused and walked the gamut between the outer circle of applicants and disappeared out the front door. "Obviously," muttered a hawk-faced woman in black bombazine, "inferior references."

The next woman to be called, a heavyset elderly woman, left the room after what seemed like moments, looking puzzled. And after that the succeeding applicant stalked out angrily after what could only have been a moment, muttering, "She's mad." The remaining women began to mutter among themselves. One by one the applicants disappeared, only to reappear after an indecently short time.

"She could be deranged," whispered a timid-looking woman sitting near Catherine. "But then," she added with a smug little smile, "my last was quite gone in the head and I stayed with the poor soul until the end."

"I," said one of the elegant women, "shall not work with a mad person. An eccentric perhaps, as my last dear lady was an eccentric, but charming withal. But not a raving lunatic."

One by one the others were shuffled in and out so quickly that Catherine doubted they had the time to present their credentials at all. The duchess, she reasoned, must be relying very heavily upon first impressions. And when the muscular woman went in, and returned so quickly that she must not have had time to have said a single word, Catherine was convinced of it. As she sat and watched, it seemed that only the two more stylish-looking applicants were given time for any decent conversation in their interviews. And yet the last one left very angrily, stating firmly to those who remained, "You are all wasting your time; this whole interview is a farce." And then Catherine was called.

Remembering to remain calm at all costs, Catherine walked slowly across the room in the wake of the butler. He opened a door, and Catherine found herself within a room facing the duchess.

She must be a duchess, Catherine thought dazedly, for I should know her for a duchess anywhere.

The room was small, but richly furnished. It had been the duke's study at one time, and it still had a very masculine air. The duchess stood ramrod straight in back of a huge mirror-polished walnut desk. She stared at Catherine. And Catherine, bereft of speech, could only stare back. The duchess was tall, and thin, and very old. Her hair was white, not the commonplace snowy white of most elderly persons Catherine had met. It was rather the color of ice, as were the two direct cold eyes that fastened upon Catherine. The duchess had a great long imposing nose and gaunt slightly rouged cheeks. She wore a gray dress and was altogether the most imposing, imperious woman Catherine had ever seen. She looked almost as though the title "duchess" was too insignificant for her; rather, Catherine thought, she should be addressed as "Your Highness."

"Well," the duchess brayed in a loud nasal voice, quite shattering the image, "now this is more like it. How did a poppet like you get in? Who are you, my gel?"

Catherine fumbled her papers out and laid them carefully on the desk. "Catherine Robins, Your Grace," she said in a low voice.

"Speak up," the duchess commanded. "If you want to companion me, you must be more forthcoming. Why does a young thing like you want to be companion to an old woman?"

"I need to find a position, ma'am," Catherine said, in a clearer voice.

"And how does your family feel about it? Got any family?"

"I have a sister—well, actually a half-sister and a brother-in-law—in Kendal, ma'am. He, my brother-in-law, does not want me to go, but my sister does approve—that is, of my desire for independence." Lord, Catherine thought, I'm making a muddle of this.

"Can't blame your brother-in-law, he must feel like a fox in a hen house. Can't blame your sister neither for wanting a good-looking baggage like yourself out of harm's way." The duchess chortled.

Catherine wondered whether she should hotly defend Arthur or Jane or herself, but the duchess was actually smiling benignly at her now, and she wanted the position so badly she let the comment pass.

"Tell me, my gel," the duchess asked, unbending enough to sit, and motioning that Catherine do the same, "got any experience?"

"Here are my references, ma'am," Catherine said, spreading out the papers. "From the vicar, and the schoolmaster, and the others from my home—"

"Not those," the duchess cut her off. "I mean, any experience of life?"

"Well, yes, ma'am," Catherine faltered, not knowing quite what the duchess was getting at.

"You'd travel with me," the duchess went on. "I travel a good bit. I meet a lot of people, all kinds of people—you ain't a shy one, are you?"

"Not at all," Catherine replied, for in truth, she was not a shy person.

"Not frightened of men, are you? Or prudish? I can't stand a prude."

"Not at all," Catherine replied, thinking she was more frightened by the duchess than by any man she had ever met.

"Didn't think you were with a saucy face like yours. So you've come to London to see the queen, eh? And hope to be my companion. Well, you're more in the line of what I'm looking for than any of those biddies out there. You have an air of real gentility. Related to anybody important?"

"My father was a younger son," Catherine said, putting up her chin. "And we were related to the Earl of Dorset."

"Then what are you doing out looking for a position as lady's companion?" the duchess cried out ringingly, looking angry and affronted for no reason Catherine could fathom.

"We never corresponded with the family much after my father's death," Catherine admitted, "and not at all after my mother's remarriage, which they did not approve of."

"Black sheep? Better and better." The duchess smiled.

"What would your family think of you flying across the Continent with me, meeting all sorts of people?" she challenged.

"As I said," Catherine went on, "there's only my sister and brother-in-law, and they want only what would make me happy."

"So they're cutting line from you? Don't blame them. What I'm saying, with no more roundabout," the duchess said, leaning over and looking keenly at Catherine, and cutting off her indignant reply, "is, are you free and footloose? Are you ready for a lark?"

"Yes," Catherine said, wondering why a companion would find life a lark, but feeling that if any came along she'd be quite ready.

"Get up," the duchess suddenly barked, and, startled, Catherine did so.

"Turn, no, turn that way. You are a good-looking gel in any light," the duchess said impassively. "But I'll bet you've been told that by the gentlemen before."

"No, of course not," Catherine protested, totally at sea, and wondering if the duchess were in fact, a little deranged.

"Haw. You're a good little actress. Sit down," the duchess said, "and I'll put the proposition to you. You can let down your hair now and be frank. Your job would be to travel with me and to accompany me on my rounds. And to make sure I'm comfortable. I have a lot of friends. A lot of gentlemen friends, and I'd expect you to make them comfortable too, in a different way. You get my meaning?"

Catherine didn't at first. The first meaning she thought of was clearly preposterous and she was ashamed of herself for even thinking it. But she certainly was conversable and tactful enough to chat up any old gentlemen the duchess entertained to put them at their ease. So she nodded, so many thoughts crossing her mind that she was momentarily speechless.

"Good." The duchess sighed. "I thought I was right about you. My usual companion, Rose, the lazy slut, has gone off and left me. And Violet, who sometimes travels with me, has gone and got herself another position. So I'm left in the lurch and I'm off to Paris in a month and demned if I'll go alone or with any of those old crows out there. So, gel, you understand?"

"Paris?" breathed Catherine, unable to take in her good luck. Was she being offered the position, in Paris?

"But let us get it clear. I travel in a fast set. You are very young. Perhaps you haven't understood. Are you worried about what people will say of your reputation?"

Catherine had the giddy instant thought of a group of old gentlemen and ladies being pushed rapidly in their invalid chairs or gambling wildly in their nightcaps while their attendants and nurses stood waiting to take them home to bed.

"My reputation?" Catherine thought quickly, searching for a precise answer that would satisfy the duchess as to her maturity and independence and put an end to this odd interview and perhaps win her the position she so desperately wanted. "My reputation," she said loftily, "is my own concern."

Seeing the wide grin on the duchess's face, she hastily added, "That is to say, it is excellent. It is widely known."

"All the better." The duchess beamed. "Fine then, gel, you've got the position."

Catherine was so dizzy with happiness that she could only sit and stare at the duchess, who was smiling at her in the most conspiratorial, friendly way possible.

                          *   *   *

In a study very similar to the one that Catherine and the
duchess sat in, one, moreover, only three doors down the street,
two gentlemen sat in front of a cozy fire and smiled at each other
in a conspiratorial, friendly way.

"Sinjun," cried the younger one, waving a brimful brandy
snifter at his friend, "a toast to the luckiest of chaps. I swear you
are. Did you see the eyes on that filly? Blue as a summer sky.
And moving in here right under your nose. All I have on my
street are retired army gentlemen, and Sir Howard with two of
the ugliest daughters known to mankind. And you've got the
dowager and her lovelies right on your doorstep."

"I've also," drawled the taller man, putting down the papers
he held, "got all this work you've brought me. And if I've read
it right, it means I have some traveling to do."

"But not immediately, dear fellow. You've time to set things
up. We don't expect you to hop off immediately. And in the
meantime, what a lovely diversion you've got right here. 'Is
this the Duchess of Crewe's address?' she says. Why, that
means she's practically under your roof already. You just have to
nip down the street and collect her."

"I don't," the taller man said, stretching out his long legs,
"traffic with the duchess's companions."

"But in her case, you could make an exception; Sinjun. She's
a stunner, and new on the town too."

"If she's in the duchess's employ, I doubt it. At any rate,
Cyril, I seldom pay for what should be free."

"Oh, I didn't know you were purse pinched," the younger
man laughed. "That'll be news to La Starr. How did you acquire
that new bracelet she was sporting last week, for nothing?"

"I don't pay cash on the line." The taller man smiled. "Because
I don't like to stand in line, and the dowager's doxies traffic in
volume, as you know."

"What a lost opportunity for you then," Cyril mourned.
"Still, a toast! To the fairest wenches in London, to the dowager's
doxies."

"I think not," his companion demurred.

"Then one to the old lady herself: to the dirty dowager."

"No," his friend said gently.

"Then curse it, Sinjun, you propose a toast. I'm desperate for
a sip of this '94."

"Very well." The taller man took his glass in hand and intoned, "A toast: to work." And he handed the papers to his friend. Cyril groaned. "To work," he sighed, and dashing down the drink, he bent over the papers.

Chapter II

The Dowager Duchess of Crewe sat back in her late husband's favorite chair and waved her butler away. She lifted the glass of port that he had brought her and raised it in a silent salute before she allowed herself a sip of it. And then, alone in the study, she leaned back in her chair and sat, eyes closed, smiling to herself. Even in repose she retained her air of dignity and power. Even while relaxing she maintained her rigidly imposing countenance. With her gleaming white hair pulled back to show her strong features, seated behind the massive gleaming desk, she presented the perfect picture of a woman of consequence, a rich stone in an exquisite setting. She was a fine figure of a woman. It had not always been so.

For all women, and men as well, there is one point in life when they are beautiful, truly beautiful. There are some rare fortunate few who retain beauty all through life. But for most, they must make do with that one moment of physical beauty. And no matter how ill favored, every person experiences that moment. Nature is kind in that fashion, but she is unpredictable.

Thus, when the midwife cries in delight, "It is a girl, and a perfect, beautiful girl!" there are times when that is strictly true. At that moment, never to be repeated, the baby is indeed one of the most beautiful infants ever seen. For others, their summit of physical perfection comes in the toddler years. Still others are graceful, beautiful children and visitors will often comment, "She is a beautiful child; she'll be a real heartbreaker when she's grown." Alas, that is often not true. For that particular child the epitome of beauty may exist only in that one afternoon of childhood. Later the snub nose may lengthen, the plump jaw grow rather like a lantern, the bright hair dim, and the glowing promise never be realized. For her, the moment came and passed in early childhood.

Still others are the envy of all their acquaintances in the years of early youth. For one brief incandescent time, the girl is lovely. But it is only for that time, never to be repeated. Others do make beautiful brides and the assembled wedding guests may swear they have never seen a lovelier bride and not perjure themselves. Yet, let as little as a few weeks go by and the vision is gone. Some are beautiful in the months of impending maternity, some as young mothers have an unearthly radiance that rivals religious paintings, some reach a glowing peak of ripened beauty in their middle years. For all, if they but live long enough, the moment will surely come. But it did not come for the Duchess of Crewe for almost seventy long and barren years.

Born as a simple "Mary," fifth child and second daughter of the Earl of Appleby, she was a thin and red-eyed infant. Raised in the shadow of three hearty, boisterous brothers and a jolly older sister, little Mary looked rather like a shadow as a child. She was thin and pale with mouse-hued hair, and where the Appleby nose sat well on her father and brothers' faces, it overshadowed all else on her lean countenance. Sister Belle had mother's impudent nose, and grew to be a buxom, dashing sort of girl. Mary remained thin and gray-faced, although she elongated considerably as she grew and soon towered over both her mother, elder sister, and one of her brothers.

Nature, having given an impeccable lineage, an earl's castle to live in, and an impressive dowry to lure suitors with, did not see fit to overendow her with intelligence, beauty, or personality. Hers was a lonely childhood, but she did not seek refuge in books, as they were too difficult to read, or fantasy, as it was too much trouble to invent, or friendships, as there were too few children up to her weight in status or fortune.

When she reached the age of twenty-four, her father was reminded that he still had one great hulking girl at home who had received no offers even though she had been dutifully togged out and brought to London each season. He was a forthright man and it was a simple matter to remedy. After a hard day's hunting with his old school friend, Algie, Duke of Crewe, it was discovered that Algie had a son who was ready to be shackled into matrimony. At twenty and seven, George was a very eligible parti. He was no vision to set a maiden's heart thumping, being

Edith Layton

rather squat and square. He had not done too well at school, and his conversation consisted solely of horses and hunting, but he had the right breeding, fortune, and when his father quit this world he would be a duke. At dinner that night, between the buttered crabs and the haunch of venison, the matter was settled to all concerned parties' satisfaction.

At the wedding, the bride was not beautiful. Impending maternity only made the prospective mother ungainly and uncomfortable, and when her first child was born, no unearthly radiance transformed the new mother's face. Nor did it for the second, third, or fourth child. After the fourth heir arrived, duty done to king and country, George, now Duke of Crewe, devoted his amatory attentions solely to his amiable mistress in town, to his own, and his wife's, great relief.

Mary, Duchess of Crewe, had led a long good life. But something was missing. Some small niggling worm in the apple troubled the Duchess of Crewe obliquely during all those long privileged years. Not being a clever or introspective female, she never examined the problem too closely. But it was there, and it grew as the years went on.

For with all that she had had, she had never had attention, or at least any she had not paid for. No heads ever turned when she entered the room, as they had for jolly Belle. No one ever cried, "We must have Mary to our masquerade, she is such fun!" Rather they remembered that the Duchess of Crewe should be invited. George, while he lived, accepted that she was his wife as he accepted the fact that the title was his from the moment he could toddle. Her children knew that she was Mama, and that she must be visited every day for an hour when Nanny brought them to her. The world knew the Duchess of Crewe, but she was not in demand. For such a large female, she was, withal, seldom noticed.

In the natural way of things, if the duchess had succumbed to a chill in her sixth decade, she would have passed an unexceptional sort of life. The world would have briefly noted her passing and gone on smoothly. But her health was vigorous and two great events changed the course of her life forever when she contemplated her seventh decade.

First, George died, and she noted his absence more than she had ever noted his presence. And secondly, nature at last blessed her with beauty. It was nothing short of miraculous, almost like the transformation of a plain window pane after frost has touched

it in the night. For age came to the Duchess of Crewe and
brought a great transformation overnight.

It turned her gray-speckled mouse hair to the color of silver. It
hollowed her cheeks, turning mere leanness to high imperious
cheekbones. At last, her unfortunate nose found a face that it
fitted, and, thinned down, it stood high and hawklike, a perfect
object for two glittering myopic eyes to peer down over. Her
rigid, angular body suited an old woman to perfection: In youth
it had been awkward, in her dotage it was imperial. Her height
was no longer uncomfortable; it became regal. She had been an
unobtrusive woman; she was now an imperial old woman. Nature
kept its promise at last.

For the first time, Mary, Duchess of Crewe, excited attention
and admiration when she entered a salon. Strangers in the street
glanced at her. She was an ornament at the theater. No one ever
again forgot her after an introduction. When she appeared, heads
turned, and the gentlemen showed her every courtesy. Even the
greatest arbiters, the other society matrons, deferred to her. At a
great age, the duchess suddenly discovered all the unfair advantages of physical beauty. But equally suddenly, it was not
enough.

Much as a born actor after his first taste of applause, the
duchess discovered the one ingredient that had been missing in
her flavorless life: attention. And as much as she received, it
was not enough.

It was only an unsatisfactory brief shower, falling after a long
parched life. She wanted more than a taste of it. Now, at a time
when many of her contemporaries were content to settle back and
watch others live their lives, she wanted to begin hers. She
wanted to bask in that rare and lucent light that had always
eluded her, the full glare of public attention. But there were
impediments.

She was aged, she was female, and she was alone. Her
children had all grown, married, and presented her with batches
of uninteresting descendants. She could not look to them. She
had few friends, and no close ones. And none of them could
have given her what she wanted.

She was done with tea parties and tame entertainments. She
sought glory. It hardly seemed fair or just that now that she had
been presented with a new face and a new aspect, she should
languish in obscurity. She felt as a young girl might when her

body ripened to a woman's, that there was an attractive stranger within her that she must introduce to the world.

She had heard of the sort of life one could lead if one were wealthy, titled, and attractive. She had heard of, but never seen, the gambling establishments, the fast parties, the masquerades and travel adventures of those select few who cared for nought but pleasure and excitement. And knew that as a duchess she could have entrée to any of them, once. But that there would have to be something special about her to permit her constant presence.

It was a set, she had heard, made up of the cream of the gifted: the poets, the musicians, the authors, the intellectual, the beautiful, and the amusing wealthy eccentrics. She had now presence, beauty of a sort, and wealth. She would have to see to the rest.

Her first companion was a Lady Wiggins, a noble woman who had fallen upon hard times. Together they had traveled to Bath and to Brighton and had received an invitation to a house party at the country seat of a notoriously rakehell lord. All that she had heard was true. She found excitement, gaiety, amusing company, and a sense of privilege. She was accepted, admired, but then, ultimately ignored. For she had no special cachet, no entertaining conversation, no wit, nor even scandalous history.

Her next season, she traveled with Mrs. Coalhouse, a younger woman with pleasant looks and a genteel manner. And although the duchess now cultivated the affectation of taking snuff, and had gone so far as to purchase outrageously expensive antique and imported snuff boxes, this eccentricity was only duly noted and not remarked upon. For in an age where the reigning eccentrics kept upward of a hundred dogs, or traveled without male companions to the Near East, or rode horses into drawing rooms, a handsome elderly female who took snuff was not much noticed. Even her newly emerged forceful personality was not enough.

The following season, in a sort of desperation, she combed carefully through all the applicants for the position of companion. She stopped checking their references and began to note only their physical persons and personalities. For if she could not develop her own startling personality, somewhere in the recesses of her mind she reasoned that she could buy the services of one. Her choice settled on one Miss Violet Peterson, who was nothing like any lady's companion the duchess had ever seen. She was, to the duchess's myopic eye, more like the sort of female who ran the gaming halls and parties she had lately been to.

Violet was young—still in her twenties, the duchess thought, although a clearer eye could have said thirties with more certainty. She was buxom, and red haired, and staggeringly attractive. Her dresses were all slightly too extravagant: a bit too low, a bit too colorful, a bit too embellished. But she was bright and alert and cheerful as a songbird. Men's heads swiveled when she flounced into the room. She was, the duchess thought, sometimes a bit too cheeky, but there was no harm in the girl, no harm at all. If it came to that, she was good company, even though it was not company the duchess was after, but the admiration of company.

It was during that first season with Violet, at the country home of a notoriously dissolute duke, that the first whispers about Violet came to the duchess's ears. The whispers grew louder at Brighton, and by the time they got to the scandalous Lady Chester's country retreat, they were a roar. One late evening at the faro table, a noted gossip, a beau of the ton, eyed Violet as she left the room a few moments after their hostess's husband had signaled to her and he leaned over to the duchess. "I say," he said in a loud stage whisper, "did you know that your companion has spent more time between our host's sheets than her own? And for a price higher than the stakes we're competing for?"

Two high red spots appeared on the duchess's cheekbones. All the others at the table were pointedly looking elsewhere, but all were listening. If her sensibilities were offended, the duchess knew it would be social death in this room to admit to it. She decided to brazen it out, and, in a somewhat confused state of agitation, referred instead to what she felt were Violet's good qualities.

"Let the gel be," she said in stentorian tones. "She gives good service. Worth every penny she asks."

The duchess was a raging success after that. She and Violet were welcome to every affair they wanted to attend. If they were not welcome at the sort of parties and houses that the duchess was used to frequent during her long years of social correctness, well, she had put all that behind her now anyway. Attention was paid to the pair of them wherever they went. The duchess, through no overt act of her own, was now considered an amusing, clever, and charming eccentric. She even had the felicity to overhear society's pet bad girl of the season whisper to her cicisbeo, "There goes the Duchess of Crewe. Isn't she delicious? So dignified, so correct, such presence, such wit, to have a common trollop as companion. Plying her trade in the best houses. Oh, it's such a clever comment on society."

So the duchess turned a deaf ear to propriety, and only cautioned Violet not to get above herself or to involve her employer in any of her doings, and to fulfill her duties as companion before she set off on any "larks" of her own. And Violet, who had been, in her turn, actress, opera dancer, kept woman, and then, only in dire financial trouble and fear of turning to the streets, desperate enough to try for the position of lady's companion, was all too eager to agree.

After another season with Violet in tow, Rose came along. Claiming long friendship with Violet, Rose begged for any position in the duchess's household. The bailiffs were at her door, Lord Lawrence had withdrawn his protection, and she, at thirty-three, was too long in the tooth for any more ingenue roles in the theater. Rose was blond and billowy and friendly, and within months the duchess had two female companions in tow. And her reputation was assured.

Polite society might shun her, her children might plead impotently, but she had a title of her own, and money of her own, and a tenacity of character that only the none too intelligent might claim. It was possible, her children's lawyer said patiently, that they might, after a scandalous, arduous court battle, proclaim her incompetent, but again, it was possible that they might not. The dowager went her way unmolested to all the resorts and masquerades and parties she desired, and she desired them all for all the attention she had starved for all those unawakened years.

And if she heard the whispers about "the duchess's doxies," as the satirists were quick to dub her companions, she pretended not to hear. The contrast between her rigid aspect and her companions' life-styles tickled those she sought to impress all the more. And if she saw the caricatures in the shop windows of "the dirty duchess," she was careful not to recognize their subject. Her dignity in the face of such vilification was an exquisite delight to her champions. Yet, all the while, in some recess of her mind, she took it as tribute. There was the distinct possibility that if her children had not been so browbeaten and afraid of scandal, they might have won their case.

And now in this chill winter of 1814, she had narrowly escaped missing another promised treat. For Violet, that wench, had only just sent notice she wasn't coming to Paris as she had netted the Marquis of Wolverton's protection. And Rose, that simple ingrate, had come and prated on about true love and the reformed gambler with whom she was going to settle down.

Even the Duchess of Crewe could not advertise for a trollop. And she had no notion of how to go about acquiring one as companion. One couldn't just pick a girl off the streets. And she could not very easily ask her butler or a footman to frequent a house of ill repute and choose any stray female. And she certainly could not be seen going to one herself. She never chose to think of exactly how her companions earned their extra keep. The whole thought of what transpired at those houses made her ill. So she had cast her net again, asking employment bureaus for a companion and hoping to luck upon, by accident, another woman like Violet, in the same way that she had gotten Violet, through the applicant's own bold deceit.

For three days she had interviewed women of all classes and sizes and condition. To some that she had felt were marginally suitable she had hinted at her purpose and their duties. Those who had understood had left in a huff, or stared at her blankly, apologized, and left. But then this lovely little wench, Catherine, had appeared. As pretty as, or prettier than, the selfish ungrateful Rose and Violet, and not so long in the tooth either, the duchess thought. And she seemed ready for any rig that might be running. The duchess finished off her port and rose to stare out the window. There was a great deal to get done. Travel arrangements to make, dresses to buy, reservations to plan ahead. But her major concern was settled. She had another companion. One who would really make them stare in Paris. And give her employer an international reputation.

After the coach had left them at the hotel, Catherine and Arthur spent the next two hours in a corner of the lobby, in hot debate. She was weary and excited, and would have loved to have been somewhere more private and comfortable. But Arthur was shocked at the idea of discussing anything in their rooms. She might be his sister-in-law, she might have lived in his house for almost four years, but she was a single woman. And he was a man not related by blood. Arthur had very exact notions of propriety.

He refused to postpone their discussion till dinner, for he knew that heated conversation was bad for the digestion. So they sat at a little corner table, beneath a very sick potted palm, and spoke in hushed, but agitated tones.

"She is a duchess, Arthur," Catherine insisted again, "and very dignified. And if she wants a young companion, I am sure that it is so that she may be cheered up a bit."

"I still," he said, as he had said for the past hour, "do not think it a good idea. You do not know her, or her family, or the conditions under which you will be employed."

"Arthur," Catherine cried loudly, and then ducked down and flushed for she had not wanted to raise her voice, "you knew all that when I first went to apply for the post. And yet you took me anyhow."

Arthur flushed a little himself and, because he was by nature not a devious man, admitted, "I just thought that it would help you get the whole mad notion out of your system."

"You didn't expect me to get the post!" Catherine accused.

"No, I didn't, and to tell the entire truth I still don't know why you did. One"—and here Arthur raised his plump fingers— "you haven't the experience. Two: You are far too young to companion a dowager in her dotage. Three: No matter how well born you are, you have never had traffic with the nobility. Why hasn't a duchess a whole slew of acquaintances and relatives who could recommend a companion to her?"

Seeing the momentary hit he had made, Arthur went on, "Four: You don't know London. And Five: It is dangerous to travel abroad to Paris, even if Napoleon is mewed up on Elba now and the hostilities have ceased, with a female whom you and your family do not know."

"One," said Catherine in a hot whisper, "she doesn't care about work experience. Two: I am twenty-one, old enough to be able to be good company for any female. Three—oh, dash it, Arthur, I do want this post. She is a duchess and wealthy so I won't suffer any privation; truly, I can't see how I would. And perhaps it is just that she is lonely. And, after all, dear Arthur, it won't be forever. She said just for the season, to see how we will suit. It is October now; by summer I should be home again. And if I am not happy with her, I shall come home to you and Jane and the baby, and be a good devoted auntie and never stray again. Only I'll have earned the wages to buy the baby a present all on my own, at last. That is, if you will have me back?"

Arthur patted her hand in embarrassment. She looked so woebegone. Her bright blue eyes were brighter with unshed tears, and a little crease had appeared on her white forehead. He felt like a beast.

"Of course, we'll have you back. We want you back so much we don't want to see you go." He laughed, and she laughed with him at his unfamiliar excursion into humor.

"But I do worry about you. You are such a bright girl, Catherine, but you haven't any experience of the world. I worry about you over there across the channel with a strange female in charge of your destiny."

"Oh I make no doubt," Catherine laughed, "that she will sell me into bondage, and have me locked into a dank rat-ridden cell if I don't do her bidding. Arthur, do understand, it's not that I love you and Jane less that I wish to be independent; it's that I love you the more."

"But if you feel that way, no matter what we say, why come so far, to London, to be a menial? Why not contemplate marriage? You are a fine-looking girl, Catherine." Arthur was a little shocked by his presumption, but he was earnestly trying to counsel her, and was casting all inhibition to the winds.

"Oh, I do contemplate it," Catherine said ruefully, creasing her gamine face into a parody of sorrow and causing Arthur to chuckle. "But who is there to contemplate me? With all of two shillings as dowry. Arthur, there is no one for me at home. Perhaps there might be someone for me in London, or Paris."

"Your head's been turned by those two dandies I saw you asking the duchess's direction of when you got out of the coach," Arthur accused.

"No," she said, "they were way above my touch. And one doesn't meet one's future husband in the street."

She rose and shook out her skirt.

"Now, Arthur, shall we cry off this battle? You know, and I know, that the thing is done. Or are you trying to starve me into submission? I haven't eaten in so long, I shall forget whether to use a fork or my fingers. Come, let's have a lovely reconciliation over dinner."

Arthur sighed and rose, conceding defeat, and heeding the insistent clamor his stomach had been setting up for past hours.

They sat in the hotel's dining area and chatted amiably through all the courses. And by the time evening came Arthur bade Catherine good night at her door without one further premonition of doom about her future employment.

In the morning they breakfasted in solemn silence, and then

Arthur collected his bags and Catherine's. She wanted to accompany him to the stage to say good-bye, but he insisted on loading her case into the hackney to drop her off first. "You must never go unaccompanied, Catherine," he said sternly. "You must write us your address in Paris," he cautioned, "and be quick to come home immediately if anything goes awry."

It was a bright morning, and the hackney found the duchess's house with no trouble. As Catherine made to leave, Arthur stayed her. "Here," he said gruffly, reaching into his pocket, "no young woman should go without funds," and he pressed a small purse filled with coins into her hand.

"But I shall be earning money," she said, returning the purse. Then she bent swiftly and pressed a quick kiss on Arthur's cheek, which made him color up. "I do love you and Jane," she said in a shaky voice. "And I do thank you for all your concern."

And then quickly, before she should embarrass herself and Arthur again, she stepped out of the coach. Her trunk was handed down to her, and she stood on the curb, in front of her new home, and waved farewell to Arthur. The last look she had of him was of his worried face at the window.

Then she turned and went to mount the stairs to the Duchess of Crewe's house. There was no fog this morning and no mysterious gentlemen to unsettle her by saying that it was exactly the right place for her. But it was, and she went up the stairs.

Chapter III

As soon as the maid had left her, Catherine went to the window of her new room. And when she saw that she was safely two floors above the street level, and that there was no way any eyes but pigeons' could peer into her room, she turned and went directly to her bed. And sat there, bouncing up and down, giggling softly to herself just like a child. For if this is what Miss Parkinson had meant about a companion's life being a difficult one, she did not think she could have borne an easy one. The luxury would have flattened her completely.

She had, late in the night, when all of London had lain sleeping, been too afraid and too apprehensive to sleep. For once she had realized the position was indeed truly hers, she had at last the leisure to be anxious about her future and the opportunity to have all the second thoughts Arthur would have wished her to have. It had taken all her courage to be confident and light-hearted when she had taken leave of Arthur.

But once she had presented herself at the door, the butler had signaled to a footman, who invisibly signaled to a maid, and she had been, with no further comment, taken to her new room. And such a room! Catherine thought that no cosseted daughter of an earl could have been housed so extravagantly.

The room was large and airy, with windows overlooking the street. It was furnished with graceful taste in hues of green and white, picked out with pale yellow. After a few minutes of dazed delight, Catherine shook herself mentally and went to the wash pitcher. After only a few seconds of admiring its graceful gold trimmings, she poured water into a bowl and resolutely scrubbed her face and hands. It was time for work. Later she might have earned the leisure to simply sit and admire her room. She braced herself and went downstairs to begin her duties as companion to the Dowager Duchess of Crewe.

All her fine resolve was wasted. The butler informed her impassively that Her Grace was still abed, and, further, that she had left no message for her new companion. So Catherine spent her first full day of gainful employment too wrought up to properly luxuriate in her new quarters. Instead, she paced the room awaiting her employer's summons.

It did not come that day, nor the next, nor even the next. Catherine had time and to spare to memorize every detail of her delightful room. She was informed, each time she asked, that the duchess was variously occupied: at her mantua maker's, with her man of business, or dining out with friends. And, no, she was answered blightingly each time she inquired, there were no shawls to be mended, nor was there any knitting to unravel, nor even letters to copy out. In short, there was nothing for her to do but to wait upon Her Grace's pleasure. The members of the duchess's staff were uniformly polite to Catherine, but all those she encountered as she drifted through the house in search of occupation seemed in some indefinable fashion to look down upon the new female in their midst. Contemptuous, and rightly so, Catherine felt, of a female who was clearly not earning her way.

As the week wore on, Catherine began to wonder why the duchess had bothered to employ a companion at all. And once, in a small hour of the night, she sat straight up in bed in horrified alarm as she wondered whether the duchess was so advanced in years as to have forgotten the existence of her new companion altogether.

However, in the sixth day of her employment, while she was reading through a volume of poetry, Catherine received a summons to be present at her employer's side. She put down the volume with slightly trembling hands, smoothed down her wayward hair, and pinned a smile to her lips. At last, she would begin.

The duchess was sitting up in bed when Catherine was shown into her chamber. Even in bedclothes, she looked imperious and dramatic. She squinted up at Catherine and then motioned her to sit down. She seemed to be consulting a list she had on her lap, along with the dregs of her morning chocolate.

"There you are. Been settling yourself in, gel?" she boomed at Catherine.

"Yes, Your Grace. I have been waiting for your summons, and ready to be of whatever assistance you require."

"Why would I require your assistance here, in my own house?" the duchess asked with amazement. "I have everything I need here. Got Gracie—she's a lady's maid who knows her business." And here Gracie, who'd been picking up about the room, sniffed disdainfully, met Catherine's eye for one bleak moment, and then went back to work. "And that old stick of a butler, Griddon, to see to the running of things, and Mrs. Johnson to order up the house. No, I don't need you yet, gel. Can't keep calling you gel, neither; Robin's the name, ain't it?"

"No, Your Grace. It's Catherine."

"Catherine then. I'm getting all my plans in train for our little jaunt. Paris! It's been years, and now we can go again. Parties and folderol, and good fun. I can't wait. I called you here to see if you're ready."

"I'll be ready to leave whenever you are, ma'am," Catherine said. "At a day's notice."

"A day's notice." The older woman guffawed. "Not likely. Not with what all I've got to get readied. What are you wearing?" she demanded suddenly, staring at Catherine fixedly.

Catherine glimpsed down at herself in horror, wondering whether she'd spilt something on her gown. But no, it was the neat pristine gray one she'd worn the first morning. It had been nearly a week since she'd arrived and she'd worn each of her gowns in succession, so if it was Thursday, it would have to have been her gray.

"It's ghastly," the duchess went on. "Ain't you got something livelier?"

"I do have one gayer frock," Catherine heard herself say, thinking of her simple sprigged tea gown, the prize of her wardrobe, that she kept for visiting at home, and that she had worn to a house party with much favorable comment.

"It won't do. I don't know what your game is, and I don't care. Maybe there's some that like a gel that looks like a nun, maybe there's a few that will find it amusing, but it won't do. You've got to dress with some dash. I can't have a little mouse, no matter how saucy a mouse, trailing through Europe with me. You've got to be togged out right."

Catherine thought with panic of how she could dress up her meager wardrobe with dash, for in truth, she realized, a companion couldn't look shabby. Although her dress was considered proper by Kendal standards, this was, after all, London.

"Good thing I took a good look," the dowager grumbled. "Get me my paper, and some ink, and a pen, gel."

Catherine hastened to obey the duchess's command, and brought her writing implements from her inlaid desk. The dowager mumbled to herself as she scrawled a note, pushing aside coffee cups and napery as she did so.

"There, good as gold. Go to Madame Bertrand, she's the one Violet used to go to, and she looked fine as fivepence. Even Rose gave up her modiste when she saw what an eyeful Violet looked when Madame Bertrand got through with her. She'll set you up."

"But," Catherine protested, accepting the note the dowager thrust at her, "I haven't received wages as yet, and I don't think I can order a new gown as yet."

"I'll stand the nonsense, gel, and I don't want you ordering one gown. Give me that note back. I thought you was up to the mark. Why did that demned Rose have to go and get herself tied up?" the duchess complained as she scrawled another line on the bottom of her note. "Go out today and get yourself suited up in style. Got looks, but no style."

The maid who suffered to accompany Catherine to Madame Bertrand's sat opposite her and looked everywhere but at her. She was a plump downstairs maid, and found getting into the carriage a treat, and had even vouchsafed as much to Catherine. But when Catherine had agreed eagerly, and tried to begin a lively conversation, the girl had recalled herself and shrunk back into silence. The duchess, Catherine thought, must be a high stickler for the social order of her servants.

They rode in stately silence through the streets of town till the coach stopped in front of a plain shop window on one of the busier business streets. One dress was artfully arranged in the window, and a great deal of drapery covered up the rest of it. But as there was no name or even number visible, Catherine hesitated to alight. The coachman, a jolly-looking young freckled fellow, held the horses and sent a footman to lower the steps.

"You're here," he said, leaning down and looking into the coach, and giving the downstairs maid a ferocious wink. She colored up and pursed her lips and looked expectantly at Catherine, so that Catherine had no choice but to dismount.

Opening the door to the modiste's establishment was like

opening the door onto a new reality. Whereas the outside of the shop might have been discreet to the point of plainness, the interior reminded Catherine of what she had always imagined a harem to look like. There was a quantity of rich fabric tossed about a large carpeted room. Several couches and divans and chairs stood at odd angles everywhere. Bolts of scarlet velvet, royal blue gossamer, and shining emerald silks lay opened and half opened, spread out for display over all unoccupied surfaces.

There were a few women dressed in dazzling style peering at the bolts of fabric, and, to Catherine's surprise, there were also a few fashionably dressed men lounging or sitting and gazing at the women and each other through quizzing glasses. There was a low babble of talk as she entered, and, to her chagrin, the conversation seemed to come to an abrupt stop as she stepped into the shop. Both the women and the men, Catherine realized, were staring at her with undisguised curiosity.

She held her head high and motioned the maid to sit, and when a small black-eyed woman approached, wearing a quantity of measuring tapes about her neck, as if they were a priceless necklace, Catherine held out the duchess's note.

"I am Catherine Robins, the Duchess of Crewe's companion. She sent me here to purchase some gowns."

There was stifled laughter from somewhere to Catherine's left, and the other occupants of the room began talking again, some, however, still staring at her fixedly.

"Right," said the little woman smartly. "She says you're going to Paris. You're dressed for a convent now. Come along, I'll take things in hand."

She led Catherine, who was trying to hold her head high and ignore the attention she had caused, to the back of her shop. There, in another room, were several tables, each with a row of girls stitching. She walked past them and took Catherine to one of a few curtained partitioned stalls. As Catherine stood undecided as to what she should do next, one of the curtains billowed and a ravishing-looking woman stepped forth. She was tall and statuesque. Her hair, great golden masses of it, had come loose with her dressing, and she swung her hips slowly as she stepped up on a little dais in front of a mirror in the center of the room. Her heavily lidded eyes lit up with satisfaction as she caught her reflection.

"Perfect," she breathed.

Catherine stood transfixed. She had never seen a gown so low in the front that most of its occupant's person seemed to threaten to spill out at any moment. The fabric above the high waist seemed sufficient for a waistband, and the magnificent creature in the gown surely needed three times that much before she could go out in public. Still, she had to admit that the startling vibrant blue color and the extreme cut of the gown made the woman in it an unforgettably vivid picture.

"He'll be pleased," the woman said and smiled at herself in the mirror. "But I want him to see me in the amber, so he'll come across for that one." And, without further ado, the sensational-looking female reached behind her, unbuttoned a few buttons, and quickly slipped out a few pins. Then with a shrug, she stepped out of the gown, leaving her entire person, Catherine noted with shock, nude from the waistline up, and only wearing a gossamer-thin demi-train below.

Catherine gaped. She had seen her sister nude, of course, on rare occasions when they were growing up. And seen herself, when she was undressing. But this female was as unaware of her nudity in front of strangers, even though they were all female, as a child might be. Although, she thought quickly, as she watched the woman's eyes linger lovingly on her own reflection, she was not quite unaware of herself after all. And there was nothing childish in her expression of self-satisfaction. She swept past Catherine into her cubicle agian. "Bring the amber one quickly," she ordered. "He grows bored quickly."

The middle-aged woman looked at Catherine impatiently. "Come along," she said. "Let's have a look at you without that nun's habit on. Come along, strip it off and I'll be back to have a look-see. La Starr's in a taking, and I have to get her amber gown seen to if she's to get it from her gentleman today."

Left alone, Catherine hurriedly removed her dress. She held her discarded gown in front of her chest as she waited, chilled, for the dressmaker to return. There was a small mirror in the little alcove, she noted, and she realized that the other female could just as easily have seen herself there in privacy, without swaggering out to display herself in front of strangers.

As she waited she could hear the voices of a few other women admiring their gowns or calling for changes in them. None spoke in the accents she thought acceptable for a lady. Bored, and feeling cold, she watched her reflection in the mirror. Her black hair had come loose from its pins again, and there was a high flush along her cheekbones. On an impulse, seeing her reflection

clutching her gray gown in front of her, and hearing no one
approaching, she lowered the gown from in front of herself. She
gazed at the reflection guiltily. Hers, she thought aimlessly, were
higher and a better shape than the other females'. And then,
scandalized by her train of thought, she whipped the gown in
front of her again and held it in a death grip.

"Let's have a look," the dressmaker said, bustling into the
alcove with her. "Take that gray rag away; I can't see through
it."

Catherine lowered the gown again, shrinking with embarrassment.

"Right," the little woman said briskly. "You're a knockout
all right. The dowager's grown some taste, leave it to her. I
know just the things that'll do. Almost the lady, that's the
ticket," she muttered to herself, and left again.

"I can't," Catherine cried out, fifteen minutes later, as the
dressmaker told her to turn around. "I can't possibly appear like
this in public. I am a companion, not an actress. This gown is
lovely, but it is not seemly." She had been resigned to the
duchess providing her with a new wardrobe; after all, one's
employer had the right to dictate in matters of an employee's
garb. But this gown and the others that the dressmaker had
shown her were out of the question. At the dressmaker's brisk
insistence, she had allowed herself to be pinned into it, but she
knew it was entirely unsuitable in the dressing room, and now,
in front of the mirror, in front of the other girls at their sewing,
she knew it was impossible.

It was of a rich and ruby red, and it was so low in front that
even her spanned hand could not cover the naked expanse it
showed. Looking down, she could clearly see her breasts as they
appeared to her when she was in her bath. The reflection showed
little less. The waist was high and its folds clung and draped
about her lower person so that she seemed to have been mired in
some rich red sea kelp that outlined all her lower body. Her hair,
untidy from changing so often, had loosened and curled. The
whole effect was that of a wanton.

"No," she said desperately, "I know the duchess would
never approve."

The dressmaker snorted.

"In a pig's eye, my girl. Didn't I have the entire dressing of
Violet? And then Rose? Never fear, the duchess will approve.
Come," she said, more kindly, "it's the very thing. It's all the

rage. You're going to Paris, my lady, and anything else would make you a dowd. And the duchess can't abide dowds.''

Seeing the indecision on Catherine's face, the dressmaker began to chuckle, as if struck by a new idea.

''Come, let your maid see it. She'll tell you what all the fine ladies wear, and what the duchess likes. Come along, come with me.'' And taking Catherine by one cold hand, she pulled her into the outer room.

Catherine allowed herself to be tugged forward by this intractable little woman and before she had time to think of the audience that lay outside the door, she found herself the center of their attention.

She stood, cheeks high in color, eyes wide and expectant, in her incredibly indecent gown, in the midst of all the strangers waiting in the front room. There was a sudden quiet as she entered. Conversation ceased as they caught sight of the lovely young woman before them. Catherine held her head high and wished to disappear into the ether as she heard the dressmaker, through the pounding in her ears, ask the little maid what she thought the duchess would say. But curiously, the dressmaker's eyes were not on the little maid, but rather watching the tall blond-haired female she called ''La Starr'' in the bright amber dress. The blond woman had been posing and turning and posturing in it, showing it off to a gentleman, before Catherine appeared. And the moment that Catherine appeared in the doorway, the gentleman's eyes left her and did not return to her. She stared angrily at Catherine.

Catherine looked over in their direction and saw the amused gray eyes staring at her insolently. It was incredible how she had not forgotten a detail of his face since that morning in the fog. He stood leaning against a mantel, his long athletic form impeccably clothed in gray again. His face resembled, Catherine thought, a picture she had seen of a red Indian, with his cool angular good looks, high cheekbones, and black hair. But his look held mockery and disdain and an infuriatingly belittling humor.

He glanced over at the dressmaker. ''I applaud you, madame,'' he drawled, ''as I am certain the duchess will. You have turned a little country mouse into a dazzler. Congratulations.''

He walked slowly over to where Catherine stood poised for retreat, although perversely refusing to flee in the face of his impudence.

''I see you found the right place, little one.'' He smiled with what was not at all a smile. His eyes lingered at her breasts, and while her hands itched to fly up and cover herself, she only stood stock still and tried to return his stare with all the dignity she could muster. "See if you can make my little Starr something on this order," he said over his shoulder. "It is a most impressive display of . . . taste." And then, with a careless shrug, he turned and went back to the blond female, who was darting glances of the purest dislike at Catherine.

"Who," Catherine panted, stripping herself out of the hated dress with fever in the curtained alcove, "was that insolent man? That popinjay, that man who spoke to me?"

The dressmaker spoke through a mouthful of pins.

"Who?" Catherine insisted, buttoning herself all wrong in her haste to get back into her good, decent little gray dress again.

"He is the Marquis of Bessacarr," the dressmaker said placidly. "A neighbor of the duchess's. I expect that's how he knows you. And you should be flattered that he did. He doesn't acknowledge everyone, you know."

"He need not acknowledge me," Catherine insisted, setting herself aright again. "He need not ever acknowledge me again."

Catherine left, with her maid in tow, carrying the few parcels the dressmaker had readied for her. The rest, she promised would be delivered as soon as might be. She had turned a deaf ear to all of Catherine's protests, telling her she knew well enough what would be a suitable wardrobe for the duchess's companion.

Catherine swore to herself, on the way home in the carriage with the stony-faced maid, that she would sit up nights if need be, adding on fabric to those indecent bodices. Style or no, she was never again to be ogled in that fashion.

Madame Bertrand sipped her tea and chuckled at her work table. It had been worth it, even though it had cost her some trade, just to see the look on La Starr's face. Brazen little hussy, going to her competitor for her dressing when she was in funds, and coming back to her dear Madame Bertrand when she was sailing the River Tick. Madame Bertrand knew her clientele well—they were the cream of the demimonde. And she had discovered that La Starr was going to a society modiste when she was in clover. But now, when her protector, the marquis, was growing bored with her, she had entreated her old friend to let

her pose in a few gowns to see if he would bite and purchase
them for her. But he had paid for only the blue one, after all.
And after seeing that black-haired new beauty, he might not buy
her any others either. Well, Madame Bertrand thought, there
were plenty more where La Starr came from, both for herself and
for the marquis.

"Sinjun," the blond woman cooed at her companion as they
walked down the street, "did you not like that amber gown? I
swear I thought it would suit you down to the ground."

"It would hardly suit me, my dear. Amber is not my color,"
he said in a low amused voice, "and it did not suit you so well
either. But that is not strictly true. Truly, I grow weary of
clothes shopping with you. I think in future you should go
yourself. I will draft you a check, my dear, to better enable you
to do so. Oh, don't look crushed. It will be a very substantial
amount—just recompense for the delightful time we have spent
together. But I think the exclusive nature of our acquaintance is
over. After all, I plan to be traveling again soon, and it would
not be fair to tie you to one companion now."

"Travel to Paris, for example," she said spitefully, "where the
duchess might have a companion to compensate your idle hours?"

"Hardly," he said, with real amusement. "Her companions
are not so exclusive, you know. And it was the exclusivity of our
relationship that I valued. As well as your own delightful self.
One may admire a thing without wanting it," he said slowly,
"much as one may admire a public prospect, such as this
pleasant well-worn thoroughfare, without wanting to spend all
one's time on it. It is too public a place, after all. Private places
bring more pleasure."

Mollified, she sauntered along with him.

"Sinjun," she asked sweetly, "shall we have a farewell party
exclusively and privately together tonight? At my expense?"

He smiled down at her.

"You do me honor," he replied.

"You will have to do me a great deal better," she said
roguishly.

And, laughing, they went on, in total understanding and accord.

The gentleman was not laughing a few short hours later. In
fact, St. John Basil St. Charles, Marquis of Bessacarr, paced the
floor of his study in a singularly humorless state.

"Damn it, Cyril," he swore, with unaccustomed vehemence, "I thought it was to be Vienna. That is where all the business is going on. Why in heaven's name did he decide upon Paris? It is over and done with there. What earthly good can I do for you there?"

His friend sat and watched the marquis in his travels around the carpet.

"Sinjun, the old chap is never wrong, you know. I thought it was to be Vienna too. But he said that he had enough of his fellows there. What he needs, he says, is a good ear in an unexpected place. Paris, he said, and it is Paris he meant. You will be seeing him soon yourself, and doubtless he can explain it better than I can. But he fears treachery on all sides, and his man in Paris is a looby, he says. 'Sinjun's the chap for it,' he says. Everyone will accept you as just another merrymaker, and you can find out whose loyalties belong to whom. It's a hotbed over there now, he said, with some supporting the old Bourbon and some still working for Bonaparte. He won't be easy in his mind about Bonaparte till he's two years dead, you know."

"And that I can't blame him for," the marquis said, sinking at last into a chair. "But I had felt that I could do more good in Vienna. I have done before, unless he's come to doubting me now?"

"Nothing like it," his friend assured him. "He still thinks you one of the best agents he has. But you're well known in Vienna now, for all your subterfuge. You've practically got the stamp of the foreign office upon your forehead, he says. And you can't work well unless there's *some* doubt as to your aims, you know."

"It's not so bad as that." The taller man grinned. "But I'll grant that there may be a suspicion there that I'm not just another disinterested tourist. But Paris just now is filled with fools, with empty-headed nits who've gone for the fun and games of it. And I suppose I'm to be just another one of them?"

His friend nodded with a sympathetic smile.

"Ahh, my reputation," the marquis sighed, passing a hand over his forehead. "My lamentable reputation."

Cyril laughed aloud at that. For the marquis had posed as many things, many times, in his jobs for the foreign office. Aside from that, if there was ever a man who cared less for his reputation in the ton, Cyril did not know of him. The marquis had never cared for what any other soul in the kingdom thought of him, or any other soul in Spain, or France, or Italy, or any of the places to which he had traveled since he had enlisted his services in the war against Bonaparte. It was that, the old chap said, coupled with his winning manner and his natural intelligence, that had made him such an invaluable asset to their operations.

"Paris it is, then," the marquis said derisively. "I will have to pack my dancing slippers."

Cyril rose to go and stretched himself.

"I suppose," he yawned, "that you'll be taking Jenkins? Where is he, by the by? I haven't set eyes on him in some time."

"Down at Fairleigh, taking care of estate business. He's very good at that too, you know. But he'll be here like a shot when he gets my message. He's like an old gun dog—one sniff of powder and all else flees from his mind."

"Just like his master, eh?"

"Don't let him hear you say that; Jenkins has no master. He chooses to stay on with me and work for me. We have no title for his duties as yet, not even after all these years. He is estate manager, overseer, accountant, and, most of all, friend. As it is, I'm delighted to just be his friend and be able to employ him. He's the one man I trust in this whole weary world."

Cyril turned back at the door and pulled a hurt face.

"Oh, you don't trust me, Sinjun?"

"Not so far as I could toss you, old dear." The marquis smiled slowly. "For if the old chap told you to place a knife in my ribs, you'd do it without a backward glance."

"I'm hurt, old fellow, wounded to the quick. For I would give a backward glance, you know. To see if Jenkins was after me with another knife."

They laughed and parted with a handshake.

The marquis went to his desk to write a note to his estate manager, valet, traveling companion, assistant, and friend, Jenkins. He smiled to himself and was actually laughing softly as he added a last flourish to the note. That would get the old boy running, he thought. A hint of subterfuge, spying, lying, and the possibility of mayhem, and Jenkins would drop anything he was doing to come along. Cyril was right, he thought, Jenkins was just like him. When they had met those years ago in Spain, they had each recognized it. The marquis had been on the crown's business, and Jenkins a batman who had just lost his officer. Exactly who had saved the other's life when they had met they had never resolved, but each had instantly appreciated the other. Regardless of class distinctions, education, and lineage, they had banded together, recognizing their common bond.

There was a time, the marquis thought, the smile fading from his lips, when style and reputation had meant everything to him. More than honor or love or duty. And only now could he jest about it, only now could he remember it without shrinking, as though remembering a thing he had read once in an old book rather than lived himself.

For he had been born to a title, and born to a dignity. Yet before he had reached his majority, his father had gambled it all away, as well as his mother's health and life, all save his title. And he had inherited nothing but the title and a mountain of debts. And a handsome visage and a strong body and agile mind. He had gone out and earned his money, at tasks and trades he chose not to mention to the world, and invested the proceeds wisely and husbanded them well, and not only rebuilt his father's lost fortune but added to it as well. But all the while he had worried about his dignity and his reputation. And what would become of him if people knew his methods.

He had done all so that he could present an unblemished name to the world. He had cared about his world and what it thought of him. And all that he did that enriched or amused him—all the trafficking in trade, all the consorting with women of the demimonde, all the gaming and the pleasures—he had tried to hide from the world.

"Ah," he thought, scowling, it pained him to think of it even now. He had been such a callow fellow. And it had, in the end, cost him dearly. The one woman whose mind he admired the most, whose temperament most neatly matched his own, he dallied with and then dropped, because he had felt her face did not match the ideal of what the world would think his marchioness's face should be. And by the time he discovered how he missed her and how unimportant a face could be, only important if that certain face bore a smile for him alone, she was gone to another man wise enough to know the difference between a package and its wrappings.

And there had been another woman, whose face was so glorious that he forgot to look into her heart. And whose position and status were so low that he did not seriously think of her for his marchioness, for he thought the world would not either. So he only offered her a paid position as his mistress. But she too had

found a wiser man, who had looked beyond the surface and not
thought of the world's opinion, and offered her his hand as well
as his heart. And he, the marquis of impeccable birth and
reputation, had been left with an impeccably empty heart.

Such memories were only cold ashes to rake over. Valuable
only because he had learned from his mistakes, they had served
their purpose well—let them lie at rest. He had found occupation
in serving his country; spying suited his temperament. He no
longer cared for appearances; he, of all men, knew what a sham
reputation and titles could be. He had learned to look beyond the
obvious, to seek the truth beneath the surface clutter. And so he
no longer cared for his own name; his reputation was no longer
of any importance to him.

And the cream of the jest was that once he had left off caring
and dissembling and trying to impress the world with his purity,
his popularity soared. And his reputation, which no longer interested him, was pronounced to be of the highest. He gamed
openly—he was called a daring gentleman. He wenched openly
—he was called a dashing ladies' man. His growing cynicism
was thought to be wisdom; his rudeness, wit; his unapproachable
air, dignity. He sought no wife and was deemed the most eligible
of the ton.

Someday he would have to marry, he expected, but he would
remain heart-whole. He could not see himself letting his estates
go to his only sister's eldest, a spotty, disagreeable little boy
who whined. But even though the marquis had reached the age
of five and thirty, he was in no hurry to be bound in matrimony.
He thought of marriage in much the same way that a sinner
thinks of confession and redemption, as something to be done at
the last moment, on the deathbed preferably.

For with all of his wide experience with women, the marquis
did not trust his perceptions of them too far. He shied from
involving himself with them seriously, as he had been wrong
once too often. He was scrupulously honest, however, with them
and about his expectations of them. He enjoyed them physically
and had learned to give them pleasure as well, and asked no
more of them than that, and promised them no more than that.
This attitude caused him no impediments to his desires. There
were too many females eager to accept him on his own terms.

And those few who tried to change the terms were soon
brought to realize their folly.

The marquis glanced at the note in his hand and rang for a

footman to collect it from him. When the difficulties with France were finally irrevocably ended, he supposed he might find boredom at last. An emptiness might enter his life without occupation that did not offer such danger and interest. But he had learned to push such thoughts away. For now he was content to be a superior spy, and that was all that he cared to dwell upon.

St. John, Marquis of Bessacarr, darling of the ton, peer of the realm, patron of the frail sisterhood, social lion, and most superior spy, impatient with waiting for a footman to answer his summons, stepped out, on his way to a farewell dinner with his mistress, to send a message to his one true friend, his accomplice. And the message was to come to London instanter. For the assignment was at hand and they were off to Paris!

Chapter IV

The trunks began to pile up in the great hall, as their growing number had already outstripped the confines of the back pantries. The duchess did not like to travel with any discomfort. So there were innumerable indispensable things to pack.

The duchess's modiste, a staple of the ton who would be horrified if her name were mentioned in the same breath as Madame Bertrand's, was giddy with ecstasy over the amount of clothing she was flogging her girls to turn out in time for the duchess's departure. Catherine no longer measured the time till their going by the calendar, but rather watched the trunks slowly take over the hall. By the time, she reasoned, that Griddon could no longer pick his way to the front door, the time of their departure would be at hand.

No one could have awaited their departure more eagerly than Catherine. Despite all the splendors of the duchess's accommodations, it had been a lonely time for her. Not even the lowest servant in the house had ever had the inclination or the time to chat with her. Thus she had passed her days in sewing or reading or gazing out the window at those more fortunately occupied, afraid to leave the house lest a summons from the duchess come while she was out. Only a few times had she dared hasty trips to the shops, and those only when there was a purchase she must make. On those rare occasions, it was a treat to be able to converse with the tradespeople she transacted her business with. There were times when the purchase of a spool of red thread had been the highest point of Catherine's day.

The only person she ever encountered in the street whom she knew, and he only by accident, was the duchess's near neighbor, the lofty Marquis of Bessacarr. When their paths crossed, he invariably would take note of her, to her distress. For he took special care to say something cryptic to her in passing. "It's a good life, isn't it, little one?" he said once, smiling, and, "My regards to your employer. Why does she still keep you under wraps?" he greeted her another time. Each time she steadfastly and properly ignored him. And each time he said a thing which seemed to amuse him, and which perversely always troubled her far into the night.

But today she was to have conversation. She stood in the duchess's bedchamber again, waiting to be noticed. For today she had come at her own request.

When finally the duchess had given Gracie instructions for the securing of yet another new trunk, this one for bonnets alone, she had time to look up at Catherine.

"How are you going, gel?" she asked pleasantly enough. "All packed and ready to scoot with me? Did Bertrand deliver as promised?"

"Oh yes, ma'am," Catherine breathed, still embarrassed about the amount of clothing the duchess had thought necessary for her companion to have. Her fingers still ached from all the midnight sewing she had done to tame some of Madame Bertrand's more outrageous creations, and her conscience still pricked about the secretiveness of her stitchery.

"But there is a thing that I have to discuss with you." She hesitated. This was difficult, although she had spent the better part of yesterday preparing herself for the interview.

"You see, Your Grace, there is the matter of my"—Catherine swallowed—"wages."

It did not sound so terrible once it was out, so Catherine rushed on, "I have been with you since October, and there have been certain expenses I have been forced to make. Expenses of a personal nature," she hurried on, so as not to seem grasping or ungrateful for her food and pleasant housing, and not wishing to go into particulars, since most of her money had gone to laces and trimmings to alter her wardrobe.

"And as this is my first position, I did not think to ask originally as to when I would be paid. I do," she went on with painful honesty, "realize that Your Grace has seen to my every comfort here, but Christmas is upon us, and so I wondered if I could ask that the wages I have already earned, only those, be given to me so that I might send a few things home before I depart.''

It was so difficult, Catherine thought, to talk about money. And so very foolish to feel like a greedy, grasping creature when one was only asking for what one had earned. But there it was, it was unseemly for a female to discuss money. Perhaps that was why it was so unseemly for a female to be actually employed.

The duchess looked hard at her for a moment, squinting her eyes to get a better look, which was something she seldom did, preferring on the whole to see the world in her usual pleasant myopic blurred focus.

"I usually pay my companions quarterly," the duchess intoned, suddenly on her high ropes, and making Catherine quake at her own stupidity in not having discussed the matter on her initial interview to save herself this present embarrassment.

"But," the duchess said, with a sly little grin, "I understand your predicament. You're probably used to much more ready in your pocket. I have kept your wings clipped since you came here, haven't I? But that's only because I wanted to spring you as a surprise when we got to France. Watch their eyes bug out when they saw you. No use to having rumors spoil the treat beforehand. So you're feeling pinched because I've kept you from your usual source of income, eh?"

Catherine had not a clue as what the duchess was getting at, but then suddenly realized that she must mean that Arthur and Jane weren't there to provide for her as they usually did. Since that was true enough, too humiliatingly true, Catherine felt her face flush in embarrassment.

"Well, don't fret. You've been a good gel, and there's a treat for you. I'll give you the first two months' wages now and you can go on a spree with them. But once we get to France, that won't be a problem, will it?"

Catherine could think of no heavy expenses she could incur when she began her travels. Pourboires for servants could be taken from her pocket with no stress, since she didn't intend to spend every penny the duchess gave her now. So she nodded in happy agreement.

"Thought not," the duchess answered. "But mind, I told Rose and I told Violet. I don't want to know about it. Do your duty to me first and be discreet about the rest, and we'll rub on well enough."

There was no reason, certainly, Catherine thought, to bother the duchess with the small matters of tipping foreign servants, so she agreed again.

"We'll get you your wages now," the duchess said, ringing for Gracie to get her her cash box, "and I suppose you'll want the same arrangements Rose and Violet did. I'll be your banker on our trip, and when it's over I'll hand it all over to you in a lump sum, or you can have it quarterly. It'll be like an extra cash bonus whenever you get it." The duchess chuckled. "Money in the bank."

Catherine took the money that the duchess handed to her, too grateful to count it. It seemed like a great deal, and even more, as it was the first money she ever earned by herself. And as far as the total sum of money being an extra bonus, it would be far, far more than that to her. The duchess, she thought gratefully, could have no idea of how penny pinched she really was. At the thought of the independence of spirit that the lump sum would buy her—the freedom to choose whether to work again for some other woman, or to take her earnings and pay Arthur and Jane back some small portion of what they had given her so that she could live with them again with ease and spirit—Catherine smiled with pure joy.

"Money's a great thing. Ain't it?" the duchess crowed, seeing the girl's rapturous face.

"It is, ma'am," Catherine sighed. "It is indeed."

"Get on with it, then," the duchess said, at first amused, but now bored with the chit's obvious greed. She immediately went back to chivying Gracie again about the whereabouts of her favorite feathered bonnet.

Catherine was as careful as a new mother with her firstborn child as she decided how to spend her wages. This time she had drawn Annie, a sharp little kitchen maid, as female escort. Annie was as distant and silent with Catherine as the others of her position. But Catherine had gotten used to the peculiar notions of status that prevailed in the duchess's household.

After hours of searching in the shops as carefully as a master chef searching for a perfect cut of meat, Catherine selected a warm but exquisitely made colorful shawl for Jane and a set of six beautiful enameled buttons for Arthur. Both presents were practical enough to please their sense of propriety, but extravagantly styled enough to be kept as personal treasures. And, best of all, both were small enough to be sent without incurring the world's expense on her shoulders. She was sure that Griddon

could be asked to parcel them up for her, and that he would
know how to go about posting them safely. For Catherine had
never had to send a package to anyone before, never being far
enough from home or knowing anyone far enough away.

To be sure, she thought, frowning slightly as she made her
way back home, setting Annie to wonder if Her Grace's fine
trollop had seen her wink at the butcher's boy, Jane's papa had
lived far away and traveled further. But there was never any
question of anyone posting anything to him, as he had never left
a forwarding address.

Her own father, that dimly remembered handsome blue-eyed
dark-haired man, had died when she was six. Mama had gone on
alone, till she had met Jane's papa. He had been a slight, blond,
elegant, and altogether charming widower. And Mama's heart
had gone out to the outwardly blithe man with his little motherless,
sober blond girl, only twelve to her own orphan's seven years.
And if it had not, Catherine thought wryly, he would have
pirated it anyway. For he was a persuasive man. Merry and
laughing, charming and light spirited, he had invaded their house
and swept Mama away with him. But only so far as the vicar's.

For after they were married, he had soon grown bored with
Mama and two little girls, as he had grown bored with everything that he had encountered in his life. Soon he was charming
and delightful only to his drinking cronies, and soon after that,
having found a safe harbor for his little girl—say that much at
least for him—he was gone altogether, off on his own journeys.
In search, he had said, of his fortune.

And he had left Mama with Jane and Catherine both to raise as
best she could on what little her first husband had left her. When
they had heard of his own death a few years ago, somewhere in
Ireland, his own daughter had not even shed a tear. Small
wonder, then, that Jane had not looked for a handsome, dashing
stranger to carry her off, after a childhood full of a handsome
dashing father who had carried her everywhere and then abandoned her. When prim and proper Arthur had stepped out from
behind the counter at his shop to ask to keep company with her,
she had accepted with alacrity. And though Catherine had not
known Jane's father too long or too well, she too was wary of
gentlemen with easy smiles and pleasing graces. Not, she reminded herself, that she was much in the way of meeting such
gentlemen, or any gentlemen at all, these days.

Catherine quickened her pace, as the wind was beginning to

bite fiercely, and the pavements at last communicated their chill through the bottom of her handsome kid slippers. She had been out shopping far longer than she had ever planned, and she was anxious to get back and get her parcels seen to, so that she could dream of Jane and Arthur's pleased expressions when they saw the bounty she had sent.

She was so intent upon her thoughts that she did not see him till he was almost abreast of her, although Annie had seen him coming from far down the street.

He tipped his hat, which he wore at a rakish angle, to Annie, and as she tittered, he swept it off altogether with a flourish as Catherine raised her eyes to him.

"Good day to you, little one," he said pleasantly enough.

Although she had never acknowledged his greetings before, Catherine knew it would be quite rude to simply pass him by and cut him dead. He was a neighbor to the duchess, and the duchess seemed to hold him in some awe. So Catherine reluctantly inclined her head in greeting. His words had been innocuous enough, but she had seen the same amused gleam in his eyes.

"All ready for your little trip?" he inquired politely.

"Yes. Thank you. Quite ready," Catherine answered, wishing he would end this interview, for she was not at all sure, all things considered, that it was proper for her to be speaking with him.

"Yes," he drawled, seeing her impatience and hesitation, "you'd best be hurrying home, little ladybird. Your house may well be afire. Reinforcements have arrived."

At Catherine's puzzled glance upward at him, something in his aspect changed, and he reluctantly withdrew his gaze from her clear blue eyes.

He replaced his hat jauntily and added, "You'd best see to your bonnets, child. The competition bids to be fierce this year." And again he nodded and went on down the street, leaving Catherine with the usual mixture of feelings of chagrin and confusion, and Annie pink with pleasure at having been noticed by such a fine gentleman.

Catherine gave her coat to the footman and saw Griddon coming toward her. She began to explain about her parcels and how she wanted them sent, when he cut her off gently, "Her Grace has been asking for you. She's in the study. With a visitor."

Catherine flushed with guilt, thinking of how on the one day that she was wanted, she was out. She reached the door and tapped lightly upon it.

"Come in," the duchess called.

There was a woman sitting at the desk opposite the duchess. A magnificent woman. Her red hair was a tumble of curls, pulled back with a simple green ribbon. Her figure was full and imposing and her green walking dress was afroth with lace and frogs and knots. Her eyes were large and brown, with the darkest, longest lashes Catherine had ever seen. Her lips were full and very red and pouting, and she had, as she looked at Catherine, something of the imperious expression the duchess herself affected.

"Look who's here," the duchess said wryly. "Look who the cat's brought back. It's dear Violet. And she's consented to come with me on my little jaunterings."

"Go now." The duchess waved at Catherine. "I just wanted dear Violet to get an eyeful of you and see how indispensable her services were. She and I have some business to iron out. I'll call you later. Go now." She waved again, as Catherine stood there, staring like a ninny at the magnificent lady who made her feel all of two years old.

At last Catherine nodded and fled up the stairs.

Once in her room, she shut the door quickly, laid down her parcels with unsteady hands, and pulled the curtains closed. She was reacting, she told herself a few moments later, when she got her thoughts under control, just like a two-year-old who has seen a stranger who's frightened her. Why don't you, she scourged herself, go and creep under the bed while you're at it, to make the picture complete?

After a few moments, she had herself adequately under control again, and her face was very sad when she at last met her eyes in the mirror. "So be it," she thought resignedly. "You cannot really lose something you have not had." And, in all honesty, she had not been the duchess's companion yet, and she had not, she reasoned, lost a position she had never actually filled. "At least," she told herself, with a little of her usual good humor, "there's very little packing to do," as she saw all her new suitcases neatly arow in the corner of the room, ready for departure.

"So," the duchess said, smiling hugely, "what do you think of your little replacement, Violet?"

"Quite the ingenue," Violet answered in her high reedy voice, "but I don't think she's up to snuff."

"She's a stunning little baggage and you know it," the duchess went on, quite pleased with the agitation in her erstwhile companion's face.

"I should think you'd want to travel with a female that knows her way about. A responsible sort of companion. That little tart looks like she's still on mother's milk. She'll land herself in the suds before you know it, or pack it all in for some layabout's promises before you even reach Paris," Violet said in the thin little voice that had been her downfall in the theater. For although the gentlemen had cheered every time she swept across the stage, no one past the middle rows had ever heard a line.

The duchess acknowledged the hit with a shrug. "Perhaps, but you'd be there to show her the ropes, wouldn't you, dear Violet?"

The magnificent female in the green walking dress relaxed the tight set of her shoulders. Up to this point she had not known if the old dragon was actually going to take her on again. She'd had to do some fast and glib talking, and then when the young smashing-looking girl had appeared in the doorway, she had thought that all was lost. But resiliency was her best asset, so she masked her surprise and said laconically, "Oh, I'll see to it that she doesn't embarrass you. I know what I'm about."

"All because you're anxious to see Paris, eh?" the duchess prodded. "I'm pleased that you have acquired this sudden bent for travel. But of course, since Wolverton came down so handsomely with you, you wouldn't require any help from me with your wardrobe this time."

Violet saw the old woman's eyes mocking her, so she gave in at last, feeling that a half a loaf was better than none.

"No, he didn't. He made up some wild story about me sneaking about with an actor on the sly, and used that as an excuse to simply pull out, without leaving me a farthing. As if," she added, her bosom swelling, "I would sneak about with an actor, of all things, without a penny in his pockets and nothing but a handsome face to recommend him, and risk Wolverton's finding out."

The duchess nodded sympathetically, knowing that was just what Violet would do.

"And dear Rose, have you heard from her?"

"Haven't seen hide nor hair of her, and that's the honest truth. Last I heard, she was off on the road with that new love of hers. He'll drink her out of house and home before she knows it unless I miss my guess."

"This is all quite sordid." The duchess sighed, ringing for Griddon. "And I don't think I care to hear about any more of it. I'll take you on again, Violet, although I was most displeased about the way you were so ready to leave me in the lurch. But I do have a reputation to uphold, and traveling with two companions is what my set is used to see me doing. But I won't hear of you changing your mind again. Do your duties, keep the new girl in line, and you will find I will be pleased."

When Griddon appeared, the duchess asked him to call Miss Robins down again.

"Catherine," the duchess said as Catherine, white-faced and subdued, came to the door, "this is Violet Peterson. I have spoken about her. She finds herself suddenly able to join me again and will be going to Paris with us."

"I understand, ma'am," Catherine said in a small voice. "And when do you wish me to leave?"

"Why, next week," the duchess said, "when I do, of course—don't be such a gudgeon."

"I shall have to see to the stage schedules," Catherine said quietly. "Would you be so kind as to write me a recommendation so that I can secure future employment?"

Violet stiffened and gave Catherine a look of offended shock.

"Your new little miss don't think I'm a fit companion to travel with," she shrilled.

"Violet don't fit your nice notions of propriety?" the duchess growled, in her iciest dignity.

"Oh no, that is not it," Catherine foundered, "but I thought, when you said that she was coming with you, I thought you no longer required my services. That is to say, now that you have your original companion back, I did not see what need you would have of me."

Catherine had researched the duties of a companion as best she could before even coming to London. But some things were basic, even back in Kendal. An elderly female, or an incapacitated one, or even a healthy able young woman of means could not live in society without proper female companionship. If there were no female relations in the home, and no indigent women in some branch of the family who would be glad of a home to be pressed into service, a companion was hired. A companion served as aide, or as company, sometimes as nurse, and most often just as figurehead for propriety's sake. But she had never heard of any woman requiring two paid companions. And that seemed to be just what the duchess was now implying. Perhaps, Catherine thought, with an amazed sense of guilt, she had not looked into the social habits that prevailed in the higher echelons of society as well as she should have. And now she had unwittingly offended Violet.

"I have often told you about Violet and Rose. I frequently travel with two companions. I have a position to uphold," the duchess said, at her iciest, feeling obliquely accused by the mock innocence of this young upstart of a girl.

"Then I am sorry for the misunderstanding," Catherine said gladly. "I should be delighted to travel with Miss Peterson, really I shall," she said, looking beseechingly at the rigid Violet, and feeling a surge of delight at the thought of having someone to talk to at last nearer to her own age. "And I am relieved to find that you still want me."

"Go, then," the duchess said with unexpected relief. "Go and get acquainted. You'll be seeing a lot of each other, and I like my staff to be in harmony."

"So you've got the green room," Violet commented as she and Catherine made their way upstairs to Violet's room. "Rose, she used to have that one. What did you do before the old lady hired you on?" she asked disinterestedly as she walked unerringly into the room adjoining Catherine's.

Catherine, a little shocked at the familiarity with which Violet spoke of her employer, but not wanting to appear to be a prig and start the relationship off on the wrong foot, let the remark pass and merely said, "I lived with my brother-in-law and stepsister."

"And I lived with the pixies at the foot of the garden," Violet mocked, sweeping into her room and going straight to her looking glass.

Catherine looked nonplussed as Violet stripped the ribbon from her hair and examined her face in the mirror.

"Oh, all right, I'll play the game too," Violet said wearily. "You lived with your brother-in-law and stepsister. Is it your first time in London then, s'truth?"

"Yes, and it's all been so strange to me."

"Lord," Violet sighed, "I'm going to be going across the face of Europe with Juliet. Well, you really landed in gravy hiring on with the dowager. She's a right old sort once you learn her ins and outs. Just watch your step with her, though. She's half tiddly, but the other half comes up when you least expect it.

I remember once when Rose snuck out with that wild major before the duchess was ready to call it a night. Wasn't there an uproar about that, though? I thought old Rose was going to be chucked out in no time flat. But all was rosy again in the morning. Rose could never pick them. All for love, that's Rose. And not a penny in her pocket now to show for it. Not that I'm in clover either now, but after this jaunt I expect to have a few guineas put away, and you never know what gravy boats there are in Paris, do you?''

Catherine didn't know what to answer. Evidently Violet and Rose had both been up to some larks when the duchess's back was turned, and she supposed that the tedium of working for the duchess had to be relieved by some shows of spirit, but she honestly had no similar experiences to relate. So she simply smiled in a hopeful, friendly way at Violet.

Violet caught Catherine's expression in the reflection of her mirror. She stared thoughtfully. So the little miss was going to play it all airs and graces and not let her hair down? So be it, it takes all kinds, she thought. Rose had been more forthcoming, a right sort of girl. If this little chit wanted to play at being a society debutante, it was her business. And her dark hair and gamine looks and air of innocence might be a good contrast to Violet's own more spectacular looks. Just as Rose's blond buxom placidity had been a good foil for her own Titian vivacity.

But then, just for one moment, Violet caught one clear look of both their faces reflected in the oval of the mirror. Catherine's pure fine-grained white skin contrasted with her own powdered complexion; Catherine's clear startling blue eyes, with her translucent skin that allowed a faint blue tracery of veins to color her lids, contrasted with her own heavily soot-darkened lids and lashes; and the younger girl's faint blush of color above her cheekbones contrasted with her own heavily rouged cheeks. Then there was the chit's plump and dusky lips as opposed to her own richly red salved mouth, and, most damningly, the faint web of lines at the corners of Violet's eyes were not echoed on the girl's smooth face. No, Violet decided, only from across a room could the contrast between them be to her own benefit. She knew her assets as well as any banker knew his financial situation. Her own full figure and brazen coloring would catch the gentlemen's eyes long before they noticed the quiet beauty of this little miss. But standing side by side, Violet could only suffer by comparison. Her decision was made unerringly and irrevocably—she would stay away from Miss Innocence, stay far away in public, for her own good. And as far as when they were alone, time would tell if the chit would drop her air of sanctity.

"I'm for a quick kip," Violet yawned, and, without further comment, she began to unbutton the bodice of her gown. She stripped down her clothes, as though she were alone in the room. Catherine hastily retreated, calling a good-bye that was only acknowledged by a nod and another huge yawn.

Really, Catherine thought, seeking the refuge of her own room, the women of London thought no more of nudity before other females than they did of nudity before a cake of soap. She wondered if she should write of the phenomenon to Jane in her letter next week.

But when she wrote her next letter to Jane, she mentioned not a word of it. For Arthur, she remembered, would most likely be reading Jane's letter over her shoulder. She wrote instead of the quiet Christmas she had spent, and the expectations she had of her journey. She closed by inquiring after their health and wished them all the joys of a new year. She sealed the letter and blew out her light. Then she went to her window to gaze at the moonlit streets of London for a while. She watched some stray merrymakers reel past her observation post at the window seat and then she crept into her bed. She fell asleep as the bells rang out, and so celebrated the first moments of the new year of 1815 with quiet blameless sleep.

Chapter V

The deck of the packet to France was thronged with the fashionable of England and the Continent. Catherine tried not to goggle. There were gentlemen in the first and last cry of fashion, their capes billowing out in the wind, their hats defying every gust. The ladies wore rich garments and trailed retinues of more plainly dressed servants. Everyone boarding seemed to know each other, and the duchess nodded and smiled her tight little smile at gentlemen who bowed and ladies who stared. Gracie, like so many of the other servants who scuttled mutely and inconspicuously after their employers, only kept her attention on her mistress. But Violet, Catherine noted, behaved exactly as the duchess did, nodding and acknowledging old acquaintances. Evidently, Catherine thought, the companions of great ladies were treated exactly as their mistresses were, even though they were, in effect, no more than servants just like Gracie.

The duchess's retinue made their way to their berths. The duchess paused at the door of her cabin and looked at Violet.

"I shall rest. You know I cannot abide the sea. The mere sight of it makes me ill. But Gracie here knows what to do for me. I suppose you don't want to just languish in your cabin, eh? You'll want to see how the land lies. Well, get on with it. Let me know who's here and who's going where. But mind your manners. And take her with you," she added, pointing to Catherine. "Let them get a look at her before we sail. That'll tickle them right enough."

Violet looked as though she would balk at the suggestion, making Catherine feel like an ill-bred little sister who has insisted upon

58

coming along with the grown-ups and so is hardly tolerated. But then Violet sniffed, "She's free to walk the decks, I'm sure."

Violet was dressed, Catherine thought, as they turned from Her Grace's room, as though she were going to a high tea rather than sailing across the channel. She wore a bright burnt orange ensemble, and from the way she held her head as her fellow passengers turned to stare at her in the corridor, she acted as though she were the hostess of a large seagoing fete. Catherine felt mousy in her own rich, warm blue velvet cloak beside the glowing Violet.

As they were going out into the fresh cold sea air of the deck, Catherine noticed a small altercation taking place between the captain and a stunning attractive blond female. Although she too was dressed in the height of fashion, and was almost as theatrically brilliant as Violet, she wore an expression of consternation and seemed to be arguing with the captain. As they approached, Catherine heard Violet give out a low startled exclamation.

"Coo, now here's a turn. Look who's landed on us."

"There," the blonde cried, noticing Violet as she drew closer, "just ask her. That's the duchess's companion. She will tell you."

"Excuse me, miss," the captain said, wiping his brow, "but this lady says that the Duchess of Crewe is expecting her. She does not have her ticket, however, and I do not like to disturb Her Grace, and so perhaps you . . ."

He trailed off, looking perturbed.

"Hello, Rose, old thing," Violet said, with a slightly twisted smile. "Allow me to present Miss Catherine Robins, Her Grace's new companion."

The blond woman looked stricken, but recovered quickly to say, "There, you see, the duchess's companion knows me. I'm sure Her Grace won't be angry if you take me to her. In fact, she might be very angry if you do not."

"It's true that the duchess knows Miss Tomkins," Violet said loftily, to the blond woman's evident relief. "I'm most surprised to see you here, Rose, and I'm sure Her Grace will be curious about your presence as well."

Rose turned to the captain triumphantly. "There, did you hear that?"

The captain shrugged, content to have the burden of decision taken from him. "Very well," he said, "but we · sail in an hour."

Rose turned to go below deck and gave Violet a radiant smile. "You're a good old thing, Vi," she whispered, "and I'm not forgetting."

"Is that," Catherine whispered to Violet as they strolled on, "Her Grace's old companion Rose?"

"Don't let her catch you saying 'old,' " Violet smiled.

"Whatever is she doing here?"

"With Rose one hardly knows," Violet said disinterestedly. "Perhaps she's companioning someone else. Perhaps she's short of the ready and wants to touch the old girl's heart before she sails for a guinea or two. Time will tell."

Violet spotted someone she knew in a clutch of travelers who were standing and joshing with each other by the rail, surveying late arrivals as they hurried up the gangplank. She turned and eyed Catherine obliquely. The wind had whipped color into the girl's cheeks, she noted. And her eyes gleamed bluer than the slate-blue sea beneath them. Her hair spilled out from the blue bonnet, tugged into curls by the sea winds' damp fingers. She looked as fresh and bonny as a young doe. Violet pursed her lips.

"I see some old acquaintances," she said quickly. "Do you continue on your walk. Once the boat begins to move, you may not feel like staying above deck. So here's your opportunity to catch the lay of the land. I'll see you later."

And, with a nod, she left Catherine's side and disappeared into a crowd of people.

Catherine walked on alone. She felt uneasy about walking by herself in a crowd of strangers, for she knew it was not the sort of thing a young female should do. At least, she ammended, not the sort of thing she should do in Kendal. But the duchess had told her to go for a stroll, and Violet seemed to find nothing amiss with it. It would seem, she thought, a poor-spirited thing to rush below decks now and huddle alone in the cabin when all the world was up here on the main deck. That had been just as she had been doing, she thought, since she came to London, huddling alone while the world went by her window. Well, now she was to be one of that world. It was certainly time, so she walked on, watching the others, observing the scene.

However, she did not observe much of it. She was so flustered when one young gentleman swept her a bow and gave a white-toothed smile, and so distracted when another elderly gentleman grinned most improperly at her, and, finally, so devastated when a trio of young women stared her up and down with cold disdainful eyes that she hardly had time to make the sort of observations she expected to. So she found herself a quiet corner of the rail and positioned herself there, staring pointedly out at the shore, so that anyone seeing her would think she was waiting for an escort to board the ship and come to her side. That, she felt, was a safer pose than merely perambulating the deck looking for insults. For it seemed, the fashionable world had the same opinion as regarded young females alone as did the world of Kendal.

It had been, she congratulated herself, a clever ploy, for no one bothered her now. However, she could see little of what was going on behind her and had to content herself with hearing bits of the conversation that flowed around her. Mostly, people were gossiping, she concluded. Talking about who was here and whom they expected to see. They spoke of "Lady This" and "Lord That." She heard them joke about someone's bonnet, and someone else who had put on a few stone since they were last seen. They spoke of nicknames such as "old Bertie" and "Sly Betty." All seemed to be code names, as when they giggled over "Viscount Viperous" or "the Dirty Duchess" and "the Deacon." It was odd, she thought, that no one seemed to be speaking of the trip that was to come but instead only gossiping about who was there. She could not know that in the duchess's world people traveled not to see new things, but to see who else was traveling with them and who they knew that would be at their destination upon their arrival.

And so she was almost relieved when she heard a familiar voice at her elbow address her. Although the same voice caused only consternation every time she had heard it, this time it was with almost a feeling of pleasure that she listened to its deep laconic tones. At least it was familiar and she felt no longer so alone.

"Well," he said, "and so the little country mouse takes to the sea at last. Are we to have the pleasure of your company all the way to Paris? Why, I suppose we shall," he smiled not waiting for her answer. "I had quite forgotten that the duchess was never one to miss a gay party. Ah, but my manners—allow me to introduce you, Jenkins, this is the Duchess of Crewe's latest companion, Miss . . . ah, my lamentable memory. Miss?"

"Catherine Robins, Your Lordship," Catherine said quickly, to avoid further embarrassment, worrying about whether it was proper to introduce herself, and then once she had, wishing to bite off her tongue for admitting she already knew his name and rank.

The gleam in his gray eyes showed her he well knew her predicament.

"Allow me to present Robert Jenkins, my friend and my traveling companion."

Catherine, turning and dipping a little curtsy, was further confused when she saw the gentleman she had been introduced to. For while the marquis, she noted, was dressed quietly but splendidly in dove gray and black in the peak of fashion, the shorter, muscular older man at his side was dressed as soberly and unobtrusively as any of the valets she had seen in the trail of their employers. Could it be that he was introducing her to his valet? Catherine hardly knew anymore what was proper in this strange milieu she had entered, and, throwing propriety to the winds she smiled up at Jenkins when she saw the sympathetic look on his grizzled homely square face.

"How do you do," she said.

"Oh he'll do fine, now that he's met you," the marquis went on. "As who wouldn't? You glow, my dear, you positively glow. Life with the duchess seems to have suited you to a tee. Do you know, Jenkins, that when I first met Miss Robins, she did not even know a street address in London? In fact, I flatter myself that I was the first to meet her, when Her Grace was conducting interviews. Of course, I shall not be the last. But from the moment I saw her, I knew that she would put an end to the stream of elderly parties that were quite obstructing the street in their eagerness to find employment with the duchess. It was becoming difficult to go out of doors, with the roadways thronged with elderly indigent females. Rather like stepping out into a massive sewing circle every day. There were so many old dears littering the walkways, it was becoming a traffic hazard. But then, as I laid eyes on Miss Robins, I knew she would put an end to it. We owe her a debt, Jenkins, for clearing up the public thoroughfares."

Jenkins shot the marquis a look, Catherine thought, of censure.

"Delight to meet you, Miss Robins," he said in a gravelly voice, "but you must excuse me now. For I've things to see to."

He bowed and took his leave, but the marquis seemed content to lounge at Catherine's side. He leaned back against the rail.

"Quite a change for you, isn't it?" he said to Catherine, in the same light bored tone that he had used with Jenkins. Rather, she thought angrily, as if he were still talking to someone else, even though there were only the two of them there now.

"Here you are, in the cream of London society. But you don't know a soul and can't yet get a taste of it. Her Grace has kept you cloistered, hasn't she? Now that's at an end, and you're free, but there isn't a familiar face about. Except, of course, for Violet, but she's feathering her own nest already. I," he said, with mock bravado, "shall help you. For, God help me, I know every soul aboard this packet. There," he said, turning his eyes toward a red-faced gentleman with bulging eyes, "is Old Hightower. Buried two wives and looking for a third rich enough to make matrimony worthwhile again. He lives in high style, but don't be fooled. His estates are mortgaged to the hilt, so he'll need to be quick about finding someone who hasn't heard of his financial distress. That's why he's off to Paris. Don't waste a second on him, little one, regardless of the diamonds at his throat. And there's Prendergast. Comely enough—there, that sort of a willowy-looking chap. . . . Fancies himself a deep thinker, and he'll make up a poem for you the moment you flutter those incredible eyelashes at him! But that's all you'll get. He does have a fortune, and he'll likely keep it forever, for he doesn't spend a groat if he can help it. He's a perennial houseguest and as tight with a penny as a drum. And ah, there's Lord Hunt— pass him by, child, pass him by. Drinks, you know, and forgets all of his promises in the morning. But now there, by his elbow, there's Sir Lawrence. That's one to keep your eye on. Old, but not infirm yet, and a chap who comes down handsomely when he's pleased. And he's not hard to please. And yes, there's Richard Collier, quite a prize despite that weathered look. There's many a good year left in him, and there's not a party he's likely to miss."

Catherine drew breath in fury. She cut the marquis off just as he was gesturing toward the poor old gentleman being pushed aboard in his bath chair.

"I do not care about prizes and the personalities you have been so kindly explaining to me. My job is to be a companion. And whatever you may be thinking, please disabuse yourself of the notion that I am looking for a husband. I am here to be Her Grace's companion. To work, not to set my cap at anyone.''

The marquis stopped and looked at her with an arrested expression in his eyes. He stared down into her face, seeing the genuine anger and disturbance there. His eyes lingered for a moment on her lips, and she dropped her gaze, flustered both at her temerity in scolding him and at his intent regard.

Then he gave a shout of laughter that caused others on the deck to stare for a moment at them.

"Wonderful," he said. "The intonation, the indignation, the heated countenance, all wonderful. Unless, it could be . . . No, I am not so wet behind the ears. Still," he said, in a considering way. "What do you think of dear Violet?"

"Why, she is a delightful companion," Catherine said stoutly.

"And what of the duchess's outline of duties?" he asked in a warmer tone of voice.

"Unexceptional," she replied.

For once the marquis himself seemed puzzled. He gave her one more lingering look and then straightened.

"We shall see," he said cryptically. "I hope you are a good sailor, little mouse, for the wind is picking up. I shall see you again, I am sure." And bowing, he left.

Everything proper, she thought, with chagrin, while being everything improper.

Catherine watched him stroll away, stopping every few moments to bow or have a few words with other passengers. He was, she thought, watching his tall straight figure, quite the handsomest man aboard, but then she noted, watching the expressions of the females he greeted, she was not alone in thinking that. If only he were not so familiar and so puzzling, she sighed as she watched his slow progress across the deck.

And as she watched, he was stopped by Violet. Violet raised a glowing face as she flirted up at the marquis, and soon the two were deep in conversation. While Catherine stood watching intently, the marquis caught her at it. He looked up at her with a glance of rueful amusement as Violet motioned toward her. And then, before she could turn her head away, he gave her a curiously knowing smile. Then he linked Violet's arm in his and the two strolled away.

Catherine quelled her momentary feeling of dismay and then resolutely turned her face toward shore again. What was it that Miss Parkinson had told her so gently?

"A female who is a companion, no matter her birth, must always remember that she is not the social equal of her employer or of her employer's friends. However elevated her birth, she is yet an employee, and she must never imagine otherwise or she will be laying herself open to insult."

Good advice, Catherine thought; perhaps I should work it in needlepoint and hang it above my bed, for I should not forget it for a moment. And neither, she told herself sharply, should I care about the marquis' choice of companions. And she stayed at the rail till they began to call ashore and the wind turned bitter enough to drive her below.

Once she reached her cabin again, Catherine opened the door without preamble and then stood motionless in the doorway. For there was Violet, her hat and slippers off, lying back against her bed pillows, talking animatedly with Rose. And Rose, the duchess's former companion, had made herself comfortable and sprawled out all over what Catherine had assumed to be her own bed.

When Catherine appeared, the two let off talking, and it was Rose who spoke up immediately, "There you are, Catherine. I'm happy to meet you. Seeing as how we're all going to be traveling together, I wanted to meet you. I was in such a state up there, I didn't have time for a word. But now, all's tight and we can have a nice coze."

Violet watched them with a highly amused expression as Catherine stammered, "Oh, then you're accompanying someone to Paris, as well?"

"Oh, Lord love you," Rose beamed, "I've gotten my old job back. But don't look so downcast. It'll be heaps of fun for us. Imagine, the duchess is going with three companions this time! She thought it was a right old joke too. I do confess, when I saw you with Vi here, I thought I was sunk, I did. But I got down on my knees to Her Grace and told her all my troubles. I groveled, I did. I was that afraid she'd pitch me out. It would serve me right, but then where would I be? She gave me a hard time, calling me all sorts of a fool, and what could I say when she was right? Giving up a soft berth with her to fly off with a gamester and letting the world go hang—it was madness. Yes, Vi, you were right. A leopard don't change his stripes. And he going off with another like that, leaving me high and dry without even fare to get back to London. But first thing I do back in town is to go haring back to Her Grace. And then I hear she's off to Paris! Think of it, me giving up Paris like that.''

Rose shook her head in distress at herself. She was beautiful, Catherine thought, in a very different manner from Violet. She was fair and blonde, with a full figure and a warm, comfortable manner. She had fine large brown eyes and a high bosom and a head of flaxen hair, and was fully as red of lips and dark of lashes as Violet. But she was not so elegantly stylish as Violet. Rather, she was comfortable and plushy looking, and as she prattled on in her soft voice, it was impossible not to warm to her.

''So I borrowed here and I borrowed there,'' she said, ignoring a trill of laughter from Violet, ''and I hied myself to the docks just in time to catch Her Grace. And still, I don't think I turned the trick till I said to her, I said that everyone would be positively agog when they saw her with the three of us in tow. A redhead and a blonde and a brunette. I said, what could be more smashing? More eye-catching? More distinguished? And then I saw her thinking and I went on that she'd be the success of the Continent—her name would be on everyone's lips, I said. And she upped and said, 'Yes, I think you're right.' And so here's old Rose. Coming along to Paris with you. And you needn't worry, for I won't step on your toes at all. Vi here can tell you I'm very amiable, and I'll never stand in your light. I know I'm not terribly bright, like Vi here,'' she said, looking imploringly at Catherine, as though Catherine's opinion meant the entire world to her, ''and neither am I so elegant as you. You look a treat, just like a young lady should. So I won't take the shine out of you. But I needed this job, truly I did, so say you'll be friends and we'll have a jolly time. For if I've gotten your nose out of joint, it will be rotten for us all, and I'll feel badly for having upset everyone.''

''No,'' said Catherine, ''I don't mind. Why should I? If that is what Her Grace wishes, why should I cavil? But I truly don't understand,'' Catherine said sadly, shaking her head and sitting down in one of the gilt chairs in the cabin, ''why someone would need two companions, let alone three. Especially when she doesn't seem to even require one, what with her personal maid seeming to do all the work for her.''

''You see?'' Violet said in disgusted tones, lying back on the bed again, ''it never stops, not even when we're alone together.''

''I think that's horrid of you,'' Rose said indignantly to Violet.

"Live and let live, I say. She don't mean no harm by it. She's probably born to better things, like Henrietta was, back in Tunbridge Wells. Never you mind, Catherine," Rose said pleasantly. "You go on just as you want to. I just wanted to make sure you knew that I mean no harm. And that there's plenty to go round for all three of us, seeing as how the duchess means to hit all the high spots."

Catherine looked at Rose and felt a distinct frisson of unease starting somewhere in the region of her stomach that had nothing to do with the motion of the ship.

"Enough of what to go round?" she asked slowly.

"Oh, Lord," Violet groaned, and most inelegantly flopped over on her stomach and held a pillow over her head.

"Enough gentlemen, of course, dear," Rose said, with puzzlement. "Enough gentlemen for us all to go around. There's plenty of fish in this sea. And even though there'll be three of us, we're all so different, there'll be money enough for all of us to make. I'll never cut into your takings, dear," she said, eyeing Catherine's pale face with distress. "Never fear, we'll get on beautifully, like three sisters."

Chapter VI

Not many people were above deck now. The sky was lowering and the motion of the boat had already sorted out the good sailors from the bad, sending the latter below to suffer in privacy. And even those who did not mind the rolling sea, did not care to brave the chill winds and stayed below as well. Catherine had discovered that she was a good sailor, or perhaps it was just that she was so distressed that it would not matter to her if she were in the center of a tidal wave. Her own thoughts were in such turmoil that the motion of the ship could not match them for turbulence.

She stood at the deck and gripped the rail tightly with her mittened fingers. A great many things made sense to her now—from the duchess's servants' attitudes to the attitude of Madame Bertrand, to even the marquis' mocking comments. Her face flamed when she thought of him and what she now knew he had meant every time he spoke to her. But she was not a stupid girl, and the fact that she had seen nothing in her situation that was not glaringly out of line distressed her almost as much as the opinions of the marquis and everyone she had met in the duchess's service.

For there was no doubt in her mind now. The artless Rose had prattled on and on till she had erased all doubts. She had been hired on only because Rose and Violet were not available, and Rose and Violet had been beautiful women, and young, at least far younger than the general run of ladies' companions in the marketplace. But there was no doubt, as incredible as it seemed, Rose and Violet were women of low repute. Catherine thought of all the euphemisms she had ever heard. They were demireps, they were fancy pieces. Oh, Lord, she thought, have an end to it, they were women who catered to the darker needs of strange gentlemen, whatever you called them.

And here she was, Catherine Robins, unmarried daughter of a younger son related to the great house of the Earl of Dorset, brought up as properly and as poorly as a churchmouse, traveling companion to a duchess and two highly paid cyprians. And presently almost penniless and precisely in the midst of the English Channel. I truly am "at sea," Catherine grieved.

She tried to marshal her thoughts. For she had to decide on some plan of action immediately. Every moment brought her closer to France. The worst, she thought sadly, was done. She had hired on—she had been introduced into the household of the Duchess of Crewe. And all those that had seen or met her most probably thought her on a par with Rose and Violet. What is done is irremediable, she thought vehemently, in an effort to think clearly, pushing aside intrusive thoughts of the disdainful marquis. It was the future she had to think on.

Her first impulse was to cut and run. She felt sullied by her new knowledge and sick at heart at her new understanding of Rose and Violet. The best thing would be to turn and go at once. But then she did some sums rapidly in her head. She had spent a great deal of her money on those foolish lace and brocades she had bought to embellish and repair her gowns. And most of the remainder of her income had gone for Jane and Arthur's presents and gratuities to the servants in the duchess's London house when she had left. If she should decide to turn right back and go home on a return ship when they landed at Dieppe, she would have barely enough to reach her home shores. Then there would be the problem of how to obtain enough funds to pay the many stage fares to see her home to the north country.

How could she even think of borrowing from either Rose or Violet? She could not approach them and say, "I cannot travel with two females as low as you are. My sensibilities are wounded to be even considered in the same light as you. So please lend me enough money to go home." And if she shuddered to think of how respectable people thought of her, she now also had a few guilty feelings about Rose and Violet's opinions of her. For no sooner had Rose done with her long and artless talk than Catherine had stared at her and blurted, "I did not know! I had no idea," and had rushed, shocked and shamed, from the cabin.

That, she thought, furious with herself, had been unnecessary and cruel.

The major problem, she tried to think dispassionately, was the duchess. For she did not know her well enough to know what her true opinion of her companions was. The dowager was such a dignified, socially secure woman that Catherine found it hard to believe she knew the truth about her companions. She had always spoken of Rose and Violet's doings in terms of their "high jinks" and "larks" and "nonsense." It was, Catherine thought desperately, entirely possible that the old woman was naive enough to think they were just innocent romps. Or equally possible that the duchess's mind was turned with age, and that she truly did not notice such goings-on.

The duchess had made it clear that she would hold her wages till the trip was done, or pay quarterly, and, in truth, since paying a sum of money a few weeks past, she owed not a cent to Catherine. All of her wages were yet to be earned. Why should the dowager just hand over monies to a companion who quit her employ the moment they had begun their journey?

And, Catherine thought with a start, if the duchess's companions had such a reputation, how could Catherine ever find decent employment in London again? For the duchess would never write a reference if she quit so precipitously. But more, even if she did, such a reference would not be worth the paper it was written on.

After a half hour in the biting wind on the rolling deck, only two things were abundantly clear to Catherine. One was that she did not have enough resources to get safely home by herself. And two was that she did not have the resources to go safely on with the duchess. Yet every moment the ship bore her onward.

She bent with her head cradled in her arms, by the rail of the ship, cold within and without, until a light touch on her arm recalled her to herself.

"Why, Miss Robins, are you ill?" Jenkins' voice asked softly.

She looked up to see his concerned face close to hers. His was a lined and weathered visage. His hazel eyes looked as though they had squinted against many suns, and his short-cropped brown hair and neatness of person made him seem a comforting figure. He was old enough to be her father, and looked as though he might consider himself as such. She was tempted to blurt out her whole wretched story to him, stranger though he was. But then another familiar voice said, "The sea is not always kind to newcomers. Our little country mouse has strayed too far from her farmhouse.''

Catherine's head shot up and she looked with a mixture of embarrassment and defiance at the marquis. ''I am not ill,'' she said. ''I was only thinking about things. And I lost track of the hours.''

She wondered suddenly if she could confide in him. He, alone of all the people on the ship was a familiar face. He would certainly have the resources not to miss advancing the small amount of money to see her safely home. If only she could strike the right conciliatory note, perhaps he could even give her some advice, for he was a worldly man. She hoped that he would unbend for a moment to give her the chance to speak freely. Jenkins, she saw, was watching her with a kind, concerned expression. She kept her gaze on the marquis as he stood and looked down at her with eyes as fathomless as the slate-gray sea they were crossing and she began to pluck up her courage.

Before she could speak again, he smiled, not at all kindly, and said in an explanatory fashion to Jenkins, ''No, she's not a bit afflicted with mal de mer. So put away your vinaigrette, Jenkins. Rather, I think, Miss Robins is afflicted with a surfeit of companionship. Her cabin is literally bulging at the seams. The fair Rose has joined Violet, and now the duchess has a veritable bower of pretty flowers in her employ. Rose, Violet, and Catherine. That does not have the right ring to it. You ought to change your name, little one, to Forget-me-not, to ensure your standing with the duchess. And the gentlemen. Miss Robins is here, I think, Jenkins, because it is difficult for a little young country flower to keep her head high in the presence of two such spectacular blooms as Rose and Violet. But never fear,'' he said, laying one gray-gloved hand across her cheek to tuck back in an errant wind-whipped curl. ''There are many gentlemen aboard who are weary of hothouse blossoms and who will welcome a fresh young English nosegay such as yourself.''

All of Catherine's fears and shame coalesced into one direct and burning emotion of hatred toward the marquis. He stood there smiling, he who had been her one possible lifeline, and dashed all her nebulous hopes of escape to bits with his words. She had thought to confide in him, but before she had been able to breathe one word, he had begun a frontal attack upon her. She dashed his hand away and looked at him with brimming eyes.

''I find your humor ill bred,'' she said. ''And your inferences impertinent. Good day." And she turned on her heel and walked off. After one moment's silence, she heard a laughing "Bravo!" called in the distance behind her.

"Didn't she carry that off well?" the marquis laughed. "Like the dowager herself. She is a quick study, I'll be bound."

"I think you're being a bit hard on her, lad," Jenkins said reproachfully.

The marquis' face hardened and he turned to look out to sea.

"She's only a little artificial flower, after all, Jenkins. Don't tell me you're touched and believe her role as ingenue?"

"As to that," Jenkins said, turning to face the sea as well, to get a last glimpse of home, "I couldn't say. But no matter what she is, she's only a girl. It's not like you to get so spiteful, especially toward a woman. I saw you chatting up Violet as nice as can be. And she's a right old tart."

"But she's an honest old tart," the marquis answered slowly, "with no dissembling. Our Miss Robins aspires to play the grand lady; it's that, I think, that tickles me."

"Don't seem to tickle you. Seems to gall you," Jenkins said.

"Perhaps. Perhaps it is just that I value honesty. And I might like her very well if she would drop that facade of purity."

"Well," said Jenkins at length, "facade's what it's all about, isn't it? With all of them? Pretending to be attracted and then pleasured, with a fellow pretending he don't notice the pretense. That's all part of the trade."

"And probably why I don't patronize such businesswomen," the marquis said loftily, till he caught Jenkins' eye and then laughed lightly. "Or at least such obvious tradeswomen. You old wretch, you make me admit my every pretense."

"Seems you were interested enough in our bold little Violet," Jenkins ruminated.

"It always pays, Jenkins, to have the friendship of such females. For there's a great many pillows that they have their ears to, and a great deal of information they can, all unwittingly, be privy to. So although I don't have any designs on Violet, and well she knows it, it does pay to be in her good graces."

"Then, why are you going out of your way to alienate the little beauty?" Jenkins asked innocently.

"Be damned to you," the marquis said pleasantly, and as he cuffed Jenkins' shoulder, they both began to laugh.

"It's just that 'tis pity she's a whore," the marquis finally said, when Jenkins thought he had forgotten the subject.

"You can't be sure of that, either," Jenkins finally replied.

"Oh yes, and Violet may be contemplating a life in the convent. Give over, old friend."

"Then meet her price and see."

"I'm not interested in the question," the marquis said, yawning.

And it's not often that you lie to me, Jenkins thought, looking at the marquis' profile, or to yourself.

"It's not such a bad crossing, for January," Jenkins said eventually, to dispel the marquis' frown.

"What? Oh no, it isn't," his companion replied, and they talked of ships and crossings till the wind blew them below to seek refuge as well.

Catherine went back to her cabin, because she had nowhere else to go. And because she wanted to make amends to Rose and Violet.

She had no idea, as she crept back in, of what a fight had been raging before her return. For Rose and Violet now sat calmly, looking through their belongings, not speaking a word to each other.

But the moment Catherine had risen, ashen-faced, and fled, they had both sat there in stunned silence.

"Oh Vi," Rose had wailed after a moment, "see how you've made a mull of it? You told me she was one of us, up to every trick, young as she was. And though when I first laid eyes on her I doubted it, really I doubted it, still you told me she was a deep one. And now, you see, you was wrong. She's just a little innocent and I've gone and shocked her to the bone. Oh I could bite out my tongue."

"Don't be a fool," Violet countered, sitting up and throwing away her pillow, with a look of furious dismay on her face. "It's all part of her game, I tell you. She never drops her guard, not for a moment. All meek and mild, and she'd stab you in the back in a minute. I know her kind."

"That you don't," Rose shouted with unaccustomed heat. "For where would you ever meet such a sweet young innocent?"

"Stupid cow," Violet charged back. "If she was such a sweet young innocent, what would she be doing signing on with the old torment for?"

"Well, that's it exactly," Rose sniffed, overtaken with remorse. "She'd hire on with Her Grace exactly because she didn't know what she was about. For we did leave the dowager in the lurch, and that you do know. And when she asked me for the name of a replacement, I didn't give her any, 'cause I wanted to leave the door open, in case things didn't work out. And it's a good job I did. But I'll wager you didn't give her a name neither. So she must have hired on this little pretty, just 'cause she's so pretty and young and know-nothing.'' And Rose dabbled at her eyes with the edge of the bed covers.

"I never thought you were such a flat, Rose,'' Violet sneered. "To be taken in so by an act of innocence.''

"Well, it's true that I've been taken in, many times, by the gentlemen,'' Rose said slowly, "for I don't understand them at all, I think. Or maybe it's just that I keep expecting things of them that just ain't there. But I do know women. And I'll stake my life on that little thing's honesty. For if she was up to snuff, why shouldn't she come clean with us? You've done a terrible wrong, Vi, that you have.''

Violet, assailed by self-doubt, struck back instantly. "Rose, I vow Carlton took half your brains with him when he took all your money. Do you think the old fiend would run the risk of hiring on a good girl of good birth and reputation?''

"And I think you've gotten hard as nails, Violet; of course, she would, seeing as how she's half turned in the head. And well you know it too. Didn't you just say on our last trip as to how it wouldn't be long before the old cow would be in Bedlam, and how we might never meet on another jaunt together again? Not that I ever approved of how you refer to Her Grace. Because dicked in the nob or not, she's still a duchess, mind. Mad as hatter though she may be. So, of course, she'd hire on some sweet young thing. And a sweet young thing she is. I've never seen her on the town, and you haven't neither. Oh I feel like a brute, Vi, really I do, and you would too, if you hadn't grown so hard.''

"Well, I haven't grown so hard as your head, Rose,'' Violet shrieked in a voice that would have stood her in good stead in her first chosen profession, the stage. "And don't you start blaming me—it was your babbling, your going on and on about your exploits that sent her flying, not mine. I was close mouthed as can be with her. So don't you put the blame on me.''

"You've grown cruel, and hard, yes hard, Violet,'' Rose stated with ponderous calm. "And I'm sorry for it.''

The two fell silent, avoiding each other's eye. And they went about pointedly searching through their portmanteaus, deep in their own thoughts, in exaggerated silence, till Catherine tapped lightly and entered their cabin again, after her time thinking on the deck.

Catherine spoke very quietly.

"I am very sorry," she said, in the voice of a small child who has committed some grave misdemeanor and is determined to beg forgiveness as nicely as she is able, "about the way that I behaved. It was unconscionably rude on my part. Perhaps it was just that I was angry at myself for not seeing what was afoot. I quite deceived myself. And it was wrong in me to have given you the impression that I was disapproving or angry at you. For, you see, I was angry, but only at myself."

"Oh there, there, my dear," Rose cried, seeing the girl standing head bowed and alone in the center of their little room, "we didn't take anything amiss, did we, Vi? So you must not apologize, certainly not, right, Vi?"

"Right," Violet said, looking uncharacteristically conscious. "Not a thing to apologize for."

"That is very kind of you," Catherine said, and then, turning her large anxious eyes to both of them in turn, she asked, hesitantly, "But there is something I must ask you. And it is very difficult for me, so please bear with me for a moment, and pray do not take offense."

"Oh we shall not," Rose hastened to tell her, looking very anxious herself.

"It is just this," Catherine began. "Does Her Grace, that is to say, this is of primary importance to me, does the duchess know and condone your, ah, activities that go beyond companioning her?"

"As to that, you see, my dear, we really could not say," Rose said nervously. "Her Grace gives us free time once she is abed and no longer requires our presence. She is a very free, that is to say, a very—"

"Liberal," Violet put in quickly, seeing Rose stumble.

"Yes, an exceedingly liberal employer. And she does not care what we get up to when she is not abroad. That is, so long as we are discreet and do not embroil her in any of our activities."

"Then," Catherine ventured, raising her head, "you are not required to—to do," she stammered, "what you do?"

"Oh, Lord love you, no," Rose laughed in relief. "That is not the case at all. Why, just ask Vi, she traveled with Her Grace for a season before I signed on."

"Rose speaks no less than truth," Violet said hastily, "for the duchess hired me only as companion."

"Just so," said Rose in satisfaction.

"But I do not understand, surely she must have heard . . . she does not care, then, you say?"

"The duchess," Violet said quickly, "enjoys the attention we bring her. She enjoys the notice she receives when we are with her. As to what she may have heard, we cannot say."

"So, then," Catherine went on, thinking aloud, "she does not expect me to, she does not require me to . . ."

"Oh never, I'm sure," Rose said in horrified tones. "She never discusses such things with us."

"Then I can stay on," Catherine asked hopefully, "and only be a companion, and nothing else? No matter," she said, with a little shake of her head, "what anyone else thinks? I cannot see how I can turn and leave now. And once I return home to Kendal, I shall, in any event, hardly be running into anyone that I have met here. Kendal is such a long, long way from London and Paris in so many ways," Catherine thought aloud, "that it hardly matters what anyone in the duchess's set thinks of me. So, after this journey, I will retire and go to live out my life back home where no one has ever heard of the duchess to begin with. Not," she said, aghast at her ruminations, "that you would not be welcome in Kendal. Or that I think anything—"

Violet cut her off with a wry smile.

"Give over, Miss Catherine. If you are a nice little thing from the country, if you are well born, of course you're shocked to flinders to find yourself with us. We're hardly the sort of companions a well-bred miss hopes to find herself with. But that don't bother us. So you're staying on then?"

"If you think, and I truly ask you please to tell me the truth, that I can go forward with the duchess and not be expected by her to—to pursue another trade."

Violet gave out a little yip of laughter.

"Oh, that's a nice way of putting it. I suppose your pockets are to let, then?"

Catherine nodded sadly.

"Well, we can't help you out there neither. For we're both in the same case. But once we get ashore, we can remedy that, and if you want, we'll advance you the funds to skip out." Violet looked almost as shocked as Rose and Catherine did at her sudden burst of generosity.

"Oh no, no," Catherine protested immediately. "That wouldn't be right." Catherine thought suddenly of the names she could put to someone who profited from a cyprian's earnings and then blurted, afraid that her companions might know the nature of her thoughts from her horrified expression, "I would not ask you to be responsible for me. For if I can go on solely as a companion, as I was engaged to do, I can see the journey out and then take my earnings and go home."

"Of course you can go on with us. In fact, we can put the word about the gentlemen that you are not"—Rose paused—"of a sporting disposition."

Violet winced at Rose's effort to tidy up her speech, and then, considering the young miss so sadly lost in their midst, thought rapidly. For no doubt the little beauty would draw the gentlemen like flies to a picnic basket. And then she and Rose could only profit the more from the fact that she was unwilling to go off with them. She smiled with perfect charity at Catherine.

"Rose is right, we'll tell them, never fear. And there is no reason to concern yourself as to the duchess's caring one jot one way or the other. She'll be glad enough if you only play the companion well. All she wants is for heads to turn when she appears. She don't give a tinker's damn as to what you do to occupy your free time. Whether you sew a fine seam alone in your room or dance naked in a fountain, it's all the same to her. And that's the truth."

"Very true," seconded Rose.

"And," Violet said triumphantly, "you yourself said no one at home is likely to ever know what the duchess and her set is about. So cheer up. It will be a good journey. Rose and I will be amiable enough. And all the duchess wants of you is to keep by her side in good looks. You can just put all else out of your mind."

"You two must think me a fool," Catherine said sadly.

"Oh no," Rose protested. "We were all young once. Only, perhaps, not quite so young."

Catherine laughed. And then she looked at her two fellow companions.

"I think I shall grow up quite a bit on this journey."

"Travel is broadening," Rose agreed complacently, ignoring the weary look Violet shot her.

Chapter VII

The crossing, all agreed, was not so bad as it might have been. There were those, of course, who had been taken ill by the vessel's rocking over the January seas, and those who had been, as they expected, ill no matter what the conditions of the weather. But it might have been worse—there had been only the cutting wind and the winter's cold. Travelers who were more experienced with the vagaries of the channel's weather could only be grateful that there had been no pouring rains or wind-driven squalls of ice.

As the shores of France loomed in the distance, the passengers began to assemble themselves for departure. Catherine had spent the remainder of her journey hugging her newfound knowledge to herself and attempting to try on a new public face. For, knowing what she did, she reasoned there was no way she could delude herself into forgetting it for a moment. If she could not go homeward, she must go onward with a new attitude. But which one?

She could not appear to be constantly disapproving, because she felt that would make her a sanctimonious fool, to go on with people of whom she patently disapproved. The only hope for it, she thought sadly, was to maintain an air of irreproachable dignity. To carry on as though she well knew what people thought, but was too sophisticated to care. No, she thought, not sophisticated, for that she could not simulate as she was decidedly not a woman of the world. Rather, that she knew what was happening about her, but chose not to notice or care. That was, after all, just what she was doing. Her attitude must be then, she thought, much as her employer's was. Tolerant and uncaring.

And if she felt any squeamish qualms about having to affect any sort of attitude at all, and not simply give the whole matter up and fly off to try to get home in any manner that she could, she consoled herself by recalling that a young woman alone and without funds in the English countryside might be thought of as a great deal worse than one employed in the entourage of a duchess of the realm.

So Catherine stood, head high, surrounded by her trunks, on the deck of the packet and watched as the vessel began its docking procedures. And when the Marquis of Bessacarr strolled by with Jenkins at his shoulder, Catherine found her newly born affect of worldliness sufficient to allow her to acknowledge his presence with a smile and a nod in his direction.

He paused in his steps, for they both realized that it was the first time she had ever admitted his presence without his first having approached or accosted her. He smiled in his faint cynical manner and came to her side.

"So you have forgiven me my rash speculations? I am glad of it. I was, I fear, afflicted with the tediousness of the journey, and I let my tongue run away with me. How pleasant it is to see that you have compassion as well as beauty, little one," he said, bowing over her hand.

Catherine smiled politely at him and at Jenkins, and said, she noticed, without the usual fast beating of her heart or dryness in her mouth, "Certainly. There is nothing to apologize for."

It was amazing, she thought, now that she understood what all his sly references to her meant, her feelings of confusion in his presence had fled. It was as though she were a different person he was speaking to, and as though they both were part of an amusing play. Newly confident, she only smiled demurely when he gazed thoughtfully at her.

"I understand that we are both to be guests at Sir Sidney's little house party."

She knew nothing of the sort, but only said carelessly, "I am sure it will be most pleasant."

"Oh, delightful, I'm sure," he said, with a puzzled look at her. "And I shall be envied, for I think that Jenkins and I are the only gentlemen to have made your acquaintance as yet. For I see that you do not join your companions." He gestured toward Rose and Violet, who were chatting with a group of gentlemen.

"No," she said a little nervously, "but please excuse me, as I think the duchess requires me now."

She nodded and fairly flew off toward the duchess, who, she was sure, had forgotten her existence entirely for the moment.

She had convinced herself that the world's opinion did not matter. But yet it seemed, despite her best efforts, that one gentleman's opinion mattered very much. She discovered she could not bear the contempt in his eyes.

"Oh, there you are, Catherine," the duchess said, seeing her slip into the outskirts of the impromptu circle that had formed around her.

"This is Catherine Robins, my newest companion," the duchess said to the general interest of the group of elderly persons around her. "Rose and Violet you know of old. But Catherine here has only just joined me."

There were several murmurs of introduction and interested looks in Catherine's direction. A moment later, she found herself forgotten as the discussion turned to accommodations that were considered acceptable in Paris these days. Catherine had a good chance to covertly study the group that surrounded her employer.

They were all old, she thought with relief—indeed, some seemed ancient. A few of the gentlemen still sported periwigs, and the women were either thinned by age, as was the duchess, or blatantly plump. Some were dressed in high style and others sported garments that seemed to have come straight out of museums. One poor old gentleman, Catherine noticed, sat trembling in his bath chair, attended by an impassive valet. It was he who was going on, in a high, tremulous voice, about how the conditions of travel had deteriorated since his last journey to the City of Light.

"Of course," said the thin, pale old gentleman at Catherine's side, "that was before the flood, you know. Poor old Richard used to dance attendance on Pompadour herself, when they were both in nursery, I believe," he said, laughing. "And Cleopatra as well, I'll warrant."

Catherine turned to the speaker. He bowed and then looked at her with frankly approving eyes. She did not mind his obvious interest, because he was so very old and innocent looking. He had been tall, she guessed, in youth, but age had shrunken him, and now he appeared slender and almost translucently fragile. He had a thin coating of gray hair and his face was gentle and lined. His whole attitude, from the sober hues of his clothes to the quietness of his voice, gave her the impression of a gentle, kindly old fellow. So she smiled wholeheartedly at him.

"Ah, the duchess has picked herself a lovely this time," he said. "I hope you do not mind me being so personal, but at my age, alas, all I can do is admire loveliness in all its forms."

In truth, Catherine was growing weary of hearing nothing but references to her physical person, but it was impossible to mind anything this kind old gentleman said.

"Thank you," she said softly.

"Hah, look at the Vicar," cried the duchess. "Just got in a new flower and he's already buzzing around her."

"But never fear, little lovely," cackled one old female in a dizzying collection of shawls and scarves, "for he's lost his sting."

The assembled old people began laughing, and Catherine noticed that the man they called "the Vicar" laughed along with them.

"That is true," he said ruefully, "but Miss Robins seems to be a perceptive child, and so suffers my attentions nonetheless. We shall meet at Sir Sidney's, my dear, and show these doubters that I can still, at least, dance to a tune or two."

Catherine nodded her agreement, and further sounds of merriment were stilled as the vessel, now tied securely to the dock, began to let its passengers off.

The duchess debarked in state, leading her ensemble of four females—Gracie directly behind her, and then Rose, Violet, and Catherine—carefully picking their way down the gangplank.

"So exit the old hen and her delicious chicks," the marquis remarked to Jenkins from his observation point against the rails.

"I tell you, Jenkins," he said, in low tones, dispiritedly, "I cannot like this employment. Pitched into the midst of these posturing, empty, pleasure seekers. I'd rather be in the thick of some action or in any other company but this. Having to play at their games, play at being one with them is wearing. Fiend seize the old chap, I'll gather whatever I can and be quit of this charade as soon as possible. I cannot think I can learn enough of import for this trip to be worthwhile. I boarded this packet just to be in step with them. And what have I discerned so far? That Lady Scofield has left her lord for a dancing instructor. That he does not care so long as she takes care not to return too soon. That Lord Hunt is on the prowl for a French mistress, that old Bertie expects to make a killing at the gaming tables, and old Philip has to, else he cannot return home at all. That the Dirty Duchess has three females for hire in her train, one of them with the airs of a lady—oh, all of this, I am sure will thrill the old chap and save our dear country.''

''Aye,'' Jenkins said softly, ''but you've not set foot on La Belle France yet. And you've not put your eyes or ears to work yet. It's in Paris where the meat of the matter lies.''

''And I have to stop off at Sir Sidney's and prattle with the lot there first,'' the Marquis sighed.

''That you do,'' Jenkins nodded. ''For if you pass up an invitation such as that, they'll surely smell a rat. You're a pleasure-loving lad, and no pleasure lover would pass up such a treat.''

''Then let's haul ourselves off there instanter,'' the marquis decided, uncoiling his long frame, ''for the sooner it's over, the sooner we can go on. And,'' he said, eyeing the duchess's party as it disposed itself into a coach in the quay below, ''I might just seek some pleasure there as well.''

''Well,'' said the duchess, with satisfaction, ''now we're off. Sir Sidney has rented a house, and a great many good people are to be stopping off there before Paris. And so shall we. You've done well, Catherine,'' she said with pleasure. ''The Vicar's an astute man, and he likes the cut of you. And I noticed that everyone is bowled over by my three companions, Rose, you were quite right. Now, I shall take a brief rest and hope that it is not too long till we reach Sir Sidney's. I grow weary of so much travel, but I think it is best not to chance some local hostelry this night. Far better to spend the first night at Sir Sidney's establishment. For while it may be a foreign house, it has an Englishman in residence.''

And, so saying, the duchess gave a satisfied grunt and closed her eyes. Rose, Violet, and Catherine sat rather closely together on the seat opposite the duchess and Gracie. Their luggage traveled in one vast heap in the coach behind them.

''I saw you in conversation with Sinjun, Catherine,'' Violet whispered, when she thought enough time had passed for the duchess to have found the slumber she sought.

''Sinjun?'' Catherine asked, confused.

''The Marquis of Bessacarr, the handsome lord you were chatting up, on deck,'' Violet answered. ''For his friends call him so.''

''Go on with you,'' Rose tittered. ''Sinjun. Don't you just wish you called him so?''

Violet sniffed. "Well, I had quite a nice coze with him earlier. And he did ask after the new 'chick,' as he called her."

"But 'Sinjun' indeed." Rose snickered. "As if you two were bosom bows."

"He's too high in the instep for me," Violet said calmly.

"All he'd have to do is crook a finger, Vi, and you know it. But he never does. He chats with us, and he says such lovely things so charmingly, but there's an end to it," she told Catherine.

"Not," Violet put in, "that he's a hermit. But when he has the like of Gwyn Starr in London. And Belle Fleur, and almost any female like that, he doesn't tarry with us."

"And Lady Spencer last season, I hear. So don't be alarmed if he says things to you, Catherine, for he's only tarrying. And don't bother yourself about the Vicar's attentions either," Rose whispered, "for he's old as the hills. I hear he was a terror years ago, but now he just sits back and watches like the duchess. So rest easy about him as well."

Catherine nodded, both pleased and a little embarrassed about her two fellow companions' new solicitude on her behalf. But before they could offer her any further advice, the duchess opened one sharp eye.

"If you ladies want to prattle all the way, kindly let me know. I shall ride with the baggage."

And the three of them fell to guilty silence as their coach rolled on through the city and outward, into the unknown center of France.

Catherine was stiff in every limb by the time the coach rolled into the great courtyard. She did not know how a woman of the duchess's years could wake so quickly, and look about so brightly, as they reached their destination. It was true that the dowager had slept soundly for all the hours that Catherine had been looking out her window, trying to get glimpses of the life and people in this new land. But still, she seemed more alert and rested now than the girl who was decades her junior.

It was night, yet the great house seemed to blaze with light. Liveried footmen leaped forward to greet them and Catherine could see that other coaches were unloading other newly come passengers as well. In the gloom dispelled by the torches the footmen were bearing, Catherine could make out familiar persons from the boat, alighting from their carriages. The house itself, she saw with wonder, as she stepped stiffly out onto the circular drive, was massive. Gray and distinguished, it seemed a palace to her. She had never beheld so old and imposing a residence.

But neither her employer nor her companions seemed impressed. They had seen English country seats before, and this monumental old château was simply another stopping-off place for them. It had been the proud home of a French duke, who had fled during the revolution. Sadly, when the Bourbon had been placed back upon the throne and Napoleon left to lord it over only a small island, the duke was too impoverished and defeated by age to return. Instead, he hoped to better his heirs' conditions by letting the château out, for an exorbitant fee, to those who could afford it. And Sir Sidney and his shocking wife could afford it well enough. They had come over to France the moment hostilities had ceased, much to the relief of Sidney's more correct relations, and lorded it there in the ancient manner ever since. They never needed to journey to Paris at all for gaiety, Sir Sidney often said happily, since all those who mattered in Paris would be sure to come to him, either before or after they visited the great city. And so life in the great house had been a constant party since they had arrived.

Sir Sidney and his blatantly beautiful wife (an actress who had been lucky beyond her deserts, Violet whispered to Catherine as they went up the great steps to the front portals) were busily greeting their new guests.

"Ah, Duchess." Sir Sidney, a portly little man, beamed. "So you have come to grace our halls as well. And dear little Violet, and this must be Rose," he chortled, chucking Rose under her chin. "You see, we hear all here at Beauvoir. But who is this little darling? Never say, Duchess, that you have three exquisite companions now?"

The duchess permitted herself a little smile. "I do say it, Ollie. Good evening, Lady Sidney. So good of you to have us," the Duchess said, knowing quite well that Lady Sidney had nothing to say about who shared her house with her.

But her host and hostess had already turned to greet other arrivals, Sir Sidney chuckling that every time the packet came from France, he sent orders to his servants to make up the beds, for the British were coming. It was with relief that Catherine followed in the train of the duchess up the staircase, off the huge stone hall to which no amount of torches or candles could lend warmth.

A flustered housekeeper showed them to spacious, lavish rooms that Catherine was too weary to admire. Before settling in, Catherine scratched softly on the duchess's door. Being told by a perfunctory Gracie, already in her night shift, that the duchess was going to retire, Catherine was happy to wash and slip into bed. She had time only to murmur a silent thanks that she had gotten so far without difficulties before sleep took her far from the duchess, the château, and France.

Catherine knew that her employer never rose before noon, and in the hours that she wandered through Sir Sidney's house, she came to understand that no female of rank did otherwise. Only the lower servants and she herself were up and about in the morning. A few gentlemen, she heard, had gone out early to ride with Sir Sidney over his countless rented acres. But she was well used to being alone, and contented herself in prowling the halls and investigating the premises, storing up details to regale Jane and Arthur with on some later, quiet country evening.

Still, she thought crossly much later on, as she struggled to do up her buttons while changing for dinner, if she could only get into the habit of sleeping the day away, her state would be vastly improved.

Rose tapped and entered her room just as the early dusk of a winter's day descended. Catherine stared at her in awe. For the comfortable, companionable Rose of the day seemed vanished. In her stead stood a startlingly beautiful woman. Rose wore a low gown, the color of her namesake. Her blond hair was swept up in a flurry of ringlets, a sparkling necklace sat upon her ample breast, and she glittered when she walked. A heavy perfume hung over her, and her bright eyes seemed heavily lidded and glistened in the candle's glow.

"Oh, don't you look fine?" Rose said happily, turning to Violet, all in flaming red, with red plumes twined in her curls, as she stepped into the room behind her. "Don't Catherine look lovely? I told her to get rigged out fine, and so she did."

"And she didn't even ring for a maid. And so you should have, Catherine, to help you dress. Even though mine couldn't get out a 'how do you do' in English, and just chirped 'wee-wee' whenever I asked her anything."

Catherine could see nothing exceptional in her looks beside her two co-companions. She wore the simplest of light-green garments that she could find in her wardrobe, with a sash of darker green beneath her breasts. She had built up Madame

Bertrand's bold bodice so that only some of her white shoulders and breasts showed above it—not at all like Violet and Rose's deep expanses of exposed breast. At the last moment she had bound up her dark hair with a green fillet, and the only ornament she wore was a simple gold pendant that her mother had left her. She felt she looked the servant to Violet and Rose's great ladies.

But they saw, tentative and graceful in the candlelight, a slip and sprite of refreshing girl, so simple and refreshing as to overwhelm their finery and make them seem tawdry.

Violet sighed. "You're either the boldest thing in creation or the most innocent. I'm not sure I want to know. Come, we're dining in state with the 'great lady.' After that, simply stay away from darkened corners or stay at the old dame's side if you wish to escape trouble."

"Don't rally with Sir Sidney, dear," Rose cautioned as they went on slippered feet to the duchess's room, "for he's a right old caution. And don't dance with Lord Lambert, nor Jimmy Crawley neither. And don't flirt with Sir Harold, for he's up to no good, and don't agree to see Viscount Hightower's collection of snuffboxes, because he hasn't got any, and, no matter what he says, don't offer to help Jamie Prendergast when he comes all over faint, for he's fit as may be, whatever he says."

Rose's admonitions went on, with Catherine losing track of her whispered warnings and only vowing fiercely to herself to avoid all members of the opposite gender, footmen and waiters included. At last the duchess appeared in her doorway, nodding complacently at her entourage and quite taking their breath away. For she was in her best looks, all in lavender, tall, erect, and stately. She breezed down the stairs, as regal as a visiting dignitary, with her three companions behind her and her devoted Gracie watching from an unobtrusive darkened part of the upper stair.

They dined in a great room with a blazing fireplace that was big enough, Catherine thought, to accommodate a forest full of logs. Their table was set up under two huge chandeliers whose candles lit their plates and faces as daylight, but left the shadowy retainers who filled their dishes and glasses as faceless as wraiths. Catherine might not have been able to swallow a morsel if it were not for the fortuitous fact that she had been seated next to the gentleman she had met on the ship whom the duchess had called "the Vicar." He was actually, he admitted, the Baron Watchtower, but his intimates called him Vicar because of his quiet, cautious ways. Catherine found him a dear, gentle old fellow and enjoyed his calm good humor and his easygoing ways.

She wondered what he was doing in this ribald company, for all about them the other guests, led by their host and hostess, were laughing loudly and drinking freely and calling to each other from all parts of the great table, in a manner, she thought, that was not at all seemly. But the Vicar spoke no more than the truth when he told her that though he was too old for such pleasures, still he enjoyed being part of such merry company. She could not know that in his time, the Vicar, so named because all his actions had so outrageously belied his manner, had been one of the most absolute dissolutes of his era. There had been no pleasure of the senses that he had not engaged in, no deeds too outrageous for him to attempt. He had never married, never having been so inclined toward women. And when he had noted an excellent nephew coming of age, he had decided the fellow would do a great deal better with his title than he ever had, and so had gone happily on with his own proclivities. Now he was truly burnt out and content, at last, to be just an observer of the scene. But since he had nothing in common with the tame socially correct world, he traveled in the duchess's set, preferring to spend the last of his years among those who understood his past rather than those who pretended to ignore it.

Catherine, he thought, watching her animated face, and seeing the candles reflected in the blue depths of her eyes, was in way over her head. This amused him, and he made a note to follow her adventures. For, for all his pleasant ways and gentle, amused acceptance of life, he was fully as selfish as the duchess and would never make a move to help a fellow creature if in some way it did not help him. Like the duchess, he had no interest in the passions between a man and a woman, but instead of spending his time gaining the attention of others, as she did, he derived pleasure from simply watching the follies of others. Catherine, he thought, would be an entertaining little creature to watch. There was every possibility she was what she appeared to be. And every possibility she was not. He was delighted to devote his attention to her throughout the long and riotous dinner.

After dinner, the ladies absented themselves from the gentlemen for only a brief time. The servants scurried to set up gaming tables in the great room to the left of the staircase, and musicians filed into the other room to the right. Catherine stood with Rose

and Violet in the ladies' withdrawing room, but when the great
doors opened, with a hasty farewell they both left her. She
quickly sought out the duchess, who was seated at a card table
with another elderly female and two middle-aged gentlemen.

Catherine, not wishing to call attention to herself to the point
of summoning a chair, stood at Her Grace's shoulder in the
shadows of the candlelight. After a few hands of a game Catherine did not know, the duchess glanced up at her.

"I thought so," the duchess grumbled. "My luck never runs
right when someone's watching the cards. Run away, gel, I
don't require you now. You're setting my luck to ruin. Run
away, gel, and amuse yourself. I won't need you any longer
tonight."

Catherine wandered out of the gaming room, for she did not
wish to wager anything herself and could not just stand and
watch others. She decided that as no one yet had gone back
upstairs, it would be socially incorrect to do so. So she went into
the large room where she could hear the music and watch the
dancers swirl about, to look around for the Vicar to keep her
company.

She stood in a dim corner, although not a truly darkened one,
as Rose had cautioned. For in those dark recesses of the room
she could make out dimly the figures of men and women, close
together in intimate conversations. The waltz was played, and
she saw Violet sweep by, her red gown swinging out with each
step, in the arms of a tall, bulky gentleman with side whiskers.
Rose, whom she could pick out by her dress, was in close
converse with a short gentleman with a booming laugh. The
Vicar, she thought, must be intent on remaining as unobtrusive
as herself, for he was nowhere in sight.

So she stood and watched the scene before her. At one moment she saw the marquis dancing with a willowy woman in
black; at another, she saw Rose again, this time with their host,
laughing uproariously with him. She occupied herself with watching the changing couples for some time. But then her own hiding
place was discovered. The aging gentleman she recognized as
Old Bertie, his face gleaming with exertion, bowed and without
a word hauled her, protesting weakly, off to the dance floor. She
was not a bad dancer, she knew, but dancing with Old Bertie
was one of the most harrowing experiences she had ever had. He
gripped her too closely with his hot, wet hands. He trod upon her
foot every other measure, and he clutched her closer to his

protruding stomach every time she managed to get a little distance between them. When the music ended, he stood there and grinned at her.

"Right," he said, mopping his forehead. "Now how about it, eh lass?"

"Oh no," Catherine said quickly, to whatever he was proposing. And before he could reach for her again, she took advantage of the crowd and slipped away from him to the darkest corner she could find. But upon reaching it, she found that she had intruded upon a couple in intimate embrace, and, drawing in her breath sharply, she muttered an apology and made her way to another recess. Breathing more slowly, she found she had discovered an excellent outpost, very near to a window, and very near to some draperies, in only dim shadows, not absolute dark. She had barely caught her breath, when her heart sank as she saw the gentleman approaching her.

"Old Bertie's in a dither," he laughed. "He's searching for you everywhere. 'Where's that demned little green gal got to?'," the marquis imitated perfectly in Bertie's accents. "However, don't worry, I won't let on a word. You're quite safe here. But I would suggest standing near to a green drape next time. This golden one sets your gown off too well. Come, dance with me this time. I have ten years on Old Bertie, and he won't trifle with you when you're in my arms. In point of fact, you'll be safer from him there than in the embraces of these curtains."

In some ways, Catherine thought, waltzing with the marquis was worse than dancing with Old Bertie. For although he was a graceful dancer, and although he did not hold her any closer than was seemly, she was far more aware of his lithe well-muscled body next to hers than she had been of the round mass of the older man's. He drew her near once, and the clean scent of him was sharper in her nostrils than the overheated miasma that had consumed her in Old Bertie's clutches. Far worse, though, was that he said not a word to her while they danced, and when she looked up, he gazed down at her with an unreadable expression. She was relieved when the music finally ended and he walked her back to a dim corner.

He stood next to her, looking down at her still while she searched for some light word to dispel the strange silence that surrounded them. At last, when she was about to begin to tell him some nonsense about what a lovely night it was, he spoke.

"Jenkins is right," he sighed, so close to her now, she could feel his warm breath on her cheek. "It is far better to find out for oneself. And the question has been troubling me more than it should. For though you do indeed, in this glittering company, look like Bertie's 'green girl,' the proof is in the tasting, isn't it?"

Before Catherine's mind could register what he said, she found herself in his arms, completely captured there, and being expertly kissed. The shock of his lips, so warm and unexpectedly gentle, quieted her for a moment. The experience was so oddly delicious that she stayed there, savoring it until a split second later the intensity of feeling that arose in her recalled her to her good senses. She was transformed into a fury the moment the realization of his action came to her from far beyond her amazed senses. She struggled free from him and, glaring up into his bemused, newly gentled face, she, her mind whirling with possible methods of retribution, kicked him forcefully on the shin.

It hurt her, she groaned, realizing suddenly the thinness of her dancing slippers, more than it hurt him. In fact, through her fury and the pain of her smarting toes, she saw him throw back his head and heard him roar with laughter.

"Oh, Lord," he laughed, his handsome face free of his usual cold expression, looking young as a boy's. "You don't kick a man who's just taken advantage of you, Miss Robins, not in the duchess's exalted set. It's just not done. In the first place, it doesn't hurt your attacker enough, and in the second, it's most unheard of. You take your hand, child," he said, taking her trembling hand in his, "and you put your fingers together and swing. You slap the fellow for all he's worth, if you want to make a point of purity.

"If you do not," he said, drawing her closer again, "you make some token gesture, such as a weak verbal protest, or perhaps a gentle little kick." He smiled. "And then, token protest being made and accepted, you submit gracefully to his and your own will."

And after this astonishing speech, Catherine found herself being held and kissed once again. This time she did not tarry to taste strange new sensations. She pulled free and, taking his excellent advice, swung her hand across his face. He seemed as startled as she was by her action. The sound her slap made, she thought as she turned to look for an exit through a cloud of outrage, should have stopped all the dancers in their tracks, although no one turned or seemed to notice. She raced quietly through the crowd of people and made her way up the great stairs to her room. Once inside, she locked the door and sank onto her bed. Unconsciously, she slipped off her slippers and massaged her aching toes. But it was only her lips, still tingling, that she thought of.

"She tasted sweet enough," the marquis smiled to Jenkins as they stood on the fringe of dance, "But I'm afraid she wasn't ripe for the picking, I forgot to discuss the going price for green girls this season. That seems to have been my major mistake."

"It could be," Jenkins said, "that she hasn't got a price, or leastways one that any in this room can pay."

"And it could be that I've taken too much wine, out of boredom. And attempted, clumsily, a highly bred doxy, for the same reason. It's just as well, friend, that I didn't find myself entangled with her. For we do have to be up and out early this morning, don't we? There's no more to be got out of this pack of merrymakers. We'll have to be off to Paris tomorrow, now we've made our token stop here."

"It seems," Jenkins said, carefully and conspicuously staring at the faint red palm print that still lingered on the marquis' cheek, "that some fruit hangs too high out of reach, even for you. You seem, lad, to have got lashed by some branches."

"But it happens," the marquis laughed, rubbing his cheek, "that she was only following my explicit instructions."

Chapter VIII

Catherine was furious with herself. She paced her room, for once gladdened that there was nothing to be done during the day in this great, rambling home the Sidneys entertained in. For she did not think she could bear to make polite converse and exchange idle pleasantries when she was so bedeviled by her own thoughts.

It had only been a kiss, she thought—there was no need for the incident to overset her so. But it had. And that was the fact with which she had to deal. She had, she told herself strictly, been kissed before, so there was little sense in making such a pother about it. In fact, she remembered, she had been kissed exactly three times before (she had kept careful track). Once, when she was just fifteen, and Fred McDermott had been seventeen. It had been a hasty little kiss, stolen while they were at a picnic. And had been memorable in that it had excited not her senses, but rather her pity, since Fred had been horrified by his impulsiveness and had spent the rest of that lovely summer Sunday apologizing to her and castigating himself.

When she was seventeen, Mrs. Fairchild's son-in-law, on a visit from Sussex, had taken too much port, surprised Catherine in the hallway of his mother-in-law's house, and delivered an overheated, messy salute upon her lips, along with a great deal of unpleasant fumbling, until she had broken away and run off. But then it had been a shameful incident, and Mrs. Fairchild herself, some months later, was overheard to confide to Jane that her daughter had not picked a "right 'un" and was suffering for it.

The third kiss had come when she was twenty and had gone walking out with Tom Hanley. Tom had been a pleasant-looking chap, an aspiring law clerk on vacation from London, visiting his aunt in Kendall. But that relationship had not gone beyond a few visits. For at their last meeting he had seemed preoccupied and solemn. And when he had left her, he had kissed her once—one brief chaste kiss—and then he had looked at her and sighed deeply. Within a month Catherine had heard of Tom's engagement to a young woman in London, daughter of one of the partners in his firm.

So, Catherine thought, it was not as though she was inexperienced. But nothing had prepared her for the embrace she had received last night. She could scarcely believe how overwhelmed she had been by the marquis' attentions. And she did not know how she could face him again, for surely he must have known how she felt. And if he did, she was sure that it would only reaffirm his belief in her immorality. And as for her kicking him! But in truth she had been outraged—she had never struck another being since her childhood. She had to do something, and, fool that she was, she had kicked a peer of the realm. And then slapped him. And that, she was sure, was worse.

When the pangs of hunger recalled Catherine to her immediate world, she decided that she must carry on as before. She must assume an icy dignity in the marquis' presence. She must not allow herself to look for him or to scan the company for his presence. For if she continued to be fascinated by him, she would, she chided herself, end up in the same case as Rose and Violet in some fashion.

As Catherine dressed for dinner, she took special care with her appearance. She rang for the little French maid and managed to communicate well enough, even though she realized with sinking heart that her long-ago French lessons were hardly adequate to equip her to ask for fresh water properly. She wore her finest new gown of a deep sapphire blue, just to show him that she had not been overset by him. And brushed her hair and drew it back in a severe and startlingly sophisticated style to show him that here was no little miss to trifle with.

When she went down to dinner, she looked neither to the left nor the right, but seated herself in the manner of a grande dame. She chatted lightly and superficially with the Vicar, who seemed vastly amused at something and who enjoyed her company in a very proper fashion. It was only when the dinner was over and the guests were at their regular pursuits of gaming or dancing, or meeting with one another in darkened parts of the house, that the

Vicar, who stood at her side watching the dancers told her that
the marquis and his man had gone.

The house party, he told her in an aside, was already beginning to break up, and since the marquis had left, others were
beginning to make noises about going on to Paris. "Which much
displeases our host," the Vicar said, "since he needs to keep his
house full. Otherwise he is left alone, with only thirty servants or
so, a few constant hangers-on, and, of course, dear Lady Sidney."

Catherine felt deflated. And noticed that the music, dancing,
and chatter all around her seemed suddenly less interesting, less
enthralling. While the marquis was in evidence she had always
felt on the verge of an adventure; now all this newfound splendor
seemed oddly flat. And she murmured her sympathies for her
host with compassion.

"Oh, don't pity dear Ollie overmuch," the Vicar said, grinning,
"for he has found compensation, as you can see."

Looking up in the direction the Vicar nodded to, Catherine
saw her host, smiling and whispering, deep in conversation with
Rose. Rose towered above him by several inches and had to
hang her head down to hear his whispered comments. But as
they watched, the ill-matched couple seemed to come to some
sort of understanding, and Sir Sidney, with a little bow and
beaming smile, left the room. Catherine could see him going
upstairs. It was rather unusual, she thought, for the host of such
a great house party to absent himself from his guests, especially
since if he needed anything above stairs, he had a clutch of
servants he could summon.

But as the Vicar kept watching Rose silently, with a gentle
smile upon his own face, Catherine did the same. And saw that
within a few moments of her host's departure, Rose brushed
some invisible lint from her skirt and then quietly left the room
to go up the stairs quickly in Sir Sidney's wake. "Business as
usual," yawned the Vicar. And Catherine felt her heart sink. It
was one thing to know of Rose and Violet's interests; it was
quite another to see them in action. Catherine felt deeply ashamed
although she had done no more than watch.

Throughout the evening she clung to the Vicar's side like a
devoted daughter. Her attendance upon him seemed to afford
him great pleasure. And when he pointed out Violet's departure
with an ancient viscount, she was so glad of the Vicar's presence,
and so determined to stay with him, that he had to gently, and
then less gently, hint to her that he wished to absent himself for

only a few moments; he would return immediately, but he really had to be alone for a few moments. When she saw that he was gesturing vaguely in the direction of the gentlemen's withdrawing room, she grew dizzy with embarrassment and vowed to stop clinging to him like a limpet.

But when, in his absence, she found herself approached by no less than three other gentlemen with speculation in their bold, assessing eyes, she gave up her resolve and fairly flew to the Vicar's side again when he reappeared. And there she stayed till she saw the duchess making her stately way upstairs to her room.

For the next days Catherine stayed close in her rooms during the day, and took tea with her companions, but said little to them. For she had seen them disappear with such a variety of gentlemen each night that she felt she was not yet able to converse normally with them. She did not want them to see her revulsion, for in all, they were pleasant and helpful enough to her. And yet she could not reconcile their actions with her own standards, much as she lectured herself about tolerance and different values for different persons during the long days that she was alone in her room. At nightfall she would dress with care, for the duchess's eye was sharp, and on the one occasion when she tried to dress demurely and unspectacularly, the dowager had barked that she didn't employ sparrows—what was the matter with the gel anyway? And she would spend each evening in close converse or, at least, in close companionship with the Vicar.

She soon discovered that he thought her situation vastly entertaining, and, further that he really did not care about her predicament at all so long as it afforded him pleasure in observing it. Sadly, she began to discover that he was using her in much the same way that, she had to admit, she was using him. So it was with heartfelt relief that she heard the duchess declare, after a week at Sir Sidney's establishment, that they had tarried long enough. "The company's becoming flat," the duchess said, sending Gracie about her packing. "We'll take our leave tomorrow. I hear Paris is brimming with fashionables, and I'm eager to be off."

The Vicar had made one great sacrifice and was there to see them off the next morning. Their host and hostess were still abed, having made their good-byes in the night. As Catherine prepared to step into the coach with the others, the Vicar stayed her for a moment. There was a vaguely sorrowful look in his eyes as he took her hand.

"Good-bye, Catherine," he said. "I wonder if we shall meet again? I think not, for I do not go on to Paris. I am one of Ollie's constant hangers-on, you see. I am not one to lecture on morality, I fear, and I cannot offer you any assistance. For not only do I live upon the sufferance of my fellowman, but I am too old, too lazy, and, in the end, too unconcerned with my fellowman and woman now. But I do tell you, for what it is worth, that you do not belong here. Country chicks cannot keep company with parrots and cockatiels, you know. And it is mortally easy to become that with which you constantly associate, by slow degrees. You cannot hide forever, Catherine. And there are all sorts of lures in this wide world, especially for young things. I should know," he said, shaking his head. "I have set enough. Go when you can, Catherine," he whispered, bowing over her hand. "And go while you can. Home, where you belong."

"Thank you," she said, more chilled by his words than she dared show. "And I will. I promise, as soon as I am able."

He smiled sadly and then laughed quietly.

"Whatever you do decide, never fear, I shall know of it. For I hear of all things—that is what makes me so valuable a guest. Good-bye, my dear. It was pleasant being needed as a man again for a few days. Good luck."

He handed her into the coach, and, with a wave, they were off.

"Well you certainly made a conquest," the duchess grinned before she settled herself to sleep, in her usual traveling mode. "The Vicar don't give a demn for anyone in the world, but he seems to have been taken with you. But he don't spend a brass farthing on a female," she laughed, and allowed Gracie to tuck her up into a cocoon of wraps for the journey.

This time the duchess was in no hurry. For, she said to her companions as they dined that night in a small wayside inn, she was "shaken to pieces" by the journey and "wearied unto death" by the constant partying at Sir Sidney's.

They traveled on for two lackluster days, and it was only on the final approach to Paris that all of the company seemed to awaken at last. Rose and Violet were in full spate, commenting on the city, on the people they expected to see, and the fashions they glimpsed. Catherine was shocked to see that they did not even notice the poor, whose districts they had to ride through to get to the center of the city. The men and women in rags, far worse than any she had ever seen in England, the hovels in which they lived, and their hordes of huge-eyed starving children were not commented upon at all. But once the carriage drove through the wide white avenues where gentlemen and ladies of fashion promenaded, they noted every detail of every garment, and priced them down to their least penny.

The duchess beamed upon their excitement, but she told them she "had seen the town before." Yet even she was soon talking about hunting up some dressmakers and getting togged out in "Frenchie fashions again." By the time they rolled up in front of their hotel, the duchess was quite eager to alight and begin her inquiries as to where the gaiety was to be found.

The concierge was as obsequious as the duchess could have wished and groveled so much before her that she was in high good spirits when shown her rooms, even to the point of not beginning her usual tirade against the sanitation and grace of the establishment until he had bowed himself out of her presence. She had a large and airy chamber overlooking the street, and her companions' rooms were arranged around hers.

The duchess sat back with a grin of triumph.

"Well, gels, here we are in Paris. All dressed up with no place to go. Here, you Violet and you Rose, get yourself suited out fine and go down to the lobby; let the word go out that I have arrived. Then we'll see those invitations pour in. Catherine, you're free to do as you wish. Go tag along with the girls if you like. But be sure to tell everyone that you meet who you are and that the Duchess of Crewe has arrived. That should do it. Now, Gracie, my hair, if you please."

And sitting back and enjoying her hair being brushed, the duchess closed her eyes and planned a future full of balls and fetes and sensations.

In spite of the duchess's confidence, Catherine was amazed, when she answered the duchess's summons at an unusually early hour before noon the next day, to see her sitting at a little desk, sorting through what seemed to be a dozen invitations.

"Tonight," the duchess said to her companions, "dress up smartly, for we're off to no less than Count D'Arcy's ball. We've been asked to Lord and Lady Lynne's, and to Madame Martin's but we'd be fools to pass up the count's invitation, for that's the smartest of them all. Bound to be royalty there as well.

So do me justice, lassies,'' she said, in an unusually gay manner, ''and who knows where we may be bound tomorrow night?''

''The old lady's in high alt,'' Violet said as they went back to their rooms to pick through their wardrobes for suitably dazzling gowns.

''She thinks,'' Violet explained to a puzzled Catherine, ''that if she's daring enough, she'll yet get an invitation to an audience with the king. But she's out there, you know. For it may have been possible before all the nobs got their heads lobbed off for being royals. Now the throne's uneasy, I hear, and they don't want too much truck with a dizzy set like the duchess.''

''And what makes you so worldly-wise?'' Rose asked cheekily.

''I spent some time with old Ollie, you know, and he had a few words for me.''

''A very few words, I'm sure,'' Rose said, laughing.

Catherine colored, but Violet shot back, ''Jealousy won't get you anywhere, old Rose.''

''It happens,'' Rose said, with suppressed laughter, ''that I spent some hours with old Ollie too, and he don't waste much time on talk.''

Catherine turned to her room quickly, so as not to hear much more of their chatter, which was turning more rancorous and more detailed than she wished to hear.

''Catherine,'' Rose called, giving Violet an admonitory poke, ''do come to our rooms tonight before we leave. We'll have to see if you've togged yourself up in enough style. For when Her Grace gives orders for us to dazzle, you daren't do less or your head will roll.''

Catherine gave herself one last glance in the mirror before sighing and turning to go to Rose's room. She could not, she thought, do better. She wore a high-waisted gown in creamy white satin, and bound her hair back with a pure white ribbon till only a crown of curls relieved the severity. The only touch of color was the azure of her eyes and the little gold pendant she always wore. She felt that if she were going to see royalty, she must dress in a distinguished, but unostentatious manner. The neckline of her gown, she realized, was lower than that of any of her others, but it had looked so perfect just as it had come from Madame Bertrand's that she had not dared tamper with it. Now, glancing in the mirror, even though the slope of her breasts showed daringly it no longer seemed so dashing—not, she amended, shocking at all compared to the dresses of the females she had seen at Sir Sidney's. The Vicar's words about becoming like the company one kept drifted into her mind, but she banished them quickly, and went out in search of Rose and Violet and their opinion of her dress.

When Rose called for her to enter, she stepped in, only to stand stock still and stare at Rose and Violet. For Rose was sitting at her mirror with the top of her gown down, chatting animatedly with Violet while at the same time carefully applying rouge from a little pot to the tips of her breasts. Catherine stood and goggled as Rose looked up. For a moment she looked only at Catherine's gown and cried out, "Oh don't you look a sight! Pure and cool and just lovely!"

And then, when she saw the expression on Catherine's face, she looked down at herself and sighed.

"It's to give my gown a better look, you see," she said hurriedly, rapidly completing the job of anointing her nipples with carmine, and then blowing upon them and lifting the top of her gown back on.

"It's to give the gentlemen a better idea of the wares," Violet said languidly.

Catherine looked at Rose in her thin salmon-colored gown and saw that the rouge did indeed emphasize the small part of Rose's bosom that was covered by cloth.

"And," Violet said, in a cool voice, "to give them an extra treat a little later. If a chap's going to spring for the pleasure of Rose's company, he expects to find something out of the ordinary. And a little color in unexpected places adds excitement."

Rose got up and looked daggers at Violet. She opened her mouth to make some rejoinder, but before she could, Violet moved.

"See here, Catherine," she said, walking over to her, letting her drink in the splendor of her spangled black and silver gown, "Rose here and I, we are what we are. And it's no good pretending that we're all jolly little cousins off on a spree. I've been fighting with old Rose here all day, and there has to be an end to it. We can't watch what we say and what we do every moment you're about. We're out of leading strings a long time. I told Rose there's no sense in our having a to-do every time I say something she thinks isn't fit for your ears, for we'll only come to cuffs all day if we go on so. If you're to travel along with us, you'll have to take us for what we are."

Catherine swallowed hard. And then she spoke.

"I know that, Violet. And yes, you are right, I cannot be an ostrich with my head in the sand. I knew that back when we met and I decided to accompany you. So Rose, there's no sense in fighting with Violet. She's quite right, you know."

Rose still seemed agitated, but then she had a sudden thought.

"You know, Catherine, it won't be all bad for you. For you will know what you are about. Far more than most young misses do. For there's heaps we can tell you about gentlemen."

"Oh Rose," Violet laughed, "now that far I would not go. We really cannot tell this little miss all that we know."

"Well, not all." Rose pondered. "But if more young misses knew what we know, fewer gentlemen would have to seek us out."

"And we'd be at a charity kitchen. Give over, Rose, do. We don't have to instruct Catherine. Not with her looks and style. It's only that we won't have to act so unnatural when she's about, and we'll all get on splendidly."

Rose seemed satisfied and went back to gazing at herself in the mirror. She adroitly rubbed rouge into her cheeks, applied salve to her lips, spit into a little dish of black and with one finger swept shape and sultriness about her eyes. Noting Catherine's silence, she asked anxiously, "Is what Violet says acceptable to you, dear?"

"Oh yes, of course," Catherine said, knowing full well that hypocrite that she was, she did not at all relish the thought of hearing all of their confidences. In fact, she wanted to hear none of them—she only wanted to run to her room and quake. But, she amended, she wanted more. She wanted to be home, safe at home again.

But as the silence in the room became ominous, with Violet smiling at her loftily and Rose looking at herself in the mirror uneasily, Catherine felt the burden of conversation fall upon her and searched for a safe, conciliatory topic.

"You can tell me how to go on," she said. "For if we are to be honest with each other, I do not know how to . . . ah, discourage a gentleman, without being rude."

Violet grinned wickedly. "That's hardly the sort of advice to be asking us."

"Oh Vi, give over, do; we can too tell Catherine how to go about things," Rose said, annoyed.

"What you want to know," Violet went on, "is how to stay

out of trouble. And I'm afraid we're poor persons to ask that of.''

"Well, Vi, you're a spiteful thing today," Rose said, angrily. "I think it's just because Catherine's looks knock ours all to pieces tonight. She hasn't got a spangle nor a feather," she said, eyeing the profusion of jet plumes set into Violet's elaborate coif, "and still she looks a treat. Well, then, I'll tell you, love. There's things you mustn't do with gentlemen and you'll find yourself safe as houses. You mustn't open your lips when you kiss, for one thing.''

Catherine went pale. This was not at all the sort of advice she had requested, but before she could speak, Violet began laughing.

"Oh Rose, and what of Sir Alistar?''

"True,'' Rose said thoughtfully, "for he don't bother to kiss at all. Well, then, Catherine, I should say that so long as you stay upright at all times, you will avoid difficulties.''

Violet held her hand against her bodice—she was laughing so richly.

"And what of young Perry and Lord Sulley, then?''

"Oh,'' Rose said, "and telling you to keep all your clothes on, which is what I was about to add, wouldn't do then neither, I suppose. Well then, Catherine, I'll tell you the best advice I can then.''

Rose screwed up her face in thought and then smiled triumphantly. "You must never do a thing with a gentleman that you have not done before. And you'll go on splendidly, I'm sure.''

At that, Violet's mirth got so out of control that she was gasping, and even Catherine had to join in.

Rose herself was chuckling good-naturedly. But when Catherine stopped, she decided to turn the subject as quickly as she was able to.

"Am I dressed properly then?'' she asked.

"A treat,'' Rose agreed. "But perhaps a little too refined. You never know with Her Grace. She wants you to catch all eyes. Here,'' Rose said, plucking one white rose from the floral arrangement on her table. "Do put this in your hair, there on top, midst the curls, yes. That looks just as it ought. Now then,'' she said, squinting thoughtfully at Catherine.

"Yes, I'm sure I'm right. You do look lovely, Catherine. But who will see you across a room? Not that there's anything the matter with your coloring—it's all milk and cream. But there's the problem. In candlelight, you'll just fade away.''

"You're right, Rose," Violet said, taking a professional interest. "Footlights and party lights drab out a girl's coloring. A bit of lip salve, a bit of rouge, that's the ticket.''

And before Catherine could protest, they steered her to Rose's dressing table. Rose carefully applied salve to her lips, and though she was sure her furious blush would stay their hands, they carefully applied high color to her cheeks.

"Now don't blink or move," Rose warned, "or you'll blind yourself. S'truth.''

When Catherine gazed at herself in the mirror again, she dared not breathe. An exotic painted creature with darkly lashed huge blue eyes, pink cheeks, and violently red lips stared seductively back at her. Her hands went automatically to a cloth to wipe the vision away, but Rose stayed her.

"No, Catherine. That's just what Her Grace will expect. She'll dress you down if you come pale and ordinary. Now you look just as you ought. So leave it be.''

Rose and Violet accompanied Catherine to get her wrap, so Catherine could not even touch her face though she swore she could feel every gram of the cosmetics lying heavily upon her. They lingered in Catherine's room awaiting the duchess's summons. And when Gracie came to tell them to be ready, Rose took a small vial from her evening bag and went to Catherine's dressing table. She carefully put a drop from the vial in each eye and handed the vial to Violet, who did the same. Catherine saw, as if by magic, how huge and glittering their eyes now appeared to be, just as she had often noticed their eyes to be at night; she had assumed it was due to their excitement and candlelight.

"Belladonna," Rose explained as they prepared to go. "Gives your eyes a sparkle like nothing else. I didn't offer any to you, dear, for it's a thing you have to get accustomed to. It blurs things up, you know. So when you look your best, you can't see a blessed thing. The lights all dance, and sometimes you can't be sure of recognizing who you're talking to, for you can't make out their face properly.''

"Sometimes," said Violet cryptically, "that's a blessing, too.''

Rose and Violet proceeded to the duchess's chamber with the slow, stately tread that Catherine now saw was necessary for them when their eyes were so unreliable.

The dowager was swathed in silvery gray, with so many

diamonds shining at her throat and hair that Catherine felt sure
her companions could only see a sparkling blur of her rich attire.

The duchess stared at Catherine. "Now, that's the way I like
my companions to look," she crowed. "You'll have every eye
upon you. You're finally getting the hang of it. And Rose and
Violet, you two are bang up to the mark. Let's away. Don't wait
up, Gracie, for this is to be a late evening."

Gracie nodded as they left, knowing full well she dared not
slumber till her mistress was safely tucked in bed again.

Catherine tried to sink back into the shadows as she sat in the
coach. And she tried to be less aware of the startled looks that
James, the duchess's coachman, gave her when she stepped out
into the blaze of light and torches outside Count D'Arcy's
residence. She felt, as she trailed along behind Rose and Violet,
deeply ashamed of her new appearance, and of the spectacular
effect it was having upon those who turned to stare at her.

As their little party was announced, all heads turned to the top
of the stairs to see the quartet make their way down the grand
staircase to join the company. Her eyes almost as blurred and
dazzled as Rose's and Violet's, Catherine saw that these were men
and women in the most elegant clothes and jewels that she had
ever seen. The company was composed of the titled and the
infamous—poets, mistresses, wanderers and actresses, the rag
and tag of émigré Europe, and the foremost pleasure seekers
from her own land. All collected together and flashing their eyes
and gems and costumes beneath the light of a thousand candles
while musicians tried to drown their converse with light music.

Many stared at the haughty Violet and buxom Rose. Many
gaped at the regal duchess and her train of demireps, whose
reputations had preceded her here. And many gazed with delight
upon the delicious child with the figure of a grown woman and
the face, even beneath the paint, of a lovely gamine.

Catherine tried to ignore the sensation they had caused and
that her employer was obviously reveling in. She stared about
her in shame and despair . . . until her eyes caught and held one
familiar face high above the crowd. A face that she had been
unwittingly looking for. He had been watching her, she thought
in deeper despair, and there was no doubt in her mind as to his
thoughts. The marquis looked at her, at her face, at her neckline.
His handsome face was immobile, but the contemptuous disdain
in his gray eyes was readable even from across the room.

Chapter IX

"Sinjun," complained the petite dark-eyed woman, "you have been neglecting me. You've been here all night and you haven't danced with me once. You were not used to be so reluctant to enter my arms," she said coyly, tracing patterns with her fingertip upon his sleeve.

"Cecily," the marquis drawled, "you were not used to be Lady Smythe. Now that you are a respectable married woman, you cannot want to pick up our old ties. What would Alistar say?"

"Oh, pooh," she fretted, stamping one foot—an effect, he noted with amusement, quite lost in the throng of people. "I haven't seen him all night either. He's probably off somewhere with that Italian trollop of his. We have a very modern arrangement, Sinjun," she wheedled. "We each go about our own business, and no one's the worse for it."

"Cecily, my dear," the marquis said, beginning to edge away, "why should you try to reignite an old burned-out flame, when I have seen that devastating M. Dumont there has not taken his eyes off you for a moment?"

The woman wheeled and turned to look for her admirer and, not finding the rapt young face of M. Dumont anywhere nearby, she turned again to rate the marquis for his little jest and found herself standing quite alone.

With an exclamation of dismay, she flounced off to see her husband, to rail at him for his pursuit of foreign females.

"Oh, Lord, Jenkins," the marquis said in a low voice, when they met at one side of the card room, "for every true rumor, there are a hundred false ones. I have a list of many names now, it's true, but coming here this night has added nothing. For no sooner do I get on the trail of something, when there is an interruption."

"Your past catching up with you, lad?" Jenkins grinned.

"There's that, but I am quite expert at sidestepping. But more importantly, there's Beaumont. He's here, and he's everywhere tonight. He seems to be dogging my footsteps. And whenever I look into his eyes, I see tumbrels rolling. He suspects everything, but can prove nothing."

"He can do nothing," Jenkins said, lifting his glass of wine and holding it to the candle's light. "We're at peace now."

"Now. At this moment," the marquis sighed, "but if the scales tip, I would be first on his list."

"Whose field does he play in now?" Jenkins asked before draining the glass.

"Ah, now that," the marquis said, shrugging and then pausing as a waiter came close, "is a neat question." He took another glass of wine for Jenkins and one for himself, and they toasted each other until the waiter drifted off into the crowd and they were alone again.

The marquis began drinking his wine and then stopped suddenly to stare at his glass. "Now that," he said, "is criminal, such stuff to be even decanted in the land of the grape itself." He looked around casually, then continued, now sure of their privacy. "If we discover which pockets he has his hand in, we'll know for a certainty which way the wind is blowing. Our estimable commissioner . . . of what is it now? Taxes, water? No matter, our friend Beaumont is an excellent weather vane. He catches every nuance of the winds of fortune. That is how he has gotten and held his own fortune. Be sure that he will never put a foot wrong. In fact, I think that if we were but privy to the workings of his mind, there would be no need to compile all these names. For whatever the fate of France is to be, be sure that Beaumont will know it a half hour before the king himself."

"Aye," Jenkins rumbled, "but as he's not one to give an Englishman the time of day, best keep your ear to the ground."

"But not too obviously, of course," the marquis sighed. "Instead I shall ogle the ladies, drink more than is good for me, game for all I'm worth, and submerge myself in every bit of frivolous gossip. There are times, Jenkins, when I long for no more than a cozy fireside. I grow old, I think."

Jenkins gave a rude chuckle. "Oh yes. I can just see you

there, dandling your grandchildren on your knee, graybeard. But in the meanwhile, until you can delight in such homey pastimes, I notice you're spry enough at your job. You haven't taken your eyes off the duchess's newest doxy all night. Is it that you think she holds the secrets of the succession behind those lovely blue eyes?''

The marquis seemed taken aback for a moment and then drawled in the offhand languid manner Jenkins knew so well, ''No, that's an altogether different game. Miss Prunes and Prisms has arrived in Paris and finally shows her true colors. Or true paints, if you want to be more exact. She's obviously been after big game all the while. And I'm just curious to see to whom she attaches herself. For there's a lot to be learned from seeing to whom such a pricey little package delivers. Rose and Violet will ply their trade with whoever has the price of a night's entertainment. But these more expensive frigates will only sail off with someone who is prepared to come down handsomely for them. I think our little miss will show us the way the winds of fortune are blowing almost as well as our old friend Beaumont.''

Jenkins glanced around the room before saying dryly, ''But she hasn't sailed off with anyone as yet. The last I saw of her, she was trying to blend in with the furniture.''

''She's only waiting for her opportunity, Jenkins. She's after more than her weak sisters-in-trade.''

''You are too harsh on her.'' Jenkins sighed, shaking his head.

''Still thinking she is but a sweet little miss caught in the coils of misfortune? That's not like you, old friend. She comes to her first Paris fete, rigged out to the nines, painted and gowned like an actress. Did you see her entrance? She attracted more notice than a queen. The old girl's beside herself with happiness. 'The Duchess of Crewe is a succès fou,' they are all saying. That little rhyme will be the catchword of the season.''

''Look sharp, lad,'' Jenkins said, turning away. ''Beaumont's eyes are upon us. He's talking to that waiter. His men must be everywhere here.''

As the marquis drained his glass and prepared to leave, Jenkins smiled and whispered one farewell. ''You have to get your mind back on business. Why don't you just meet her price and then you will be able to forget about her and get on with it.''

The marquis walked over to the entrance to the great room where the dancers were whirling about together to the strains of a waltz. He watched them as he spoke with a young sprig just out of Cambridge on his first tour, who was chattering away excitedly. It was possible, he thought with a wry grin, to stand and chat with almost anyone at such an affair without even listening to half that was said. A sage nod, a small smile, or an occasional laugh when the speaker seemed to have delivered himself of a witticism was enough. He was the lofty, cynical Marquis of Bessacarr after all, wasn't he?

As the young man happily prated away, passing on all the secondhand tidbits he had amassed, Sinjun listened with half of his attention. The other half was focused on the amusing little playlets that passed before his eyes.

Lady Devon was playing her husband false with a handsome Austrian. Mademoiselle DuPres was batting her lashes at an old gentleman who had escaped the guillotine and come back to tend his lately restored estates. Mademoiselle DuPres knew, Sinjun thought, that the old chap would now need a wife to help him people his lands again. And Hervé Richard, who had been a man of substance and power when Bonaparte had led this land, was jealously watching his brother Pierre, who had been a beggar then and who was now a rich man deep in the Bourbons' confidences. The wheel of fortune had not yet done turning, the marquis thought, and that was why he was here tonight.

The marquis' eyes narrowed as he followed Hervé Richard's angry gaze. For his brother Pierre, as stout and overfed as his beloved friend Louis Bourbon, was dancing with Catherine Robins. Pierre smiled and bobbed, his red face beaming, while the girl seemed to be in an agony of discomfort. Was she never done with playacting? the marquis thought violently. She had captured the plum tonight. Pierre was a rich man now, and his presence at court gave him power and influence. And still she acted the shy virgin. But it seemed to be a useful ploy, for Pierre looked delighted with his little prize.

As the marquis watched, Beaumont, as neatly clad and unexceptional a little man as ever, came up to Hervé's side and began whispering to him. So Beaumont had some interest in watching the little playlet as well? Beaumont seemed to be consoling Hervé, who everyone knew burned with jealousy of his estranged brother. Now why should Beaumont be interested in Hervé? Sinjun's thoughts raced. Hervé was déclassé now, abandoned and impoverished. He had not followed his leader into exile, but he was financially and socially as much of an exile as Bonaparte. If Beaumont sought his company, then indeed something was in the wind.

"But, Sinjun, you say nothing. Don't you agree?" the little lord at his side asked.

The marquis recalled himself with difficulty. "Why, I'm sorry, Peter, I was distracted. What did you say?"

"I don't blame you. Not a bit. She's a smasher all right, isn't she? I wish I had the blunt to interest her," the young man said sadly, looking over to where Catherine danced.

"Now, now, Peter, she's too rich for your blood," the older man laughed. "And mine too, I think."

"Never say so," Peter replied, laughing. "Why, good English gold outweighs French any day."

The two men laughed, and then the younger, seeing the marquis' distraction, bowed and went off in search of more congenial company. It was good to have spoken with the marquis, for he was a man of the world and one whose name would excite much interest and envy among his friends when he returned home. But he was a strange fellow, after all, so bored that he seemed half asleep, those gray eyes half masted and quiet throughout their whole discourse. Peter essayed the same look as he made his way to the punch and found he almost stumbled against a footman as a result. Practice, he told himself sharply, that would be the answer.

But there was no boredom in the marquis' eyes as he watched the interminable dance go on in front of him. He watched Catherine dip and sway in Pierre Richard's arms. Her figure was exquisite and her face entrancing, even under all the paint. The swept-up dark curls revealed her white vulnerable neck. The marquis found that his hands were clenched. There was no use for it. He was interested in her. He had been from the moment he had seen her. Jenkins was right. Though she might be nothing more than a cyprian, certainly less discriminating than any of the wenches he usually consorted with, he did desire her. And his fascination with her was only getting in the way of his mission here. He must have her and be done with it.

In the morning, he knew, when he paid her, all the mystery would be vanished. He would have known all there was to know of her. Or all he wished to know of her. The attraction was strong, and it was dangerous for him to be so attracted. In the past, he had consorted with women whose conversation amused him or whose personalities somehow made the mercenary side of their relationship less sordid. He did not know if Catherine Robins could even read or write, much less make pleasant discourse. He did not care. For he had no wish to be ensnared by a woman ever again. It would be enough to have her, and thereby end the interest he had in her.

For he could neither gather information nor observe dispassionately when she was about. No sooner did he get on the track of some new development that might be of interest to his cause than she would appear and chase all such thoughts from his mind. For instance, he thought angrily, he should not be watching her dance with Pierre Richard and be as consumed with futile jealousy as Hervé Richard so evidently was. He should rather be at Hervé's side now, listening to his spiteful rage, as Beaumont was. For when a man was consumed by passion, he was often indiscreet, and when a man like Hervé Richard was being indiscreet, there was a chance that there would be a great deal to learn. No, his fascination with her handicapped him and he grew angry at himself. And so, indirectly, at her.

There was only one remedy he could think of. And he knew that before the night was out, he would have taken it. He was not such a coxcomb as to think he was irresistible. But he was experienced enough to know that she felt the same tug of interest that he did. And he did have money, money enough to assuage her conscience for giving up such a potential honey fall as Pierre Richard.

The dance finally ended, and while Pierre executed a courtly bow, Catherine took the opportunity to dip a sketchy curtsy and begin a hasty retreat to the wall where she had been standing before the weighty Frenchman had sought her out. But before she could return across the floor, she was intercepted by another gentleman. He looked much the same as the partner she had just abandoned, except that he was slightly taller, slightly less obese, and dressed in clothes that were far less grand.

He bowed, and the music struck up again. Before she could leave, he took her hand and led her into the dance. There were gasps and those on the sidelines broke into excited babble as the dancers swung into the first steps. The marquis was not the only one who stared at the dancers now.

And neither was he the only one who made his seemingly unhurried but nevertheless rapid way to her erstwhile partner's side. Monsieur Beaumont also began to make his way through the crowd to the flushed, angry gentleman. But Beaumont, whose legs were shorter, had to stop after getting halfway there when he saw the marquis lean to speak with his quarry.

"Good evening, Pierre," the Marquis said pleasantly in his perfect French. "I see that the new young English cocotte is becoming quite an attraction. Even your brother cannot resist her."

The stout gentleman muttered, as much to himself as to the marquis, "But he is a beggar now. What does he think he is doing? It was only through my intercession that he was allowed to stay on in Paris. For he is my brother, after all."

The marquis smiled sympathetically, knowing full well that Pierre would never allow his brother to go into exile totally, and thus miss seeing his more successful sibling's triumphs in society and at court. Just as Hervé had insisted on allowing his Royalist brother Pierre to stay on through his charity, when Bonaparte swept all before him.

"She could not refuse him, poor little sweet," Pierre said, never taking his eyes from the couple before them, "but I shall tell her, soon enough, that he has nothing to offer her. He forgets himself. It is through my sufferance that he is here at all tonight."

"Perhaps," the marquis said with a smile, "he thinks his fortunes are about to take a new turn."

"What?" Pierre said, distractedly, his attention so focused on his brother, who was whispering into the delightful young woman's ear, that he scarcely heard the question.

"No, no, never," he said vehemently, his attention reverting to the marquis. "I keep Hervé and his wife and children in food and necessities as it is my duty as a brother to do. But I assure you, he won't get an extra sou from me to carry on with a demimondaine. And so I shall tell her, never fear. Hervé shall not have her, never fear."

"Doubtless," drawled the marquis, watching Hervé clutch Catherine closer and shoot a triumphant look at his brother. "But I wonder what he is telling her now? Perhaps he feels he will soon be in clover again?"

"Never!" Pierre barked, his little eyes jealously watching the couple's progress. "For his star is no longer in ascendancy. It shines only on the little island of Elba. Paris is mine now."

"Perhaps," the marquis mused. For Hervé's bid at taking away Pierre's new plaything was not unusual. The two brothers were famous in Paris for their competitive relationship. The wags had named them Cain and Cain years before, because, as society said, neither one was innocent enough to be called Abel. Still, this was a daring gesture for Hervé to make. And one, the marquis thought, that might not have been made solely out of rage and jealousy. It might have been an ill-advised gesture; however, it might just as well have been only a premature gesture showing that Hervé thought the direction of his fortunes was indeed about to change. It was true, as he had told Jenkins, that one might learn a great deal from merely watching clever demireps. For they seemed to gravitate to money and power and point it out as surely as any compass could show the North Star.

When the dance ended at last, Hervé made as if to delay his partner, for he had seen how quickly she had fled his brother. But Pierre was quick off the mark this time, and as Hervé reached for Catherine's arm again, Pierre approached his brother and signaled forcefully that he wished to speak to him. While the two brothers broke into low and volatile argument, to the amusement of watchers, the girl made her escape. And when the marquis looked away from the snarling brothers, she was gone.

Beaumont looked about him rapidly and then turned on his heel and went into hurried conference with a footman. But the marquis only strolled away, seemingly aimlessly. He smiled to himself as he wandered off into the direction that he had seen the white flash of her gown disappear. An association with her, he thought, however brief, would be of some real value after all. For his own personal interest now seemed to dovetail with his professional interest in the girl. After they had parted, he might be able to work out some arrangement with her whereby she could report back to him on whichever of the two brothers with whom she finally chose to consort. A word from either camp would suit him well. He would have to be sure that he left her with pleasant memories so that she would be willing to cooperate with him. And he would have yet another partner in his inquiries.

He knew she would not fly to the duchess's side, for that was where the brothers would look for her first. Nor would she have gone to Violet or Rose. For both were deep in the process of securing business for themselves at this hour. Thus, the marquis reasoned, if she had disappeared into this section of the house, she must have sought a room where she could be alone to weigh the offers of the two brothers.

The marquis eased open two doors off the main hall before he found her, standing alone, holding her hands together tightly, staring into a fire in Count D'Arcy's unused library.

"What a problem," he sighed softly, entering the room and closing the door securely behind him. "Two such eligible suitors. And no one to give you advice as to which one to select. Hervé is, one admits, a trifle more comely, but after all he has four years on poor Pierre. But then, Pierre has the ear of Louis, and the purse and privilege as well. Yet again, as you surely must have heard, there are all sorts of rumors flying. And it is altogether possible that after one month of bliss with Pierre, you might find that Hervé was the one in power after all. His emperor is away just at the moment, but one never knows, does one?"

She turned and stared at him as he came up slowly behind her. Her eyes, he noted with amazement, were filled with tears and she wore an expression of grave despair. Had Hervé threatened her then? he wondered.

"I want nothing to do with either one of them," she whispered. "Nothing at all. I just want to be let alone and stay with the duchess just for a little while longer, just till I can get home."

As he watched, amazed, tears began to run down her cheeks. He took out a handkerchief and dabbed at them.

"Ah no," he said in his gentlest voice, "for how can you face the company again if you go on so? You shall ruin the work of art you have created upon your face. See? Although I can repair the damage, I will not be able to recreate the effect, for I've left all my cosmetics home again, alas."

At his words, she looked up in despair, and began to sob. He gathered her close in his arms and stroked her smooth bare shoulders. When she tried weakly to pull away, he only held her closer and whispered soft words of comfort to her.

"No, no," he said tenderly, pushing back some tendrils of hair from her face. "What can be dreadful enough to make you weep? It cannot be so terrible, can it? For here you are in the heart of society and you are so greatly sought after. Why, you are a stunning success tonight. So lovely that the world of Paris is at your feet. And you are so wretched? Come, come, tell me what is the matter. It may be that I can help you. For I have come to help you, you know."

He felt her warm and vital, close against him, and he held her close, whispering all the while, and then he laughed and planted a brief passionless kiss against her hair, which, he noted irrelevantly, had the scent of the rose she wore there.

"No, now you are turning my jacket to ruin. What will

Jenkins say? For it is not raining tonight. You will quite turn my reputation with him, you know, for I am not used to reducing females to tears. He will wonder what dreadful things I have been up to, to transmute lovely laughing girls into fountains."

She drew away, looking ashamed. And after taking his handkerchief and dabbing at her eyes, she looked at him, he thought, with something very much like wonder.

"It's all such a mull," she said, controlling her voice with effort. "And I'm sorry to have wept all over you. But it has been so dreadful. I did not want to be a social success. No, I did not. I only wanted to fulfill my duties and stay in the background. But then that great fat Frenchman took my hand, above all my protests, and made me dance with him. I didn't want to create a scene, for I thought he could not understand English and my French is so poor. But once we were dancing, I found he spoke English as well as I. And he . . . he made me the most dreadful offer. That is to say, he supposed me to be something I am not. And no sooner had I gotten away from him when the other took me up. For a moment"—she smiled weakly—"I thought it was him again, but it turned out to be his brother, saying almost the selfsame things."

"What sort of things?" the marquis asked with a glow of interest in his eyes.

"Promising me all sorts of things," she said, closing her eyes and waving her hand in dismissal. "Carriages and gowns and jewels. And no matter what I said to both of them, they seemed deaf to my every word and only assured me that they were in earnest."

"They both promised great riches?" the marquis asked abruptly, an alert look upon his face.

"Yes, yes," she said. And seeing his abstraction, she said shamefacedly, "I am sorry to have gotten so familiar with you, Your Lordship, and I thank you for trying to set me right again. I shall be leaving now, for even though the duchess is at the tables, I shall ask her to give me leave to return to the hotel. I feel a headache coming on," she explained hurriedly.

"No, no," the marquis objected, capturing her hands and smiling down at her. "Let's have none of that. You owe me no thanks, for I have not done anything for you as yet. And let us have no 'Your Lordships' please; my friends call me Sinjun, and you are my friend. For we have known each other a long time, haven't we? Only we have let a lot of silly misunderstandings get in the way of our friendship. Tell me, Catherine, what is it you want of this journey that neither Pierre nor Hervé can give you? For I am here to help you. We are fellow Englishmen, in a matter of speaking, here in a strange land,'' he added, seeing her hesitate.

"I want to go home," she blurted, looking up at him, an incipient sob in her voice. "That is all. It was wrong of me to come. It is wrong of me to stay."

"Then why do you stay?" he asked in a low voice.

She hesitated again as he drew her a little closer and said, "Say it, Catherine. For have I not said I am your friend?"

"I must wait until mid March at least," she said gravely, not looking at him, "for the duchess pays me quarterly. And only then will I have the fare to go home."

The marquis stiffened imperceptibly, and then he laughed low in his throat. Ah, the little fox, he thought maliciously, it is true. A bird in the hand is worth all of a Frenchman's promises. So be it, he thought, we begin. Yet still he was aware of a strange surge of bitter disappointment. It is only, he thought rapidly, that it was, after all, so simple. Once they begin to speak of money, it always becomes so simple.

"Well then," he said, the lines of cynicism deep in his smiling face, "that is easy enough to remedy. No need to shed one more wasteful tear. For I have enough in my pocket at this moment to see you home. And more than that in my other coat at home. I shall see that you are able to travel home in style, little one, with even a companion of your own to see you safely arrived. I am only sorry that I cannot be that companion. For I must stay on here awhile longer and cannot now make any plans to leave."

"Oh no." She shook her head. They were standing so close to each other that he could feel the ends of her curls tickle his cheek. "I could not borrow from you, Your Lordship. . . ."

"Sinjun," he whispered, pulling her closer.

She resisted his embrace and went on in a small voice, "For I don't know when I could pay you back. Even though you are being so charitable, it would not be right of me to take your money. No, it would not be fitting. I can wait until March, truly I can. It is just that it is good to have someone I can talk to. Someone who understands."

"Why, there is no need for paying me back, little Catherine," he said gruffly, again wishing she would drop this game, and wondering if their whole relationship would be filled with this tedious denial of the truth. Would he have to ease her to bed above little halfhearted protests? Remove her garments, all the while quieting her sham of maidenly terrors? Would he have to put up with this mockery of innocence even as he bedded her? It would grow boring. He knew there were men who enjoyed simulated force in their amorous adventures, but he was not one of them. He wanted wholehearted cooperation. And so he sought to disabuse her of the notion and put an end to the charade.

"Little Catherine," he said, raising her chin with his hand and looking straight into her enormous eyes, "you would earn the lot." And seeing her eyes grow wider, he said quickly, "But I would, I promise, try not to make it a hardship. And I am generous. Although I usually prefer relationships that are open at both ends and can grow into long-standing ones, I am pressed for time. So I shall settle as much upon you for a few days of pleasure as I usually do for a few months. For it will not be your fault that we cannot continue. And though I do not pride myself upon being the answer to every maiden's prayers, I know I can be far more congenial than either of the Richards. You will find it more than pleasant, little one, I assure you. I have wanted you for a long time, and I know that you have not been unaware of me. So let's have an end to dickering. I will pay you—" He paused and then named a sum which he knew was more than generous, more in fact, than he had wanted to pay, but he was unsettled by the strange quietness in the room. "And I promise you will not have to exert yourself to earn it. Now, it grows late. Come, we'll go back to my rooms, and you will see for yourself how delicious it will be."

He drew her closer, bent his head, and kissed her lightly, and then, as he lost himself in the deepening kiss, he became aware of pain. For she was tugging sharply at his hair.

He released her abruptly. She was staring at him in horror.

"How could you?" she shrilled.

His thoughts reeled. Had she expected more? But that would be impossible—no man would pay more. Not even Louis himself.

"You are as bad as those others." She wept freely now, the cosmetics running across her cheeks, making her seem, not ridiculous, he thought, but somehow even more childlike.

"No, worse," she cried, pulling free of him and rushing to the door, "for you said you understood. And I trusted you."

"But what is it that you want?" he asked, standing alone and confused.

"I want to go home," she sobbed, and ran out the door.

The marquis did not go after her. He simply stood and stared after her, and then aimed a fierce kick at a chair, sending it flying.

What was her game, he wondered, savagely angry at her and at himself. Why should she come to this party painted like a doll and gowned like merchandise in a window if she were not looking for trade? Why should she be in the trail of the Dirty Duchess at all? Or thick as thieves with two other low tarts, if she were not what she appeared to be? And why should she maneuver so shamelessly to charm the coins out of his pockets? Somewhere, deep in his fury, the marquis felt the dim remembered pain of his past. He had been wrong before. Devastatingly wrong. And had sworn never to be so shortsighted with women again. But this time, how could he have been wrong? For it was not his perception alone.

How could he have been wrong when all the signs, all the world, and even she herself, in her request for money, had told him, unerringly, that he was right?

Chapter X

The duchess sulked for a day. She went on at tea about ungrateful little wretches, she complained at dinner about green little pieces, and went to bed grumbling about wicked, deceiving, brass-faced little hussies. But by the next day, when ever more invitations poured in, she had forgotten her anger at Catherine. For the chit was the talk of the town, and everyone had gotten a look at her, and wanted more, and then she had just disappeared.

The duchess was mollified when the spate of invitations flowed in. She had been a success, she knew it. What was it the Frenchies called her? Ah yes, "The Duchess of Crewe, le succès fou." A crazy success, that was it. That was one thing with these foreigners, she thought, pleased beyond her expectations at the evident splash she had made, there was no prudishness about them. No whispered condemnations. No sly little jibes. They took her to be a woman of the world. And a great many gentlemen had bent over her hand and looked at her with frank admiration. That was just as it ought to be, she sighed, holding the invitations as though they were a winning hand at cards. For though she had no interest in gentlemen any longer, nor indeed ever had for that matter, it was delightful to be so famous. When she at last returned home, there would be no more snickering. She would be such a success on the Continent that she would have to be admired not only in her own set, but in the highest circles in the land.

When Catherine crept in the next day, pale and shaken, the duchess only smiled at her benignly, all rancor forgotten. "Get some rest, gel," she said pleasantly, "for we're going to a levee

tomorrow night and I want my gels looking their best.'' And she
waved Catherine a royal dismissal.

Catherine walked slowly back to her room, where she had
hidden herself since the D'Arcy ball. She was in desperate case,
she knew, but she could not see her way clear yet.

How was she to get out of this coil? she mourned. She would
not beg Violet and Rose for funds, she swore; she must not. For
that would make her, in her own eyes at least, as culpable as
they were. She must find a way to tolerate this life at least for a
few more weeks, at least till mid March, when her quarterly
salary came due. For she knew the duchess would not advance
her a penny to go home, but surely, when the time came, her
employer would be honor bound to pay her justly earned wages.

She tried not to think of the marquis. For when he had
followed her to that empty room where she had sought refuge,
she had looked into his eyes and honestly thought she had found
honesty there. And so she had, but not in the way she wanted.
He had said he understood; he had neither said nor done anything
untoward. And had asked for her confidence. He was the only
safe refuge, she had thought. And so, like a fool, she had told
him her true situation. And discovered that he still thought her
no more than a conniving light-skirts. And, she thought, in
sorrow, how could she blame him? Her cheeks still reddened
when she imagined the construction he had put upon her telling
him of her need for money.

But he had seemed so genuinely friendly and caring. She had
looked into the depths of those softened gray eyes and had wanted
him to take all her problems on his own broad shoulders. Worse,
she remembered, when he had kissed her, for one tiny moment
of time, she had wondered what it would be like to stay in his
arms, to stay close to him, and go on further with him to taste
the ''delicious'' experiences he promised her. It was as the Vicar
had cautioned her—that if she stayed with her companions, she
would become as one with them. And so, she told herself
sharply, she had.

She had worn cosmetics and a gown that would have sent
Arthur and Jane to the top of the boughs. She had danced with
every lecherous gentleman who had leered at her, and capped the
whole thing by complaining to the marquis that she had no
funds, almost forcing his offer to her. She must, she knew, get
away before she actually became as Rose and Violet were. For if
she had doubted that such an impossible thing could ever come

to pass, she had only to remember the moment she had stayed, drowned in pleasure, in the marquis' embrace. How long before staying with him would seem like the only sane thing to do? She must go.

And if, she told herself strictly, staring at herself in the glass, she had to put up with insults, with sly appraisals, with comments about her condition, then she had merited it. She had brought it upon herself, and if, as a consequence, she suffered for it, that was all to the good. It would be a fit punishment for her. It would have been far better to have taken the ship on its turnabout journey home, once she had known about the duchess's companions and the life they led, than to have stayed and exposed herself to such an existence. Better, she thought, to have begged and scraped her way home alone than to go on in luxury under a false flag.

By the time that Rose and Violet came to her room for their usual afternoon tea, Catherine felt herself to be under control. And when Violet said, with a sneer, that Catherine had gotten herself quite a following, Catherine stood, and said firmly, "There has to be an understanding between us. I did not want this. I do not want this. If I could, I would leave now. But," she added, raising her hand in denial, "I want to make it clear that I want no charity, Rose. Nor any sympathy, for I've gotten myself into this coil. But, if you would be so kind, could you try to bear with me till a few more weeks go by? Then I shall take my quarterly earnings and go home, straightaway, as I should have weeks ago. Till then, please just try to accept me as I am, as I promised to accept you. And if you would, try, as you promised, to discourage any gentlemen that ask after me. Now let's forget about it. I have only to wait and let time pass, and it will all go right."

At first, it did. The next night, at the levee the duchess had promised them to, Catherine had to use all her resources to stay afloat. The gentlemen ogled her as before, and the ladies stole speculative glances at her. When the duchess went to the card room and Rose and Violet vanished with their own quarries, Catherine found herself pursued by the gentlemen again. She refused to dance, telling all who asked her that she had turned her ankle. But that only netted her a circle of admiring men, all vying to procure her a drink or tidbits or to keep her company. It was, she thought, better than having to dance, and the number of men who surrounded her ensured her safety from unwelcome suggestions as to her future.

She had worn a very conservative, almost demure gown and had refused Rose and Violet's offers of cosmetics, and so when she recognized the marquis as he strolled by her complement of admiring suitors, she raised her chin and met his eyes, unblinking and unmoved. He smiled at her and shrugged and then turned to his companion, a lovely Frenchwoman, and walked on. She felt a hollow glow of pride in herself and went on chatting with a very young, very charming Frenchman.

But toward the end of the evening, her dancing partner of the previous affair appeared. Pierre Richard seemed agitated when he saw her among her coterie of admirers, and stared hard at her and frowned. But then she noted that a smallish dark-haired man in conservative dress plucked at his arm and engaged him in conversation with many a smile and nod in her direction. This seemed to soothe him, and Catherine saw the rest of the evening out with relief, with nothing but a great deal of conversation filled with innuendos to parry.

At an émigré English couple's house party the following evening, Catherine saw both Richard brothers again. They seemed to exchange harsh words, and then each retreated to opposite corners of the room, from which they glowered at her separately throughout the evening. Really, she thought, it would be amusing— they were making such cakes of themselves in their admiration for her and their hatred for each other—if it were not for the fact that, separately, each had the power to frighten her very badly. They were like two overgrown evil children squabbling over a desired toy. But there was no dancing that night, so she could stay well away from both of them. The small dark man was there as well again, and he seemed to spend an equal amount of time with each brother, as did, Catherine noted through exaggeratedly careless glances, the marquis.

They met again at many parties and fetes as the days spun by. The same set of people seemed to revolve constantly about each other. When a fresh face appeared, everyone converged upon it with alacrity. Now she knew why the duchess and her followers had been greeted with such extreme admiration. For surely, Catherine thought, it was a very small world they allowed themselves, and since they insisted on partying constantly, and with the same persons, any newcomers must be met with joy.

By careful maneuvering, Catherine saw to it that she was

always surrounded by gentlemen. It was difficult to smile and pretend coy pleasure in the face of their incessant compliments, but it seemed to keep her safely away from any individual proposals. Her admirers ranged from callow young English boys residing in France for their education to dissipated roués who seemed to know her game very well. But all of them, by some miracle of fate, were content to beg only for her company at each affair. She could not know that they wagered nightly on the odds as to who the clever young doxy would eventually choose to be her protector.

The Richard brothers saw her many times after that night when they had each danced with her, but they no longer solicited her presence; rather, they watched her greedily from afar. The small dark man, she discovered, was a M. Beaumont. She learned that he was a person of some importance in the government, although his duties and title remained nebulous. Still, he was regarded by all with much awe and some fear. The marquis, she saw with an admixture of relief and dismay, no longer sought her out either, but only acknowledged her presence with a nod and a knowing smile. And each time she saw him, he was partnering a different but equally striking woman of the worldly sort. All the others whom she had met that first night in Paris she saw constantly as well.

Privately, Catherine now appreciated the quiet backwaters of life in Kendal. For she found that despite the fine apparel she wore and the fulsome compliments she always received, and the constant improper hints she had learned to refuse without shock, there really was no adventure or excitement in such a life. It was, she thought, fully as tedious in its own way as the many quiet evenings spent at home.

And while the duchess and her companions disported themselves freely in many homes and private ballrooms, they never received that coveted invitation to appear at court. Just as the dowager had been shunned in the highest circles in her own land, so she was ignored in a similar plane of society in France. The Marquis of Bessacarr might be welcomed to a fete in loftier circles, might even make his bow at the Tuileries, and have the ear of Louis himself. But the only time the duchess and her companions met the cream of Parisian society was when some of them came down to her level to gape at the goings-on of her notoriously wilder set.

Rose and Violet, she noted, were as busy as farmers during

the haying season, reaping their crops while the sun still shone. The only thing that shocked Catherine about their activities now was how steadily she grew less shocked by their activities. They were happy, and Catherine reckoned she was lucky to remain and pace out her days and nights unscathed, except in her sensibilities.

But Catherine grew uneasy and counted the days till mid March. And her uneasiness had little to do with Rose and Violet or even her own situation.

For there was a growing undercurrent here, in conversation and gossip, at the gay parties they visited, and even in the city itself, that she could not put a name to.

As it happened, she was not the only one aware of it. One afternoon, as she sat mending one of her frocks and gossiping with Rose and Violet in their rooms, Violet suddenly sat up and began to prowl about restlessly. These afternoons with Rose and Violet were some of Catherine's easiest moments as she counted the days till her release from the duchess's employ. She had grown used to their ways. She barely looked now when they sat about with their wrappers half opened, and barely blushed when they swapped stories about their gentlemen friends. For, Catherine noted with relief, with all Violet's speeches about their not minding their tongues any longer when she was about, they still greatly abbreviated their reminiscences in her presence.

Catherine had grown very fond of Rose, who, when not on her nightly errands, sat and sewed and smiled like the friendly farmer's daughter that she was. Violet was not so easily taken to, Catherine decided, for she had an acid tongue, and was not so scrupulously clean in her habits as Rose. In that, Catherine saw, she was not much different from many of the French ladies of fashion she had seen. For she had seen many a swanlike neck ringed both with diamonds and with grime. Still no one else seemed to mind, as both the gentlemen and the ladies appeared to be bathed in perfume and did not seem to consider water as useful as cosmetics.

Now Violet, pacing the room, cut off Rose's detailed description of a certain Austrian woman's tiara that she'd remarked upon the previous evening by saying sharply, "There's a lot going on here now, and, truth to tell, I wish to heaven we were in Austria too. There's too much afoot here, and too many whispers. I cannot like it."

"Whatever do you mean, Vi?" Rose asked, stretching

luxuriously. "It's ever so gay here now. So many dos, so many lovely people. Why should you want to hurry off now? The pickings are good enough."

Violet gave her a scornful look.

"You wouldn't know your hat was afire till you smelled the smoke, would you, Rose? It's like the top of a stove here now. I've been keeping company with an Italian, as it happens, and all of a sudden, last night he ups and informs me that he's off for home. And when I ask him why, he says, things are getting too hot in dear Paree."

"Why, Vi," Rose said ingenuously, "he must have been too old for sport, is all."

"Idiot!" Violet spat out. "Don't you see beyond your nose? There's talk Bonaparte is coming back. And where would that leave us?"

"We're English," Rose countered. "What difference does it make to us?"

"You talk to the fool," Violet said to Catherine in disgust.

Catherine looked up at Violet's worried face. "Have you told the duchess? Does she know? Perhaps she'll leave now if you tell her."

"The old cow is in the same case as dear Rose here. She wouldn't know the Little General was back till he was atop her."

"Not the duchess," Rose said, aghast. "She don't go in for that sort of thing."

Violet flounced back to her room in high dudgeon. But Catherine did not answer any of Rose's confused questions. All it needs is this, Catherine thought fearfully, Bonaparte returning. But perhaps, it occurred to her, her face brightening and reassuring Rose, if war broke out again, the duchess would return home. And all my troubles would be at an end. And then she felt guilty and shamed that she would be small spirited enough to actually welcome a war just to suit her own selfish purposes. Rose was quite worn out with trying to read the varying expressions that chased each other across the other girl's face.

"Really," she said at last, giving up the attempt, "Violet does take on when she's been dropped. Like the world was coming to an end."

"I think," the marquis said, as Jenkins helped him into his jacket, "that it's at an end. I think we can leave at any moment. Keep our gear in readiness. We have the names or, at least, all that we can humanly be expected to have. Enough of those at the Tuileries who are supposed to be supporting Louis, but who will stab him in the back if they have a chance. And enough of those who plot for Bonaparte's resurgence. We can do no more. If all the whispers have any credence, we shall be lucky to get out with our skins intact.''

''A few of Beaumont's lads have been watching this hotel,'' Jenkins said calmly.

''Yes, and a few are at every affair we attend. I should dearly love to know when Beaumont moves, to see what jump he makes. But he's too clever to move until the fat is already in the fire.''

''Aye, there's a lad who keeps his bread buttered on both sides. Last night, he kept the early evening with the younger Cain and lit the midnight oil with the elder. He's keeping all his exits clear.''

''He would not be alive today if he didn't,'' the marquis said, giving himself one glance in the glass. ''For it's no small feat for him to have held power in both regimes. He bends enough to last out every storm. And as he has no true backbone, it's easy enough for him.''

The marquis strode to the door. ''One last party, old friend,'' he said, ''and then I think we'll be gone whilst we can. Beaumont shouldn't at all mind finding us in his net, if the tide turns his way. I only hope those other poor devils we'll be dining with have as much sense.''

''True,'' mused Jenkins, following him. ''It's hard to think of the old duchess rotting away in the Bastille.''

For a moment the marquis paused, and Jenkins watched his face carefully to see if his arrow had landed.

Then the marquis smiled a cold hard smile that made Jenkins grimace.

''The old woman is so far gone, I doubt she'd know the difference. As to her camp followers—since that, I think, is what you were referring to—they are the sort that follow a trade that can be plied under any change of government. For men remain the same no matter what uniform they put on, or, as in their case, put off. Stop being a sentimentalist, old dear. I offered the girl a soft berth, and she turned me down. She's after a seat nearer the throne. Any throne. And good luck to her. And good riddance,'' he added grimly, motioning Jenkins to follow him.

*   *   *

Catherine gazed in wonder at the home she entered. She had been to a great many parties, so many that her head whirled thinking of them; they all seemed now to coalesce into one noisily splendid affair with richly gowned and garbed people saying the incessantly same things to her and to one another. But this home was so stately, so lavishly furnished, that she gaped anew. The staircase was decked with flowers; so early in March it was rare to see such perfect blooms. She saw many of the guests pause to stare at the masses of violets entwined everywhere.

Early on in the evening Catherine lost track of the duchess and her two other companions. She made her way to a chair in an unobtrusive corner, ready to plead distress with her ankle again, and was pleased and surprised to find that in the crush of people, her usual admirers seemed to forget about her.

She was sitting and watching the merrymakers when M. Beaumont came up beside her and bowed. Catherine nodded. In all the time that she had seen him, he had never approached or spoken to her. But now he smiled and asked her leave to seat himself. She smiled back and nodded again. She had learned much more composure in the weeks that had passed. Though her days were spent in her room, her nights had been filled with parties such as this one. She had gained so much aplomb that she turned to Monsieur Beaumont and was able to study him with candor before he turned to speak.

He was a neat man, she thought, of no special age. Small, well turned out, and unremarkable in every way.

"Mademoiselle Catherine," he said, with only a slight accent making "Catherine," sound droll, as if it were "Cat-arine." But so many of the French, she had often noticed, had trouble with the "th" in her name. "We so often have seen each other, I think. Yet we have never actually conversed. How delightful it is to find you alone, and on the very night that I wished to have private conversation with you."

Catherine kept her face impassive. She hoped this quiet little man had nothing improper to offer her, but he seemed to have nothing but calm appraisal in his small dark eyes.

"I see that you have been very circumspect, unlike the dear duchess's other two companions."

Catherine's eyes widened. She knew that she could not defend Rose and Violet, as it would make her appear a fool. But she did not like to hear them condemned, so she simply kept her face blank.

"No, no," he said sweetly, raising his hands. "I do not say a thing against them. They are two lovely English flowers, truly. And so many of my acquaintances have found their company so amusing. So I shall say nothing against them. But you, my dear, have been so much less . . . free with your person, shall we say? It has caused much talk among us. Why should the sweetest of them all withhold herself? they are saying. Why? I myself have wondered."

Catherine grew anxious—she did not care for the way this conversation was tending. For although she had become adept at countering flattery, and even immodest suggestions, this cool appraisal of her presence with the duchess disconcerted her.

"And then I thought. And then I knew. You are not a fool—no, not at all, Miss Catherine. You have refused my friends, even those of the highest rank. And you have refused even the much-admired nobleman from your own country. Yes, I know. And why?"

Catherine began to speak, but he cut her off with a shrug and a wave of his hand.

"No, no explanations please. The thing is clear to me. The others settle for small rewards, and small adventures. You are much wiser. You seek something more lucrative, more permanent, with more advantages. You see the long view, while your fellow companions see only the end of their delightful noses. We are two of a kind, mademoiselle. I understand you well."

"Indeed, you do not," Catherine flared, rising. "You do not understand at all."

M. Beaumont put his hand upon her arm and forced her to sit again. Catherine stared at him, for whatever insult she had been open to, no one yet had tried to forestall her physically. But this quiet man held her firmly in her seat, and, glancing upward, she saw many faces hastily avert themselves from her obvious distress.

"I am a man of some small influence, Miss Catherine," he said with a smile. "I would advise you to stay and listen to me. I have connections in many places, Miss Catherine, and if you do not listen to me here, I shall be forced to have you taken to some place where you will listen. I have that power, you see."

Catherine sat and looked at the small man. She quietened, and he took his hand from her arm.

"Much better," he smiled. "I do not like to insist upon my way unless I have to. Do not be alarmed, Miss Catherine. I appreciate your beauty—I am a man, after all—but I do not covet it. No, I am happy with my own dear, cher ami. I do not require your presence for myself, no matter how lovely you are. But you see, I do understand, no?

"Now if you go on as you are doing, you will end up with nothing. For you do not know how to go on, that is obvious. The dear duchess, she is quite old, and quite silly. And your two companions, they would advise you to squander yourself, as they do, on any fellow that comes along with a few francs jingling in his pocket. They do not understand grand designs. I do. As you do. But you do not know which way to turn yet, do you? Quite wise," he said, as she shook her head violently in demurral at his words.

"For my poor country is in such a state right now that even we do not know how to go on. He who rules now may be in the streets tomorrow. Change has only begotten more change. You are so right not to cast in your lot with one who may lose all in a moment. Take my dear friend Pierre Richard. Tonight he will go home and sleep on fine silks in a room next to a king. But tomorrow?" M. Beaumont shrugged. "So who could blame you for casting him down? Or, for that matter, for repulsing his poor brother Hervé? For at the moment Hervé has nothing. Nothing but his charming self."

Catherine sat trapped while the small man beside her smiled smoothly at her. She felt a danger emanating from him unlike any she had yet faced.

"But that is only for the moment. Great things are in the wind, my dear. And great things are called for. So"—he straightened and stared at her—"this is what I have come to say. Give up your ties with the duchess. She has served her purpose—you will get no more from her. In fact, she may soon have no more to give. Come with me; I shall steer a clear course for you to the rewards you have been seeking. I shall find you a comfortable arrangement before the week is out."

"You are wrong," Catherine whispered. "I shall not leave the duchess."

"Oh," M. Beaumont said deprecatingly, "you think I wish to share in your reward. Put that from your mind, please. I seek nothing from you. Rather, my reward shall come from seeing you well placed."

"No," Catherine said, staring at him, "such a thing is unthinkable. You misunderstand."

"It is quite thinkable. If you think the duchess will object, please speak with her. I have already, and she is quite willing to end her association with you, so you need not worry about any problems from her. And none in the future, I assure you. I have taken over your fate. You are in good hands, never fear. Just have your bags packed by tomorrow morning, and all will end more pleasantly than you ever hoped."

"Tomorrow morning?" Catherine gasped.

"Perhaps that is too sudden," he said with a smile that did not reach his eyes. "Tomorrow evening then. I know how you ladies have to make farewells and pack every little thing. Although, I assure you, you could come to him with nothing but what is on your back and he would be pleased. He will smother you in riches, I assure you."

"To whom?" Catherine asked, staring.

"To my dear friend Hervé, of course."

"Never," Catherine said, rising again.

"A very pretty show of reluctance. I quite see what has won everyone over. And I cannot blame you for thinking me misled. For until now poor Hervé has had nothing to offer. But things will be greatly changed, and quickly, I promise you. He will soon be able to afford you—more than that, to treat you as a queen."

"No," Catherine protested, "it makes no difference, I tell you."

"I have no time for playacting; the decision has been made without your consent. It is over, Miss Catherine," he said, rising with her and gripping her wrist till it ached.

"This is my country. It is my domain. It is my wish. You will please to make ready for your journey. My man there will see you to your hotel. And my man will take you to M. Richard tomorrow evening. We will meet again, and by then you will see how foolish your fears have been. But do not try to evade my orders, Miss Catherine," he said, pressing her wrist till she had to bite her lip. "For my name is known, and no good will come of it."

Catherine looked around her frantically and saw no one willing to come to her aid, even though she was in evident distress. Rather they turned and ignored her. Hopelessly, she craned her neck, looking for a glimpse of familiar gray eyes, familiar broad shoulders, but the marquis was nowhere in sight.

"You see?" M. Beaumont said. "I am known everywhere. Now go, Miss Catherine, and make ready for your new and more pleasant life. I do you a great favor, Miss Catherine, and someday you shall thank me."

He released her, and she drew back. An impassive man in footman's livery stood at her back.

"Take Miss Catherine to her rooms, Claude," M. Beaumont said, and he watched as the footman steered the dazed girl toward the door.

Done, he then thought with a sigh. That was a good piece of work. Hervé would babble with gratitude when he told him. Pierre would be beside himself with rage, but much good that would do him.

Henri Beaumont had weathered many political storms by catering to the right persons at the right moment.

He had never heard the old English folk song about his legendary English counterpart, the infamous Vicar of Bray. But he would have understood the chorus, in which the vicar supposedly boasted that "Whatsoever king may reign, still I'll be the Vicar of Bray, sir." For whoever took power, Henri Beaumont would serve him well. The trick was in knowing the precise moment to shift allegiances, the exact moment to bestow favors. It was all in the timing. And if foolish Hervé Richard wanted this little English miss, he would have her as a gift from his friend Henri Beaumont just before the tide rose, just before Hervé knew that soon he could have anything in France that he wished. Even his own brother's head, if he wished. Though—and here Henri Beaumont gave himself the luxury of a rare, real smile—Hervé getting the woman his brother wanted and flaunting her before him would be better than getting his brother's head on a plate.

He had separated the little English cyprian from that fool of an old woman. He would serve her up to Hervé, who would be undyingly grateful. For he did not know what M. Beaumont knew. He did not possess the small piece of paper with the few coded words scrawled on it that M. Beaumont had received this very night. The few words that let him know that Hervé's great good friend and former ruler would soon be his, and everyone's, Emperor again.

Chapter XI

"Her Grace ain't back yet," Gracie sneered. "As you should well know. Why, the clock ain't even struck twelve."

"Please," Catherine begged. "Please, Gracie, let me know when she arrives. At any hour, at any time. I shall be waiting, but it cannot wait till morning. I must speak with her this night, whenever she returns."

Gracie folded her arms over her narrow breasts, an expression of great satisfaction upon her usually grim face.

"It's Mrs. Grace to you, young woman, and don't you forget it," she said slowly, eyeing the trembling young woman. "And Her Grace needs her sleep when she comes in. Why, she usually is so done in, poor soul, that she just tumbles into bed and don't stir till morning."

"Mrs. Grace," Catherine pleaded, "it is of utmost importance. Truly. You must—" And seeing the expression on the older woman's face, she quickly amended, "Please, please, just tap upon my door when Her Grace returns. I am sure she will want to speak with me as well. I know she will," she pressed, seeing the indecision on the other's face.

"All right," the older woman grumbled. "But don't be surprised if she sends you off with a flea in your ear. For having a chat with her 'companions' ain't what she's used to when she comes dragging in after one of them big dos."

Gracie turned abruptly and closed the door in Catherine's face smartly. One of those cats got her tail caught in the door at last, she sniffed with contempt as she caught a last glimpse of Catherine's stricken face. It's the Lord's judgment upon all of them wicked females.

Back in her room, Catherine slowly removed her shawl with trembling fingers and sank down upon her bed. Her first thoughts were of self-condemnation. She had dithered, and her selfish, cowardly procrastination had led her to this. For if she had been truly virtuous and truly courageous, she would never have been caught in such a coil. If she had thought herself derelict in remaining in the duchess's employ, it now seemed that she never really understood the full extent of the danger she had placed herself in.

And yet, she thought, groaning to herself, she should have known. Step by step, her complacence had led her to this, as surely as in any morality tale she had ever suffered through at Sunday sermon. She had accepted all, by slow degree, just as the vicar had warned her. A few months ago, if anyone had told her that soon she would be able to accept as commonplace nightly invitations to strange gentlemen's beds, she would have been appalled. Or if they had said, straight-faced, that she would have permitted a nobleman's ardent embrace without deadly shame, or even, in the quick of her soul, welcome it, she would have thought them mad. And perhaps, worst of all, if they had hinted that she would have been able to suffer blithely the reputation of a light-skirts, she would have laughed in their faces. But all of this she had done. And see what it had come to.

One cannot wear the feathers of a bird of paradise without being hunted as one. Why should anyone believe her now? And, she thought, rising and pacing in her agitation, it had gone beyond explanations. For M. Beaumont would not care to hear weak excuses. He had seen her as a cyprian, so he had decided to use her as one. She must speak with the duchess, collect her wages, only a few weeks before time, and go now. For she wondered if even the duchess's influence could prevent M. Beaumont from going ahead with his plans. And yet a small persuasive voice in the deeps of her soul still whispered that she would not have to leave yet—that she would not have to brave the world alone as she went back to England, that the duchess was still her employer, was still a woman of title and influence, and would still protect her.

It might be, Catherine thought, as she paced her room and listened for every creak in the old hotel walls for the duchess's return, that now the dowager herself would have had enough and would wish to return home as well. And then Catherine would find the entire incident just a frightening, cautionary false alarm.

So she persuaded herself as she waited; so she consoled herself as the hours ticked by. For she could not face the thought that she was trapped, that her future had been taken out of her own hands.

When the tap came upon her door, Catherine started. It had been so long a wait that she was sure Gracie had not told the duchess after all, out of spite.

Catherine straightened, ran her hands over her hair, licked her lips nervously, and went into the dowager's rooms. She had practiced her speech, but it died upon her lips as she caught sight of her employer. For the duchess had changed, as if in a moment. As if she were some once-vigorous plant that had been touched by the icy finger of winter.

She stood, Gracie hovering by her side, waiting for Catherine. But she seemed not to stand so straight as before, and to be rather oddly shrunken and debilitated. No longer a regal and imperious peeress of the realm, but only an old woman. The icy eyes that had gazed sharply at life and its pleasures seemed watery and weak in the candle's glow, and when she spoke her voice was querulous and edged with self-pity. Catherine gaped at the transformation. She did not know that it was only that the duchess's brief late flowering was passed, that her moment of spectacular beauty was over. It had been inevitable, for no beauty remains forever, but its flight had been hastened by terror and anxiety.

"Well, good riddance," the duchess said, staring at Catherine, but instead of backing the words up with a haughty stare down her long nose, her eyes seemed to waver.

"Your Grace," Catherine began, recalling herself after the shock of seeing the dowager so transmuted, "there has been a terrible mistake."

"No mistake," the duchess said. "You've found greener pastures. Can't blame you. You're young, with the world ahead of you, and you've seen a better chance and grabbed it. Violet told me you would, and she was right. So go, and be demned to you."

"I don't want to go," Catherine cried. "I want to stay with you. M. Beaumont told me that you had agreed to my leaving, but I swear I don't want to go. I had no idea of what he had in mind. And I want to stay with you. Please tell him that he was mistaken."

The duchess sank into a chair.

"Why shouldn't you want to go, eh? He said there would be riches aplenty for you."

"But Your Grace, please," Catherine said, going to the duchess and sinking to her knees by her feet, "please listen. You know that I served you faithfully."

Gracie gave a short bark of laughter.

"No, listen," Catherine pleaded, "I came as your companion. I didn't know about Rose and Violet then. And when I discovered they were accompanying you as well, it was too late to turn back."

Catherine faltered, for how could she claim that the dowager's two companions were nothing but highly priced prostitutes and that she, knowing all, had not been the same?

"I have been only your companion," Catherine said fervently. "I have done nothing else, I promise you. I am not right for the life M. Beaumont projects for me. You must know that."

"I don't care what my girls do when I'm not about," the duchess said, turning from Catherine. "I don't know and I don't care. What they get up to is their business, so long as they don't involve me."

"But I have got up to nothing," Catherine cried.

"It was a mistake," the duchess mumbled, "all a great mistake. I should have hired on someone who was up to snuff, who wouldn't enact such tragedies."

"But it would be a tragedy for me," Catherine protested, rising to her feet and staring down at the duchess. "Can't you see that? Can't you just tell M. Beaumont that you refuse, that you wish me to stay on with you? I promise to be no further trouble."

The dowager avoided Catherine's eyes and instead began to talk rapidly to Gracie.

"I told him I wanted to keep the chit. I told him I was a woman of some influence. I told him that he had colossal nerve to try to dictate to me—the Duchess of Crewe. But he didn't back down. No, he didn't. Do you know what he told me? He told me I had no influence in France. That he had power over my life and death. That he could clap me in prison, duchess or no, and leave me there to rot away until my countrymen would extricate me. He told me that soon the English would all be in his power. And when I told him he was speaking fustian—and I did, Gracie, I did, I was so angry at the fellow—do you know what he told me?"

Gracie took the duchess's hand and soothed her with, Catherine saw in amazement, a look of great contentment upon her homely face.

"He told me," the duchess whispered, "that I was only a mad old woman. Only a senile old woman of no account. And that after a week or two in his cells I would be less than that. He told me I should be locked up for my own safety. That he had the power to do so. And that by the time my family found out, it would be too late for me. Too late for me! 'The Duchess of Crewe is a succès fou,' he said, and then he laughed and said it was no more than the truth, that I was a crazy old woman. And that everyone knew it and laughed at me, as they laugh at inmates in a madhouse. And then he said that that was just the thing! He would put me in a madhouse, and no one would question him at all. He had the power, he said. He does, Gracie, he does."

"Your Grace," Catherine said, but at the sound of her voice the duchess turned to her and cried with some of the old power in her voice, "Go, go from me. I never want to see you again. You have brought me nothing but misery. I should never have taken you on. Butter wouldn't have melted in her mouth, Gracie, I swear it. And now look at her. Begging me to let her stay. I cannot, don't you see? She will bring me to ruin. He wants her and he shall have her. Gracie," the duchess quavered, "I shall want to go home now. Yes, I want to go home."

"Let me come with you," Catherine begged.

"No, no," the duchess cried out in a strong voice, "for then he will not let me go. Get away. Get away."

Gracie marched to where Catherine stood. She placed herself so close to her that Catherine had to back away.

"You stop bothering my lady," Gracie commanded, suddenly forceful and demanding. "You let her alone. You and the others was nothing but a passing fancy for her, like I always said. She's come back to her own sweet self now and she wants to be shut of you and your kind. So the gravy boat has docked and you let her alone. I won't have you battening on her anymore. Take your things and go where you always belonged. To the gutter."

Catherine went white. The hatred in Gracie's eyes chilled her. There was no hope for her here, not anymore. She thought quickly and pleaded once more, "But if I am to go, please, Your Grace, my wages. For I haven't enough funds to get home alone.

And I have worked for you. Please do not strand me without funds."

The duchess rose and went to her dressing table. She opened a drawer and with palsied hands withdrew a small box. She took a handful of coins and flung them onto the floor.

"Here, here. Take your money and go. I never want to see you again."

Catherine went to retrieve the coins and almost stopped and let them lie when she heard Gracie sneer. "It's the money all right. There's never enough for her kind."

Catherine had to swallow back a biting reply and stifle the impulse to leave the money and flee with her self-respect intact. But she knew that self-respect alone would never extricate her from her problem. When she had hastily counted out the amount she knew she had earned, she stood again. There was some satisfaction in noting that she had left the better part of the coins still lying upon the floor.

"I have taken only what was due me," she said stiffly, "and I am sorry, Your Grace."

"Get out now," Gracie commanded, arms akimbo and advancing upon Catherine. "Go and good riddance." Her voice softened as she looked back to the duchess. "Leave Her Grace to me now. I'll see her right, just like I always have. I didn't desert her when she took to the wild fancies she did, and I shan't leave her now that she's come back to her senses. But you get out."

Catherine heard the door slam behind her, and the sound was ominous. If M. Beaumont had such power as to terrify and override a duchess, what chance had she against him? She could not turn to the marquis, although her thoughts had turned to him a dozen times this evening. For if she went to him, he would only think she had at last decided to take up his offer. Somehow, she was sure that he could stand against M. Beaumont, or anyone in the world, for that matter. But to go to him would be to say she was his. Why should he believe otherwise? And in some small part of her mind Catherine knew that if she went to him, she somehow would become his. And even if he then took her to safety, she would then be lost to herself forever, and be in time no less than Rose and Violet. She would have become, no matter how she examined it, or how many excuses for her behavior she invented, a woman who sold herself to a man, and forever beyond the pale of decent people. And she was done with excuses for her outrageous behavior.

She knew she had enough money to reach the coast now. And enough to take a ship to England. But she knew that M. Beaumont would not let her get that far. So she waited for Rose and Violet to return. Now they were her last hope. They were clever and women of the world. Doubtless, they would have some idea of what she could now do.

Dawn was staining the sky with its gray light when Catherine at last heard some movement in Rose's room. She leaped to her feet and, after gazing anxiously about the empty hall, tapped on Rose's door.

"Who is it?" Rose whispered.

"Me, it's Catherine. Oh, Rose, let me in," she pleaded, suddenly afraid that Rose, too, would deny her.

But when she entered Rose's room, she saw only her familiar smiling face grow suddenly concerned when she glimpsed Catherine's ashen countenance in the growing light.

"Whatever is the matter, Catherine?" Rose asked, drawing her to the bed to sit. "You look as if you'd seen a ghost. Never tell me that Her Grace's heart's given out? That she's taken a bad turn and left us? For she looked like death itself when I last saw her. And when I went to her, she just shooed me away and told me to leave her be. I should have stayed," Rose mourned. "Poor old dear."

"No, no," Catherine said, "she's well. It is something else. Oh, Rose, you must help me. For I'm in desperate case."

Catherine took Rose's arm and, feeling the frozen hand which clutched her, Rose stopped chattering and sat quietly while Catherine poured out her story.

"Oh, that's a rum case," Rose sighed, when Catherine had done at last. "That's a fine predicament."

Rose stood and shook her head and looked consideringly at Catherine.

"You do have a problem, Catherine," she said, "and I have got to be right out with you, dear. The easiest thing for you to do would be to go with Beaumont. Hervé Richard ain't a bad sort. He's clean, and he's got something blowing in the wind for him. And," Rose added, absently rubbing her shoulder, where Catherine could now see in the brightening dawn light, there was a fresh set of bruises, "he ain't got any strange ways about him, so far as I have heard. No, he's a straightforward chap who wouldn't want nothing special from you."

Catherine recoiled and hastily averted her face. The look of horror, however, had not escaped Rose.

"No," Rose sighed, "I didn't truly think so. Ah, Catherine, forgive me. I didn't mean to hurt your feelings. It was just an idea, you know. Forget I said it, do. For I know you're a good girl, and I wasn't thinking straight. We have just to get you away from here without Beaumont twigging to it, and all will be well. How to do it is the question."

Rose and Catherine sat silently in the room as the light increased, each thinking alone. When Rose heard a movement from the next room, her face brightened.

"That'll be Vi. She's just the one. She's far more longheaded than I, and she's a wonder at getting herself out of tight corners. I'll just go get her."

Before Catherine could look up from her miserable contemplation of the carpet, Rose had fled the room, and before a few more moments had passed, she returned with a tired-looking Violet in tow. In the fresh light of morning, Violet's dramatic orange costume seemed tawdry, and her carefully made-up face seemed blurred and exhausted.

"Here she is," Rose sang. "Oh Vi, we need your help, for our Catherine's got herself into a terrible problem."

Violet turned her weary smudged eyes toward Catherine's woebegone form.

"If she's gotten herself in the basket," Violet yawned, "she's just got to turn round and go home. She can't be increasing in the duchess's employ. The old girl don't want a squalling brat on her hands."

"Oh Vi," Rose cried, genuinely staggered, "you know better. Catherine ain't in the family way. And she don't want to be in the game, neither, and that's the problem."

Violet flung herself upon the bed and lay so still while Rose explained Catherine's situation that Catherine feared she had fallen asleep. But when the tale was done, she opened her eyes and looked at Catherine narrowly.

"You want to skip out, then?" she asked.

"I must," Catherine said. "But how? And I must do it now, for Beaumont will be here to collect me by nightfall. But how shall I go in broad daylight?"

"It's not impossible," yawned Violet. "I've done it myself. Remember in London, Rose, when that poxy viscount was after me?" She laughed. "I made a monkey out of him, didn't I?"

Rose nodded eagerly. "So you did, Vi, but this is Paris, and Catherine and I ain't so wise as you. What's she to do now?"

Violet studied Catherine's abjectly sorrowful face. Her thoughts raced behind her sleepy facade. So the Richard lout was about to come into riches and wanted a fine English female? Well, she'd do just as well to console him when he'd lost the one he had his heart set on, wouldn't she? She watched Catherine—she had nothing against the girl, but business was business, and it wouldn't suit her to stick her neck out and defy Beaumont. But if there was some profit to be made from the girl's disappearance, well, there were no flies on Violet. The problem was, she thought, how to get the chit safe away without Beaumont twigging to the fact that she'd helped. After a moment she smiled.

"Rose, you goose. The answer's plain as the nose on your face. Catherine, do you take those things you find necessary, and only a few things at that. Here, wait a tick," she said, suddenly galvanized, and the two other women stared at her in wonder as she leaped up and ran lightly to her room.

She returned in a few moments. "Here," she said, placing a worn portmanteau at Catherine's feet. "I always carry it in case I have to skip fast. It's old and battered, but it won't attract attention."

Catherine looked at the worn case and had to agree. Indeed, it looked as though it had been used in the days of Violet's grandmother.

"Now you take only a little with you, and when you've all secured, act sharp, because time isn't on your side. Then, you come back here. And then, Rose, you take Catherine down to the stables. James is there, and he's a right caution. What he don't know about Paris, the Frogs themselves don't know. He's a game 'un and up to anything. And if your pretty face don't tempt him to help, Catherine, your good gold coins will. For he's always on the lookout to make some extra. And he don't like foreigners above half. Now shoo, go to it, Catherine, time is wasting."

Catherine fairly flew to her room and collected those few items she felt necessary. She left all her fine dresses and bonnets and slippers without a backward glance, only taking those few dresses she had originally come to the duchess with. She flung toothbrush, hairbrush, and underthings into the portmanteau.

When she was done, she hurried back to Rose's room.

"Good," Violet smiled. "Now Rose, you take her down the servants' stairs and James'll do the necessary."

Rose paused and then asked, "Catherine, let me see your purse."

Dutifully, Catherine handed it over to her.

"Oh, this will never do," Rose cried, "for you're a pauper. Look, Vi, how far can she go on this?"

Rose hurriedly went to a box in her closet and came back with coins that she poured into Catherine's purse above her horrified protests. "No, no," Rose said adamantly, "I couldn't sleep nights thinking of you starving in a ditch. We're friends, aren't we?" she asked, suddenly stopping and looking hard at Catherine.

To refuse Rose's money, Catherine realized, would be to deny her friendship.

"So we are Rose," she whispered, "and I am grateful. Someday I hope to pay you back."

Satisfied, Rose nodded sharply. "Here, Vi, open the coffers. For you're fast with advice, but tight with your purse. What do you want Catherine to think?"

With ill grace, Violet left, to come back and add her mite to Catherine's growing treasure. "But understand," Violet said quickly, "if anything goes amiss, you're not to prattle about where you got the funds."

Catherine smiled bitterly and met Violet's worried eyes. "Do you think M. Beaumont will wonder at my riches?" she asked.

Violet seemed satisfied, but she added, "And I hope you'll not cry rope at us, if he does find you. Do you promise to leave us out of it?"

"Of course," Catherine said softly. "But I think if he does find me, he won't care how I failed or who helped me fail."

"But you won't fail, Catherine," Rose said quickly. "For James is as sharp as he can be. We'll have to think of something Catherine can wear to escape notice, Vi," she added, biting her lower lip.

"Leave it to James, Rose," Violet answered. "He's up to all the rigs. Now get her out of here. And then I'm to bed. For I'm worn out."

Rose bustled ahead to the door, to see if any servants or guests were in the corridor.

"Half a mo," she said cheerily, like a little girl up to some midnight pantry raid, "I'll go ahead and check out the stairs to see if all's clear."

"Violet, I thank you," Catherine said softly, when they were alone, "for I know it's a dangerous thing for you to do. And I know that you never really approved of me."

"I like things straightforward," Violet murmured, suddenly less bored. "And it may be, Catherine, that I don't like being constantly reminded what I am by some great-eyed innocent girl. It's well enough with Rose, and the gentlemen I accompany. And the old duchess is daft anyway, you know. But it just may be that I like to think of myself as only a clever businesswoman, and I don't care for the constant presence of someone who is so very much aware of what a bad business mine is. You don't hide your thoughts too well, you know. And while I've come to terms with myself a long while ago, you keep reminding me of what I am and where I'm undoubtedly going. I wished to be an actress once, and the trick of being a good actress is to believe in your part. You shake that belief, Catherine, and I don't mind telling you, I'll be relieved when you're gone."

"Thank you anyway, Violet," Catherine said, wondering whether she should give the older woman a farewell embrace, for wherever she herself was headed, she did not think they would, in any case, ever meet again. Violet settled the matter by taking Catherine's hand and shaking it.

"Good luck," she said simply, and then, with a smile, she added, "and stay away from wicked companions in the future."

"Come, come, don't just stand there, Catherine," Rose whispered in exaggeratedly conspiratorial tones. "Time is wasting. Come, come, let's go, for the stair is clear."

Violet lifted an eyebrow in Rose's direction and said with some asperity, "Stop looking so sneaky, Rose. You'd make anyone suspect you of anything. It's a good job you never tried for the stage. Good-bye, Catherine, keep a good thought." And then she gave a tremendous yawn. "Lord, I'm beat. I think I'll sleep the afternoon away, and if anyone knocks upon my door, they'll see that I haven't done a thing but sleep since I returned. I haven't seen a thing, I haven't done a thing. Just like you, Rose, just like you."

"To be sure." Rose tittered in her excitement. "And where dear Catherine's got to, how should we know? We've been just two sleeping beauties, haven't we? Come, Catherine, the time is right."

Chapter XII

Catherine followed Rose down the servants' back stairs, bumping her portmanteau against the wall at every turn. They went quickly, Catherine hiding, flattening herself against the wall at every landing as Rose scouted to see if the way was clear. But it was early dawn and they achieved the sanctuary of the stables without any mishap. Once there, in the dim light, with the strong scent of horses and hay in their nostrils and only the curious nickering of the horses to greet them, Catherine relaxed at last. Rose nodded with satisfaction, for none of the grooms or coachmen were afoot in the stalls area, and there was no sign of any human activity.

"Do you wait here now, Catherine," Rose whispered, and she bustled off down the line of stalls and disappeared up a stairwell at the back of the stables. Catherine absently stroked the neck of a mare and wondered how Rose knew her way so surely through the stables, for she herself had only seen horses and carriages emerging from them during the days and nights that they had rested at the hotel. After a few moments during which Catherine worried about the increasing daylight and started at every restless sound the horses made, Rose reappeared at the other end of the stable and motioned urgently for Catherine to follow her. Catherine followed Rose up the turning wood stairs and found herself on a level above the stable proper. There were several doors off a wide wood-planked hall, and Rose led her unerringly to the door at the end of the corridor.

"Are you decent now, Ferdie?" Rose whispered as she tapped softly at the door.

The door swung open and James stood there, stuffing his

shirttails into his trousers. He yawned, then grinned wickedly at
Rose.

"Ah, Rosie, you never asked that of me before," he grinned.

"No nonsense now," Rose snapped, all business as she motioned Catherine to follow her into the room.

It was a garretlike room, with a wooden floor and a high
sloped ceiling. A simple bed and dresser with a lamp occupied
one wall, and the other wall had a large window overlooking the
stable entrance. James gave Catherine and Rose a sweeping bow
and then sat down on his bed and smiled sleepily at them.

"Your visits are always welcome, Rosie, my love," he said,
"but you don't often bring me extra helpings. Whatever will our
little Miss Catherine think?"

Rose flushed a bit and then said hurriedly, casting a worried
eye at Catherine shrinking back against the far wall, "None of
your games now, Ferdie. I told you. The poor thing is in trouble.
And Vi said, and I agreed, that you're the very one to spirit her
out of here. And quickly too, for that devil Beaumont is after
her, and he's no easy boy to cozen."

"Ferdie?" Catherine whispered, wondering if her fear had
turned her comprehension, for it was James, the duchess's coachman who was grinning happily at her.

"Oh, that," James laughed. "The old girl calls all her coachmen James, but it's Ferdie Robinson at your service. So you
want to nip out and leave the old girl in the lurch?"

"No, that's not it," Catherine said quickly, "for she's washed
her hands of me. M. Beaumont has frightened her badly."
Catherine grimaced involuntarily. "He wants to give me to
Hervé Richard. He thinks I'm . . . that is to say, he believes me
to be . . ." Catherine found herself at a loss for words, since
with Rose standing next to her, how could she describe what
Rose and Violet were without giving offense?

But James/Ferdie just laughed and Rose looked on benevolently.

"Oh aye, I know. All of us here know, lass. You're not in the
same game as dear Rosie here, and we've often wondered just
what your game was. For I swear I've brought you back to the
hotel a dozen times alone when you could have had company
easily, and I knew back in dear old London town you was in
above your head. I thought to drop you a word even back then,
but I've learned the less said, the safer your head. So now you're
in the soup, eh?"

"Oh James—that is, Ferdie—" Catherine faltered.

"Keep it James, lass, or you'll be stammering all morning."

"James then," Catherine said, gathering up her courage at the friendly expression on his plain, homely face. "I must go. I cannot do as M. Beaumont wishes. I cannot stay. Indeed, I should not have stayed so long. But see, I have all this money. I only need enough to take the packet back to England. You may have all the rest, but please, if you know of a way for me to leave safely, help me now."

"Keep your brass," James said, with a wave of his hand.

Catherine's heart sank and Rose bridled instantly.

"Why you are a beast, Ferdie Robinson. After all we've been to each other. And after I thought you were a right sort!" she shouted. "It's as well I never went along with you and your high promises. You'll leave my friend to go to strangers for help? Oh, you are a rum cove, you are."

"Hush, hush, Rosie," James said, quickly rising and going to Rose and capturing her in his arms. "Did I say no, love? I only said I wouldn't take her money. And so I won't. For she is your friend, love, and I wouldn't charge her for a favor. Anyhow, I don't like Beaumont, and I don't like the duchess, and I don't like this whole setup. I've only stayed on to earn some more shekels, puss, so I can set you up proper if you ever say yes."

Catherine noted the satisfied little grin on Rose's face with some shock. For she had never seen Rose so content as she seemed now as she coquettishly tapped James on the chin and sighed, "I knew I was right in you, Ferdie. You are a good lad. Ferdie is the wisest thing in creation, Catherine," Rose said comfortably. "So rest easy, he'll think of a way."

"They'll be expecting you to fly," James said thoughtfully. "We've got to confuse them a bit, that's all. We've got to get you safely away from here to Saint-Denis. That's only outside the city a way, and there's a diligence that stops there that goes to the coast. You've only to hop on it and you're in Dieppe again. Then skip on a packet and you're home."

"But how?" Catherine and Rose said in concert.

"Some sort of disguise," James muttered, pacing and thinking.

"A widow!" Rose exclaimed, clapping her hands together. "That's the very thing! With a long black veil. And you could pretend to cry a little, couldn't you, Catherine, dear?"

"And all they'd have to do is lift the veil," James put in, "and then she'd be crying in earnest. Rosie, love, when we do buy that inn, it's you who will greet the guests, and I that will run it. For it's your face that's your fortune, puss."

Rose subsided sadly. She walked over to Catherine while James stood, lost in thought.

"It's true," she sighed, "I'm not longheaded at all, you know. And I'm not getting younger neither. I most likely will buckle up with Ferdie. And follow his path. For he wants us to set up an inn on the road to London, and after this trip I think I'm done with this old life. I had such dreams of fortune. Now I think I will be very glad to be plain Mrs. Ferdie Robinson."

"Never plain," James said, turning to them. "It's a disguise we're after. Now how can we change this lovely English beauty into something Beaumont's lackeys will ignore?"

Catherine thought for a moment and then she clapped her hands together.

"James! Rose! I have the very thing. I've seen it done on the stage. And I've read about it often enough. I'm not very tall, you know. I can dress as a lad."

James looked skeptical, but Rose was delighted.

"The very thing," she cried.

"I don't know," James said, but, at Rose's urging, he shrugged his shoulders. "It's worth a go, I suppose. Wait here. There's a room downstairs with some old kit left over from lads that have stayed here and skipped. I'll be back in a flash. If Beaumont's coming to collect Catherine, we'll have to move smartly."

Catherine wrung her hands in anticipation. "I know I can do it, Rose. I've seen it often enough. And they'll be looking for a girl. I'll pull my hair back and I'll swagger a bit. . . . Oh Rose, it has to work. I cannot bear to think of what will happen if it doesn't."

Rose's enthusiasm began to fade as she looked Catherine up and down. Some of her doubt communicated itself to Catherine, and by the time James arrived with an armful of old clothes over his arm, he encountered two white-faced grim-looking women.

"Try it," he said simply, handing Catherine the old faded clothes.

Cathering looked about nervously.

"Where can I change?" she asked anxiously, looking about the room for an alcove or a closet.

"Yes," James grinned, "there's no doubt, you are a lady. Here, Rose, let's go into the corridor and catch up on some gossip. The lads here have seen you often enough; it won't arouse comment. Might arouse something else though,'' he added, with a grin.

"Hush, Ferdie,'' Rose giggled, poking him in the chest. But they grinned at each other and turned to go.

"Open the door, when you're done,'' James whispered. "But Catherine, best close your eyes first,'' he added while Rose smacked at him coyly and simpered happily.

Catherine moved far from the window into a corner of the room. She quickly stripped off her gown and clambered into a faded, patched pair of pantaloons. They were tight about the hips, but, she reasoned, as she did up the closings, they felt so strange on her that she could not know if they fit or not. It's rather, she thought, as she quickly did up the buttons on a much-mended white shirt, as if a gentleman got into skirts. How would he know if they were the right length and fit? She felt a fool as she hurriedly pulled back her masses of raven curls and tied them severely with a simple black ribbon. But, she thought, as she stuffed her discarded gown into her portmanteau, she would gladly suffer feeling a fool for a space of time in exchange for freedom. She was so badly frightened that she felt she would go to any lengths—like a fox who would chew off its own leg to get out of a trap—to be free of her present situation.

Drawing in a deep breath, she glanced down at herself. She was barefoot, the pantaloons were fastened, the shirt seemed to fit. She slowly swung open the door, and, taking James's advice, she averted her eyes and whispered urgently, "James! Rose! I'm ready.''

And then she stepped back into the room, to await their approval.

Rose came in first with a little laugh and high color in her cheeks, and then stood, stock still, and gaped at Catherine. James followed languidly and then stopped at Rose's side and stared. He gave a low whistle and then said slowly, "I've never seen a lad like you, Catherine, my girl. But I surely hope there's more such about in this cold, cruel world.''

Catherine looked from Rose's shocked face to James's frankly admiring one, and then looked down at herself again.

"Don't I look right?'' she asked.

James started to laugh, and laughed till he had to hold on to the side of the dresser for support.

"Oh girl,'' he sputtered, "you do look right. But not in the way you could wish.''

Rose tittered as well. But then a considering look came into her eyes. "Oh, Catherine," she finally sighed, "you could have made a fortune. You could have had such a career."

"Here, Catherine," James finally said, steering her toward his dresser, where he had a small faded-looking glass in the corner. "See for yourself."

Catherine felt the color flooding her face as she stared at the image in the gray speckled glass. She might as well have been nude, she thought with shock, the blood roaring in her ears. The white shirt strained its buttons over her high breasts and emphasized them. And the pantaloons clung to her hips and legs like another skin. She was, she thought, in confusion, seeing her body's slim but rounded outline—the most indecent-looking female she had ever seen,

Desperate, she turned and blurted, "If I bound myself . . . here. And if there were another pair of pantaloons, but perhaps larger. . . ."

"No, Catherine," James said kindly, "for it wouldn't do. There's not a portion of you that don't look like just what you are, a full-blown woman."

"But," Catherine protested, "I've heard about it being done. I've read about it as well. Women can disguise as young men."

"Some women, maybe," James chuckled, never taking his eyes from her frame, "but you, Catherine, never."

"But you do look a treat," Rose said helpfully. "Ever so gay. Such a nice figure of a woman, Catherine. It's very flattering in its way, dear."

"Don't be a bufflehead, Rosie," James put in, wrapping one arm about Rose's shoulders as Catherine sat down wretchedly upon his bed. "She don't have to look good—she has to look different."

"All I look like," Catherine grieved, "is a fool. Which I undoubtedly am. I've landed myself in this wretched state because I have been a fool. So it's only right that I look like one. Like a fool, like a zany."

James's eyes narrowed as she sat there hanging her head and crossing her arms in front of her breasts.

"Now you've hit upon it, lass," he said unexpectedly, causing Rose to turn to round upon him for his unkindness. But before she could assault him for his cruelty, he was gone, out the door.

"Don't despair, Catherine," Rose said, sitting beside her and patting her shoulder. "I told you Ferdie is clever. He's not beaten yet. All he has to do is to get you out of this hotel and you'll be safe as may be. And I know he'll do it."

But Catherine only shook her head and did not try to restrain the tracks of tears that were slowly coursing down her face. She could not grasp the enormity of her failure. She could not imagine what she could do if M. Beaumont acutally came to claim her for his friend. She now knew that she had never really accepted that he would, or could. There had always been the possibility of escape in the back of her mind. Now, she felt, that was impossible. And now, for the first time, she had to face defeat. How, she thought frantically, ignoring Rose's murmured assurances, could she go on? It was one thing to bear the insult of being thought of as a prostitute. But she knew she could not actually be one. Her thoughts raced each other around in her mind, and she felt a despair such as she had never known.

"Here," James said triumphantly, suddenly appearing in the door and swinging it closed with his foot.

"Mop up, girl," he said, busily separating the garments in his arms. "Stand up, put out your arms. Come on, Catherine, buck up. Time's running. We have to be off now. We have a chance while it's yet early. Once morning comes up full and the light's better, we cut our chances in half. Now turn. No," he said, pulling off the jacket he had put on her and trying another. "Here, Rosie, you help. She's like a dummy. Get her arms into this. Aye, it's the very thing."

Catherine stood and let them push her about, buttoning up the jacket they had forced her arms into. She tried to wipe her eyes, but Rose was busily adjusting her sleeve. As she began to collect herself, James wheeled her round again and began to adjust a large battered hat upon her head.

"There," he said, standing back a pace and peering at her. "No, not quite. Half a tick," he said, and slipped out the door again. By the time he returned, Catherine had managed to slow her labored breaths and wipe her streaming face on the sleeve of the jacket they had put on her.

"Hold still," James ordered, and while Catherine stood dumbly, he, to her dazed horror, took some of the dirt from the handful he had acquired in the stable yard, streaked it across her cheeks, and added a dab to her nose. Then he pulled the brim of her hat further over her forehead.

"Perfect," he exclaimed, and then he steered her to the glass again. "Now look, Catherine, that's the ticket."

Catherine saw a bizarre vision facing her in the looking glass. It was small and woebegone. It wore a battered sloping hat down over its eyes. Its face, the part that was visible, was streaked with tears and mud. The patched and misshapen jacket that it wore hung to its knees. Its sleeves ended inches below its hands. Just the bottoms of the pantaloons showed, and bare feet completed the vision.

"A zany," James breathed. "A want-wit lad. Just a scruffy little lack-brain French boy."

Rose gave out a long satisfied sigh.

"There was a lad like that in the town where I grew up," she said with amazement. "He had a good heart, but he was a simpleton. You look just like him, Catherine. Oh Ferdie, you are a one!"

"They'll be looking for a desperate lovely young beauty. They won't cast an eye at a little simpleton wheeling along with a coachman. We'll walk right out of here, under their noses. And we'll go by foot to my friend Jacques, the other side of town. He's a Frenchie, but he's all right. We can't take any of the horses from here—they'll know them. But Jacques owes me a few favors," he smiled reminiscently, "and he'll lend us the nags. He works for some jumped-up tradesman. I'll get you to Saint-Denis right and tight. Then you board the diligence and you're off!"

"Shall I use this voice?" Cathering said in gruff tones, her spirits rising by the moment, infected by James's enthusiastic confidence.

"Oh, Lord," James said, "you still sound a female. And your French ain't too good, is it?"

Catherine nodded sadly.

"Never mind," James said briskly, "we'll get us a note. In French. From your folks saying as how you're just a poor simple lad going to visit your grandparents in Dieppe, and would any stranger kindly direct you right. Then you don't have to speak at all. Just be mute. You can show the note, and your fare, to the coachman on the diligence. Then when you get to Dieppe, you board the packet. Get out of your disguise. Then get the captain aside and tell him the story. Tell him all. He's bound to be an Englishman and he'll see you safely through."

"I can't write French too well, but if someone dictates it . . ." Catherine said doubtfully.

"Never mind," James said dismissively. "Your hand's probably too good. Our simpleton's not from an educated lot. We'll get Jacques to pen it. It will look better if it ain't spelled or written too fine. All set?"

"But she has no shoes!" Rose cried, aghast.

"Now I'm thinking like a noddy," James groaned. He went out the door again swiftly, mumbling that time was wasting.

"I told you," Rose sighed happily, "didn't I? He's a caution. And he's right. For you do look a fright. Nothing like the pretty lady they're on the catch for."

Catherine peered at herself from under the worn brim of the hat and laughed merrily.

"Thank you, Rose. That's the finest compliment and the most welcome one that I've heard since I came to France."

She amused Rose by striking foolish poses in front of the glass and flapping the long arms of her jacket. She looked, she giggled to Rose, like a ninny, there was no doubt of that. The worn jacket must have belonged to a giant, she opined, and its threadbare shape could have accommodated both herself and Rose. With the hat pulled over her eyes, she cavorted for Rose's delighted applause, looking, they both agreed, a veritable model of a fool. James returned carrying a pair of scruffy well-worn boots in his hand.

"Boots is the one thing they never leave behind unless they're dead," he grumbled, " 'cause they cost the earth. But here's a pair someone must have outgrown and then couldn't flog to anyone before they left. They're in sad shape, but that's all to the good. Put them on quick, girl, for folks is beginning to stir already."

Catherine struggled to fit the boots to her feet.

"I can't get them on," she cried in anguish. "My feet are not so large, but these must have been a child's, for I can't fit into them."

"Here," James said, bending and helping her to tug them on, "it just needs some force."

With concerted effort, Catherine and James managed to pull the left boot on. When she stood, Catherine stifled a cry of pain.

"Oh, Ferdie," Rose complained, "you never are going to send her off squeezed into those. Why, she doesn't even have stockings. She'll be in agony."

"There's no stockings about," he said sternly, "and the agony will be worse if Beaumont finds her."

Catherine bit her lip. If these were the only boots available, she would not quibble. She would wear them if they had hot coals in them. It would be poor spirited to lose all for the sake of momentary comforts. She reached down for the right boot, but James stayed her hand.

"Where's the blunt you've got?" he asked.

"In my portmanteau," she answered, puzzled.

"Get it out, Rosie," he said.

Rose looked at him with consternation, but obeyed. She handed Catherine's purse to him with a questioning look.

He spilled the coins and scrip into his hand.

"Here," he said, wrapping the coins in a square handkerchief he pulled from his pocket.

"Frenchie scrip won't be worth beans in England. Take the gold, wrap it like this, and keep it for home. There's pickpockets," he said, wrapping the little parcel tighter and tighter, "and thieves, and portmanteaus can be lifted too. You use the poor man's safe, Catherine, and you'll be right and tight. Here," he said, "stow it in your boot."

"But there's hardly room for her foot," Rose protested.

"Then she can swim to England," James thundered, "for if someone lifts her good British gold, she's a beggar."

"But," Catherine said, "if someone robs me, they'll discover what I am."

"Even if they do," James said grimly, "with your money safe in your boot, you can still go home."

Seeing her sudden stillness, he went on more slowly, "So you don't speak to a soul, and you just nod and show them the note. And even if worse comes to worse, you'll always be able to get home. For whatever else they may take off, it won't be your feet they're interested in. But if you're clever, they won't go near you, for you look poor as any beggar boy in Paris. So calm yourself. And hurry."

Catherine took the little cloth-wrapped parcel from James and firmly laid it in the bottom of the right boot.

"Lay on, Macduff," she said bravely, as James helped her tug up the boot.

"Talking warm don't suit you, Catherine," Rose sniffed.

Catherine laughed shakily and stood. When she began to walk

to the door in response to James's hurried admonitions, she had to limp.

"All to the good," James commented, seeing her altered gait. "It completes the picture."

Catherine and Rose waited in the darkened entry of the stable while James sauntered out casually to get the "lay of the land."

"Rose," Catherine said, clasping the other woman's hand, "I shall never forget you. You have been more than good to me. I do not know if we will meet again. I hope not in France, at any event. But I shall never forget you."

Rose clasped Catherine to her and hugged her tightly. As Catherine returned her embrace, Rose gasped a little, and, drawing back, Catherine again saw the fresh red bruises on Rose's shoulder.

The older woman looked down ruefully at the angry marks on her shoulder.

"You see, Catherine," she shrugged, "it's not a good life. And not one that I wanted for you. I choose it, so it's not the same for me. But not for you, love, for you are a lady. Anyway"—she smiled seeing Catherine's eyes glitter suspiciously beneath the downturned hat brim—"I'll be leaving it. We're to start that inn, Ferdie and I. So do you look for it one day. On the road to London. With a stable, and fine food, and flowers in the back. And Ferdie says he'll call it The Rose and the Bear, after us two. Now you go on, dear, and never look back."

James came back to the door of the stable.

"Say your good-byes, girls, for we're off, my simple lad and I. It's a lovely clear cold morning. Get back to your rooms, Rosie, and sleep the day away. You don't know a thing, Rosie, you don't know a thing."

But Rose hovered in the doorway and watched the lanky coachman and the small, ragged, limping little urchin flapping by his side swagger out into the street together. Clapping his hand around the young innocent's shoulders, the man began to sing a simple French rhyme, and the mismatched pair thus ambled on down the street. M. Beaumont's man only looked up and noted their passing. Then he turned his eyes up to the window where the English miss was, waiting and watching for any movement there. He doubted his employer's warnings that she might try to leave by stealth. Why should she, he mused, as the ragged pair of layabouts passed him, when she was set to go straight into the lap of luxury? Some females, he thought idly, blowing on his chilled hands after his long night's vigil, had all the luck.

Chapter XIII

Even though her feet ached, even though her right foot felt like it trod upon a fiery cobble every time she took a step, Catherine kept pace with James, and even swung her battered carpetbag in rhythm with the little song he chanted. For she felt freer and lighter than she had in days. They had walked blocks from the hotel. And no one seemed to give them a second glance. James marched her through the poorest district in the city, through crowds, yet no one bothered to take note of their passage. In her disguise, in dirty borrowed clothes, she suddenly felt more herself than she had all the nights she had been gotten up in her new finery. For that disguise, she reasoned, had been more alien to her than this one.

At least, she thought, as she gratefully rested on a barrel outside of the stable where Jacques, James's friend, worked, she would have a tale to tell her grandnieces and nephews when she grew old. For even now she was beginning to turn her thoughts homeward. Home, toward Arthur and Jane and the haven she looked forward to enjoying again. She might not, she thought, swinging her feet aimlessly as she waited, ever be able to tell Arthur the entire story. But she would tell Jane. And Jane would understand. Her adventuring days were over. She would be glad to go home and be a good auntie.

But the worm of ambition still gnawed at her. She might, she mused, someday be able to write of her adventure, perhaps under an assumed name, and earn a few guineas so that she would have some money of her own, and not be a burden upon Arthur forever. Then she hastily put her thoughts away. For it was ambition that had landed her in her difficulties, and she vowed to

be done with it. Still, a sudden thought made her laugh aloud.
And a nearby groom looked at her and shook his head over the
way even a stray current of air could amuse a simpleton. For she
very much doubted if Arthur would ever believe that his correct
sister-in-law could be dressed as a scruffy idiot, chewing a straw
and giggling to herself in the heart of the city of Paris. Oh Lord,
she thought, drawing in a breath in sad realization, what a
desperate pass I have come to.

James came out of the stable looking very pleased with himself.

"Here," he whispered, bending over her, "Jacques believes
you to be the son of a friend of mine. The less said, the safer your
head. I decided to name you Henri, in honor of your friend
Beaumont." He laughed. "And I thought 'Gris' would be a nice
short last name for you. Now," he continued, puttting a bit of
paper in her pocket, "there is your note. It says, as best as
Jacques could pen it: 'Here is my son Henri. He visits his
grandparents, M. and Mme. Gris, in Dieppe. Please see him
safely there, he has not much wit.'

"And now," James said, rising, "here are our horses. They're
too good for peasants such as us. But we have to stir stump. I
have to be back at work by evening. That's when the old woman
stirs. So mount up and we'll be off. You can ride, can't you?"
he said suddenly, in her ear.

Catherine eyed the huge black mare she was to ride and
swallowed hard.

She nodded. She had ridden back in Kendal, when Mama had
been alive. But always sidesaddle. Still, she thought, as James
threw her up atop the horse, she would do what she had to.

Seeing her there, clutching the reins with whitened knuckles
and struggling to stay right, James nodded.

"You look just as you ought," he grinned wickedly. And as
they rode off, he laughed to himself, watching his companion
struggle to stay upright. "Just as one would expect."

It seemed to Catherine that they rode for hours. But she knew
that it was only her body protesting her means of transport. The
horses steadily made their way through the crowded city streets,
and when the crowds began to thin, she thought she could see
James relax. "Now, we must travel," he called to her, and they
picked up their pace.

By the time the sun was high in the bright afternoon sky,
Catherine didn't know which part of her anatomy ached more,
her feet or her seat. But she was curiously happy, even in all her

discomfort. Once they reached open country, she even found herself humming in time with the beat of the horses' hooves. She wanted to whisk off her absurd hat and sing. For she was free. The air was cold and sharp and clean against her face. The decision had been made. And it did not matter what sort of a fool she looked, for no one knew her. And in her anonymity lay her safety and her passport to freedom.

She was almost sorry when James drew the horses in at a farmhouse and signaled her to dismount.

"I will go and make arrangements for the horses to be watered here. Then we'll walk to the inn where the diligence stops. For it never hurt to be extra careful," James said consideringly. "These nags are too good for the likes of us and you never know who notices such things at an inn. Se we'll hoof it there ourselves. I'll collect the horses on the way back."

While James went to the back door of the farmhouse, Catherine leaned upon a wooden fence. When the farm wife came out to look at the horses and glanced curiously at Catherine, she quickly drew her hat brim down further and gazed at the ground.

James dickered with the woman in his rough French, and then he came back to Catherine and slapped her on the shoulder, almost knocking her from her feet.

"*Allez idiot!*" he roared, "*Il est tard. Allez, allez.*"

She strode after him and breathlessly kept pace with him till the road turned and they were out of sight of the farmhouse.

"Did you have to be that convincing?" she complained, limping quickly after him.

"It does grow late," he said worriedly, glancing at the sky, "and she wanted to offer us some cider and a bite to eat. But I couldn't risk it. It wouldn't do for me to be gone when Beaumont comes. He'll twig to me in an instant when he finds you're gone too."

Catherine felt extremely guilty. For she hadn't realized the penalty that would fall to James if it were discovered that it was he who had helped her. So she merely nodded and tried to keep pace with his long strides. Her feet burned in the tight boots, and her right foot felt as though it were afire with each step she took upon her secret cache of coins. But she knew it would be selfish and dangerous for James if she slowed her pace, so she held her lips together tightly and forced herself to match his steps.

As they walked, James offered advice.

"It might be crowded on the road. And if it is crowded, there are always folk who'll take advantage of a half-wit. So push yourself. Wave your note around if they tell you there's no room in the coach. Someone's bound to take pity on you. You look sad enough. But remember, don't speak. Don't trust anyone. Keep to yourself till you get aboard an English ship. Keep that portmanteau by your side. Sleep on it, if you have to. And don't take off that boot. That's your bank account.''

Catherine puffed along with James, nodding at his every suggestion. The cold afternoon eased her pain. The ground was so cold, and the sole of her boot so thin, that her right foot was numbed and the pain seemed bearable. She would board the diligence and suffer quietly. But, she vowed, the first thing she would do aboard ship, even before she took off her hat, would be to rid herself of her accursed boots.

The inn was a sorry-looking place, Catherine thought, as they came to it. It was weathered, in need of a coat of paint, and grimy. James sniffed disparagingly as they passed the pungent odor of the stables. There seemed to be a great many people, mostly peasants and tradesmen, milling about in front of the place and talking loudly to each other.

"Stay by my side," James whispered urgently as he mounted the steps to the entrance.

Once inside, James pushed his way through a group of angry-looking farmers and went up to a high desk. A harassed, very fat woman was arguing loudly with a red-faced farmer. James waited until the farmer had finished his argument and stomped off before catching the woman's attention by rapping a coin on the desk. He flipped the coin repeatedly in the air as he held a whispered conversation with her. Catherine could not catch his words, but he, too, seemed to be growing angry. Finally, he sighed and flipped the coin at the woman, who caught it adroitly and then moved on to speak to another patron.

James drew Catherine aside at the entrance to the inn, near a large crowded taproom.

"Ahh, bad luck," he sighed. "The diligence broke down further down the line. And it won't come till tomorrow. So you'll have to spend the night here. These others, most of them live nearby and will go home and come back tomorrow. But still others are staying overnight. So there's no room for a rat, she says. You can't sleep in the stable neither, for there's a whole crew of rowdies putting up there, or share a room, for they're all parceled out. So I offered her a pourboire and she says a little chap like you can sleep safe enough right there.''

James pointed to the massive fireplace that took up one whole end of the taproom. Catherine looked at him in puzzlement, a little smile on her lips, for surely he was joking.

''No, not in the fire, nit,'' he laughed. ''But on the fender there—it's wide and brick, and there's room enough to curl up warm there.''

The fireplace, Catherine saw, did have a wide brick lip that ran in a semicircle along its circumference.

''Not the best accommodations,'' James shrugged, ''but keep your hat on, curl up tight, use your carpetbag as a pillow and you'll be safe enough. This side's for the common lot. There's private rooms on the other side. I gave her a tip so you could stay and she would see you on the diligence tomorrow. So,'' he said, looking around him, ''this is as far as I take you, sweet. I have to go now. But is there anything else I can do for you before I go?''

Catherine shifted from foot to foot in embarrassment. There was one other problem, but she did not know how to ask him about it. He saw her consternation and after a moment began to laugh. He cuffed her on the shoulder again.

''I'm a looby too,'' he grinned. ''Come with me.''

Keeping her head down, Catherine followed him out a back door near the steaming kitchen. There was a small vegetable garden and then nothing but a field of weeds. James picked carefully through the garden and led her around to the side of the house. Two ramshackle outbuildings stood there.

''Go into the one on the right,'' he whispered. ''I'll keep watch.''

When she came out of the little building, the smile disappeared from James's face.

''See you don't go in again unless there's absolutely no one about,'' he warned.

''I'd like to wash up,'' Catherine whispered.

''Forget that,'' James cautioned, leading her back into the inn and the taproom, ''for it's dirt that makes the man in this case. Now,'' he said quietly, as he sat her down by the fireplace, ''there'll be a spot of dinner later. Then curl up and sleep. And then, after breakfast, board the coach and go. I don't care if you have to ride atop it, go.''

"I'd like to pay you," Catherine said in a very little voice.
"You've been so very good to me."

James grinned hugely, swept her into his arms, and kissed her
soundly on both cheeks.

"Payment," he said. "The French," he whispered, "kiss all
the time. Take care, Catherine, and luck be with you."

She watched him go and sank down at her seat by the fireplace.
Suddenly the light seemed gone from the day, and she almost,
imperceptibly, shrank into a smaller shape. She was on her own,
at last.

The afternoon passed slowly. True to James's predictions, the
crowd of people slowly filtered away, grumbling as they went.
Still, the inn remained filled, but few people entered the taproom
and those who did, ignored the simpleton sitting and staring at
his boots by the fireside. As night came, it grew colder, and
soon the landlady huffed into the taproom and brushed at Catherine.

"*Allez, allez,*" she roared, as people do at those they think are
lacking in wit, as though volume alone will get their meaning
through. "*J'ai besoin d'allumer le feu,*" she screamed, indicating the logs stacked in the fireplace.

Catherine stepped back from the bricks and let the landlady,
puffing from exertion, bend to touch a match to the tinder. Soon
a comfortable fire was roaring, and the landlady grunted in
satisfaction. She waved at Catherine again.

"*Asseyez-yous. Asseyez-vous,*" she commanded, and, after
what she deemed to be enough of a confused consideration,
Catherine sat back down again as requested.

The taproom slowly filled, and a few tired slatternly-looking
kitchen maids brought bowls of stew, tankards of beer, and
bottles of wine out to the guests. One stopped and placed a bowl
of stew and a glass of cider on the bricks at Catherine's side. She
smiled at the poor waif, and Catherine ducked her head and
began to eat, badly frightened because she had almost said
"thank you" without thinking.

Most of the diners finished, puffed at their pipes, and then
grudgingly left the warmth of the taproom and made their way
upstairs to their rooms. The heat and a full stomach should have
made Catherine drowsy enough to curl up to sleep. But the heat
had thawed the anesthetic of cold from her leg, and the pain was
sufficient to keep her sitting upright in distress. The hour grew
later, and she sat almost alone by the fire, rocking unconsciously
to the beat of the throbbing in her foot. The warmth had made

her feet swell and the boot was now like some medieval torture
device. Catherine was in agony, both in spirit and body. Her
every impulse told her to strip off the boot and be done with the
pain. And her every thought told her that James had been right
and on no account should she part with it. But the walking and
the heat were taking their toll, and she felt her leg would burst.

The interior misery she was suffering had become so acute
that she did not take note of the altercation at the desk in the
little front room for some time. But finally the sound of raised
voices reached her pain-deadened ears and she looked up. She
could see the front entrance clearly from her seat. The landlady
was shrieking at a troop of men who had straggled in. They were
a bad-looking lot, Catherine thought. Some wore uniforms that
were tattered and grimy. Some wore work clothes. But they were
tough desperate-looking fellows, and Catherine shrunk into herself,
looking at them.

Even with her poor grasp of the local patois, the sense of
what they were shouting at the woman was clear to her. These men
were traveling to Paris, they protested loudly. For they had heard
that their emperor was returning. And they were volunteering to
be of service to their country again. One great fat fellow was
roaring that the emperor would be very displeased with a female
who denied free room to his soldiers. The woman shouted back,
equally loudly, that as far as she knew Louis still sat upon the
throne and no one was going to take over her inn as housing for
an army that didn't exist. She was not turning over her establishment to the rag and tag of an army without orders or compensation.

Catherine listened to the battle rage. The gross fellow who
was the evident leader of this disorderly troop finally banged
some money down disgustedly on the counter. And then, to
Catherine's horror, the landlady pointed to the fireplace and to
Catherine.

"Allez. Avec l'idiot," she said.

The troop of men, grumbling, coughing, and cursing, made
their way into the taproom. Catherine was afraid to budge, so
she simply took her portmanteau, put it on her lap, and tried to
look as insignificant as possible. The men eyed her, and then
disregarded her and began to call for food and wine.

After they had eaten, they sat and continued to drink and talk.
Catherine was desperate for sleep, for an end to the pain in her
foot, but she was afraid to close even one eye. The fire was
dying and the night advanced. But terror kept her wide awake.

As she sat there, hoping that they would soon settle down to sleep, the fat man who was their leader looked over to her. He shouted at her in a rough patois. She was not sure what he was saying, so she simply sat still, hoping he would lose interest. But he rose and came over to her. He was huge and unkempt, with a burgeoning belly and a sly look in his eye. He shouted down at her. She drew back, both from the violence in his voice and the dark heavy smell that emanated from him.

Then, to her horror, he reached down and lifted her by the shoulders and threw her aside. She stumbled against the edge of the fireplace.

"*Je dors là,*" he grunted, and, sitting where she had been, he took her portmanteau and began to open the straps on it.

It was sheer despair that caused her to launch herself soundlessly at him, cluching for her portmanteau in a frenzy. He waved her off with one large paw and kicked out at her. When his booted foot connected with her aching leg, she heard someone howl in a high keening scream of pain, and only when she fell, cradling her leg, did she realize that it had been she herself who had made that terrible cry. The tears were streaming down her face as she watched him begin to undo the other strap, and she was sobbing in earnest, when she heard an incredibly familiar voice say in French, "So this is how brave Frenchmen disport themselves."

The landlady bustled into the room, clucking.

"*Non, non. Ce n'est pas bien.*"

Catherine, looking up from under the brim of her hat, saw in the wavering light of the drying fire, as best she could through misted eyes, the tall straight figure of the Marquis of Bessacarr striding into the room. Jenkins, she saw, was behind him.

"Now why does a grown man torment a child, do you think, Jenkins?" the marquis drawled in English.

"Let it be," Jenkins said, with a worried look at the men in the room. "And for God's sake, let it be in French."

"We are not yet at war, Jenkins," the marquis said. "There'll be time enough for that."

The man who held Catherine's portmanteau put it down and slowly stood up. But she saw, from where she crouched on the floor, even when he stood up fully, the marquis still towered over him. In a caped driving coat, immaculate, disdainful, and straight, the marquis presented a picture of authority and command. Though hate glittered in the other man's eyes, he was the first to drop his gaze, and he walked back to the fireside and threw Catherine's portmanteau at her.

He muttered something about the boy being only an idiot. And the landlady began to explain rapidly to the marquis, Catherine surmised, who and what Catherine was.

"*Pauvre petit,*" the landlady cried, helping Catherine to her feet. Then she went on to assure her in many ways, by shouting loudly and by hand signals, that she was to go back to her seat by the fire, that the kind gentleman had interceded for her, that she was safe now. Then she turned and scolded the other men, who looked at her sullenly.

The marquis looked around him.

"And how long do you think it will be, once we are in our rooms, Jenkins, before they take extra good care of the poor lad?"

"Let it be," Jenkins repeated. "You surely don't intend to stay the night down here to watch over some wretched simpleton?"

"Hardly," yawned the marquis, "but, as I recall, there's a spacious hearth in my room as well. I'll let the lad spend the night there. For these oafs will tear him apart by morning, just to revenge themselves on me, if I do not protect him now."

"Surely not," Jenkins said, genuinely appalled, "for he's flea-ridden, or worse."

"I didn't say my bed," the marquis said coolly. "I said my hearth."

Jenkins shook his head in demurral, and Catherine stood still and watched as the marquis explained his plan to the landlady. She beamed at him and hastened to Catherine.

"*Allez,*" she shouted in Catherine's ear. "*avec le gentilhomme. Allez. Allez,*" she screeched as Catherine stood frozen to the spot.

Still, Catherine noted that the marquis did not look at her again. He merely turned and went to the stairs and began to go up. Jenkins turned once and shook his head in disapproval. But the men in the room grumbled to themselves, and Catherine knew she would be safer away from them.

As she mounted the stairs behind the marquis and Jenkins, she realized that neither of them had seen through her masquerade, and that the light was dim, and she would be expected only to curl up and sleep by a hearth. And, she thought wildly, she could be gone by early light. Safe from the marquis and from the brutes below stairs, for they were traveling in the opposite

direction. Gratefully, she limped up the stairs in the marquis'
trail. For a moment when she had recognized him and heard the
firm assurance in the deep voice, she had longed to throw herself
upon his mercy and reveal herself. But then she remembered
where he had last seen her, and what James said. But tonight's
safety would do well. She hugged her bag to her chest and
entered the marquis' room as quietly as she could.

His room was spacious and well appointed. It was obviously
the best the inn had to offer. The marquis flung off his cloak and
sighed.

"This will be my sheet for the night, Jenkins. I expect these
bed linens are inhabited. Perhaps they contain more livestock
than the garments of that poor soul over there."

"English?" Jenkins asked with a lifted eyebrow.

"The poor creature hardly understands his own language. Do
you think him fluent in English?" The marquis laughed.

"Right," Jenkins said, and then, seeing Catherine sidling
toward the fire, he said softly in French, shooing her, "Sit, sit.
Go to sleep. Go to sleep, boy."

Catherine obediently put down her portmanteau and, gathering
herself up in a small heap, lay down upon the stone hearth with
her bag as her pillow.

"Take off your hat, child," Jenkins said again in French,
reaching down.

Catherine sat bolt upright and clutched her hat tightly to her
head.

"He's terrified of us. Let him be," the marquis said.

"Gladly," Jenkins said stiffly, "but I'll sleep with my door
open, for I think he's not above theft."

"I wouldn't worry," the marquis yawned. "At least not about
him. But I think we ought to speed up our pace a bit. That's the
second group of volunteers I've seen headed for Paris. The
moment hostilities arise, we are fair game. I disliked to stop over
here, but I refuse to ride through the French countryside in the
dark of night. Tomorrow, if all remains the same, we'll leave the
horses and get on the coach. With luck, we'll reach England
before the week is out. And then let them march on Paris all they
wish."

"Aye, lad. I think they'll accommodate you. But pray it's
after we're safely asea."

The marquis and Jenkins continued to talk softly about lists
and plans and plots while Catherine lay quietly at the hearthside.

She would very much have liked to have done with the whole scheme and was itching to leap up and tell them who they shared the room with. She yearned to have the burden of escape taken from her shoulders. But, she reminded herself as sternly as she could, it was in seeking the easy way, the comfortable way of life, that she got into difficulty. It was time that she took responsibility for herself at last. She sighed heavily.

"The boy's aching for sleep," the marquis said, hearing her gusty sigh. "And, for that matter, so am I. I give you good night, Jenkins. We have a long day tomorrow."

Jenkins shot Catherine a suspicious look as he went quietly into the connecting room. Once there, he did not close his door all the way.

Sinjun blew out all but one candle by his bed and lay himself down upon the cloak that he had draped over the unreliable sheets. In the semidark, he could only make out the outlines of the poor boy's form by the dying fire. Satisfied that all was quiet, Sinjun lay back and rested his head against his laced hands.

All was done, he thought. The lists lay sewn firmly in the seams of his coat. Now there would be a reliable guide as to whom they could trust, whom they would have to name enemy, and who would sell to the highest bidder. A smile touched his lips as he thought of the list. There was really no need for it, he knew them all by rote. And as for highest bidders, his thoughts wandered to the man he knew ached to arrest him on any premise. If he could leave this benighted land before the emperor returned, there would be no need of the list, and if not, he thought resignedly, he could find a way at least to get the list out safely. It was not as if there was anyone in England who would mourn long for him—it was not as if his oblivion would matter at all. He felt a twinge of despair and pushed the thought firmly away as he had trained himself to do. He was wide awake. Company in his bed would eventually bring sleep, he thought. But the serving wenches below stairs looked in as sad a state as the linens his cloak protected him from. And as for that female in Paris—his lips wrenched into an unpleasant smile—she had probably been long gone to a higher bidder. Sinjun lay back silently and waited resignedly for sleep to at last steal over him. It would be, he thought, a long wait.

Catherine sat up slowly. It had been a long time since she had heard any movement from the marquis. She had lain still for a

long time—she could endure no more. Her leg ached with a
steady throb that began to encompass her whole body. Whatever
James had said, she knew she must get her boot off. She would
take her money and conceal it somewhere else upon her person,
for no one, she told herself, should really be expected to endure
such travail.

The sound came to Sinjun's ears immediately and his face
twisted into a disgusted grimace. He raised himself slightly and
looked over toward the boy. The fool was sitting up, slightly
hunched over, and the sound of his rhymthic panting was clearly
audible. Sinjun lay back and gave himself points for his own
idiocy. Jenkins, of course, was right again, as usual. See how he
was repaid for a moment of compassion. Sinjun had spent his
boyhood in boarding schools, and he had traveled in the thick of
many various armies. Lovely, he thought grimly, I give the waif
a safe harbor and he repays me by using my room to abuse
himself in. Ah well, he thought angrily, at least it won't go on
for long. And I think I won't tell Jenkins in the morning, for it
will delight him no end.

But after several long laboring minutes had gone by, the fool
of an idiot was still at it. Sinjun wondered at his perseverance,
for the harsh breathing went on, not only unabated, but considerably louder. Slowly, with the stealth that had surprised many
enemies, Sinjun raised his long body from the bed and padded
slowly on light feet to see what the devil was going on. He felt a
moment's self-recrimination when he saw that the poor fool, far
from attempting to enjoy himself, was merely struggling to get
his shabby boot off.

With an exclamation of impatience at himself and the world
which sent poor half-wits out into it with no protection, he
approached the boy.

"Here," he said gruffly in the local argot, "let me do it."

He had expected the boy to be surprised, but not to the extent
that he was. For he jerked up to a sitting position and cowered
away.

"Come," Sinjun demanded in the same dialect, "I will help
you. Do not be afraid."

And without waiting any longer, he made a gesture of impatience and reached down to grasp the boy's boot. He held it
firmly and began to wrench it off. As he gave it a twist and the
final tug to free it, three things happened almost simultaneously.

The boot, freed from its grip on the boy's foot, came off in his hand. A small packet flew from it and landed on the floor with a damp thud beside him. And the boy cried out in English in a high, clear woman's voice, "No. Do not touch me. Please, don't."

And then as he stood dumbfounded, the boy flung his hands to his head and fainted away.

Sinjun bent over the boy and stared at him. Then, still shaking his head, as if to clear his sight, he gathered the boy in his arms and carried the insubstantial weight to his bed. Once he had lain the lad there, he gently removed the ridiculous hat and stared long at the still white face. He pushed back one dark curl from where it had fallen onto the forehead and continued to stare, genuinely staggered at the sight of the unconscious form.

"Well," said Jenkins slowly from behind him, as he sheathed his knife carefully, "it looks as though you've finally gotten her where you wanted her, lad. In your bed."

For once the marquis did not return Jenkins' sally with another. He only stood and watched the closed face beneath his.

"Here's a pretty sight," Jenkins grunted.

Sinjun wheeled around to see Jenkins holding up the bootless leg. The small white high-arched foot was blood-smeared and torn.

"This," Jenkins snorted, holding up the small bloody linen-wrapped packet, "is what did the trick. A boot's a good place for treasure, as you well know, but not when there's scarcely room for a foot there as well."

"At least," said a small frightened voice from the bed, "it was safe till I disturbed it."

Sinjun turned and looked down into a pair of wide terrified eyes.

"That," he said, with a slow smile, "is more than I can say for you, child."

He let his eyes linger on her as he lowered himself to sit beside her, and trailed one finger slowly across her jawline,

"A great deal more than I can say for you," he smiled.

Chapter XIV

Catherine's voice faltered as she brought her story to a close. The marquis had sat beside her silently as she had told it. She had no idea what expression he wore, as she had been afraid to chance a look at him. Instead, she had watched the far less threatening, more sympathetic play of expressions on Jenkins' concerned countenance. And it had been Jenkins who had insisted that she tell all in such a gentle fatherly manner that she had complied. If she had been alone with the marquis, there was every possibility that she could not have uttered a word, for when she had woken from her pain-induced swoon, his face had held menace, and his voice had implied further distress for her at his hands. But she had taken heart from Jenkins' presence. For no matter what the marquis' intentions, she doubted he would initiate any ploy against her with Jenkins in the room. Now, risking a glance at the marquis from under her lashes and seeing the unblinking gray gaze fixed upon her, she did not know which she feared more—his anger, his disdain, or his easy seductive acceptance of her.

But there was nothing seductive in the look which he now bent upon her. There was only outraged incredulity. He rose and paced a step and then wheeled back to her.

"Do you mean to tell us that you actually believed you were to be no more than a companion for the duchess? That your duties were only to be to hold her knitting or sit and have pleasant little cozes with her about her grandchildren or her rheumatics?" he asked.

She shrank back from the force of his voice, but then found herself growing angry at the tenor of his words.

"How should I have thought otherwise?" she argued, "for she was a duchess and she seemed to live at the height of respectability. Even Arthur—he's my brother-in-law, you know, and he is a stickler for propriety—could not claim otherwise. Indeed, he would have been glad to have thrown an obstacle in my path, for he did not want me to earn my own way at all. If he had had even an inkling of anything amiss, he would have thrown it up to me."

Seeing the patent disbelief upon the marquis' face, she went on with more spirit and a genuine sense of outrage, "Women such as the duchess may be common coin in your set, Your Lordship, but I assure you we have none such in Kendal. Why, if any woman behaved so, her relatives would have her clapped up somewhere to protect her from herself. Mrs. Blake is the only true eccentric we have," she mused, "and that is because she is so overfond of cats. And even so," she added triumphantly, "her children have told her if she adopts one more, they'll have the whole lot out on the streets, for people will begin to talk."

Sinjun ran a hand through his hair while Catherine could hear Jenkins' low chortling. But then the marquis turned again and said with a certain slyness, Catherine thought, "And yet, even you must have realized what her game was by the time we met upon the packet to France. For both Rose and Violet were in the duchess's trail then. Never say you thought those two particular prime bits were there to complete a cozy sewing circle? Or that they were too reticent to tell you the whole of it?"

"No," Catherine admitted in a little voice, hanging her head, "by then I did know."

"Then, in the fiend's name, why didn't you just throw up the whole bad business and hie yourself home to Kendal and rejoin your eccentric cat-loving old ladies?"

"I hadn't the funds," Catherine answered softly.

"Why didn't you appeal to someone you knew? Or tell the duchess the whole game was off?"

"She wouldn't have paid me," Catherine said sadly, "for she had already advanced me my wages for the first months and told me the rest would only come quarterly. And I did not think she would take kindly to my denouncing her and demanding un-earned money for my return home before her journey had truly begun. And I knew no one else."

Sinjun stood still and then said with a softer voice and an expression she found hard to read in the dim light, "But you did know me. And I'm not known to be pinch-pursed, and, certainly, I had not been distant with you.''

"Oh yes," Catherine flared suddenly, "you have not been. But you took no pains to conceal your opinion of me. And I was going to tell you twice, in fact. But that first time aboard ship you only began to give me advice about which gentlemen I should attach myself to for profit. Wouldn't I have presented a pretty picture if I had asked you for money after that recitation?''

The marquis, Catherine noted, looked abashed for the first time since she had met him. A brief uneasy silence fell over the room which was at length broken by Jenkins' query. "And the second time?''

Catherine, remembering the moment in the marquis' close embrace, only flushed. And the marquis, instantly remembering the same scene, for once was speechless. He only gave a low muttered curse and walked to the fire to stare at its dying embers.

Well then,'' Jenkins said with suppressed laughter in his voice, "we should see about binding up that limb of yours, Miss Catherine. For one-legged companions are not in too much demand this season. Just sit back. I'll go to fetch some clean water. No need to worry, for His Lordship can tell you I've some experience in that line, and I'll have you up and ready to travel by first light.''

Jenkins went quietly out into the passage. Finding herself alone in the room with the marquis, Catherine sat very still, not daring to break into his seeming reverie. But before long he was back, standing beside the bed and looking down at her. She did not dare to even look up at him this time, being too aware of his proximity and of her embarrassing position, occupying his bed.

"And how," he asked finally, "did you think to come through the whole of your adventures with your reputation intact?''

"Oh," she said slowly, "as to that, it hardly mattered, for I intended to go home to Jane and Arthur immediately upon my return. One's reputation in Paris and London wouldn't count for much there. For no one I know travels further than to market most of the time.''

"And how," he persisted, "did you think to return with your person intact?''

She looked up at him in anger when the meaning behind his words became clear to her.

"As to that," she said with some heat, "I felt that I could rub

on well enough if I remained alert and circumspect in my
dealings with the gentlemen in the duchess's set. And so I did.
Except, of course, in your case. For you were the only one who
attempted liberties. The others were content to accept "No" and
look around for easier game."

"Liberties!" he exploded, shouting loudly enough to make
her wince. "Do you consider a few brief embraces liberties?
When you were prancing about Paris, painted and half clothed in
the company of acknowledged tarts? I think," he said, sitting
down abruptly beside her again and taking her chin in one hand
and forcing her head up to meet his blazing eyes, "that you
should know more of 'liberties' by now. Didn't those two expensive bits of muslin you were cloistered with all these weeks tell
you more about liberties?"

"No," Catherine protested, drawing back from him and his
touch. "No, they didn't. They were actually very prim with me.
They said that they did not think they should tell me anything I
didn't already know."

The marquis dropped his hand and shook his head, as if to
clear it. He gazed at her steadily till she shrank with embarrassment. She could see belief and disbelief battling in his
expression. Then he smiled a slow easy smile that curiously both
melted and chilled her, and went on in a low sweet voice, "But
there was nothing you did not know about embraces, was there,
little Catherine?" He took a curl of her hair in his hand and toyed
with it as he spoke. "I do not remember that there was need of
too much further instruction in your kisses. You are not totally
inexperienced then, are you? Mine was certainly not your first
kiss, was it?"

"Of course not," Catherine blazed, striking his hand away,
"yours was the fourth. I did not grow up in a clam shell. And if
you count Roger Scott's, it is five. But," she admitted carefully,
"I do not usually count Roger Scott's for that was only upon my
cheek, and I have never been sure if that was his intention or if
he missed. But it makes no matter, for I was very angry with
him anyway and did not speak to him again."

The marquis looked at her speechlessly, but any reply of his
was cut off by Jenkins, who had appeared by the foot of the bed
and who shooed him away by saying briskly, "I have to do up
the lady's foot now. And if you two persist in quarreling at
midnight, you'll call the whole inn's attention to the presence of
a female in your rooms. Here now, My Lord, do you hold her

hand. For I have to put some medication upon the wounds and I think she'll be glad of something to hold on to, for it will smart a bit.''

"No thank you," Catherine said loftily, snatching her hand from the marquis' grip.

But when Jenkins poured some of the fine French cognac he had produced from his bags over her aching foot, she involuntarily grasped the marquis' hand again and bit her lip to keep from crying out.

"That's the worst of it," Jenkins said cheerily as he began to spread some unguent and then carefully wrapped her foot in strips of linen. "It will hurt like the devil for a few more moments, but then it will ease off enough for you to sleep."

True to his words, by the time Jenkins had straightened and begun to pack away his medicants and remove the ewer of water, Catherine's pain had subsided to only a low cranky aching.

Jenkins retreated to his room after bidding her a pleasant good night, and Catherine had a moment of alarm as the marquis straightened but still stood looking at her. She was about to rise and hobble back to the hearthside when he said curtly, "I'll retire to Jenkins' room. I hope you're an early riser. For we have to be off by first light."

"You may be off wherever you choose," Catherine said sleepily. "I shall wake early and go from here and bother you no more."

"Don't be absurd," he snapped. "As a woman traveling alone you'll never get past the door by yourself."

"But I shan't be a woman traveling alone," she said, smiling. "I shall be a poor zany French lad."

"In the night, you might have gotten away with it for a few hours," he said sternly, "but never in the day." He cut off her next words by saying swiftly, "And if you think you can, I beg you to remember what might have befallen you if we had not interceded with that pack of mercenary curs below stairs this evening. So you shall travel with us, unless you really do desire Pierre Richard's fevered embrace and are only trying to up your price by being a little inaccessible when M. Beaumont comes to call."

"I shall not travel with you," Catherine whispered fiercely. "And, at any rate, it is not Pierre Richard, it is Hervé, that M. Beaumont intended me for. And I would rather face a horde such as I met this evening than—"

But she could say nothing further, for the marquis had taken her shoulders and gripped them hard. "Hervé?" he said fiercely. "Are you sure he said it was to be Hervé?"

"Yes," she answered fearfully, for there was a terrible expression upon his face, and she could hear Jenkins give a low whistle from the doorway, where he stood watching them.

"Then we shall awake before first light," the marquis said grimly, releasing her and turning to go. But before he left her to the sleep which exhaustion was drawing her to, swiftly and against her will, like water flowing down an open drain, he said harshly, "And if I discover you have taken one step from this room without my knowledge, you will wish we had left you to those misbegotten wretches downstairs. You will pray for Beaumont to come and save you, I swear it."

While Catherine abandoned her struggle against the weariness that was closing her eyes to his retreating form and her mind to the thousand questions that assailed it, the marquis was ordering Jenkins back to the bed from which he had risen.

"I'll take the floor," he said savagely. "It won't be the first time and I feel the need of some penance. Hervé! There's a turn. Bonaparte must be closer than we had thought. For if Beaumont is beginning to shower Hervé with gifts, it's certain that his little corporal has quit his island empire and is on his way. Henri's not a fellow to squander his riches or to take chances with fate. He takes no risks."

"Aye," Jenkins agreed, as he took the bedcovers and rolled them into a makeshift bedroll for the marquis over the latter's angry protestations. "And he'll be like a hound on the lass's traces if he's already promised her to Hervé. For nothing makes a fellow more of a no-account than promising something he fails to deliver. And Beaumont can't afford being thought a no-account, not with big things in the wind. And won't it be sweet for him to deliver up to his new master a fine English gentleman that he can prove is a spy once hostilities are opened again? He'll have your head neatly from your neck, lad, the moment Bonie's got one toe back on the throne. It will be a double risk, traveling with the lady."

"Lady?" snorted the marquis, settling himself for sleep. "But no matter. Whatever she is, I can't leave her here. For whatever she is, she seems to have no more talent for self-preservation than she had for companioning."

"Oh, I think she's a lady," Jenkins said softly in the darkened room, "for there's no cause for a trollop to put herself to such rigs when she's been offered such a plum. And, at any rate," he yawned, "you have only to look at her and listen to her to know she's telling the truth."

"A courtesan has to be a good actress," Sinjun whispered, almost to himself.

"Ahh, you're just narked because you're merely the fourth fellow to kiss her," Jenkins laughed lightly. "Fifth, if you count the lad with the bad aim."

The reply was a pillow flung across the room and a curt, "You're a cat-footed sneak. Go to sleep. We have to be up early."

But as he drifted off to sleep, there was no look of anger on the marquis' face. Instead, one would have thought, looking at the small easy smile that he fell to sleep with while thinking of the female in the next room, that his was the best of worlds.

It was an early hour and the few birds that had braved the chill rain to greet the first light of a March morning were unheard in the finest room the inn at Saint-Denis had to offer. For a low-voiced but fierce battle was raging there.

Catherine stood, backed up against the fireplace mantel, dressed again in her outsize gentleman's jacket, with her low-brimmed hat pulled over her forehead. The marquis towered over her, advancing upon her with his hands on his narrow hips, dressed as a gentleman of fashion, but raging like a low brawler.

"You shall not go on by yourself," he said adamantly. "You shall travel with us and there's an end to it."

Catherine shook her head stubbornly.

"I know what you think of me," she insisted, "and your saying that it's your position as a gentleman to defend me makes no difference. I am capable of looking after myself."

The marquis groaned in annoyance and she went on bravely, "So unless you intend to carry me out kicking and screeching, you shall have to let me go on alone. For I do know that you have no wish to draw undue attention to yourself. I'm not entirely stupid, you know, just unlucky. And I do not desire your company," she said defiantly, tilting up her chin to get a better look at him from under the brim of the hat.

His face softened unexpectedly. Really, he thought, she looked such a complete waif in her bedraggled getup that the absurdity of her appearance and the spirited defense she was offering irrationally combined to make her irresistible.

A new train of thought occurred to him and he shrugged and turned from her.

"All right," he said quietly. "I can, as you say, do no more. I can but let you go your own way. Of course, it is true that you do know a great deal more of Jenkins and my doings than any other man in France. In fact, if you were indeed a man, we should not be expected to let you go, if only for our own safety. For there is little doubt that Beaumont has unpleasant but extremely persuasive ways about him" he added grimly. "And there is also little doubt that as much as he needs you to build up his own personal empire, he needs poor Jenkins and me. Our heads in a basket would only add to his prestige. And once he has caught you, it will be the work of a moment to get our direction from you and then, of course, capture us."

He heard a little gasp from behind him.

"I should never tell him," she said stoutly.

"Oh, you should not care to, I'm sure," he sighed. "But, of course, he has ways of making strong men tell all."

In the small space of silence that fell as Catherine remembered M. Beaumont's implacable smile and strong hands, the marquis continued, "If you were a man, I make no doubt that Jenkins would either have dispatched you already or, failing that, enlisted you in our cause. But as you are a woman . . ." He shrugged again.

"There is no need to make an exception," the little voice said sadly. "And as I do not care to be, however inadvertently, an accomplice of M. Beaumont, I shall come with you. But," she added, as she turned, "I shall expect you to treat me as you would any man."

"As a lady, never fear," he corrected her.

"No," she insisted, her voice rising again, "just as you would a man. I ask no special courtesies of you. Treat me as an equal."

When Jenkins returned to the room, there was another acrimonious dispute being waged. He smiled to himself and then called their attention to his recently acquired burdens.

"The kitchen maid was glad to part with her second best dress, as a present for my own little French friend, you understand, and for a substantial price. And, My Lord, you and I are pleased to be the owners of these splendid garments, courtesy of the landlord and his stock of repossessed clothing from guests who stayed the night and went forfeit on their baggage when they could not ante up the price of their accommodations. We shall be a trio of right Frenchies till we reach Dieppe. And,'' he went on triumphantly, "there's a sadly used old mare, for a gift to my little French mistress's father, that I managed to persuade the innkeeper to part with. For a staggering fee," he said sadly, "but it is done."

"A good morning's work," the marquis said.

"I can't wear a dress," Catherine said nervously, "for the landlady saw a little boy come up here last night."

"And so she shall see a little lad leave this morning," the marquis said over his shoulder as he inspected the garments.

"And as soon as we take the turn in the road, the little simpleton will disappear forever. In his place will be a comely peasant lass. In this," he said, holding up a simple faded-blue long-skirted frock.

"I'll bind up your foot well," Jenkins added, beginning to fold up the clothes for storage in his traveling bag, "And slit the boot so you can get into it. We'll bind it on with rope. It will only be a little way to walk," he assured her, seeing her distress.

"It's not that," she said. "It's only that I dislike being a burden to you."

"Think of it," the marquis commanded, snapping his bag together, "as being a necessary evil, if you will. For your own safety, and ours. And," he added jauntily, as Jenkins bent to help her with her boot, "I think I'll carry your treasure with me for a while, seeing as how now your strong box has been breached."

So it was that at an early hour the landlady of the inn at Saint-Denis saw the two fine gentlemen off. They had decided, they said, not to wait upon the coach, as it would no doubt be sadly crowded. The simpleton, she noted, limping badly and dragging his battered carpetbag, came down the stair a few moments after them. As her other guests were beginning to descend for their breakfast, she did not see the lad hobble off out her door. And by the time other patrons began to throng her front room, waiting for the delayed diligence to arrive, she had forgotten that she had not seen the quiet little ragged simpleton come to breakfast.

The marquis and Jenkins stood waiting for Catherine, atop their horses, as she finally hobbled to the crossroads they had indicated was far enough from the inn. But before they let her mount the speckled gray they had procured for her, they insisted she divest herself of her costume and put on the peasant's dress.

In the chill rain, Catherine stood behind some bushes at a distance from the road and changed quickly. Then she gathered up her things and emerged again by the side of the road.

The sight that met her eyes made her heart stop beating for a moment. For there were two evil-looking rogues atop the marquis and Jenkins' horses. One was a swaggering younger fellow with patched trousers and a once-white shirt open at his throat. He wore a scarlet bandanna carelessly tied about his neck. The other was a gruff, grizzled fellow with a slouched hat and a none-too-clean jacket tied about his waist with a frayed belt. She was about to dart back into hiding when she heard the marquis' deep voice call out to her. He slipped from his horse's back and bowed to her, a wicked smile upon his lips.

"You haven't seen the devil, child, just two vagabonds set on keeping you company. *Vite, vite.* We have some traveling to do."

He helped her up into the saddle, and let his hands rest upon her waist for one extra insulting moment, and then laughed at her uncomfortable expression.

"Now, now. You did say you wished to be treated as an equal. Now I'd never keep hold of a lady for so long, but any fellow would only thank me for making sure he was well seated before we took off."

Catherine tossed back her head and pretended not to hear Jenkins' snort of amusement. She was fully prepared to brood upon the marquis' impertinence, and to worry whether he had noted the shock of pleasure she had felt at his touch. But once he had remounted his horse, he slapped her old mount sharply on the rump to get her started, and they were off. Riding in the cold wind-blown mists soon took her thoughts from his warm touch and turned them irrevocably to thoughts of the fine chill rain that found its way unerringly down her collar to trace icy fingers along her back.

By the time they drew their horses to rest beside a farmhouse, Catherine was thoroughly chilled. Not much conversation had been possible as they rode the muddy lanes in the gusting wind. And now it was with a distinct shock that she felt the marquis help her down and heard his low voice whisper in her ear, "The good wife here is curious. So say nothing. Your grasp of the language, I recall, is inadequate. You're my woman, for the remainder of the trip at least''—he laughed at her upturned face—''and very shy. But your brother and I will take care of you. We've bargained for a rough luncheon and then we're off again. So sit as close to the fire as you're able.''

Catherine was grateful for the bread and cheese and rough wine that the farm wife provided, and loath to leave her perch by the fire when the marquis arose and bade their hostess farewell. But she was determined not to be a hindrance to them, and duly remounted and rode off without protest when they indicated it was time.

The remainder of the afternoon became one wet, miserable blur to her. Even in later years she could not remember the route they had taken that day. She kept her gaze firmly on the horse's ears and prayed for some benevolent god to stop the wind and rain.

By the time dusk fell, the rain had mercifully stopped, and the increasing winds were drying the lanes they traveled, turning some of the ruts to ice.

''This must be the house Madame indicated,'' Catherine heard the marquis say. And while she was still gazing numbly at the tilted roof on the weatherworn house at which they had stopped, she felt the marquis swing her down from her saddle.

''It's in bad shape,'' Jenkins said, as they entered the simple one-room house through a door that was banging in the wind.

''War takes curious turns,'' the marquis agreed, ''for when the master of this hovel died in glorious battle and his wife had to go beg to relatives, I doubt they could have guessed their home would ever provide succor to their dearest enemies.''

Seeing no chairs or furniture, Catherine simply lowered herself onto a wooden box by the side of the fireplace.

''You do have a propensity for gravitating to hearthsides,'' the marquis noted. ''I wonder at such a sit-by-the-fire being able to pick herself up to travel the Continent in such high-flying fashion.''

But seeing how weariness had stilled her tongue, he left her and set about building up the fire and held low converse with Jenkins about securing the horses in the half-timbered barn that remained.

After a welcome dinner of cheese and bread that Jenkins had foraged earlier, and after warming herself thoroughly by the fire, Catherine stretched and began to take lively note of their surroundings again.

The marquis sat at ease across from her on a box he had found in the barn, and Jenkins sat cross-legged on the floor, gazing into the fire.

"I suppose," Catherine said conversationally, "that it won't be too long before we reach Dieppe, will it, Your Lordship?"

"Oh, Catherine," the marquis answered. "Have done with 'Your Lordship.' We are not precisely in a drawing room here. I doubt the mice will be offended if all the proprieties are not observed. At any rate," he went on, pleased to see blush upon her cheek, "It would be nothing wonderful if you did not blurt "Your Lordship" the next time we were in a crowd of Frenchmen, if you persist in calling me that. I should hate to lose my head due to an overnice attention to the correct social forms of address.

"But no, I am sorry for it, but it will be long before we reach Dieppe. It will be never. No, don't startle. I haven't formed the intention of becoming a lifetime resident here. It is only that too many people knew you were bound for Dieppe. Indeed, I think soon half the English in Paris will be bound for Dieppe, and it will be the logical place for Beaumont to pick up your trail. No, we will journey to Le Havre. And we shall not find ourselves berths upon a tourist packet for we will be snugly accommodated on some fishing vessel. Brandy, lace, and smuggled souls are high trade on the coast. And I think that, sly as he is, still M. le Commissaire Beaumont will not look to find one of the duchess's doxies sharing her seat with a haddock."

Sinjun looked up to see Catherine's face blanch. She looked as though he had slapped her, and he turned in sudden uncomfortable contrition to Jenkins.

"It grows late, old friend. Let's gather in some hay to make this wretched floor pass for a feather bed."

As they rose to go to the door, Sinjun looked back at Catherine, who was ostensibly studying her fingernails with concentration.

"Forgive me," he whispered back to her. "I have a rash tongue, and I'm sorry for it."

Resting upon her pelisse, which lay over the mound of straw Sinjun and Jenkins had provided, Catherine stared into the darkness. Sinjun lay not far from her on the other side of the fireplace, and Jenkins, nearer to the door, breathing heavily.

She was warm and full and the two men in the room gave her a feeling of comfort and security such as she had not known in many weeks, but still she could not sleep. Her conscience twinged. Perhaps it was because she was just where she wished to be, she thought with sudden alarm. The sense of contentment and pleasure in the marquis' company was so overwhelming that, try as she might, she could not imagine a place where she would rather be. And yet she felt that if he but knew her deep contentment, he would be somehow displeased. He would be, she thought further, convinced that she was no better than a light woman. For what decently reared girl would be so pleased in such bizarre, irregular circumstances? She ought to be, she thought sternly, fearful and trembling in distress, not as contented as a sleepy puppy.

"Catherine," came a low whisper in the dark, "do go to sleep. For we must travel hard in the morning. We go a round-about route."

"How did you know I was not sleeping?" she whispered back.

"I could hear you thinking," Sinjun chuckled. "And I could not hear you snore."

"I don't snore." Catherine giggled, thinking again, as she had all evening, that the marquis seemed to have put off his cold, cynical manner as he had put off his immaculate garments. Now he seemed so much younger and more carefree that she had a difficult time remembering the aloof aristocrat she had met a hundred years ago in another life, in London.

"Nonsense," he replied softly. "Hear old Jenkins sawing away over there? I'll wager between the two of you, I won't have a moment's rest this night.

"Catherine," he said again, after a pause, "do not worry. We shall see you safely home again. But I wonder—how shall you explain your travels away to your family when you get home? Should I expect your brother-in-law at my doorstep at dawn with a pistol clutched in his hand? For while I consider Jenkins an excellent chaperone, I do not know if William will."

"Not William," Catherine smiled; "Arthur. And I assure you, you need not fear. Indeed, he will be grateful to you for seeing me safely from my own muddled affairs."

"I don't have to make reparation for sullying your good name?" he asked lightly.

There was a moment's silence, and then he heard her reply in a suspiciously low, broken tone. "Indeed, I do not see how anyone could have sullied it more than I."

Sinjun silently cursed himself for an insensitive clod, and then went on as if he had not heard her, "I must admit that if I knew my sister was traveling with me, that is to say, if I were not myself, and heard that my sister was traveling with me, I should be outraged and fly to her defense.''

Catherine gave a little laugh. "I did not know you had a sister.''

"Well, I was not hatched from an egg," he protested, in mock affront. "Of course I have a sister, and I had a mother and a father as well, you know.''

"Tell me about them," Catherine said sleepily.

And so the lofty Marquis of Bessacarr lay back upon his straw pallet in an abandoned French farmhouse on a cold March night and spoke into the darkness of his sister's wild extravagances and her complacent husband, and their brood of unruly children. Encouraged by Catherine's delighted response, and prodded by her questions, he told her in less merry tones about his wastrel father and his invalid mother. By the time the natural progression of his story had led him into deep water and he fell silent, wondering how to tell her of the mistakes he had made in his career, he noticed she did not urge him to continue. Instead, he only heard her muted, even breathing.

He rose and went to her. She lay like a child with one hand under her cheek and the other flung out in sleep. He knelt to cover her more securely with her coat. If she were an actress, he thought almost angrily, seeing the easy peace sleep had brought her, she was the best he had ever met.

"I make no doubt"—Jenkins' amused voice came from the shadows—"that you have put many females to sleep of nights. But I do doubt that you've ever just talked one to sleep before.''

"Go to sleep, you old pretender," the marquis grumbled as he sank down upon his bed of straw again, "or you'll wake her.''

Chapter XV

Their journey was not half so simple as Catherine had anticipated. The weather was against them. First rain, then cold to freeze it where it lay, then wind and more rain slowed their forward movement. They dared not go by coach, and yet increasing numbers of coaches, private and hired, passed them on the roads. It was as the marquis had predicted: The English—at least some small portion of the more than fifteen thousand who had arrived on French shores since Louis had been put back on the throne—were beginning to go home again.

At every stop either the marquis or Jenkins would engage the inhabitants of the small villages or farming communities in easy conversation. Rumor was everywhere, and while the farrier in one town would insist that they were at war with the pigs of England again, the one in another town would steadfastly maintain that Louis still held sway and the adventurer Bonaparte was still at Elba, safely out of harm's way.

Other incidents impeded them. Catherine's horse, never in the best condition, began to founder as they traveled further toward the coast, and they had to stop and search and bargain till they could trade it for another, younger bit of horseflesh that an avaricious farmer near Vironvey agreed to part with. When Catherine insisted on paying Sinjun for the expense, he grew angry, and their bickering caused Jenkins to comment that he felt as though he were seeing two children home from an outing that had overtired them.

Jenkins, for his part, had insisted on calling Sinjun "lord" and "sir" till Sinjun had cursed him and snarled that Catherine would understand if he dropped the pose and continued to call

him "lad" or "friend" or "enemy," for fiend's sake, so long as
he was done with posturing as a correct gentleman. Jenkins had
looked wounded and explained that those names were only for
Sinjun's ears alone, and not for use in company. And when
Sinjun rejoined that Catherine was by no means polite company,
she looked so stricken that both the marquis and Jenkins together
had to jest and make up foolish verses to old songs till they had
jollied her out of her depression.

One day they had to sit and wait out the weather in the shelter
of a disused barn. For the rain and wind were so fierce that they
knew neither the horses nor they themselves could have traveled
far. They had passed the time telling stories, speculating on the
fate of those they had known in Paris. When, at noon, Jenkins
produced an old, limp deck of cards, they had cheered as though
they had been given the rarest treat.

They had traveled together for five cold, unpleasant days.
They had slept in abandoned houses and begged night's permission to camp in barns. Their food had been rough, their beds
usually straw or their own folded garments, yet Catherine could
never remember being happier.

And the cause of her happiness, she had thought on the fifth
day, rode alongside her. Though they had been constantly together throughout the journey, and only for a few moments of
the day was she ever alone, she grew uneasy when he was not
with her. She had stolen glances at his straight back and noted
the way the wind tossed his demon-black hair back from his
forehead. Each night, like the small children Jenkins had commented on, they had chatted happily in the dark till sleep overtook them. He had been a courteous and charming companion,
and every last vestige of the cool autocrat she had envisioned
him was gone. And, above all, never once since they had begun
their trek had he looked at her with the salacious, burning looks
he had used when they met in society. He did indeed, she
thought with a mixture of relief and disquiet, treat her as an
equal.

He had often made her laugh, there in the night, when they
spoke to each other as disembodied voices. And she counted
among her life's greatest triumphs those moments when she in
turn reduced him to helpless mirth. Sometimes they spoke of
their past lives, and though she found nothing in hers that she
thought might interest him, still he pressed her to tell him more.
So she had recounted her mother's sad story, and told him of

Jane's beauty and Arthur's primness, and even, as the hour grew late and Jenkins seemed to snore in earnest, of her own desire to be a free and independent person rather than an obligation for her sister's new family to bear.

Sometimes after that first night she told him of Rose and Violet, and tried to make him see that they were nothing like one would have thought, simply common harlots. She told him of their hopes and fears and attempted to let him see that their lives, apart from their trade, were much as anyone else's. And she felt he did try to understand.

She thought he was far too hard on himself. He did not seem to be able to speak of his past without disparaging it and demeaning himself in jest. He did not appear to be able to speak of the woman he had offered for without congratulating her on her perspicacity in rejecting him. He held himself in low esteem, and she found herself tightening her hands to fists whenever he joked, there in the night, about what an empty, idle fellow he was. For she dared not let him see how very much she wished to disprove what he said. One night, as he was speaking, she almost blurted out, "No, how can you say that? You are a man any woman would give her life to please." For where would she proceed from there? If he rose and came to her and asked her to prove that, how could she then say, "No, I didn't mean that."

The only discomfort Catherine had felt beyond the physical on their journey toward home was the discomfort of knowing that if he knew her feelings—worse, if she displayed them—he would think her to be the easy female he had originally thought her.

So she kept herself under restraint. They spoke of books they both had read and liked. They joked about the people they both had met. They giggled in the night like small children afraid to wake their nanny, Jenkins. But they did not touch. And they did not speak about their new friendship. Catherine kept herself on a tight rein. She was so busy keeping her feelings tightly to herself that she never saw the looks he bent upon her, obliquely and often during their journey.

The next day the sky cleared and it was a cool morning—one of those strange mornings in the earliest spring when the air holds only a tantalizing promise of the splendors of the months to come.

"We're allowing ourselves a treat today," Sinjun said as he rode beside her. "We've come more than halfway and the coast will soon be in sight. I think we deserve a day of rest. We are on the outskirts of Rouen, and since we have heard no bells tolling or cannon fire, I think we can safely assume the throne lies secure still. So we will stop at an inn. Then it will be an easier day's journey to the coast.''

"And," growled Jenkins, "he neglected to mention that my horse's shoe is coming off.''

"Ungenerous Jenkins," Sinjun said. "Here I was convincing Catherine it was all due to my magnanimous nature and you have to tell her the blunt truth.''

"Bless your horse," Catherine cried, "for I think I would trade my soul for a chance to wash my hair and sleep upon a bed that a horse hasn't used first.''

"And," Jenkins stressed, "we must go out, His Lordship and I, to nose out the land. We'll be convivial in the taproom, Catherine, whilst you launder your hair, and find out what's to know. We need to know if we have to skulk about in Le Havre or if we can ride in like free men and charter a vessel openly. Things depend upon what state the land's in. And whether there are any looking for us or not.''

Catherine sobered at the reminder that there might yet be danger. For she had felt so secure thus far that she had almost persuaded herself that the night in Paris when M. Beaumont approached her had been nothing but a mad fancy of hers.

The inn they chose heartened her. It was clean and in far better repair than the last one in Saint-Denis.

They had spoken for two rooms. One, Sinjun had explained, was for himself and his good wife, and the other for his brother-in-law. Catherine's room, she saw with joy, when the proprietor's daughter had left her at last, after filling the large basin of water Catherine had bespoken, was as lovely as the faded beauty of an old genteel lady. The carpet upon the floor yet bore the outlines of soft spring flowers. And, best of all, Catherine thought as she immersed her hands in the warm scented water, there were soft towels and a cake of soap at the washstand.

She stripped off her peasant dress and washed herself from top to toe.Then, as she knew she would have more time alone, since Sinjun and Jenkins had the horses to see to, and then would undoubtedly luxuriate in their own room for a space, she allowed herself the bliss of washing straw and dust from her hair in the large enameled rose basin. Glowing with good feeling, she shook out a plain blue frock from her bag and got into it. Clean and dressed, she sat in a chair by the fire to comb out and dry her tresses.

But afternoon came and began to fade, and her hair was completely dry and silky soft, and still there was no knock upon the door. She began to worry and went to the window to look out. There was little activity in the stable yard below. It was only a tranquil late-afternoon scene that met her eyes. There was a small millpond, deserted save for a few geese that patrolled its tiny shores, and the only soul she could spy was a stable boy, drawing water from the well's pump.

As the hours went by, all sense of ease and delight faded from Catherine. They had been gone too long, and she worried over the dozen misfortunes that might have befallen them. She had almost gotten up the courage to go downstairs by herself, against all of Sinjun's express orders, when she heard a light tap upon her door.

She fairly flew to the door and flung it open. Sinjun stood there, looking down at her with surprise.

"I hope," he said, entering the room and closing the door behind him, "that you have no intention of stepping outside in that garb."

The joy in her face faded.

"This is just an old garment I had when I came to the duchess," she said in confusion, looking down at her simple high-waisted blue muslin gown.

Her hair, newly washed, fell riotously around her face, and she had to sweep it back to see him when she looked up at him again.

A curious spasm, almost of pain, crossed his face for a fleeting moment.

"It might not be," he drawled, in a voice she had not heard for many days, "High fashion on the Champs Elysees, "but here it is decidely not what a simple little peasant wench wears to dinner. It's as well, I suppose. For it would be better if you did not go down again till we leave."

She searched his face for the reason for the solemnity in his voice.

"We've been out, we two hearty French lads, chatting up the local gentry. And, it seems, they don't understand why we're not marching in the other direction, toward Paris. For all the able-bodied young chaps hereabouts are off to war again. They've heard that their little corporal is on the high road to glory once more. But it's not confirmed, of course. So we'll have to dine without you tonight, Catherine. We'll get you a tray in your room and we'll sit and drink with every local know-something we can find.''

Catherine tried to essay a smile. ''But Sinjun, you said it's only a day's ride to Le Havre. Surely, we can get that far before a war breaks out.''

''Catherine,'' he said, his gray eyes serious and steady, ''we may well be at war at this moment. I do not know. And if we are, then Jenkins and I are very wanted men. We are not an English peer and his valet—we are also labeled 'spies' in some quarters. I do not care to spend years skulking about the French countryside in disguise. And neither do I wish to be clapped in irons in Le Havre. For the ports are the first places the soldiers go to comb through the refugees for profit. So stay in this room and say only a shy little *non* if a maid or anyone comes to this door tonight.''

Catherine nodded and then, as he turned to leave, tugged at his sleeve. ''Must you go out?'' she whispered. ''Could you not stay and just wait till morning?''

''I must go out. There's little danger here, I think, and we have to discover how much is fact and how much is rumor. And, oh Catherine, if you get the notion of creeping below to aid us by eavesdropping or some other strategy your fertile mind conjures, there is one other bit of news. It seems that there is talk of a reward offered for the apprehension of some vile Englishwoman who stole a fortune from her employer, a certain English lady. And the word is that the miscreant is most probably headed for the coast.''

Catherine shrank back.

''You know I stole nothing,'' she gasped.

''Of course. Your purse is in my keeping, remember? It's a meager treasure you hoarded. And I don't even know if you are the female they are seeking. But M. Beaumont is a desperate character and dislikes having his will crossed. So stay safe inside, my little French 'wife,' and no harm will befall you.''

''Sinjun?'' Catherine asked softly.

''Yes?'' he answered, his hand already on the knob of the door.

''Will you come back tonight and let me know what you have discovered?''

''Of course,'' he agreed. ''Otherwise I think you'll stand and shake all the night through. Don't trouble yourself so. I said it is all rumor. And you know you are safe with us.''

Jenkins brought her a tray a short while later.

''Best if the maids stay far from this room altogether,'' he said, putting it down for her. ''When you're done, wait till there's no one about, peek out the door if you must, and when the coast is clear, put the empty plates outside. They'll understand below stairs.''

''They'll think me a poor shy retiring lady,'' Catherine said with a smile.

''There's that,'' Jenkins agreed, ''and also the fact that His Lordship explained how his little wife was enceinte, and feeling very poorly after her ride.''

Catherine gasped in indignation, but Jenkins only continued blithely, ''He's a lad who has a fine tale for any occasion. It's what has made him so valuable in his work. You should see him below stairs, drinking and gossiping, like he was a born Frenchie. All out of sorts, of course, because he's itching to go off and join up with his emperor's forces, and he's stuck with a pretty new wife, expecting her first babe, and he's got to deliver her to relatives before he's off to war. He's even made me feel sorry for him.''

Jenkins displayed her dinner by whipping a serviette off the tray with a flourish.

''There's good fresh meat—best not to inquire too closely as to its origin, though. And bread and lovely green beans. And a bottle of the landlord's best, with His Lordship's compliments. He's got a nose for good wine, you know, and he's very impressed with this local vintage. Even to the point of regretting not being able to take a case or two home with him. So he's trying his best to take as much home with him as he can hold.''

Catherine, remembering her stepfather's bouts with spirits, grew uneasy.

''But if he gets light-headed, he might let something slip.''

Jenkins only laughed.

''I've been with him years now, and I've never seen him let slip one word in his cups. He's got a hard head, Catherine, so don't you worry. But you drink up, for it'll ease your mind and let you get a good night's sleep. 'A little wine's a lovesome thing,' I once heard, and a little of anything can do no harm.''

When Jenkins had left, Catherine sat to dinner, thinking she would be lucky to be able to peck at something, her fears had so encompassed her again. But the wine was good, and the dinner miles above anything she had eaten for days. By the time she was ready to place her tray stealthily outside in the hall, she noted with amazement that she had finished every scrap upon her plate and reduced the bottle of wine by half.

Catherine did not like the sudden inactivity she was forced to here in her faded, but elegant little room. She was restless and impatient, itching to be off and doing rather than to be just a passive creature awaiting whatever fate had in store. That, she thought, was gentlemen's main advantage in life. For they could go out and meet fate head on, while a gentlewoman was expected to sit back and watch what the tides of fortune brought to her feet.

Women like Rose and Violet were able to go out and face life and try to turn it to their advantage, but a properly brought-up female could not. Perhaps, it was that, Catherine thought moodily, sipping her wine, that turned them to such occupation in the first place, rather than inherent lechery. A part of her was appalled by the new train her thoughts were taking, and yet another applauded her new expanded vision. Whatever else this trip provided, she concluded at last, it was certain that the Catherine Robins who returned to Kendal would never be the same who had left it.

The hour was late, the muted sounds of activity and voices in the inn had all but faded away, and Catherine was sitting sleepily in her chair, when she heard the faint tapping at her door.

"Catherine," Sinjun's voice called in low, conspiratorial tones, "it's Sinjun, reporting back to you at last."

She was glad to ease the door open to admit him.

He strode in and grinned at her. She sensed a high excitement emanating from him, and saw that his tanned face held a faint flush along its high cheekbones.

"All the lads are planning how high to hang old Louis. Some are even talking of how to spend their prize money when they take over London. Oh, spirits are running high downstairs," he said, walking carefully to the table and lifting the bottle of wine to peer at its label.

"Fine vintage," he commented, almost to himself. "It's a great pity I can't reason out a fashion of getting it home with us."

There was a recklessness to his speech and a glitter in his eyes, and Catherine wondered if he had indeed partaken too much of the wine he so admired. But she well remembered the condition of her stepfather when he was in his cups, and the marquis did not stagger—he walked erect, perhaps with even more of a careful tread than usual. And he did not wear a foolish grin or slur his words or sing or say inconsequential words as her stepfather had done when he came reeling home after an evening with his friends.

"And what is said of the Englishwoman who was branded a thief?" she asked.

"Oh, as to that," Sinjun said airily, "there's no description of her hereabouts save one. And that is that she is traveling in the company of two English gentlemen."

Catherine gasped.

Sinjun grinned again.

"It seems that you disappeared from Paris the same day Jenkins and I did. So Beaumont has reasoned, and one can't blame him for it, that I ran off with you just to tweak his nose. Which is a bit conceited of him, but a lovely thought nonetheless. Still, they're looking for three English citizens, and here we are, three sturdy citizens of the Republic. So there's nothing to fear. But here," he said, seeming to see her for the first time since he had entered the room, "it is far past midnight. Why aren't you in bed?"

"I waited for you," Catherine explained. "I was worried."

"And," he went on, frowning, "not even in your nightclothes. You don't have to share your room tonight. I thought you would make yourself comfortable and sleep like a proper lady, not in your clothes again. Catherine," he said, marching toward her and glowering "get into bed and go to sleep. At once."

Catherine sat back upon her bed and and told him that she would go to bed as soon as he had left her room.

"Now that," Sinjun said, sinking down to sit beside her, "truly wounds me, Catherine, it does. For we have shared our rooms for so long and you never were so punctilious before. I only came to tuck you in tightly, as a good brother should. And I have been a good brother to you, haven't I?"

He sat close to her and ran his hand gently across her hair, seeming to become engrossed in the texture of it.

"I have tried very hard to be brotherly, Catherine, though Lord knows, you are nothing like my sister. And I have been extremely circumspect. Yes," he agreed with himself, as if, it seemed to Catherine, he were speaking only to himself, "extremely circumspect. A perfect gentleman, in fact. And the wonder of it is that all these months I had thought you so available, and when at last I had you to myself, I treated you with perfect courtesy. And it has been hard, Catherine, very hard to do so. Now don't you think I deserve a reward for being such a paragon? Especially,'' he said, looking down into her eyes and bringing his other hand up so that he held her face between his two hands, ''especially since . . .''

But he did not finish his train of thought, for he bent and kissed her, gently and sweetly, and she was surprised at the eagerness with which she involuntarily returned his kiss.

Although it was only Sinjun who held Catherine, she was so lost in the warmth and delicious pleasure of his embrace that she had no thought of holding him closer to herself as well.

He moved his lips to her cheek, to her throat, and then gathered her still closer with a groan.

''Catherine,'' he whispered against her hair, ''you are lovely.''

And then he kissed her again, a deeper, darker embrace that began at last, to waken Catherine from her stuporous pleasure.

But it seemed that as she became aware of exactly what was beginning to transpire between them, he became less aware of her reaction and more lost in their embrace. His hands drifted from her back and moved to begin to trace the outlines of her breasts and waist. He began to call her still further into his provenance as she retreated from him. His kisses became more profound, his mouth as warm and rich and fragrant as the wine she tasted upon it. But these were not the sweet light movements that had so enticed her. He now seemed to be setting something urgent into motion, something that she could not control or know how to respond to. So she began to try to pull away from him, to force his searching mouth from hers.

''Catherine,'' he breathed as his hands became more insistent, ''no more pretense. Come, I know what will please you.''

But now all thoughts of pleasure, for herself or for Sinjun, were gone from Catherine's mind. In their place was panic and the realization of what he thought her willing to do with him. She struggled to be free from him and finally repelled him, crying out, ''Please, Sinjun. No. No more.''

He released her immediately when she spoke and sat confused.

''No, Sinjun,'' she cowered, fearful of the changed expression in his smoky eyes, fearful of her own reaction to him.

''What is it you want, then, Catherine?'' he asked, genuinely puzzled. ''Have I gone too fast for you? I promise to go slower then. Lord knows we have the entire night before us. I can be patient. Come, Catherine," he said, pleased with himself for being reasonable, and reached for her again.

But she pulled away and stood and when he rose to take her back, she cried out again, "No. Sinjun, Your Lordship. Please, it is late. Please leave."

He let his hands drop to his sides and stood shaking his head, but no longer reaching out for her.

"I don't understand," he said slowly. "Why are you so afraid, Catherine? You've never been so afraid of me before."

"It's only that I startled her," Jenkins said, coming up from behind Sinjun, and indeed startling Catherine with the sudden soft-footed grace of his movements. He seemed to have appeared from nowhere.

"I've something important to tell Your Lordship. Indeed I do. Come with me. Make a good night to Catherine," Jenkins said, propelling Sinjun from the room with him, "and come with me, for I've something to tell you. That's a good chap," he said, talking steadily to the marquis and leading him away. "Lock your door, Catherine," Jenkins called back to her, "and go to sleep. His Lordship and I have something to discuss."

Catherine collected herself and rushed to her door, not to lock it, but to see what Jenkins and Sinjun were about to do. But instead of leading the marquis back to his room, Jenkins, still talking softly and rapidly, led him down the stairs. From the top of the stairs Catherine could see them going to the front of the inn.

She ran back to her room and went quickly to her window and flung the casement up. Cold night air rushed in, making her realize how warm and flushed she had been. She leaned out to see where her two companions were going.

But she could see nothing in the darkness. All was quiet, no one seemed about. Then she heard a splashing coming from the pond. And a sound of thrashing water, as though some large animal had stumbled into it. She stood listening, straining her ears and eyes, but after a few moments all was quiet again.

The room grew cold as the night outside, so Catherine lowered the window again and went back to her door. She was trembling with the cold and with the force of her emotions. She had welcomed his embrace—she could not deceive herself as to that. And she had pulled away from him not only because of her fear of the unknown, but because of her horror at having let him see what her innermost emotions toward him had been. Now, she told herself dumbly, he will think me no better than what he always thought me.

After a long while she heard Sinjun and Jenkins return, heard them coming slowly up the stairs in silence. When they neared her door, Catherine's eyes widened. Sinjun was drenched. His hair was plastered to his head, and his clothes were dripping water. She thought she could perceive a slow shudder race across his wide shoulders. He turned to her and bowed before he passed her door.

"My apologies," he said stiffly. "I bid you good night, Catherine."

Catherine could only gape after him, but Jenkins paused as they returned to their room.

"Lock your door now, Miss Catherine," he said sternly. "There'll be no further disturbances tonight."

"But," Catherine whispered, "what befell Sinjun? Was there trouble with footpads?"

"No, no," Jenkins said soothingly, "no trouble at all. His Lordship only decided to go for a midnight dip. Just a moonlight swim."

"But it is freezing outside," Catherine said in horror. "He'll be ill. He'll take a chill."

"No, no," Jenkins demurred. "He *needed* a chill was what it was. The poor lad was overheated from all that fine French wine. He's a hot-blooded fellow, never fear for him. And I'm sure he'll be all apologies for his behavior in the morning. He'll be fine now, I assure you. And glad, I'll be bound, to forget this night."

Jenkins bowed correctly and then waited till Catherine had closed her door and locked it.

Sinjun toweled himself dry in silence as Jenkins climbed into his bed.

"I made a cake out of myself, didn't I?" he asked.

"Yes," Jenkins answered.

"I frightened her, didn't I?" he asked.

"Of course," was the only answer he heard.

"Well, blast it," Sinjun shouted, throwing the towel across the room, "it was the wine."

There was no answer.

"It was the wine," Sinjun said softly, "and the last vague

hope that I was right and she was just another cozening fancy piece.''

"And the fact that she said no changed Your Lordship's powerful mind?'' Jenkins growled.

"And the fact that she wouldn't have known what to do if she said yes,'' Sinjun admitted.

His companion made no reply save a disgusted snort.

"But,'' Sinjun said, lying down upon his bed, "I will make amends. Never fear, Sir Galahad, I shall put things to rights. For I've attempted to seduce a decent young female of good birth, and I know the penalty for that. I am,'' he said righteously, "a gentleman, after all. Not completely lost to propriety.''

"Go to sleep,'' was the only reply Jenkins made as he turned his back with an irritated ruffling of his bedclothes.

Sinjun lay back and gave a deep sigh. The cold water Jenkins had toppled him into had cleared the edges of his mind, but he still felt the vaporous waves from the wine cluttering up his thoughts. He had, he thought wryly, not gotten himself so inebriated since his youth, and all, he now knew, because of that damned female.

For he been a pattern card of behavior. He had watched her—noting the curve of her neck, the tilt of her nose, the inviting sway in her walk—for all these days and had pretended he saw nothing. He had been entranced by her in London, and then again in Paris, and then when he had grown to know her, she had captivated him completely. And he had shown nothing of his feelings all these days by word or action.

She had completely enticed him, he thought angrily. For by the time he had offered for her favors in Paris, she had ruined him for other women. There had been an Italian countess when he first arrived in Paris, but her embraces had palled by the time he met Catherine again. And when Catherine refused him, the little unfaithful wife of a diplomat had offered him solace. But he had lightly rejected her, thinking then that it was that he did not care for the tone of her laugh, or for the way she had of constantly clutching onto his sleeve. But, he admitted now, it had been that he had looked up and seen Catherine across the room and the sight of her had turned the diplomat's fluffy wife into something like a toad. No, there was no escaping it—he was, he admitted, well and truly caught.

Well then, he thought, so be it. He would offer her marriage. And then a small repressed uncomfortable thought wriggled into his mind from its dark hiding place. He could not bear to think of the answer she would give him. The answer that would be like another's so long ago. The remembered sad pitying look, the soft glance of sympathy, the mournful little syllable that would accompany all the unspoken sorrowful gestures: "No." And then the torrent of words about understanding, and friendships and respect, followed by the reasonable explanation that there could be no acceptance where there was no love.

Very well then, he thought quickly, I shall put it so that there has to be no word of love. Where love has not been offered, it cannot be refused. I shall put it on a basis a girl like Catherine can understand. And wait until we get back to that infamous town of Kendal, for surely her prig of a brother-in-law will understand and encourage it. For I have traveled unchaperoned with a young woman of good birth and spent many nights with her. No man of even sterling reputation can do that without destroying a decent female's hope of ever being received into polite society again. And my reputation, especially with women, is far from clear. Moreover, Sinjun thought with some satisfaction, as he lay in the dark and built his reasonable case for a reasonable marriage, I have overstepped the bounds of a decent gentleman. I have attempted her virtue. All the tenets of society demand that I offer her my name.

I do not, he thought, have to offer her my love as well. At least, he amended, I do not have to let her know that is what is being offered. For surely it is not deception, he told himself, to withhold an emotion that can only distress her. She was horrified at my embrace, but perhaps, he thought with sudden hope, she will come to love me in time. It is not unheard of for a wife to come to love her husband, even in a forced marriage. But I can protect her. I shall have her for my wife. And that will be enough. More, he thought with a last sleepy grimace, than I deserve.

Chapter XVI

Three very solemn travelers mounted their horses in the stable yard of the inn early the next morning.

Sinjun had come into Catherine's room at first light, with a breakfast for her. He had been stiffly correct and unsmiling, and had apologized sincerely for his actions of the previous night, explaining that they had been caused by the amount of wine he had partaken. His words were gracious, his manner contrite, his gaze half-lidded and impersonal. His very correctness toward her froze Catherine. For she read disdain and revulsion in his every word and gesture. And so she had meekly accepted his apology and thanked him for it. He had turned and left her room, convinced that she held him in the deepest abhorrence.

Jenkins, seeing his companions' uncomfortable attitude toward each other, only sighed heavily and kept his own counsel. And so, though it was an easy ride to Le Havre for the last lap of their journey, it being a clear and sunny, bracing day, it was the uneasiest trek in spirit that any of the three could remember making.

Their conversation was minimal, merely an asking after each other's physical comfort and brief consultations as to their direction. By afternoon, as Catherine saw the houses growing more clustered together as they rode past and when she scented the distinct salt tang of sea air, she was heartsick and disconsolate.

They rode through the main streets of the seacoast town. Many other travelers thronged there, but not so many, Catherine noted, as there had been in Dieppe. In Dieppe she had seen all sorts of crested carriages and equipages taking on finely dressed, happily chattering noble visitors. Here in Le Havre there was more of an assortment of humanity.

There were fishermen and ragged urchins and small family groups. The English people she saw were not the sort she had seen either in Dieppe or in Paris. There were knots of schoolboys with their masters and soberly dressed couples. There seemed to be a hush over the town and an atmosphere of uneasiness that could not have sprung just from Catherine's own uneasy perception of the world this day. It was as though the village were holding its breath either in fear or anticipation. All those she passed conversed in low voices and even the local people seemed to be in clusters of whispered conference. She repressed a start when a screaming gull soared overhead. She would be glad to be gone from this place.

They stopped at yet another inn. It seemed the most ordinary of places and when they dismounted, not one of the stable boys looked at them with any particular interest. Sinjun led Catherine to a table in the inn's front room. She was amazed to see his countenance change to that of a hale, jocular, rough sort of common fellow when the serving girl came up to them.

In loud happy tones he ordered some refreshment for his little wife and himself. And he added, with a huge wink, he would be pleased if she would bring some sour wine for his brother-in-law, who was joining them, for the fellow was a sour enough sort as it was. Soon Sinjun had the French girl laughing and simpering. Soon, Catherine thought sourly, he would have the girl agreeing to bring him anything, including her own person on a plate.

He looked handsome enough, she thought. His shirt was unbuttoned to the chest. The red bandanna emphasized the tanned muscular neck, and his hair had been artfully arranged by the March wind. Catherine saw the girl give her a speculative sideways look. She probably wonders, Catherine imagined, what such a fine fellow is doing with such a drab quiet little mouse of a wife. She could not know that her own eyes sparkled bluer than the tone of her simple peasant frock or that the wind had flung her dark hair into exquisitely curling tendrils. The serving girl smiled lovingly and helplessly at Sinjun again and went off to find refreshments for the beautiful young couple.

When Jenkins joined them, they fell to their food in continued silence. Only when Catherine had done and looked up did she find Sinjun watching her with a troubled expression in his eyes. It was gone in the moment she saw it. He looked at her coolly and then said in a low voice, "Catherine. Jenkins and I now have to go and find lodgings. We'll try for this inn, but I fear it's too crowded here. Then we will have to saunter over to the waterfront and look up a few local fellows well known for turning a blind eye to the cargo they carry. More importantly, Jenkins knows of a few English fellows who might be ready to start home again. For if we had our way, we'd rather go home with an English crew than find ourselves at sea with a crew of suddenly patriotic Frenchmen. So it will take time. Stay here and sip your chocolate. Speak to no one. If you spy your own sister walking by, do not speak. Do you understand?''

Catherine nodded.

"Buck up, Miss Catherine." Seeing her quiet compliance, Jenkins put in softly, "With any luck, we'll be out of here by the rising of the tide.''

Catherine watched as Sinjun and Jenkins strode out the door, telling her in French that they'd return shortly.

But the afternoon lengthened and Catherine sat mutely stirring the third cup of chocolate the serving girl had brought her, and still they had not returned. She had sat impatient and feeling as cramped and bottled up as an ill-tempered genie as the time had gone by. She watched all sorts of people pass the window of the inn, and had difficulty swallowing when she noted that there were soldiers in the town, strolling by and looking at all the passersby. A few had looked in the window at her. But aside from one cheeky young fellow who had winked at her, they seemed to pay her no special attention.

She was wondering whether it might be possible that she could be on English soil again before another day passed, when she noted a group of people who had entered the inn and had come into the room where she sat. So she turned and stared out the window, pretending to be oblivious to her surroundings when she realized that one of them had come up to her table.

"Good evening, Miss Robins," Henri Beaumont said silkily. "It is a great pleasure to find you here. I do not care for your new style of dress, but I must say you do nonetheless look as enchanting as ever.''

Henri Beaumont pulled out a chair and sat smiling benignly at Catherine. He noted the shock in the girl's eyes and the distress which had sent the color flying from her cheeks. It pleased him to see her in such distress for it had been a long and uncomfortable chase, and at least her consternation in some small way repaid him for his discomfort.

He did not blame her, he thought, watching her sit and blink at him as though he were a specter, for opting to go off with her countryman. Even he could see that the English marquis was a better example of manhood than his poor friend Hervé. After all, she was a woman as well as a businesswoman. When he discovered she had flown, and that the marquis had flown as well on the same day, his chagrin had been genuine. Still, he would have been content to shrug the whole matter off if it had not been for two unexpected factors.

One was that Hervé had been horrified to find that he was not to be presented with the English miss his brother had been so sure he would have for his own. For, as Hervé had explained, sputtering and banging upon the table, Beaumont had promised the woman to him. And he had told his brother he was to have her. And now, he had gone on, flapping his arms in fury, he would look like a fool. For while it would be delicious to be in power again, to live in splendor and deign to give charity to his brother, it would be as nothing if he had not the whole of it. What use, he had screeched, to be generous and dole out coins to Pierre? What use to see Pierre give up his splendid apartments to live in a hovel? It would not be complete if he could not see Pierre dying of envy as he nuzzled the neck of the very woman Pierre had thought to have. And implicit in every furious gesture Beaumont read the message: If Henri Beaumont could not procure him all that he desired, what sort of a friend was he? And what did he need him for when soon his beloved general would reward him so well for his loyalty?

The other factor that had precipitated Henri Beaumont's chase across the country was the man that the English female had fled with. For there was no question that the Marquis of Bessacarr was on clandestine business in Paris. Beaumont had known it, but had been helpless to stop it while peace and Louis reigned.

But now that the regime was changing, matters were different. The moment Napoleon once again set foot upon the throne, all the marquis' immunity would vanish. Even now at this delightful moment as he recovered the girl, he could not take the Marquis of Bessacarr. For, with all his far-ranging network of informants, still he had not gotten certain word of Napoleon's arrival in Paris. That he had left Elba, Beaumont knew. That he was coming to Paris was also certain. But as yet there had been no word of his triumphant arrival. And he had to wait upon that word.

Still, he thought, it had not been a wasted trip. Here was the girl. She was not a titled Englishwoman; she had no immunity. He could deliver her to Hervé and be in the excellent position of having Hervé Richard deeply indebted to him. He looked at the girl as she sat, pale and transfixed with terror, gazing at him. She was lovely, he noted dispassionately. Fleshly passion was not one of Henri Beaumont's sins. Women were in all, he thought, rather boring creatures. Power was Henri Beaumont's only passion, and he felt a distinct twinge of pleasure as he contemplated the girl he had gone to such lengths to discover.

"So," he said, placing his hands upon the table, "now you will come with me, Miss Robins."

"No," Catherine said, "I shall not. I told you so in Paris. And I say so again. For I am an English citizen and I am free to go home if I wish."

"This is so very tiresome," he said. "I know you are loath to leave your good friend the marquis, but I assure you Hervé is a generous man. While, admittedly, he is not so fine a specimen as the marquis, he is a good enough chap in his own way and you will be recompensed more than adequately for your services."

He stood and motioned to two of the soldiers who had entered the inn with him.

"Please stand and go with them quietly, Miss Catherine," he said, "for it will be no use for you to make a to-do."

Catherine rose and began to walk with the two soldiers. She knew she could leave a message for the marquis, but she feared even letting his name slip in M. Beaumont's presence. In her confusion Catherine could only hope that Sinjun had seen what was happening and was wise enough to stay away in safety.

But as they approached the door she saw Sinjun and Jenkins enter. Jenkins was breathing heavily, as if they had run a long way.

Sinjun stood and stayed the soldiers with one imperious up-lifted hand. He turned and stared at M. Beaumont. Even though Sinjun was dust covered and dressed as a peasant, still he had an air of command that communicated itself to the soldiers.

"M. Beaumont," he bowed, "how unexpected to meet you again."

Henri Beaumont stood quietly, a solemn gray-coated insignificant man beside the marquis. The two men measured each other with their eyes.

"Not entirely unexpected, Your Lordship," M. Beaumont

smiled, returning the bow. "For surely a gentleman such as yourself would have patronized finer establishments than stables and barns on his journey if he had not been at least halfway expecting to see me again?"

Sinjun acknowledged the words with a tight smile.

"And," M. Beaumont went on glibly, "I admire your caution. But you could not know that the landlady in Saint-Denis wondered why the little simple lad never got on the diligence. Nor could you have known that Mme. Boisvert in Louviers noticed that your charming French wife spoke English when she thought no one was listening. And I pride myself on reasoning that Dieppe would be too obvious a place for you to return to and Calais too far in these so troubled times."

"Very reasonable pride," Sinjun said, "but why are you taking my lovely companion away? Is it sheer revenge?"

"You know better than that," M. Beaumont said. "I must deprive her of your company. Alas, she is lovely, but she is also a thief. See what I have discovered she had upon her person when I apprehended her."

He dug into his pocket and held up a chamois purse. Lovingly, he withdrew a strand of pearls. As Catherine gaped, he took an emerald and diamond brooch from its folds and, lastly, held up the duchess's finest sapphire and ruby pendant.

"And not only that," he said sadly, "but I have also the dear lady who owns these trinkets to testify as to their theft."

He nodded to one of his minions, who quickly went out into the street to a waiting coach.

"Now what magistrate could deny the word of a titled English lady against her former companion?" he asked.

As Catherine watched in horror, M. Beaumont's man returned with the Duchess of Crewe following him. She appeared supported by Rose on one side and a wretched-looking James on the other. She was blinking in the light as though she had just been awakened from sleep. No trace of her former dignity showed, and when she spoke, it was not with command, but with a cranky querulousness.

"Yes. Those are my jewels," she said immediately upon entering, never once looking at what M. Beaumont held up in his hand. Her eyes wavered over to Catherine for a moment and then hastily darted away from her.

"And that's the gel. Now I must go. You said I could go home now. Give me my jewels back and let me go."

"I must keep the stolen goods, for evidence," M. Beaumont said calmly. "Surely you do not object to that? For if you do, you can always wait until the matter is settled and then claim them from me." ·

"No," the old woman gasped, "no. Keep them, but you said that I could go home now. I've told you all I know. I want to go home. Rose, tell him he must let me leave now," she whined.

"Certainly," M. Beaumont said, as he dropped the jewels back in his pocket. "Now that you have spoken in front of witnesses, you may go."

"But, Your Grace," Catherine called, unable to restrain herself, "and Rose. And James. You know I did no such thing. Oh, why don't you tell them it is untrue?"

But the dowager only hastily and ungracefully made for the door. Rose's face was red, but she and James only helped the old woman on her unsteady way and did not look back.

"So you see," M. Beaumont said helplessly, spreading out his hands, "I have no choice. I shall keep Miss Robins here securely for a day or two. Then we shall return to Paris and justice. But," he said slyly, "you may visit her in her incarceration if you wish, My Lord. I am not a heartless man, after all."

"And you hope I visit often, often enough to let time pass and tides turn?" Sinjun snapped.

"Oh, well," M. Beaumont shrugged, "time has a way of doing that, hasn't it?"

"Time enough," Sinjun said bitterly, "for news to come from Paris, no doubt?"

"We both await such news, Marquis," M. Beaumont said smoothly, "for even as we stand here talking, such news may be old in Paris. But, alas, there is no glass to see so far nor any voice to carry."

"And," Sinjun said carefully, "there is even a chance that such great events might miscarry, is there not? For otherwise, I think, you would not be so content to let me go."

"All things are possible," M. Beaumont said, "and I am a careful man. You are free, of course, M. Marquis. But the moment you become Citizen Marquis I shall know of it. Mlle. Robins will be safely kept in the jail here. But the tide runs high tonight, so you may visit or you may go. It is all the same to me."

He signaled to the soldiers to proceed and they motioned

Catherine to go with them. She stared at Sinjun and shook her head fiercely.

"Good-bye, Your Lordship," she said tersely. "Please do not fear for me. Please leave while you can, for I see this is a coil you cannot extricate me from. Good-bye, Jenkins. Good luck."

And, head held high, Catherine looked away from Sinjun's despairing face and followed the soldiers from the inn.

Catherine sat on the wooden bench in her cell and actually smiled to herself. For, she thought, M. Beaumont was a great one for effect. She knew that there were large clean cells above stairs, for she had seen them when she had been brought in. But here in the dank basement the cells looked like something out of a picture book of medieval tortures. They were made of cold gray stone with an ancient vaulted ceiling. The bars were thick enough to keep in a ravening murderer, and the one high window only showed a patch of light while it was still day.

She was the only prisoner, and her jailer, a close-mouthed dirty old fellow, spoke no English and seemed to be more interested in catching up on his sleep than in observing her. But M. Beaumont had been set upon proving his power to her. She shivered in the musty chill of the cell. He had succeeded. She had spent the last hours feverishly rationalizing her situation, and knew that she had her emotions under only the most gossamer-thin control. The only way she could stay rational was to tell herself over and over that at least Sinjun was free, and that perhaps he would find a way out of this for her.

Now she felt even that meager lifeline of hope slipping away. For now that she had sat here and night was upon her, a new cold voice rang in her head. Why should he risk all to save her? And even if he did, how could he possibly win her freedom? M. Beaumont had very carefully told her how impossible any escape efforts would be. They were in France; she was in a French jail.

The knowledge that she was being used as bait to trap Sinjun into overstaying warred with her frantic desire to escape the fate M. Beaumont had outlined to her. When she had insisted that she would never be Hervé Richard's mistress, he had only shrugged. It was true, he said, that Hervé would keep no mistress who wailed and wept and tried to escape at every moment. For he was not a brute. But if she did not agree to go pleasantly to Hervé and behave as a woman of her sort should, there were other places he could take her for profit. Places, he had said calmly, where she would be expected to accommodate twenty men an evening rather than one poor devoted Hervé. Places where her weeping and shouting would only be considered piquant by the patrons. And while every instinct she possessed cried for escape, still she knew she would rather suffer her fate ten times over than cost Sinjun his life.

She sat and gazed up at the little square of black, at last admitting it was a full night sky. The tide must have gone out, she thought, and Sinjun and Jenkins must be safely away. She wondered how long they would remember her after they were safe in England again. At last her control snapped and the tears began to flow. He might have at least stopped for a moment on his way to freedom to bid her good-bye.

There could have been nothing, she knew as she sobbed, between a lord of the realm and a foolish girl who had gotten herself in a tangle through her own willfulness. And she had known all the while that she would part from him forever when they reached home. But she had felt that the memory of him would sustain her through all the long years while she stayed and watched her sister's family grow. And now, almost wildly, she regretted her reactions of the night before. For if she had let him make love to her, it might have been a thing that could sustain her in the strange new life that lay ahead of her. She would live and she would go on to things that were now unimaginable, for she was by nature a survivor. But how? She almost cried aloud.

So it was that when her jailer rose and slowly climbed the stairs to a summons she had not heard, she scarcely cared who it was that he admitted.

And when Sinjun saw her, crumpled in a corner and weeping soundlessly, he caught his breath and tightened his knuckles till they were white on the bars of her cell.

"Catherine," he called to her, when he had his voice back in control, "Catherine, come here."

She turned and, seeing him, rose and came running to the bars.

"Oh no, Sinjun, you must not stay here," she cried out wildly, "for that is M. Beaumont's plan, to delay you till it is too late. You must go," she said frantically, her tearstained face striking him to the heart.

He grasped her hand through the bars and tried to think of a way to calm her, for time was short.

"Hush, Catherine," he said sternly. "Quiet. I must speak and you must listen. Listen carefully. Calm yourself, for, as you say, I do not have much time and you must pay attention.''

She fell silent at the cold imperativeness of his voice and listened, her eyes wide and unblinking.

Sinjun ran a hand through his hair and thought rapidly. He saw that her spirit was held only by his voice and that fear and shock had driven all else from her mind. So he spoke rapidly, forcefully, and clearly, knowing that her jailer could not understand the language.

"I have been very busy, Catherine. I have not forgotten you.

"Indeed, no one has forgotten you. Rose could not speak in your defense, for if she had, Beaumont would have accused her of theft as well. She and James wanted to stay to help you, but I persuaded them they could do no more. They had already made sure that the duchess signed nothing, so that nothing she said would be held against you by anyone but Beaumont. The duchess bore you no ill will, Catherine; she was only a frightened old woman. They sailed on the late tide. Violet elected to stay on in Paris with a gentleman of her choice. But none of them deliberately wished to harm you.''

When he saw tears start at his words, he quickly went on, knowing now that he could not speak of emotions, or recall emotions to her mind, or she would crumble.

"But there is a way to get you safe from here. There is a way to take you with us. But you must agree and agree at once.''

She nodded, clutching his hand tightly.

"You must marry me," he said.

He saw her disbelief and lowered his voice and said firmly, "Beaumont cannot keep you here if you are a peeress of the realm. He cannot keep you if you are a marchioness and we are not at war. Marry me, Catherine, and we can leave at first light and go home, home to England again.''

Her eyes searched his face, and he kept his countenance impassive with difficulty as he looked back at her. Now, here in this filthy jail, was no place for him to spout on about love, desire, and future happiness. He doubted that she would believe him, and feared that, even if she did, she would refuse him. For as she did not love him, her sense of what was honorable might override her instinct for preservation. So he said nothing of love and continued, "I have Jenkins here. And a minister. Yes, an accredited representative of the Church of England, trying to make his way back home with his charges. He was traveling with schoolboys when the news of Napoleon's return came to his ears.''

The jailer looked up at the one word he recognized and shifted uneasily. M. Beaumont had said the woman might have visitors and converse with them, but had warned of terrible repercussions if any escape attempt was made. Although the sound of his onetime hero's name had jolted him, he soon relaxed, remembering how many soldiers were above stairs.

"An attaché from the consulate in Paris is here as well, Catherine, though not with me, for his face is recognized by Beaumont's men. He has gotten me the special papers. We can be wed here and now. And then you will be allowed to go free. Say yes, Catherine, for your own sake.''

But she only stood dazedly staring at him.

Sinjun wondered now if any of his words had reached her, so he went ahead in a low despairing voice, "Catherine, you cannot stay. And I cannot live with myself if I let you stay. So say yes. If you marry me it will be for the best, and,'' he said suddenly, trying a new tack to bring some sort of comprehension to her eyes, "if it does not suit you to be my wife, we can procure a divorce when we are back home. I promise you that. I will not keep you tied to me forever if you do not wish it. But for now, you have only to sign a paper and repeat some words and you are free.''

At last he saw some new emotion coming into her white face and he pressed on, "For me, Catherine. So that all my work will not be in vain. For I promise you if you do not agree, I will stay here until I hit upon a plan. But by then it might be too late for both of us. I cannot live with myself as a man if I abandon you here.''

He had to strain to hear her whispered reply:

"Yes, Sinjun.'' Then: "I will if you wish it.''

Dizzy with relief, he motioned to the men behind him.

"Here, Jenkins, you just stand so that you can hear Mr. Whittaker. And Mr. Whittaker, you cannot take out your little book; you must recite by heart. Can you do that? For though the jailer looks like a fool, the book will alert him to something to be suspicious of.''

The tall, thin, balding man smiled and said briefly, "If I cannot recite it by heart after twenty-five years in the Church, Your Lordship, I am more of a fool than the jailer.''

"And,'' Sinjun said clearly, taking Catherine's two hands in his tightly, "you must alter the pattern of words. For the cadence of the ceremony might strike a note in our watchdog's mind."

"Let us see," the minister mused. "How about this, then?" And, clearing his throat, he looked at Catherine and said in a friendly conversational tone, "Dearly beloved we. Are gathered. Together here in the sight . . ."

Catherine gripped Sinjun's hand and thought only that she must do this so that he would not be caught. Tears gathered in her eyes when she thought of the sacrifice he was making. What if she were the sort of female to hold him to the marriage once they returned, making him regret his act of gallantry for the rest of his life, tied to a woman he did not want?

Sinjun carefully listened to the weird rhythm of the words so that he would know when to reply, and kept smiling and nodding as if Mr. Whittaker were only chatting and trying to reassure Catherine.

"Live?" asked Mr. Whittaker pleasantly.

Sinjun increased the pressure on Catherine's hands and looked toward the minister.

After a confused moment she said, in a thin voice, "Yes, I will."

Sinjun closed his eyes in relief and hoped only that she would never regret this moment. For although he had forced her to marry him, he vowed he would do all in his power to make her content with her state, to persuade her to one day accept him as husband, even if she could not love him.

And so in a basement in Le Havre, St. John Basil St. Charles, Marquis of Bessacarr, was wed to Catherine Emily Robins in a ceremony signally blessed with complete misunderstanding on the part of the bride, the groom, and the witnesses. As Sinjun guided her hand to sign the paper Mr. Whittaker handed her, and Jenkins assured the guard that it was just for the transfer of some of her property now that she was remaining in France, the ceremony was completed.

Jenkins and Mr. Whittaker left to congratulate each other royally at a tavern near the docks before continuing on the marquis' errands. The groom stayed the night on a bench outside the cell as he told the guard he could not bring himself to leave his *chère amie*. The guard was content—his master had told him it would suit him well if the English gentleman did not leave his prisoner. And the bride sat and watched the sleeping face of her new husband through the night.

M. Beaumont's face was wreathed in smiles when he descended the steps to Catherine's cell in the morning. So it was true, then: The marquis had stayed the night and missed one voyage out to be with the girl. With luck, he thought, he could be maneuvered into staying another. And another, it if was necessary, till the news he waited for came through.

"Good morning," he said happily, eyeing the weary girl as the marquis rose from his seat.

"Good morning," the marquis said briskly. "It lacks half past the hour of ten, Beaumont. You must have slept soundly. And now, if you please, release your prisoner."

M. Beaumont laughed.

"Ah, if it were only that easy to forget crime," he sighed happily.

"I'm afraid it must be," Sinjun smiled, "for you have no authority to arrest my wife, the Marchioness of Bessacarr. If you have any doubts upon that head, I beg you to look at these papers. There are our marriage lines. And there is a very official note from our ambassador requesting that you immediately release my wife from your custody. And the mayor of this city, as you can see from this other document, requests you comply. You would not want to disrupt amicable Anglo-French relations, would you, Beaumont?"

Sinjun smiled as he lay back against the tarpaulin upon the deck of the fishing vessel. He smiled just remembering the look upon Beaumont's face as he took the papers from his hands and read them.

Jenkins looked over from the rail where he had been watching the coastline of France begin to recede in the morning mists.

"Recalling past triumphs, lad?" he asked.

"And present ones," Sinjun agreed, looking down at Catherine as she slept, her head against his shoulder.

"There might be rough seas ahead," Jenkins mused.

"At least we are at last asail," Sinjun replied.

The ship glided smoothly home, and the two men did not break their contented, separate silence till they heard the far-off sound of cannon fire and the distant, almost toylike sound of the tumultuous ringing of many church bells coming from the direction they had so recently left.

"You left it close, lad," Jenkins whistled. "At least, you can never forget your wedding day. It was the day the news of the emperor's return finally reached Le Havre."

"I shall never forget my wedding day," Sinjun agreed, gathering his sleeping bride closer.

Chapter XVII

Catherine trailed aimlessly through the fragrant garden. The spring sun shone so warmly upon her shoulders that she had taken off her hat and held it by its strings as she wandered. She paused by the ornamental pond and watched the small golden fish glint in the sun-drenched water. There was no doubt that Fairleigh was a lovely place. It was well appointed and very commodious. It had delightful gardens filled with unexpected pleasures at every turn. Any path could take one to a statue or a waterfall or a bench overlooking a delightful view such as this one. Fairleigh also had a well-run genial staff of servants and comfortable well-furnished rooms. In fact, it had everything one could wish for in a home, Catherine sighed, except a heart. For its master was away. And Catherine did not know if he would ever return.

A month ago when she had first come here, straight from the dock where their fishing vessel had deposited them, she had been too exhausted to appreciate Fairleigh. Sinjun had traveled on to London to deliver his lists and his news of the emperor's return and future plans. He had sent Catherine straight on to his country seat. She had arrived by night, after a long and weary journey by carriage. But then sleep and ease and the security that emanated from the house had helped to mend her spirit. The knowledge that she was home and safe aided her. But Sinjun's prompt return to her side and having him near her every day had done the most to restore her.

Those first weeks she and Sinjun had roamed the grounds. He had shown her all the secret places of his youth; they had laughed and played together as though they were back in his childhood. He saw to it that the servants acknowledged her as mistress and she was easy in her mind at all times. He was such a clever, attentive companion that he almost succeeded in making her forget that this was but a temporary time for her and that she must soon move on again. He had treated her as a well-loved sister.

She did not know precisely when the change had begun. Before she had even been aware of it, it had arrived. One day he had been her eager friend and the next it seemed his air of polite and icy indifference was upon him again.

It was as if the one night they had dined by candlelight as usual, and there had not been enough hours in the evening to tell each other all they wished, and the next night he had sat listening to her with sedate half-interest until her voice had dried in her throat and conversation ebbed away. He was not cold to her, nor ever rude, but she could feel the distance grow between them. Instead of reassuring him that she was prepared now to be on her way, perversely, cowardice stilled her tongue and instead she attempted to draw his interest back. And the more she tried, the more precisely polite he had become.

But then, only a week past, she had, in a burst of misery-induced bravery, stopped him as he finished his dinner and began to bid her good night before retiring to his room. As no servants were in the room, she spoke swiftly, before any could return to complete the clearing of the table.

"Sinjun," she asked, "is it that you want me to begin the divorce proceedings now? But you will have to assist me, for I do not know how to go about it."

"Whatever gave you that idea?" he asked, sitting back to watch her closely.

"It was only that you have seemed less than pleased with my presence of late. I have tarried here but perhaps for too long. You said our marriage was to free me from M. Beaumont. And so it has. But you also said that you would free me from it when we were home. And so we are. I haven't made a move to go as yet, I know, but that is only because I do not know how to go about the thing. If you wish, we can start it in motion."

His eyes became shuttered during her speech and he sat quietly for a moment and then replied in a colorless voice, "Catherine, lay your mind to rest about that. You may stay on as my wife as long as you wish—till death do us part, for that matter. I only offered divorce if our relationship became unbearable to you. Has it?''

"Oh no," she had answered quickly. "But it is you that I am thinking of. I do not want to constrict you in any way. It would be the devil of a coil," she laughed artificially, "as Jenkins would say, if you wished to be rid of me and I just stayed on.''

"You are pleased with our relationship then?" he persisted.

"Of course," she said, "except for the fact that you have been so distant of late."

His shoulders seemed to droop, and then he at last rose and gave her a thin smile.

"It is only some trifling estate matters that have occupied my mind. Well then, my dear, since this form of marriage is acceptable to you, we'll go on just as we are. By the way," he asked, "have you yet written to your sister to inform her of your sudden nuptials?"

She faltered. For she had not as yet. Since her marriage had begun with the promise of divorce, she did not know how long she would be a wife. It seemed impossible to explain all to Jane in a mere letter. And almost impossible to tell Jane the tidings of a wedding, then follow it with an announcement of a bill of divorcement. Yet of all the things she had been able to speak freely of with Sinjun, the precise nature of their marriage was the one thing they both, by some unspoken agreement, never discussed.

"I see," Sinjun nodded as she tried and failed to explain. "Well then, my dear, I bid you a good night. Oh, by the by," he had added, as though he were discussing a change in the weather, "those estate matters I spoke of. I am off to London tomorrow. There is business to attend to. Do you care to accompany me?"

The lackluster offer he made warned her off and she answered in a low voice that she would if he wished it.

"It makes no matter," he said coldly, "but I wondered if you were interested in consulting a lawyer while you were there?"

"Do you wish it, Sinjun?" she asked.

"I have already told you," he answered almost angrily, "that is not my desire."

And then he was gone. Jenkins had gone with him and Catherine had spent the week cudgeling her brain for an answer to her problem. She was the Marchioness of Bessacarr now, but she was yet a maid. Sinjun had never so much as held her hand since

their return. She had asked if he wanted a divorce and he had
denied it. Still, he made no effort to make her his wife. She no
longer knew what it was he wanted or what she wanted. For all
her brave thoughts back in Le Havre, she did not wish to
leave him. Distant though he was, he was still Sinjun and she
could not accept the thought of being apart from him. But neither
could she bear the thought of being an encumbrance to him.

And there was also the fact that she knew divorce to be an
expensive, complicated affair and one that would put her beyond
the pale forever. It was one thing for Sinjun to have laughed at
her fears for her reputation when they returned to England. For it
was one thing for the duchess's infamous companion to return to
quiet obscurity in Kendall, quite another for her to be wed to no
less than the Marquis of Bessacarr. But he had laughed her
fears away. He had told her that as his wife she would be above
reproach. And that few people who mattered to her would have
traveled in the duchess's set anyway. And, that having been
rescued from the duchess, she would in fact, be a sort of
heroine. But being his divorced wife, she knew, could not be
easily laughed away.

She watched the sunlight play upon the water and wished she
had more understanding and experience. The worst part of her
situation was the loss of Sinjun's attention. She wondered again
what she had done to turn his friendship.

His room was connected to hers, but she had never entered it.
And so she could not have heard the angry conversation the
morning of his departure for London.

"Have done, Jenkins," Sinjun had snarled in a voice she
would not have recognized. "I am to London and there's an end
to it."

"And your wife?" Jenkins asked, lounging against the door.

"Better with me gone," Sinjun said, "for I cannot go through
with this masquerade. I am not the man I thought that I was. I
cannot be with her every moment, laugh with her, condole with
her, and yet be a plaster saint. You cannot creep into the master's
bedroom at Fairleigh, Jenkins, as you did in France, and stop the
master from forcing his attentions on his legal wife. It's just not
done, old fellow," he said with a trace of his old humor.

"And you think she would call for help?" Jenkins asked
again.

"Worse," Sinjun said. "She would probably suffer me out of
gratitude, and that is one thing I will not bear. No, I am better

off away from her. I saved the girl, Jenkins. And now she finds herself trapped in a loveless marriage, at least on her part. I am not so lost to decency that I will take advantage of her gratitude. Nor will I settle for it. Nor can I pretend to be a eunuch any longer. So I'm off to London. Perhaps time will clear the air and we will see what is to be done. And Jenkins," Sinjun said slowly, "if in your self-appointed role of nanny, you think to tell her anything of my feelings on this head, I will slit your throat."

"I have never betrayed you," Jenkins said simply.

"I know," Sinjun said softly. "Forgive me, old fellow, I am not myself."

"And so you're off to London, seeking the comfort of women?" Jenkins said quietly.

"Women?" Sinjun laughed. "I swear you know me better than that. It is woman that is my problem, in the singular. I am not at all in a plural mood, dear friend. No, I am pure of heart and I wish to remain so for a space. I need time, Jenkins. Catherine needs time. And my trip buys us time."

He had gone, and Jenkins with him as escort, and Catherine wandered the halls of Fairleigh and haunted its gardens. The morning sun played tricks with the water's surface, but she shaded her eyes with her hand and leaped up in eagerness. For she saw Jenkins strolling toward her through the garden. She flew to his side to greet him.

"Jenkins!" she cried in pleasure, "you are back. Is Sinjun back as well?"

"No," Jenkins said correctly, "His Lordship remains in town."

"Oh," Catherine said, downcast. "And how does he? Does he remain long? When shall he return?"

"As to that I cannot say, My Lady," Jenkins replied.

"What is it, Jenkins?" Catherine asked. "Why the formality? Have I given offense?"

"No, My Lady," Jenkins replied, "but you are the Marchioness of Bessacarr now, and it would not be fitting for me to call you otherwise."

"Jenkins," Catherine said, fixing her eyes upon his deferentially lowered head, "you cannot be so proper with me. Not now. Now when I need you as friend. We have traveled together. You have shared my bedroom, Jenkins," she said roguishly. "Do not say it will be 'My Lady' and never 'Catherine' between us again."

"I am a servant, My Lady," Jenkins said as he studied his boots.

"Oh, you a servant," Catherine laughed. "You are a servant in the same way the prime minister is a servant to his king. Please, Jenkins, if you wish to come all propriety when we are in company, I could accept it as a whim. But when we are alone, surely you can remain my friend? For I do need one, indeed," she said sadly. "I have no other."

"And what of His Lordship?" Jenkins asked shrewdly.

"As to that," Catherine waved her hand, "you see how eager he is for my company, don't you? I've been spending the morning wondering would I do better if I were just to be gone from this place."

"So that we three can chase the breadth of England together this time?" Jenkins said, shaking his head. "No, adventuring days are over for us, Catherine. We must learn to live with peace."

"I know," she said simply and sadly.

"Come," Jenkins said, "if you want to be friends, we must sit and have a chat as we did in the old times."

Once they had seated themselves on the white metal bench that faced the pool, Catherine turned to Jenkins.

"Why has he gone?" she asked.

"Business," Jenkins said. "Why did you not go with him?"

"I don't think he really wanted me to." She sighed, dangling her hat and watching it spin on its strings.

"Do you not know?" Jenkins asked. "A wife should know her husband's mind, not think she knows."

"But I am not truly a wife," Catherine whispered, fearful of a gardener overhearing her, but glad of a chance to speak with someone she knew and trusted. "And you know that, Jenkins. For you were part of the entire plan. He married me only as an act of gallantry, a gesture of kindness. And now," she said bitterly, "he's stuck with me. For I haven't the wit or experience to take matters into my own hands and free him from the consequences of his own good deed."

"I don't know," Jenkins mused, putting his hands behind his head and looking up into the unfolding blossoms of the tree above them. "I haven't met many fellows, no matter how noble, who would give their name to some female as a gesture of courtesy. Seems a mighty high gesture. For example," he went on contemplatively, "I should think it would have been just as easy for him to get those papers mocked up. The curate was a good chap and the mayor such a nit that he believed anything anyone told him loudly enough. Any warm body would have done to pretend to be a minister, for that matter. As I recall, the fellow from the consulate was so flaming mad at the Frenchies, he would have signed anything to dupe them. No,'' Jenkins said thoughtfully, ''it seems to me that he made a highly permanent gesture of kindness when he didn't really have to.''

Catherine sat still and blinked.

''But Sinjun's so honest,'' she finally managed to say, ''why would he tell me it was the only way to free me if it was not?''

''I'm not saying he's dishonest,'' Jenkins said quickly. ''Perhaps it was what he believed at the time. I've often found that a fellow believes what he wants to, deep down, when an emergency arises.''

''No,'' Catherine said flatly, after some thought, ''that cannot be. For he's never said a word to me about any tender feelings, not since we've come to Fairleigh. And,'' she said, a blush rising in her cheeks, ''he's never made a gesture either. And,'' she said with hurt in her voice, ''he's grown very cold towards me in recent weeks. Oh, Jenkins, what does he want of me?''

''As to that, I couldn't say,'' Jenkins said mildly, ''for he's not one to open his budget to another. But it seems to me, if you'll forgive the impertinence, My Lady, that you're the one that's got the only right to ask. And speaking of such, I couldn't ask Her Ladyship, but I can inquire of Miss Catherine, do you want to stay in this marriage?''

''Yes,'' Catherine said simply, hanging her head.

''I can't blame you,'' Jenkins commented. ''A lovely home, fine clothes, no more worries about money. It's a soft berth, it is indeed.''

''How could you!'' Catherine said, suddenly blazing with anger. ''You know me better than that, Jenkins. I couldn't care if we had to live in a barn forever, as we did in France. It's Sinjun I love!''

''Love?'' Jenkins asked, grinning when he saw her sudden dismay at the hastiness of her words. ''Well, there's a horse of a different color. Love. And so then, you are sad because His Lordship rejects his wife's love? Ah now, that I can understand. But I can't understand him turning down such a lovely female.''

Jenkins wagged his head slowly. ''Well, I don't know what

sort of maggot the fellow's got in his head, turning down the attentions of a lady like you.''

"He hasn't," Catherine said guiltily.

"Hasn't," Jenkins said with surprise. "Why, here you are languishing since he's left you, and now you say he hasn't rejected your love."

"He has not," she said in a rush, "because I haven't offered it. Jenkins, can't you see? If I tell him how I truly feel, I know, I just know what his reaction will be. He will feel sorry for me. He will offer me sympathy. Why, he's so kind, he'll stay on in a marriage with me, because he'll feel responsible. And all the while, it will all be only more courtesy. I could not bear that.''

"You could always leave if he offered you sympathy," Jenkins reasoned. "But the thing of it is, you don't really know what he'll offer. You've been a brave lass since I've known you, Miss Catherine, I wonder at you not being courageous enough to hear what his offer will be. I should think it would be more comfortable to know once and for all where you stood than just standing on air like this. I should think the only thing you'd have to lose was pride. And that only for a moment, for then you could up and say, 'Well then, thank you, but I think I'll be going along now,' and there's your pride back again.''

"It frightens me to death," Catherine whispered, "when I think of the look of sympathy that will come into his eyes. For there's nothing worse than knowing someone loves you, I should think, and knowing that they ask the one thing of you that you can never give them.''

"Pride's a curious thing," Jenkins said, as if speaking to himself. "It's a terrible thing to lose, but unlike a heart, once you've lost it, you can always grow it back.''

"You think I should bring up the matter once and for all," Catherine stated defiantly. "You don't think I should shilly-shally any longer; you think I'm making too much of my sense of pride.''

"I think," Jenkins said straightforwardly, "that the Catherine I knew would rather have things clear and in the open, whatever the cost, than dangle and waver like a puppet, or like that fine bonnet of yours, on its strings. But I suppose that now you're a great titled lady, you've taken on new airs and graces to fit your situation. And if you count a moment's discomfort above a lifetime of doubt, I can't blame you. So if you'll excuse me, My Lady, I'm off to get back to business, for Fairleigh don't run itself. And I'm sure you've got important things to do, like watching fish and wondering about when life will straighten itself out and be kinder to you."

"I'm going to London," Catherine announced suddenly. "Oh Jenkins, I'm going to London!" she cried, springing up. "Here and now. For if I wait, I will lose courage and go back to waiting upon things to come right. And they will not, alone. I have to go out and face it squarely. And I shall. Jenkins, help me to go now. If I think about it, I know I'll change my mind again."

"I'll ready the carriage," Jenkins said, moving quickly, "and tell your maid to pack like devils were after her sweet body. We can be there by nightfall if we hurry."

"But, Jenkins," she cried to his retreating back, "you've only just returned. I can't chase you back again."

"It's as well," he called back across the wide lawn, "for I discovered I've left my best boots there, and I'm lost without them."

Jenkins drove the coachman to hurry, as though they were indeed being pursued by demons. Catherine sat back and rehearsed her speech to Sinjun again and again as the coach fairly flew toward London. She did not have a word for the happy young maid sitting across from her.

She only looked out the window, not seeing the spring day flash before her as she argued with Sinjun in her mind. By the time they changed horses at the Owl and Cross, she had three excellent speeches to choose from. And by the time they had achieved the outskirts of London, there were two she was sure she'd begin with and two alternates to use, depending on his answers. She had decided that she would phrase her opening statements obliquely, to give her room to maneuver away from an outright declaration of her feelings if he so much as hinted he would be unhappy to hear of them.

In fact, she had so many excellent speeches, rejoinders, and face-saving devices at her command that by the time the coach finally slowed and came to a stop outside of her husband's town house, she felt as though she had been orating to an unseen audience for hours.

As she stepped from the carriage, Catherine looked down the street toward the duchess's house, the first home she had known in London. The knocker was off the door and there was no sign of occupation there. As Sinjun had told her, the dowager had retired from the high life and was now residing with one of her sons, happily spending the remainder of her days driving her relatives to distraction. As Jenkins came to give her his arm to assist her up the white steps to Sinjun's door, she drew in a deep breath.

He would be surprised to see her, but, as Jenkins had twitted her when they had stopped for a light luncheon, he seldom threw great orgies at his town house, so she need not worry about interrupting him at anything important. At last I am taking some positive action, Catherine told herself sternly as she mounted the steps, so there's no need for me to keep trembling like a puppy in a thunderstorm. She raised her head high and when the door swung open, she walked in calmly, as befitted the Marchioness of Bessacarr visiting her house in town.

His Lordship was out, the butler informed them unhappily, but he said more positively, since the marquis had not sent orders to cancel dinner, he would most likely be returning soon.

After the staff had made its curtsies to its new mistress, Jenkins ordered a hip bath brought to Catherine's room and told her to go and refresh herself and change. He would, he promised, send Sinjun straight to her when he returned. "Head high, girl," he whispered to her, bowing respectfully and wishing Her Ladyship a good evening.

Catherine washed and changed into a simple white at-home robe and brushed her hair. Then she sat poised on the récamier in her elegant room. She had time to pose herself in a variety of casual fashions and run through her speech several more times. She had time to admire the gracious chamber that was hers and count the exact number of cherubs carved into her bedposts, when she at last heard voices below stairs.

She forgot her pretense at languor and flew to her door to see Sinjun taking the steps of the long, curving staircase two at a time as he came toward her.

He came toward her with a delighted easy smile, but in a moment she saw it slip and by the time he had achieved her room, he wore his habitual cool expression.

"Catherine," he said politely, entering her room, "I am surprised to see you. Is anything amiss? Jenkins said you felt you had to see me straightaway."

"No," she said quietly, with admirable control, "but I felt

that I must speak with you, Sinjun, and I did not wish to put it off till you returned to Fairleigh.''

''Very well,'' he said, standing before her, ''here I am. What is it, my dear?''

She eyed him in dismay. All her rehearsed comments seemed to churn into one insoluble mass now that he stood before her. He looked so formidably immaculate. He wore high mirror-polished boots with gold edgings, clean carefully tailored buck-skins clung to his legs, and his jacket fitted closely to his wide shoulders. An intricately folded white neckcloth completed the picture of the aloof aristocrat.

''Well, Catherine, what is it?'' he asked with growing impatience.

''Sinjun,'' she breathed with difficulty, ''it is hard enough for me. But I cannot speak to you as you are now.''

Seeing a look of confusion upon his face, she said hurriedly, ''That is, you are so . . . imperious looking. You look exactly as you did when I first met you and you so frightened me. On this very street. Not at all like the man I traveled with through France. It's as if you were two different men,'' she complained, shaking her head.

He hesitated, then went to close her door. As he returned, he began to strip off his jacket. He flung it to the side and in a moment the white neckcloth followed suit. With his shirt open at the throat, he sat in a fragile gilt chair and took both hands to disarrange his careful Brutus haircut. Then he threw one booted leg over the other and grinned at her.

''I would,'' he said ruefully, ''scuff up the Hessians if I could, and if I dared face the rage of my valet. But if you wish, Catherine, I'll nip below stairs and get some earth from the garden to rub over them.''

She relaxed and gazed happily at him, for he had shed some of his coldness with his garments.

''Now,'' she said carefully, finding it easier to look at her own clutched hands than at his face, for it had been so much simpler to discuss the matter with the Sinjun in her mind than with the vital, handsome actuality before her. ''Sinjun, I must know, exactly why did you marry me?''

After a brief pause, his voice came coolly to her ears. ''Catherine, you know that as well as I. Why did you marry me?''

''Don't answer my question with a question,'' she retorted,

daring to look straight at him. "I came here to see you, to talk with you, for I do not think we can go on as we are."

"That is true," he agreed, which was an answer she had not thought he would make, and which stopped her for a moment.

"And I have been thinking," she said wretchedly, feeling all her resolve fading and all her craven subterfuges coming to her command again, "that we must not go on so. For I have come to realize that we cannot continue to live a lie. It is too hard, Sinjun. It is too difficult. I find that I cannot even explain it to you."

She bent her head and railed at herself, for she did not have the courage to suddenly declare love to this watchful collected stranger.

He came, sat beside her, and wrapped one long arm about her to comfort her, but she kept her face averted.

"I know," he sighed. "It was a bad beginning and you should not bedevil yourself. I do understand."

His nearness and the soothing tone of his voice made Catherine wish to curl up and hide herself.

"It's just," she sniveled, "that now I find that it is too much for me. Especially now when I know my own heart. And what I was prepared to say to you straight out, I discover I cannot say at all, out of fear. Fear of your sympathy, Sinjun. For I do not want that. Nor any pity either," she went on, feeling his body stiffen and his hand pause in its stroking of her hair.

"I do understand, Catherine," he said in the iciest voice she had ever heard from him, "and I do not offer you pity. Quite the reverse, in fact. I congratulate you. And so, do not worry, for you shall have your freedom just as soon as it is lawfully possible. Who is the lucky fellow? He must be a paragon, to send you haring to London to settle matters so swiftly."

She looked up at that, to find him looking at her from eyes that seemed to be narrowed and carved of marble.

A sense of outrage at having so thoroughly blundered in what she had assumed to be a perfectly clear statement of her case made her gasp, "What are you talking about? What fellow?"

"The one you have discovered you love and wish to make your true husband," he said with weary patience.

"There is no other I love," she blurted, "or could ever love. You are the only man upon this earth that I want for a husband."

The enormity of what she had said, the way she had put the whole matter, plain and unadorned, caused her to stop and stare at him with an expression of horrified guilt. She had to restrain herself from clapping her hands over her mouth.

"What did you say?" he asked, incredulously.

"Oh Sinjun," she almost wailed, "it is not how I wished to say it. Indeed, it is nothing like the way I had planned to say it. And you do not have to dissemble. I beg of you, talk frankly to me for I am not a child. And do not be so noble that you will sacrifice your future life to spare me a moment's dismay. For I will not keep you tied to me, indeed I will not," she almost babbled, for now that he had discovered her, she was trying to say all the things she had hidden, all at once.

"Catherine, Catherine," he said, taking her in his arms, and holding her closely, "what are you talking about? Are you mad? Tie me to you for the rest of my life? Why, you have done that already, and so securely that I find I cannot break free to save my life. Nor do I wish to. For I love you, and have done so for so long that I would feel empty without it. As I have done this past week."

"But you left me," she whispered, delighting in the warmth that flowed from him.

"Only so that I could save you from my attentions," he said, "for we have no millpond at Fairleigh to cool my ardors in. And I did not wish to force you to my desire, nor did I want your charity either, Catherine."

"Oh, that. But then, it was only because I did not wish you to think me like Rose and Violet," she admitted, still finding it safer to speak into his ear than meet his knowing eyes.

He laughed and she could feel the laughter deep in his chest, where her hands lay.

"And so you came all the way to London to confess your love," he breathed.

"Yes, and to straighten matters out between us, even if it meant I should have to leave at once. For Jenkins was right, one cannot stand upon air."

"Jenkins?" he asked, drawing back a space. "What did he tell you?"

"Only," she said, at last looking into his eyes fully, "that he did not know how you felt any more than I did, but that I could no longer be such a coward. That I should make a push to settle things between us rather than wait for fate to intervene once more."

The tender look that grew in his softened gray gaze made Catherine's pulse leap.

"Jenkins is a knowing fellow," he smiled. "Catherine, let us have done with pretense for all time. Will you be my wife because you love me, with no hope for escape in divorce, for I love you?"

"Oh yes, of course, Sinjun," she whispered, and then he drew her to him gently and kissed her for reply. She gave herself to his embrace and freed herself to give him back kiss for kiss and embrace for embrace.

But as his gentle hands and mouth threatened to drive all further rational thoughts from her, she placed her hands against his chest again and gently pushed him from her.

"Sinjun," she said, catching her breath, "before we go on, there is something I must tell you."

"Tell me," he said into her neck. "Keep telling me while we go on, for I will listen."

"No," she said, firmly tugging at his hair. "It is a thing you must pay close attention to. It is a thing Rose and Violet told me about marriage."

He straightened instantly and looked at her with dismay.

"I was afraid of that," he muttered to himself and spoke carefully, "Look, Catherine, you must not pay too much mind to what they told you of the ways of love. They are not respectable married females. And many of the things they have . . . ah . . . encountered are not things to which a respectable woman is subjected. So you need not fear, for I will never do anything that I think will frighten or distress you. I will only try to bring you pleasure."

"That's just it," Catherine said with satisfaction, "just as they said. One afternoon Rose and Violet were speaking of marriage. And they said that the reason they had many clients who were married gentlemen was that so many of them treated their wives with nice notions of what is proper between a man and his wife. And further, they said that if a man would show his wife exactly what pleased him, as if she were a paid companion, they would probably be a great deal happier and the gentlemen would save their money, for then they wouldn't have to seek out special females for their pleasures. But, Violet said, it was as well that they did not, after all, for then she would have to go back to the theater again, having no employment left to her. So you see, Sinjun," Catherine continued, sincerely, "you must show me everything that you desire, so that you will never have to go to other women again.''

"Everything?" he asked, arching one eyebrow wickedly.

"Everything," she said staunchly.

"Oh Catherine, my delight," he said with a look upon his face that melted her resolve to be logical, "I will, and gladly, for I do love you. I shall do my best to make you my own dear doxy."

"And I love you terribly," she said as she went back into his arms.

Since theirs was to be a marriage built upon laughter, he paused in undoing one of the tiny pearl buttons on her robe and smiled tenderly. "Then I shall have to do something about that. For I want you to love me expertly, just as Rose and Violet wished. It is only that"—he paused—"I hope I do not disappoint you. For I wonder if I know quite as much as Rose and Violet did."

And then he found an excellent way to stop her laughter before it threatened to overcome her completely.

The morning dawned so gray that Molly, the youngest maid in His Lordship's establishment, grumbled to herself as she groped her way into the kitchen to start the fire and greet the day. She yawned as she opened the back door to the kitchen and groggily watched the lamplighter begin his rounds of damping the glow of the new gaslights that lined the street. As she stood stretching and scenting the air, she heard laughter ring out in the empty street. Craning her neck, she looked up to its source.

The sound of masculine laughter blended with the high sweet trill of a woman's mirth. The sounds came from her own establishment, from the upper regions, where the master's rooms were.

Molly shrugged—that portion of the house was not one she had yet been qualified to enter.

"What I'd like to know," she grumbled, thinking of the work that lay ahead of her, and speaking to herself as she often did so early in the morning, "is what folks has got to laugh about at this ungodly hour?"

She started, as she saw she was observed, and then ducked her head in embarrassment. For it was Jenkins, that mysterious fellow who was the force behind the master's establishment. He stood on the lower step, his hands on his hips, and a wide grin on his face as he listened to the merry sounds above him. Only when the woman's laughter had ceased and then the man's laughter stopped abruptly, as if cut off at its source, did he turn his gaze from the upper window. Then he came jauntily into the kitchen bound for the servants' stairs, and a short walk to his rooms. But first he turned and smiled at Molly.

"There's a great deal to laugh about in the morning, little Molly, as you will discover one day if you are a very, very good girl. Or," he added, with a wink, "if you are a very, very bad one."

Molly flushed and went to close the back door, holding it open only a fraction longer to admit the kitchen cat, in from his night's wanderings. The cat sidled in and made quickly for his basket by the stove, glad to be in from the night, in from his weary travels, in safely from the cold gray of dawn.

The
Abandoned Bride

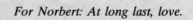

For Norbert: At long last, love.

October 1812

1 The innkeeper was very concerned about the young gentleman. The wind outside his snug establishment was kicking up for a rare blow, a real autumn storm. Bits of gravel and rag ends of fallen leaves were dashing against the windowpanes along with the rain, and the whining blasts seemed to shake the very walls of the wayside inn. Such weathers ought to have made his elegant young patron glad of his comfortable surroundings, the innkeeper reasoned, for there was nothing like a storm without to make a fellow glad of the peace within. But there the young nob sprawled in the common room, growing increasingly disheveled even as the wind increased in velocity, muttering for yet another cup of punch as though he were only another wild manifestation of the storm itself.

The innkeeper sighed and shrugged resignedly at the serving girl's questioning glance. He agreed with her unspoken comment on his guest's condition. The young gentleman certainly did not seem to be in need of any more rum punch. But the look in his eye precluded disagreement. The Quality, the innkeeper had learned from hard experience, could get devilish thorny when they were thwarted. And the fellow was Quality, you

7

could tell it from his look and his voice, even in his present condition. When he had arrived only a few hours before, one glance at his equipage and one stare at his fine clothes had sent the innkeeper hurrying to his bidding. And the first command, disguised as a request, given in that languid, cultured voice, had verified his host's first impression.

The Partridge Feather was only a humble hostelry on the North Road, but that did not mean that its owner did not have grander dreams. It was, after all, a neat, clean establishment. Mine host's wife had a rare way with simple country cooking; the linen was, if not of the finest, then certainly the most frequently darned; and there was always fresh brewed ale in readiness. It would be nothing wonderful if the gentry didn't discover the place and make it as famous and as lucrative as The Rose and the Bear in Ludlow or The Maiden's Head at Uckfield. The Partridge Feather had not been so happily designated yet in its long history, but that did not mean that a fellow should give up his dreaming. So when the elegant young gentleman had alighted from his crested coach with his lovely, laughing lady, the landlord's hopes had risen higher than the wind which now battered upon his doors.

But air-dreaming did not blind a fellow. When the young gent had signed the register with only a common surname and then given the young lady's name as a "Miss Hastings," the innkeeper's hopes had shriveled even as he had read the drying script. For if the young gentleman were a mere "mister," the innkeeper was a monkey's relative, and if he were green enough to believe that the glowing young female answered to the name written, he didn't deserve to walk upright either. For a "mister" didn't talk or walk that way, and after being a hostelier for over a decade, the innkeeper wished he had a pennypiece for every fancy piece of a "miss" that registered at his inn with a gentleman rather than a lady's maid to attend to her.

But only a fool rushed to conclusions, and the innkeeper's mama hadn't raised any nodcocks. For all the signs of mischief, the lass had looked so rare and spoken so soft, it had been hard to think worse of her. So he had been as sweet as he could stare, and had been rewarded for it. Within moments of their arrival, the young man had come down the stairs to have private conversation with his host. Then he had commenced to order up a lavish repast, as well as another bedchamber for his best man. Then he had coolly requested the services of a justice or a vicar, he declared, whichever one could make his lovely lady legally his the faster.

They were only hours from the border, where the deed could have been done in a moment, and the young gentleman knew it. But he didn't want a havey-cavey sort of wedding day to look back upon, he explained, he wanted it done both legally beyond question and before the day was out. And as he had a special license and a full purse, the landlord hastened to make preparations to do his bidding.

Between shouting orders to his wife, and sending a messenger to the old vicar, and seeing to the cleaning of the private parlor and the best suite, the landlord had only a moment to wonder at the deficiency of his own usually sound judgment. Owning an inn high on the North Road, he had often encountered young runaway lovers, and yet this time he had not for a moment considered that possibility before the young man had spoken. It was generally an easy matter for him to spot a pair bound for elopement. But then, couples bound for a wedding over the anvil usually had a hunted look about them. The fellows were invariably anxious. The females were often fearful. Their moods varied between high excitation, punctuated by bursts of brittle laughter, and frequent awkward silences, as though they were suddenly doubting their judgment or fearful of pursuing papas. But this pair had been calm and easy, graceful and smiling.

The young gentleman, slender and beautifully dressed, tawny-haired and self-assured, had stayed belowstairs for a while and condescended to drink a prenuptial toast or two with his host as he awaited his friend and the vicar. But because of the growing storm, the roads were slow, and the vicar was, after all, too old to leave his dinner beforetimes and go plunging out of doors, all haste, into the raging evening just for the sake of a few extra shillings. So the young gentleman had time for several toasts, so many in fact, that the landlord had to silently congratulate him on his hard head when he was able to mount the stairs with a steady tread as he went to reassure his waiting bride-to-be.

But then, within the half hour, he was downstairs again, his face white and set, his soft mood vanished, his words clipped and hard as he rapped out an order for more drink, and threw down coins to pay the vicar when he arrived, both for his trouble and for services he need not now trouble to render.

As the gentleman sat and drank steadily, the landlord kept a worried eye upon him. He had paid and dismissed the incredulous vicar, as he had been bade, for the young man refused to spare even one word for the angry old fellow. And now as the hours wore on and the storm picked up fury, the host of The Partridge Feather wondered what, if anything he ought to do about the situation. He could not help but worry about the young female. She had not shown her face since she had been shown her room. She might be in need of consolation, indeed, she might even be in dire distress. But a fellow could not build up a reputation as an innkeeper to the Quality by putting a foot wrong. A maid had been sent up to the room with fresh towels and water, and had been allowed to enter, so it could be proved that at least the young woman still existed. But what else might be done, the landlord could not say. For a look at the jug-bitten young gentleman showed that a word about the young miss he had arrived with might cost a careless innkeeper his front teeth, if not his life. So the host of The Partridge Feather polished glasses and took care of his other customers and kept his tongue discreetly between his intact teeth. For his conscience's sake, he thought he would have a word about the female with this "friend" when he arrived, and he entertained himself as he waited by wondering how many more rum punches it might take to put the young man beneath the table entirely, instead of only half sprawled upon it.

It was nearing midnight when the other gentleman entered the inn. By then, the room was empty save for the young gentleman. The other customers had gone, the travelers to their rooms, the local lads to their homes. The young gentleman, his snowy cravat rumpled and askew, his embroidered waistcoat unbuttoned, his tawny "wind-swept" hairstyle as tousled as though he had been out in the storm all night, was still sitting as he had all evening, brooding and drinking. He did not even look up as the other gentleman entered. That it was the expected friend, the landlord had not a doubt. Although he was many years older than the young gentleman, his refined face and sober but exquisitely cut clothes marked him as a member of the same lofty class. He paused in the doorway for only an instant and then spied the young man before the landlord could come out from behind his station. Then he walked quickly to the young man's side.

"Am I too late?" he asked urgently.

The young man raised his head at that utterance and then both recognition and a slow, bitter smile appeared upon his face.

"Too late for the ceremony?" the young man drawled, pulling himself up straight. "Too late for the hymn to Hymen? Too late to congratulate my blushing bride? Are your pockets burdened with unshed rice, my dear Edwin? Have you hurried all this way only to miss the bedding ceremony?"

"So you have done it," the older gentleman said heavily.

"So I have," the younger man agreed, nodding repeatedly to himself and to his friend. But as the other sighed and sank to a chair, the young man added reflectively, "It's all over, dear Edwin, and you have missed the lot. I declared myself, and carried her off, and procured the special license, and engaged the vicar, and ended it all just as you would wish."

"Then there's nothing to be done but to wish you happy," the older man replied sadly. "It is not as I would wish, but perhaps the best can be made of it, perhaps I was wrong, after all. But do not let me keep you from her now. I was late due to the storm, and I would not come between you now."

"Come between us?" the younger man mused, and then let out a raucous roar of laughter that startled the innkeeper, who was listening in as quiet a manner as possible. "Why Edwin, my noble Edwin, my sweet counselor, the Edinburgh Coach could come between us now and not ruffle a hair on our heads. Don't you listen, Edwin, my dear? I said it was over. And so it is. Over. Not wedded, not bedded, not saved. Over."

"Then you thought better of it?" the older gentleman asked.

"Not thought better of it, Edwin, my friend," the young man said loudly, but in what he thought were confidential tones, since he bent close to his friend, "but *knew* better. Was forced to know better. I could not do it, Edwin," he cried out in a wild sort of anguish; "when it came to it, I could not."

"It's all for the best, Robin," the older man said softly. "You know it is."

"Ah yes, as you said," the young gentleman nodded, calm

again. "Shall we drink to it? Landlord," he called out, "another, and for my friend as well."

The landlord hesitated, but when he saw the older gentleman nod in affirmation, he reluctantly left off listening to the conversation so that he could prepare two new cups of his heady, steaming punch.

"Robin," the gentleman called Edwin asked as he drew his chair closer to his young friend, "how did the girl take it?"

"Beau-ti-fully," the young gentleman said lightly. But then he began shaking his head and frowning as though he sought to clear it, and by so doing facilitate his speech as well, for now he took care to speak slowly and carefully, enunciating each syllable. "Beautifully, magnificently, stoically, a treasure of a girl. Oh Edwin, you should like her, I'm sure. No underbred whining, not a whimper."

"I'm sure I should," the older man replied evenly. "And her family, they said nothing? They will not make difficulties?"

The young man began laughing at that, and could not seem to stop. He laughed until tears started in his eyes. He laughed on an increasingly high note, until his friend took his arm and shook him hard.

"Oh leave off," the young gentleman snarled, snatching his arm away violently, his mood veering. "I'm half sprung but I've had more, and done less. Yet there simply isn't enough rum, dear Edwin, not in all the Indies, to make me forget the look in her eyes. Or to let me forget how igno— how igno-minious—fiend take it, how completely I failed. Damme, the drink takes my tongue, but leaves me my heart. Isn't that nicely put, Edwin?" He laughed.

"The family, Robin, how did her family take it?" Edwin asked patiently.

"And how should I know?" the young man grumbled, leaning far across the table to scoop up the mug the landlord had placed cautiously just outside his reach.

When their host had retreated a respectful distance, the older gentleman waited until the younger had done taking a large swallow and whispered, "You mean to say you just announced your change of plan and left her there and walked away?"

The young man put down his mug and stared at his inquisitor with as much insolence in his gaze as his unfocused eyes could maintain. "Certainly not," he said arrogantly. "What sort of a fellow do you take me for? I have not left her suddenly. She is still here. Or was here a few hours ago. Upstairs," he added, before he drank deep again.

The older gentleman drew in his breath and half started from his chair as he gasped, "She is still here? You brought her all this way before telling her?"

The young gentleman gave him a singularly sweet, sad smile, but no reply.

"You must take her home again at once," Edwin cried.

"No," his friend replied, in a curiously sobered tone. "*You* must, Edwin, I was waiting for you. No, don't say a word. I simply cannot. I have done so much, I have done all that you said was honorable, but that I cannot do, not for her, not even for you. I took her from her doorstep this morning, while her father beamed and her mother shed happy tears and her little sisters strewed flowers, or so it seemed. How can I bring her back in the night and say, 'Oh, terribly sorry, I've changed my mind'? But you can. You must. I have done so much," he complained even as he began to nod as though his head had grown too heavy for him to continue to hold upright. "You must do the rest," he murmured as he at last put his head down upon the triangle his arms made on the tabletop.

The older gentleman stifled an oath and clenched his fists in anger. But after a moment, his shoulders slumped. "So it seems I must," he breathed, almost to himself.

The landlord readily gave the older man the direction of the young woman's room and then, upon stiffly given orders, he himself went quickly to rouse up the stableboy to prepare his new guest's coach for travel again. He rushed about his task, not only so as to please the gentleman, but so that he might not miss a moment of the unfolding drama. Yet for all his hurrying out into the wind-swept night and back again, it was still several moments more before the older gentleman came down the stairs with the young woman. She wore a dark traveling cloak, and went out into the night without a backward glance at the young man now seemingly asleep, his head cradled upon his arms upon the broad-planked table.

But within a few moments, while the landlord was still staring at the closed door he had exited from, the older gentleman returned, his driving cape streaming rain.

"Robin," he said sternly, "only one thing. Wake up, Robin, there is only one thing I must know. What did you tell her? How did you tell her?"

The young gentleman opened his eyes, but did not lift his head. His voice came soft but clear.

"Why, the truth, Edwin. The truth, of course."

As the older man stiffened, the younger said, as though repeating a thing he had learned by heart for a stern schoolmaster, "I told her that I could not wed her. I told her it was because there was another whom I loved, but whom I could not wed due to cruel circumstance. I told her that it was not fair for me to wed her with half a heart. I told her the truth, did I not, Edwin?"

"Yes, Robin," the older man sighed. "I will take her home now. You stay on here and I shall come for you tomorrow evening, as soon as I may. And then we will leave. Do you understand?"

The young man raised one hand and then let it fall to the table. Edwin walked a few paces to the door and then wheeled around again. "Her family, Robin. Shall there be serious trouble?"

"I am not that sort of coward," the young gentleman said wearily. "No. What sort of trouble could there be? Papa and Mama are decidedly commoners. No, no trouble from that quarter."

"And as to what will become of the girl?" Edwin persisted.

"What do you think?" came the reply, with a curious note of bitter laughter. "She's no debutante. Do you think she'll be ruined? Refused admission to Almacks? Come, come, Edwin my dear, she'll be married before the year is out. They are not so top-lofty in the provinces, you know. This affair may even lend her a certain cachet."

"And your family?" Edwin asked quietly.

"Ah, my family," came the reply in a muffled voice. "I shall tell them only what they wish to hear." As I have told you, the young gentleman thought before he lay his head upon his arms again, and this time found the oblivion he had sought all evening.

His last customer lay still, slumped across his table, as the landlord heard the coach clatter away into the night. But long moments passed before he crossed the room to help his young patron to his feet and to his bed. For he stood and looked out toward the door for a very long while as though still seeing that white and dazed face as he had last seen it. He remembered the alabaster features, the bright, light tendrils of hair escaping from her hood, no lighter in hue than the carven cheeks, the wide eyes blind with shock as she had walked to the door. So he would remember her always, whenever sorrow touched his own life, and her face would come to him unbidden, as his personal symbol of living grief.

2 The sun had burned off the early morning mists and now the spring day had grown so slumberous and warm that the young woman had to interrupt her walk to take off her light shawl. But as she put her package down to do so and paused to lean against a wooden rail fence, she admitted that she was glad of an excuse to linger. It was true that she had been given a half day off to complete her errands. It was further true that her employer was so lenient, especially these days, that she could have delayed her return for hours and not heard a word of censure upon her return. But her conscience had always been her stern master and so she had not dawdled for a moment this morning.

She had posted her letters promptly once she had arrived in town. She had purchased her odds and ends without lingering, she had not even loitered to gossip with Mrs. Ames at the sundries store, and that good woman's expression had clearly shown that she would have been delighted for a chance for a good chat-up. No, she had been swift and sure in all her transactions, for she had known that she needn't have wasted time walking to town, she could have easily requested and gotten the use of the rig. But she had wanted a chance to stroll alone through the bright morning, she had needed the opportunity to say her own silent farewell to this countryside, and if she had taken extra time from her employer's purse for one extravagance, she could not, in all conscience, have taken more moments for others.

Now she leaned against the worn fence rail and looked out upon a sea of yellow fields and breathed deep the fragrance of the blossoms and thought: this, this she would miss as much as any other thing about the home she was about to leave forever. Her employer thought it a foolishness, and the local people hid their smiles at her preference. For hadn't they roses here in the North? And wasn't the hard-won spring this year filled with laburnum, lilac, and daffodil? And if a person fancied wild flowers, why poets had always sung the merits of the gillyflowers and marsh cups and violets. But mustard fields? One might as well admire a turnip over a tulip. Mrs. Bryce's governess-companion might be a very nice sort of young female, but what sort of person could prefer a working field in spring to a carefully tended garden?

Mrs. Bryce's governess-companion could, and did. She stood at the fence rail and saw the radiant yellow of the fields shouting back at the sunlight and thought that she had never seen such beauty. Most of the susceptible gentlemen in the district would have disagreed if they had seen her there, for the light hues of her hair made the mustard blossoms seem garish by comparison. Miss Hastings' tresses were, the smithy vowed, the color of the palest ale, and he knew no finer compliment, while Mr. Fisher, grocer and secret poet, thought that they more nearly resembled moonlight upon gold.

But her hair alone would not cause such rhapsodizing from those usually taciturn fellows. No, it was Miss Hastings in her entirety that did. Everything about her enticed her admirers—the contrast between her light, almost ice-blue eyes with their darker lashes and brows set beneath her high clear white brow, her straight little nose, her plump and generous pink mouth, her slender but surprisingly generous form, her grace, her modulated voice. Indeed, Mrs. Ames for all her kindness, often complained that a person could become ill listening to the local lads discussing Miss Hastings' charms.

Still, for all their admiration, the fellows never discussed the subject with Miss Hastings herself. For she was, after all, a lady. Well, not actually a lady, they had to admit, for she had no title or high birth, and was really only a paid governess-companion. But there was that in her voice and her attitude which placed her above them. She was pleasant to a neighbor and friendly to a fellow, but there was a distance she maintained, a coolness no sane male could ignore if ever a conversation became too personal. They could no more pay court to such a composed young woman than they could stand and gaze in rapture for half the morning at a field of mustard flowers as she was doing now.

But Miss Hastings was not merely appreciating the scenery, she was instead trying to imprint it all on her memory so that she could then take it with her wherever she might chance to go from here. She would leave soon, she knew. However much she might not wish to depart, the letter had been posted and the deed had been set in motion. It had been a pleasant situation, working for such an undemanding mistress in such a beautiful locale. But for the embarrassing attentions of a certain very young fellow, she might have been very glad to stay at it until she had reached an age for retirement. She might have been very angry at the lad, just as she had been at others of his sex who had caused her to lose other positions, but she could not even harbor a grudge against him. For she loved him. And, she thought, he could hardly have known better, for after all, he had only been in existence upon the planet for a scant sixteen months.

Six months previously, when Miss Julia Hastings had taken up her position, young Toby had spent most of his days in his cot, in his room with Nurse. Because of that, even though the woman at the employment bureau had described her duties in her new position rather nebulously as: ". . . a sort of companion to poor lonely young Mrs. Bryce, now that her husband's fulfilling his commission at sea. In time you might work with her infant son as governess as well," Julia had not paid too much attention to Toby.

In any event, Mrs. Bryce had taken up her time completely then. She was a pretty, silly little young woman, a new wife, bored and lonely in the great house her seafaring husband had taken her to after their wedding. She had seized upon Julia's company like a drowning man onto a drifting timber.

For months she had delighted in prattling to her new companion, detailing her humdrum past as though it were the stuff of epic saga. In fact, Julia came to hear the tale of her employer's greatest triumph so often that at times she felt almost as if she herself had been at the great ball where the dashing Captain Bryce had first been smitten by his lady.

But there was nothing to dislike in her new employer, and a great deal to be thankful for. As the lady's husband was a gallant captain in His Majesty's Royal Navy and as the family was well-to-do, the Bryces lived graciously. But also, since they were only well-connected and not of the nobility, they did not attempt to live in great state. Julia remembered only too clearly how uncomfortable she had been during her very brief stay as companion to Lady Wycliffe's daughter in London. That great lady's airs and graces had been, however correct, eventually quite tiresome. Julia had been almost glad when Lord Wycliffe had made certain advances toward her, for then she had an excuse to leave that noble household and could do so without a backward look.

Best of all, being so wrapped in herself, Mrs. Bryce never listened too closely to anyone else's conversation. Pleased with having been answered promptly each time she spoke, she seldom remembered that her companion never gave specific answers to her endless questions. She knew that Miss Hastings had been disappointed in love, and found that rather thrilling and romantic, where a more thoughtful and thorough gossip might not be content with only that crumb of information. But though she was thoughtless, she was never unkind. Julia had a pleasant room, she dined with her mistress, and she had a great deal of personal freedom, since her employer rose late and napped immediately after every meal.

It was because of that unoccupied time that Julia had come to know Master Toby so well. As soon as he had overcome the drunken seaman's walk of a toddler, he had begun to run wild. Julia reasoned that he must take after his absent father whom she had never met, for as he grew older he exhibited a strong free spirit that quite exhausted his old nurse and startled his mama. Mrs. Bryce had evidently always pictured herself the mother of an infant who would sit placidly at her side, complementing her gown with all the decorative advantage of a lap dog, and was at a loss for what to do with the restless, pugnacious little man-child she had begotten.

So just as she had given her babe immediately to a wet-nurse's breast and from thence quickly handed him to Nurse, she was now delighted to assign him to her youthful companion, who would hopefully tire him out so completely that he might rest easy upon her lap for the hour a day allotted him. She did not begrudge him her companion's time, for in truth, after four months she could find little new to relate to Miss Hastings, and was glad to find some useful occupation for the young woman she was paying so handsomely.

Her new duties suited Julia, for she found Master Toby far more lively and intelligent a companion than his mama. And his merry ways eased some of her homesickness for her own younger brothers and sisters. It might have gone on thus, a peaceful existence for Julia: long days interspersed with the laughter of a child, long evenings sitting listening to her employer reminisce, with occasional treats such as conversing with the villagers and assisting when the neighbor ladies came to tea. But young Master Toby had inherited his father's eye for a comely young woman, as well as his venturesome spirit.

The die had been cast the day Master Toby had struggled out of his mama's arms to seek Julia's embrace. The afternoon he had fallen in the morning room and pushed his mama away to run to her companion for solace had complicated the situation. But the day, only a week past, that he had spoken his first word had settled the matter. He could not have been expected to say "Papa," so much as his mother might have wished to include that charming anecdote in a letter to her dearest husband, as he had not set eyes upon that gentleman since he had been able to sit up unaided. But he should *not* have uttered a clear, distinct "Jool-Ee-Ahh" either, when he was expected to cry "Ma-Ma," like any other decent child. Definitely he ought not to have done so in the presence of the immediate social world, as personified by Mrs. Carew, Mrs. Templeton, and that social arbitor, Miss Mundford, the schoolmaster's sister, when they were come for tea.

"Does the lad say nothing else?" Miss Mundford had finally tittered as Toby, enthralled with his new talent, had gone on and on, chanting "Jool-Ee-Ahh" loudly and happily to the assembled company.

That very evening after her son had uttered his disastrous first word, Mrs. Bryce began to display a marked aversion to her companion. Instead of sitting before the fire with Julia, merrily dissecting the appearance, intelligence, and condition of each of her visitors of that afternoon as she usually would have done, Mrs. Bryce only stitched a bit and said nothing. Occasionally, however, she would dart little glances at her companion as though she had never seen her before and wished to have a look at her without seeming to do so. It was not long before she complained, in a very artificial manner, that the smoke from the fire disturbed her eyes and so she was off to bed. The morning did not bring her to the breakfast table and the afternoon found her so engrossed in her luncheon that she had not a word to spare. When Toby was brought down for his afternoon visit, and when he endured Mama's hug and then quickly threw himself upon his favorite and sat in her lap and tried to undo her bound-up hair so that he might run his pudgy fingers through it, the look upon Mrs. Bryce's face chilled Julia. It was that evening that she made her suggestion.

She tentatively offered to leave Mrs. Bryce's employ. And was shocked when her offer was swiftly accepted.

But it was inevitable from the moment that young Toby had made known his preference. Mrs. Bryce was, like many other self-centered persons, a very vain creature. Although she had seen Julia only as a charming companion in the past, now, suddenly, she saw her as a cunning rival. It might well have occurred in any case. If her husband had returned from the sea and chanced to pass a pleasant word with Miss Hastings, the same jealousy would have resulted. For whether the object of her affections were two and thirty years of age, or six and ten months of age, Mrs. Bryce would brook no competition.

Still, another young woman might have waited upon events, giving Mrs. Bryce time to think her feelings through, giving young Toby time to learn another, less threatening word. But Julia feared rejection as she feared nothing else in the world, and sensing rejection, she had to be the one to cut the ties first.

She spoke some confused faradiddle about her homesickness. Because she was so sick at heart, she was not the cool, composed young woman she usually was. She mentioned her difficulty in adjusting to the rural life, she murmured some foolish things about her dual duties tiring her, she even, in her extremity of embarrassment, invented the difficulty a young woman such as herself had in meeting and attaching any eligible gentlemen in her present situation. It was all so unlike her, so badly done, that her employer should have been able to see through it in a moment, and perhaps Julia wished that she would. For with all her resolve, Miss Hastings was only a very young woman still, and at twenty years of age she might be forgiven for making a noble gesture ineptly in the secret hopes that it would be seen as such and refused. But when she spoke the words, ". . . new position . . . ," the look of relief and gratification upon her employer's face confirmed her deepest fears. Then Julia had no choice but to make suggestion into concrete reality.

Of course, once the decision she most desired had been made without her interference, Mrs. Bryce felt the pangs of guilt. Perhaps she reviewed Miss Hastings' speech in her own mind later, when the immediate pleasure of it had faded. Perhaps she remembered that Julia had never seemed to be interested in any eligible male in the vicinity and had even refused to consider any invitations to possible future meetings with likely junior officers of the fleet on that happy day when Captain Bryce returned at last. Perhaps she wondered at why a girl who had seemed so content and pleased at her lot in life should suddenly be struck with the blue megrims and want to leave instantly. Or perhaps, just perhaps, there was some hope for Mrs. Bryce, and she understood just why the offer had been made and was ashamed of her own easily-read emotions.

Whatever the cause, Mrs. Bryce seemed determined to kill Julia with kindness now that she was seeking a new position. Her letter of reference was so effusive that Julia feared no one in his right mind would believe it, or if he did, would wish to hire on such a paragon of virtue who, if the letter were to be believed, belonged on an altar rather than in a paying position. Since the morning that Julia had sent her request for a new situation to the redoubtable Misses Parkinson, Employment Counselors of London, Mrs. Bryce had been showering her with little gifts to take with her when she left: trinkets and handkerchiefs, a garnet brooch, a jet pendant, floral paperweights, and enameled thimbles, all, as she said, "to remember us by." The small pile of guilt offerings grew on her nightstand by the day, and she heartily wished she could go before she had to pack an extra bag just to contain them. And then, in a blinding reversal, as if it were felt that last days would not matter, or as if her employer were punishing herself, Toby had been thrust into Julia's care so often that she had no time for herself at all and fell into bed each night feeling wearied unto death.

This morning, she had requested some time off from her duties to go to the village to see if any replies to her letters had come for her. She did not really believe the Misses Parkinson could have sent a reply so swiftly, or that she could not have waited for the post to be delivered if they had, but she had needed a space to be alone. Now, with the sun increasing in strength, promising summer and stealing away resolve as that vagabond season always did, Julia left off gazing at the sea of yellow before her. For she *had* gotten some letters she wanted to read before she returned to the house. And in truth, she could stare at the scenery forever and it would not be long enough, yet it was quite enough as well, since the first look had enshrined it in her mind's eye forever.

She found a stile a few paces along the fence and swung the steps out and settled herself as comfortably as if she were a goosegirl. Then she withdrew the letters from her package and sank back with them in hand. The reading of her post was something of a ritual for Julia. She deemed it one of her great luxuries, for it was a thing for her eyes alone, and it was indeed the whole of her private life. One of the letters, she decided, just might be from the employment bureau after all, since it was on such fine paper, but the other, smudged and slightly disreputable, was the more important since she could see at a glance that it was from her sister's hand. Feeling that she had prolonged her pleasure long enough, Julia opened the missive and, sighing happily, sat on the stile in the sunlight to read her letter.

Clarice was the one who had appointed herself family scribe, but since, at thirteen, her hand left much to be desired, Julia smiled as she bent herself to the task of deciphering her message. Soon she was far from radiant fields and back at home in her thoughts. Betty had gotten a new frock, Dorothea fancied Raymond Pibbs these days, though Dominic Ellis was still dropping by each day languishing for her, the schoolmaster said that William was doing excellently, and the splint had come off Harry's arm. Papa was working hard now that the spring sowing was begun, and Mama thought Raymond Pibbs was unsteady. And there, at the bottom of the letter, as though

Clarice had only just remembered it, was the mention that, oh yes, Harriet was increasing again.

Julia laid down the letter and stared off into the distance. Her sister increasing again! And she was only a year older then Julia. Soon she would have two nieces or a niece and a nephew. And while Harriet's house would ring with the sounds of children, she herself could only hope to procure a new post tending to someone else's children. But Miss Hastings had not gotten through the last three years by allowing herself to indulge in self-pity. She quickly banished traitorous thoughts and forced herself to be happy for her sister. But she did fold the letter away quickly, and some of the sun did seem to be gone from the day.

Thus it was that she opened her other letter absently, and had read three lines before she knew what it was that she was reading. There the words were again: ". . . Something to your advantage . . ." ". . . particularly lucrative proposition . . ." ". . . My nephew Robin, having failed in his importuning . . ." Julia read no further. She crumpled the letter tightly in her fist. What madness was this? she thought again, as she had thought each time she had received and destroyed these insane correspondences. Do they refuse to clap madmen in Bedlam if they are titled? Does the nobility not step in when an old family member loses his senses? Why has the fellow fastened upon me to plague in his dotage? she wondered.

Again, she thought momentarily of writing to some senior member of that accursed family to complain of how she was being persecuted. And again, she vanquished the thought. She would have nothing to do with them, for any reason. And in truth, writing bizarre letters could not be construed as truly menacing behavior. They would shrug it off. They could not know that mere letters could call up so much that she had worked so hard to put behind her. No one, she knew, could understand how those simple letters upon blameless paper could have the power to so completely distress her, to so easily pitchfork her back in time to the worst time of her life. A time that had in a matter of hours changed the course of her entire future, ensuring that she could never live the life of a normal female. Even Papa, whom she knew could not forget it, and blamed himself for his part in it so continually that he still dreamed on it in nightmares that woke his wife in the deepest night, could not know the whole of it.

She was so lost in her appalled thoughts that she did not hear the farm cart rattling down the road, and half the district laughed that a deaf man could hear Joseph Pringle's cart trundling along.

"Eee, missy," that ancient chortled as he came abreast of the ashen-faced girl and stopped his horse, "have you gotten a letter from a ghost?"

"Why yes, Joseph," Julia replied calmly, knotting the letter in her hand. "As a matter of fact, I have."

So of course, Old Joseph had to regale his lovely passenger all the miles back to her destination with tales of ghosts in the district. She had taken him up on his invitation to a drive home because she had been so troubled with her own company. The fact that Ruby, his ancient horse, walked even more slowly than she could was an extra bonus, for thus she could be seen to be hastening back but could still enjoy the bright day longer without even a twinge of conscience to plague her.

"Aye," Joseph continued regretfully, after a particularly convoluted tale, which Julia had difficulty following, that had to do with a spirit who seemingly, so far as she could make out, disliked wash days, "there's never been a hint of a haunt at Three Elms, so you'd likely never think on 'em, living there. But if you was to stop at the Manse, where the Mundfords dwell," he said, brightening, "you'd be up to your pretty chin in 'em. Oh," he said wisely, "not that *she'd* be like to tell you the tale over tea, not she, for she thinks 'em disgraceful, like they had to do with bad housekeeping, like mice or beetles. But there they do bide, mark me well."

Old Joseph rattled off his tales of dire midnight doings as Ruby plodded down the drive to Mrs. Bryce's house, thinking contentedly that he was entertaining the pretty lass handsomely from the way she sat silent and big-eyed, attending to him. But he could not know that it was not his ghosties and haunts that she was frightened of. Rather, she was aghast at the sudden realization of her own unwillingness to part from newly familiar friends such as himself to go to an unknown future more terrifying in its emptiness than any of the specters that capered through the Mundfords' house.

When Ruby slowed as she came to the base of the drive, Old

Joseph left off his story to comment with surprise, "Seems like you got company, missy. Could it be the cap'n's back?" There was a certain amount of chagrin in his tone, for he liked to be the first to know the local gossip. But then, when he dropped the reins and lowered himself to the ground to help the young lady down from her high seat, he stood and looked closely at the equipage and horses being held by an unknown boy. "Nay," he grunted, "I lie. For cap'n's a seafaring dog, with never such an eye to cattle. Them's spanking brutes, bang up to the mark."

Glancing at the high phaeton and the two gleaming black horses as she straightened her skirts, Julia had to agree with Old Joseph's outsize admiration. The pair of animals seemed to be of a completely different species than poor Ruby, standing head-down and patient.

"They do shine in the sun," she commented.

"Pah, shine," Old Joseph said, shaking his head at a female's foolishness, "the shine's in the brushing. Ruby'd shine too if I was daft enough to curry her half my life. No, those two could be covered in muck and still they'd be thoroughbreds. It's in the bone, missy, it's bred in the bone. You can see it in the eyes, in the points. It's spirit and intelligence and line, missy."

As it is with you, missy, Old Joseph thought as he touched his battered hat when Julia thanked him kindly for the ride before she disappeared into the house. Born and bred it is with you, too, whether you work for your bread or no. And then, casting one more admiring glance at the equipage, he clucked to Ruby. But in a tribute that would have warmed Miss Hastings' heart had she known it, Old Joseph, though he had left his seventieth year behind in the winter, gave no further thought to the fine, glistening black horseflesh he had seen in the drive, but rather let his thoughts linger instead on a mane of heavy gleaming gold hair as he drove away.

Julia was consumed with curiosity as to who would call upon her mistress in such fine state, but she would not allow herself to sink so low as to question Mr. Duncan, the butler, as to the visitor's identity. For, she thought as she mounted the stair to her room, it was enough that she had to work for her livelihood in others' homes. If she began to try to live through their lives as well, she would be lost. But she had gotten only so far as the first landing when she heard her own name being called.

"Oh Julia, my dear," Mrs. Bryce called from the bottom of the stairs. "Do come down, you have a visitor."

Julia paused so long upon the stair, frozen in disbelief, that Mrs. Bryce became impatient. If her companion had compunctions about prying into others' lives, she did not. Her little nose fairly twitched in excitement, there were high spots of color in her round cheeks, and her tight black ringlets shook, perceptibly, like little sausages hung before a butcher's shop quivering in a gust of wind.

"Do come down, Miss Hastings," she ordered in the voice of an employer.

When Julia had obediently, but dazedly descended, Mrs. Bryce clutched her companion's wrist in her hand.

"My dear, " she said in a low voice, "what a lucky chance for you! I have been waiting for your return for hours. Oh," she said quickly, "in the ordinary sense I would not have cared how long you tarried on your errands, but when the gentleman came, I could not wait for you to return. I stayed him with tea, for I didn't want him to change his mind and leave, though he said he was stopping at The White Hart, which is not far from here at all, you know, and that he would come back later. But I wouldn't have that," Mrs. Bryce said, shaking her head so vigorously that her ringlets swung like carillon chimes at noon. "For who's to say that he wouldn't change his mind? He said he had your direction from the Misses Parkinson in London."

Mrs. Bryce whispered as she drew Julia to the door to the salon, "And he said he had a position to offer you. So I could not let him go, though he's had to have his horses walked twice as he was waiting. No," she went on, as Julia paused and tried to fathom it all, "you don't even need to change your frock, you look charmingly today. But here," she said, steering Julia to a hall mirror, "only tuck some of your loose hair back, and you will do."

Julia smoothed back the strands of hair that had escaped from their moorings. Ordinarily, she would have bound it back into a smooth bundle as befitted a proper aspirant for a position as governess or companion. But here in the countryside, though the easy life-style did not delude her into forgetting her position enough to venture to wear her tresses *à la mode*, she had been lulled by it enough to fall into the habit of merely gathering her heavy hair up in back and letting it fall from a high knot.

She stared at her reflection as Mrs. Bryce hovered at her elbow. Her deep blue walking frock was simple and neat enough and she had automatically put on her beige shawl as she always did in company, despite the warmth of the day, when Old Joseph had come along. There was nothing extraordinary in her appearance, but she looked amazed into her own amazed eyes. To be offered a new position just when she most required one, was felicity indeed. At last able to absorb the good news, for these days it always took her a space to react to surprises, she smiled at Mrs. Bryce.

"Ready, ma'am," she said.

"Now I'll let you go in by yourself, Julia dear," Mrs. Bryce said, "for he did say he wished to speak with you privately . . ." Here she hesitated, for though she knew very well that it was quite unexceptional for Julia to be closeted with a strange man in her house, since for all her gentility she was really only a variety of servant, still if a young and lovely female such as her companion were anything but an employee it would have been reprehensible to allow such a meeting. But then, she reminded herself, servants did not have reputations to worry about. At least, not like proper young females did. And then, feeling guilty about how very defenseless her lovely young companion actually was and extremely guilty about Julia's having to seek a position at all, she attempted to absolve herself by saying happily, "At any rate, there is nothing to worry about, he is more than respectable. He is very high ton, actually. You ought to be honored. It was quite pleasant chatting with him until your return. He is no less than a baron."

Julia paused at the closed door to the parlor as her employer went on, "Lord Nicholas Daventry, Baron Stafford, to be precise. I should think he had a marvelous position for you, but he won't disclose—why Julia, whatever is it?"

Mrs. Bryce looked at her companion with alarm. For the young woman's milk-white skin had achieved an impossible hue, becoming so leached of color that it appeared to be transparent. Miss Hastings held on to the doorframe, her eyes wide and filled with horror.

"Julia," cried Mrs. Bryce, growing quite faint herself at the transformation that had come over the usually serene Miss Hastings. "Whatever has come over you?"

"I cannot see him," Julia said frantically, backing away from the door. "Send him away. I shall not see him."

"But why ever not?" Mrs. Bryce demanded, her pique at having this splendid solution to her problems with her companion solved and then ruined in a trice now overriding her concern for the overset young woman.

The door to the salon swung open.

"Yes, Miss Hastings," the gentleman's voice said coldly, "why ever not?"

3 It was not at all well done, not at all socially adroit. The gentleman stood at the doorway to the salon and stared intently at the shaken young woman. She, in turn, gaped back in frank astonishment at him. In the common way, Julia was to think later, it was most irregular for any female of breeding to subject a visitor to such naked, unrelenting observation. But then again, it was not at all correct for the gentleman to stand and gaze at her in such obvious, stark, unblinking appraisal either. She did not know or care to know the reason why he studied her with a growing sneer upon his lips, she only shook her head as she looked at him, wondering whether to disbelieve her eyes or her ears. For surely, one of her senses had betrayed her.

The gentleman Mrs. Bryce had said was Lord Nicholas Daventry, Baron Stafford, could not be the gentleman of that name who had composed and sent all those insane letters, one of which lay crumpled and twisted in her pocket at this very moment. This gentleman looked as though he had never committed an unconsidered or rash deed in his life. Everything about him was meticulous and correct. His clothes, from his tightly fitting blue jacket to the highly polished half boots which covered his buff-kerseymere-clad legs, fitted his trim, athletic

30

form to an inch. His neckcloth, arranged in a perfect waterfall, was dazzling white, and his linen was no less well cared for than the white hand which held the quizzing glass he observed her through. His hair was dark and curling, his skin clear and of a flawless matte texture that any young woman would weep for. The watchful eyes were gray-green and well opened, ringed round with thick dark lashes. But even with these graces there was little else that was effeminate about the haughty face with its well-carved features: the thin aristocratic nose, the strong chin, and the high sculpted cheekline.

Whatever else this unknown gentleman was, Julia thought, with an admixture of relief and embarrassment at her reaction to his name, he could not be her unwanted correspondent, for he could not be above thirty years of age and he radiated health and fitness. But as she continued to stare at him, as if to reassure herself of the accuracy of her perceptions, the mobile lips opened to speak.

"Now that you have assured yourself of your ability to recognize me should we meet again, Miss Hastings, do you think you might be able to explain why you cannot have converse with me?" he asked in a chill voice.

Julia flushed, both in chagrin at her own actions and in anger at his less than gallant reminder of them.

"I apologize, my lord," she said stiffly. "Obviously, I mistook you for another."

He made no reply save for sketching a brief, ironic bow as Mrs. Bryce, sensing that the potential storm had blown over, rushed to say with evident relief,

"You see Julia? Just as I said. The baron is here to speak with you about a new position. I shall leave you now, my lord," she simpered, "and hope for a happy resolution to your conversation."

As Mrs. Bryce left the room, with an arch look given along with her curtsy to the baron, Julia experienced a moment of rebellious rage which she had to tamp down. For she had not been introduced to the gentleman, neither did it seem that he expected her to be. Rather she had been brought in for his inspection as though she were livestock he were thinking of purchasing. But her talents were there to be purchased, in a manner of speaking, she thought sadly. And she was only a servant, and she ought to be used to it, she reminded herself quickly, so she collected herself and stood,

her eyes downcast, waiting for his next utterance. When it came,
it did nothing to restore her spirits.

"Who did you think I was?" he asked abruptly.

Taken by surprise, Julia spoke up more rapidly than she
might have wished.

"A gentleman with a very similar sounding name has been
writing to me," she began, "offering me bizarre propositions . . ." But then, realizing that the receipt of such letters
might imply that she had sought such correspondence in some
way, she added quickly, "Indeed, I do not know why, he is an
old fellow, wandering in his wits, and I can only assume that he
has seized on me as his victim due to some aberration that age
has wrought in him. I had thought to bring the matter to the attention of the authorities, but so far I have taken no steps as I
have hoped the matter would end of itself. Pray disregard it,
my lord. I'm sorry that such a distastful subject came up at all,
but that is why your name so unsettled me. My employer says
that you have gotten my direction from the Misses Parkinson
and have a post to offer me?" she continued, blaming her original misapprehension upon her employer's bad diction and attempting to get the conversation back to a more normal level to
discover what had brought him to Mrs. Bryce's home.

He stared hard at her and then said smoothly, "I do indeed
have a post to offer you and had you bothered to read my letters
instead of dismissing them as 'bizarre propositions,' you would
have known it before this. As it is, I got your direction from the
Parkinson sisters, yes, but only after I had first gotten their direction from the Bow Street runner I had employed. You've
been a difficult young woman to locate, Miss Hastings.

"Sit down." Julia heard the baron command, as her
thoughts were scattered by his words. She did take a seat, for it
seemed that she suddenly required one, but even as she did she
found that overriding all the confusion in her mind was the ir-
relevant thought that he might have asked her to sit politely
rather than insisting so rudely. But he spoke of Bow Street run-
ners as though she were a common criminal, and he claimed
authorship of the letters in the same harsh voice. She fumbled
into her skirt's pocket and with trembling fingers withdrew the
missive she had received that morning.

"You wrote this?" she asked in bewilderment, as though
that were the hardest fact to fathom of all.

He looked at the rumpled paper. "Yes," he replied in a hard voice, "and so I can see why I had to travel all this way to meet with you. Really, Miss Hastings, I was prepared to be quite generous. This race you have run me does not up my price at all."

Julia did not even bother to take in his words, as she was still thinking on what he had first said. Her only reply was to murmur in wonderment, "Bow Street!"

"Why yes," the baron said bitterly, as though the subject was as distasteful to him as it was to her. "It was necessary to obtain their services. You cover your tracks well, my dear, and have moved about frequently, and your family was singularly unhelpful in providing a clue as to your whereabouts."

Of course, Julia thought, catching onto that one warm thought in this cold interview as though it would thaw the chill of fear that had gripped her and restore her clear thinking. Of course, Papa would have nothing to do with anyone from that wretched family. So, "Of course," she said, raising her head to look the gentleman in the eye, "for they know I would want nothing to remind me of that episode in my life. Really, my lord," she said with more spirit, as if the very mention of her family itself had called them all back to her in truth and that they stood ranged beside her now to shore her confidence, "I cannot understand why you are come here. Nor can I understand the necessity for the letters. Three years have passed. For me, it is as though a lifetime has passed. What profit is there in raking up the past? I admit, I was going to marry your cousin. But I did not. There's an end to it. Why should you bother to seek me out now?"

"My nephew," the baron corrected her absently, as he turned to look out the long windows.

"Your nephew?" Julia asked in bewilderment. "But Robin always spoke of his uncle as 'Old Nick.' He always spoke of him as his mentor, that is why I thought you—"

"Addled and confused with the weight of my years?" the baron supplied, leaving off gazing out the window to look hard at her. "I am four years Robin's senior, Miss Hastings, but I am, nonetheless, his uncle. And, I assure you, in full command of my senses. It is Robin that has left off his," he added angrily in an undervoice.

As Julia only gazed at him with incomprehension, he went on in annoyance, "Come, Miss Hastings, I have not traveled all this way to entertain you with our family history, which I am convinced you know as well as I do myself. It is Robin that I speak of. Three years ago, I will freely admit, I opposed the match. Events have transpired that have caused me to change my mind. You have won. Oh, I do not say that I will be delighted to see you wed my nephew. I'm sure you know better than that. Let us have the truth with no wrappings on it. Say rather that I will contrive to accept the union. In short, Miss Hastings, I am prepared to remove all obstacles.''

Julia only gazed at him as though he were demented, so he went on angrily, ''As I said in the letters you were so contemptuous of, I will pay the piper. Not only will I countenance the union, I will pay you a sum to ensure that you accompany me to Robin's side. But be aware, Miss Hastings, that if you seek to continue your way of life after the wedding, or disappoint Robin in any fashion, it will not go easy for you. I am still Robin's 'mentor,' as you say, and I have some social power. So, I tell you now, as I did not, for obvious reasons, in the letters, if you should decide against the marriage, I will make that decision worth your while. There is no way you can lose in this, my dear,'' he added when he saw that she did not speak.

''What are you talking about?'' Julia cried.

The baron made a sound of annoyance, then walked to her and raised her chin in one cool hand so that she had to look directly into his now narrowed eyes.

''I leave for the Continent in a week. Accompany me and you shall have . . .'' and then he named a sum so large that Julia gasped, despite herself. With a smile of grim satisfaction, he went on, ''Marry Robin and you will, of course, have the run of his purse. But husbands are notoriously unreasonable creatures, and there is no guarantee that he will not grow economical with the years. And you are not inexpensive, I'll wager. Refuse to marry him, once and for all, and you may find that decision even more lucrative. But we do not have to cross that particular bridge as yet. We shall have time to talk about it on our journeys, never fear.''

Noting her absolute stillness and still looking steadily into her eyes as he held her chin fast, he went on gruffly, ''You needn't fear for your safety, if that's what's troubling you. I won't pitchfork you into a nest of Frenchies. We shall circumvent them entirely. We go by sea to Greece. There's no danger,'' he insisted, as he waited for response to flicker in her wide eyes, ''but only profit in it for you.''

Julia struck his hand away, and rose to her feet. She found herself shaking, her rage was so complete and so completely contained.

"You may not be addled with age, but you are certainly mad," she said wildly. "I do not want to marry Robin. Nor does he wish to marry me. I have not laid eyes upon him for three years, nor do I wish to ever see him again. I do not know what maggot you have gotten into your head, but I am nothing to your nephew. I haven't heard from him, or seen, spoken, or thought of him for three years," she cried, knowing that this last, however, was untrue.

For she could not count the times she had thought of him. Once, each time she had to apply for a new post, twice, each time a gentleman looked at her and she remembered that terrible night and reminded herself that she would be no fit wife for any man, and a dozen times at least, each night she lay awake and thought of the bleak future she had bought for herself in that reckless past.

The anger left the baron's face, and he only gazed at her with resigned and weary patience.

"Oh yes," he said with an undercurrent of disgust evident in his low voice, "and all those letters he wrote to you were writ on the wind, were they? And all those tantalizing replies you sent to him were figments of his imagination? Come, Miss Hastings, have done with it. You have exacted your revenge. I am come to you, if not precisely on bended knee, then at least with full pockets. You can ask no more. Indeed, I will give no more. Are you coming with me then?"

She shook her head in the negative, as much to attempt to clear it as to deny him.

"It is no use," he said angrily. "I don't know what game you play, but I do know all. I put it to you bluntly then," he said on an exasperated sigh, though Julia could not see how much more bluntly a gentleman could speak.

"Look you, Miss Hastings," he said, facing her directly and speaking as though he were containing himself with much effort. "You cried off that once, the very night of your wedding, fearing, and rightly so, that Robin's family would come down upon you if you wedded him. He left for the Continent to recover from the incident. But he did not. God knows why he did not," the baron said, scowling, "but he did not. He wrote you to that effect. You ignored him. His letters grew more and more plaintive, and then you began to encourage him. For months you led him on, only then to announce that it was quite impossible to ever reunite with him, as you were already wed. A master stroke, Miss Hastings. A neat revenge. A creative and most superior lie. I congratulate you, indeed, perhaps I even understand you. He was, as you intended, utterly crushed. In time, perhaps, he could recover from even that. But now, you see, he has not the time to spare.

"His father lies dying, Miss Hastings," the baron said roughly, "and though there was never any feeling between them, Robin must return to his home. He cannot go on denying his heritage, solacing his wounds with excess upon the Continent. No one of the family can persuade him to return. Not even I. But you can, and you must. Even if you were indeed wed, with three babes at your knee, I would insist upon it."

Julia hugged her arms around each other in front of her. She was badly frightened. Although the baron was young and vital, spoke coherently, dressed perfectly, and seemed sane, it was becoming apparent to her that she was alone in a room with a lunatic. Mrs. Bryce might not be far off, she might even be eavesdropping upon this weird conversation. The butler certainly would be within shouting distance. But Julia feared that if she were to call out for assistance, the baron might become uncontrolled or destructive. She tried to remember all the advice she had read about such cases, and remembered only that she must try to remain calm so as not to excite him the more, and that she must not call him insane or risk sending him off into a rage.

She drew in a deep breath and then said softly, reasonably, as she backed slowly to the door, "No, my lord. I'm so very sorry, my lord, but I cannot. Indeed, I think you have the wrong opinion of me."

He showed strong, even, white teeth as he threw back his head to laugh harshly and she winced, despite her resolve to be collected.

"Now how could I have gotten that opinion?" he asked, halting her backward movement by staring pointedly at her and her proximity to the door, his eyes alert and amused. "Could it be from the interviews my agent obtained? You passed seven months with the wealthy Mrs. Pomfret in Leeds, and then you were summarily dismissed because of the attentions you received from her eldest, a seventeen-year-old lad. Six months with the Honorable Miss Carstairs as companion, dismissed abruptly when Miss Carstairs noted the unseemly approval with which her noble fiancé soon came to regard you. Ah,'' he went on with a theatrical air of discovery, as he took a paper from his pocket and scrutinized it, ''A blameless year with old Lady Wingate in the Midlands, terminated perhaps because of her vile temper, I grant. But also perhaps because she abhorred males and there was never a susceptible one in sight? And two months, fancy that, only two months before Lord Wycliffe's interest came to the attention of his lady. Really, Miss Hastings, you ought to have known that the lady has the eye of a hawk and the gentleman already enjoys the services of that Turner woman.

''And now,'' he went on, taking his attention from his notes, putting the pages back in his pocket; and glancing up just as Julia was about to make a lunge for the door, ''leaving dear little Mrs. Bryce and her charming Toby, whom you profess to adore, in the lurch because you are homesick? Or because, truthful for once, you have told her there are no eligible males in the district? Yet, according to the townspeople, Miss Hastings, you have many admirers here. But, I will admit, no wealthy ones.

''Oh, I have done my homework,'' he sighed, noting her grimace and misconstruing her complete distress at his false interpretation of true events. ''And I know your history as well. It makes for colorful reading. But you have not been as good a scholar, my dear. Did you not remember that Robin is in line for a more august title? When his father dies, he will be no less than a marquess. Now how can you think to do better? You cannot have anyone in mind with more pleasant prospects. You will come with me next week?''

But Julia had been moving, inch by inch, quietly to the door. Now that she felt the handle firm against her spine, she drew herself up and said clearly and decisively, as she turned the handle unobtrusively behind her back, ''No. I shall not. I am not what you think me, no matter what bits of paper you have amassed about me. I do not wish to ever see Robin again and I tell you that I have not even been in contact with him once since that night we parted. It is all a mistake, my lord.

''And,'' she added with relief, as she at last felt the door sway open a crack behind her, ''I wish never to see you again as well. And I shall certainly not leave with you for anywhere, at any time.''

But Julia did not have to race from the room, shrieking for help as she sought a hiding place from a violent madman as she had envisioned herself doing. The baron merely stood still for a moment and looked at her as he might look upon something found wriggling upon the earth after a rain. Then he bowed, and as she shrank back and poised to run, he simply walked past her and out the door. But he turned back to face the salon as the butler approached with his hat and driving cape. He ignored Mrs. Bryce, who came to wish him good day, and gazed only at Julia.

"Oh, but you shall," he said softly, as though taking a vow. "One way or another, my dear, you certainly shall."

The next few days were among the most uncomfortable Julia had ever passed in her brief span. For now her employer exhibited not only the symptoms of jealousy, but those of deep distrust as well. Julia attempted to cope with the uneasy atmosphere as she had done in such situations before, by occupying herself completely with her tasks and by so doing blinding herself to hateful reality. But as the days wore on and she still did not get a response from her letter to the Misses Parkinson, the situation became increasingly less tolerable. The present so neatly imitated the past that the same learned responses were called into action. Thus, on a heavily scented late spring night almost a week after the mad baron's visit, Julia began to pack her bags.

Just as she had fled the comforts of her home when gossip and innuendo had become too distasteful to bear, now, even without assurance of a new situation, she prepared to bolt again.

Mrs. Bryce was admittedly in an untenable position as well. Whether the captain's good wife had stood in an adjacent room, or ordered the butler away so that she could actually put her ear to the door, there was no doubt that she had heard every word the baron had uttered in private to Julia. Now her sense of propriety obviously warred with her notions of morality. She could not bring herself to admit to having actually done something so crude as eavesdropping. So she could neither condemn Julia for her scandalous behavior, nor discuss the accusations with her to get at the truth of the matter. Instead, she consistently cast shocked glances toward her, or studied her with badly concealed amazement. She seldom directly addressed Julia if she could help it, yet her every action showed that she could not decide whether her governess-companion were something as exciting as a shameless Delilah, or merely as contemptible as a common lightskirt. In any case, Julia had not the heart to bring the matter up herself.

For even if she told no less than the truth, the truth itself was enough to have her dismissed and lose her the foolishly effusive recommendation she would need to secure a new position. For, Julia thought as she opened her largest traveling case, although she had not deliberately committed any of the crimes she had been accused of, the bare facts were sadly true. She had been no more than kind to Jamie Pomfret, the young son of her first employer, and he had fallen immediately into calf love with her. His obsession had shown itself in no more than bad poetry, but it was that overheated verse that his mama had found, and it was her shock at the depth of her beardless boy's ardor which had caused Julia's dismissal.

Mrs. Pomfret had been a fair-minded female and Julia had gotten her letter of reference. Similarly, her second period of employment had ended abruptly. Yet even as the Honorable Miss Carstairs had swallowed down her disappointment, she too had resignedly penned a glowing commendation. "For it is not your fault, dearest Julia," the Honorable Miss Carstairs had sighed. "I know that Teddy will be a sadly unsteady husband, and there is nothing for it, because you see, I am unfortunate enough to love him. I know the world will hold many other decorative females, but at the least, I must remove a source of unhappiness from my own household. So you see, my dear, I'm sorry for it, but you must go."

Lady Wingate's temperament had estranged her from every one of her relatives, and considering the amount of her estate, that was no mean accomplishment, but still Julia had managed to endure her company for a full year. That, Julia thought now, as she arranged her linen in the traveling case, was not due to virtue, nor was it any moral credit to her. She had stayed on solely because the Misses Parkinson, while sympathetic, had firmly told her that a succession of brief periods of employment would look badly upon her record, however much she might be blameless in their cause. On the precise day to a year after she had arrived to companion Lady Wingate (Julia was sure of that reckoning, as she had kept track with a pen on a calendar upon her wall, just as any other prisoner might), she offered up her resignation. Surprisingly, her dreadful old ladyship had written a perfectly unexceptional reference as well, perhaps because

she had been amazed that any employee could have stayed on
with her for that long a time.

Lord Wycliffe and his despicable actions, Julia thought, as
she resolutely fastened up her largest traveling bag, did not
bear refining upon. And so, even as she began to carefully wrap
and stow away the last of her possessions, Julia could not find it
within her to blame Mrs. Bryce. For, on the face of it, she supposed that she might well appear to be a mercenary, conniving,
husband-hungry opportunist. Yet, even if she could explain all
these things away, there still was one basic truth that was
unalterable and inexcusable.

When she was seventeen, she had gone off unchaperoned
with a wealthy young nobleman to be wedded to him, and had
returned the next night, accompanied by a different gentleman,
still very much unwed.

It could not matter that she had not cared a jot for his riches
or title, or that she had gone with the full cognizance and approval of her family, or even that she had vowed that she had
returned, as she had left, a maid. The thing that was not done
had been done. Her good name was as lost to her as her betrothed clearly was.

Her family had rallied around her, and it made no difference.
Both love and guilt impelled them to support her. Though
Mama had wept for her daughter's distress and her own short-
sightedness, and the other children had stoutly defended their
sister, Papa had blamed himself the most.

He had no word of censure for Julia. For it had been he who
had listened to the sincere young nobleman when he had come
to ask permission to pay his addresses, and it had been he who
then had weighed all the risks of an elopement and had finally
agreed to it. How easily Robin had brushed away his doubts,
admitting in straightforward fashion that, yes, his family might
protest or have an eye on a more equal match for him, but that
nonetheless he was resolved to wed only where his heart lay.
How plausibly and convincingly he had added that as his family loved him, they would come in time to accept his choice of
bride, and come to love her as well, but only after the wedding.

Robin had insisted on elopement, explaining reasonably that
he would not have his family think his new in-laws in any way
coerced him to his decision. However much Julia's papa shrank
from the idea of a run-away wedding, foremost in his mind was

the question of how he could deny his daughter happiness with the handsome and clever young gentleman. But deep in his heart, clouding his clear judgment, there also arose the question of how he could ever hope to obtain a better match for her. She was a mere estate-manager's daughter, and to see her securely wed to a member of the nobility, even if the thing had to be done in secrecy, was more than he had ever dared envision.

Ill-advised as it was, young as they both were, it was this secret dream of advancement for her that decided him. It was, in the end, simply too good an opportunity to ever come again. But if it was greed for his child that caused his acquiescense, it was the remembrance of that greed which was to torment him later.

But who could have resisted Robin? Julia wondered now. Light and laughing Robin, who had sworn to Papa with earnestness evident in every word and gesture, that as he loved and respected his daughter, he would so care for her throughout her life. And if he had conquered practical Papa, he had completely swept away Mama and overwhelmed all the children of the house, herself included.

At seventeen she had known no real beaux, though it was said in the neighborhood that she was bidding fair to becoming a beauty. When Robin had arrived suddenly to visit with her father's employer, Lord Quincy, he had seemed to her to be a prince from out of one of the fairytales she had just left off reading. When he deigned to speak with her that first time they met on a country lane, she had been staggered that he had even noted her existence upon the earth. He might have become, as he should have become, an idealized standard of masculinity that she could base her future choice of husband upon when she had grown to adulthood. But he had continued to meet her by chance, and then by happy accident, and then, finally, by secret arrangement. And he became instead of her distant ideal, her betrothed.

However much her family had comforted her after she had returned home that night, exhausted and confused, it had not been enough. It could never be enough to shield her from the criticism of the outside world. If Lord Quincy and his family had been appalled at their factor's daughter's sly behavior when he had, full of pride, prematurely announced her wedding to their honored guest, there were no polite words to describe their reaction to her ignoble return. Neither could Julia discount neighbor women's whispers, nor could she pretend to ignore their menfolk's calculating stares for long.

It soon became apparent to her that she had not only destroyed her own future, but that she had jeopardized others' as well. The local people shook their heads and opined that Mr. Hastings had got above himself, thinking to marry his daughter into his betters' class. Lord Quincy and his family decidedly agreed. It wasn't long before Lord Quincy himself began to drop ponderous hints about renovations the estate needed that a younger man might find easier to implement. "Can't teach an old dog new tricks," he had jested, sending his factor home that night looking a score older than his actual years. Julia had four sisters, one already of an age for matrimony, and as the attitude of the local bachelors changed toward her, it subtly altered toward her sisters as well. They never said so, but when Dorothea went walking out with young Alan Baines, and came running home alone, her face flushed and stained with hastily wiped tears, her sister knew what had transpired as surely as if she had been there to see the familiarity which had been rebuffed.

No, it was time for her to be gone, Julia had vowed, despite all their pleas for her to remain. A shadow cannot fall if there is no one about to blot out the sun, she insisted. And so, armed with a letter from the vicar, whose job it was, after all, to forgive all transgressors, and a letter to the Misses Parkinson, whose job it was to find jobs for all idle young females regardless of their morality, she went.

The family saw her off again with tears in their eyes. But this time they did not shed tears of happiness, and this time she did not return.

Julia finished her packing and stared about the room, which now looked naked without her little picture frames upon the nightstand, and her sister's samplers on the wall above the bed. A jumble of oddments still remained upon the nightstand, however. She had decided that in light of present circumstances, it would not be fitting for her to pack away those many tokens of esteem her employer had pressed upon her during her brief orgy of atonement.

As she lay down upon her bed, Julia thought of Toby, whom she had left an hour ago, rosy and talc-covered, still damp from his bath and the sleep which had overtaken him just as the princess lost her golden ball down the well. That memory she would take with her, she mused on a sleepy smile, and the visions of the mustard fields, this room, Old Joseph, the village people, even Mrs. Bryce in those days before the deranged baron had called upon them. She would stay on a few more days and then, even if the letter she awaited did not arrive, she would go. She had done it before, Julia thought as she herself fell down into a soft gray well of sleep, and however much it pained her now, she consoled herself by remembering that the present would soon become the past. And she had become an expert at living with the past.

The gentleman entered the room as he was bade, and walked to the older gentleman seated at the huge satinwood desk. At least, he thought it was the satinwood desk, but there were so many books laid out upon it that the exact nature of its surface was difficult to ascertain. He smiled as he watched the other man carefully place a bookmark, or what he had decided would do for a bookmark but was rather a jay's feather that he extracted from his pocket, in the center of one particularly large tome.

"Nick, my boy," the older gentleman then said, rising and coming forward from behind the desk with every evidence of delight large upon his thin, patrician features. "I had not looked to see you here. I thought you were off to the Continent, about the King's business, or the family business."

"And so I thought too, sir," Baron Stafford replied, taking the proferred hand in his, "but I've had to change my plans."

"I'm not a bit sorry," the older gentleman said, gesturing to his visitor to take a chair by the window, as he himself now did. "I should think any friend of the enemy knows your face as well as Bonaparte's by now, and Robin is quite old enough to be accountable for himself."

"Actually, the home office quite agrees with you on the former, and I very much doubt your infinite wisdom on the latter, but in any case my hands are tied and I must wait a while before I leave, it seems," the baron replied with barely concealed annoyance.

"Petulance does not sit well upon you, Nick," the older gentleman chided.

"Bad as that?" The baron laughed, relaxing and stretching out his long legs. "Then I apologize, sir, for it wasn't my intention to sulk. But I had hoped to have this business with

Robin resolved and I've met up with an unexpected impediment." He frowned as he left off speaking.

At the questioning look upon the other gentleman's face, he said with some irritation, "The young woman in question refuses to cooperate."

"She must be a very strong-minded female to resist your blandishments," the older man said, smiling, but then his face grew serious and he reached out to tap the baron's knee, as though to reinforce the importance of his next words. "Nick, my boy, let it be. Robin is his own master now. He's of an age."

"Marlowe's sinking, sir," the baron replied, just as seriously. "Even the King's physician don't give him more than a month. My aunt is weeping all over everyone in sight, including the gardeners if they come close enough, and it isn't for Marlowe's sake, as you might think, it's all for Robin. 'Ah where's my boy,' she cries, and looks accusingly at me as though I could produce him from a hat. And that isn't so bizarre, sir, for I used to have some sway over him, far more than anyone in the family, you know, even more than you had, sir, and I can't convince him to return. But his light lady might, if she would, but she won't."

"Then there's no more to be done, my boy," the older gentleman said gently, seeing how his visitor had fallen into a brown study.

"But there is, and I shall," the baron swore, his face growing closed and hard.

"Robin is no green youth any longer," the older gentleman mused, "and I'm not at all sure you shouldn't just let him be. He may know best."

"As he knew best when he ran off with that bit of muslin? Come, sir, it was good luck, not good sense, that saved him when she decided to sheer off. No, it's clear that he stands in need of some counsel now."

"He is your nephew, Nick, not your son," the older gentleman said softly.

"But he hasn't a father, or at least Marlowe might have sired him but he never did more," the baron explained earnestly. "And who is there to guide him? At least I had you to set me straight when I was about to make a cake of myself in my youth, and you were not, strictly speaking, my father."

Ah, that episode still rankles, the older gentleman thought, but he only said calmly, "I did marry your mother."

"Devil take it, sir," the baron muttered. "You know that's not what I meant. I could not have had a better father than you had I ordered one up from the deity."

Ignoring his stepson's embarrassment, the elder gentleman went on, as though musing aloud, "I have not thought of that incident in years. That young woman you were involved with was a pretty little creature, I quite sympathized with you. In fact, it was not her lack of birth that disturbed me at all. You know I don't place much emphasis on social lineage, and neither should you. Why just think of the odd branches on your own family tree: the Spanish lady that Elizabethan rogue brought back from his travels, the moneylender's daughter your wastrel Royalist ancestor wed, your great-grandmother who came from a humble cottage. They only strengthened the stock, you know. Weak links tend to crop up in those socially-pure inbred families. Why look at the Bryants, they go back to the Normans, without a misalliance, and they haven't produced a chin for generations."

"Then why did you pay off my little filly to be rid of her?" the baron asked coolly, though his white cheeks had grown flushed during his stepfather's discourse.

"Ah, because, as you well know, she had more than no breeding, she had no heart, and no morals," the older gentleman said. He paused and then asked quietly, "Does Robin's light of love remind you of her? Then it's no wonder you've become so exercised about it. Is she such a pretty little creature then?"

"No," said the baron abruptly, "she is not." He paused and then added bitterly, "She is beautiful."

4

The stagecoach driver was being extremely conscientious, or so at least one of his unhappy passengers thought. For the fellow seemed to be taking great care not to miss one rut or hollow in the road. Perhaps, Julia thought as she raised her hand again to secure her bonnet, he was doing some sort of audit for the government bureau in charge of public roads and it was his duty to painstakingly record every deficiency in them. Then, when the coach lurched over a particularly deep depression, she clenched her teeth tightly to ensure that they did not rattle out of her head and left off thinking about the driver's hidden motives and only prayed that her traveling cases were more securely anchored than their owner presently was.

When the coach had righted itself again, the fair-haired young woman attempted to do the same herself. Julia whispered a polite "Excuse me" to the matron on her left, who had taken most of her weight when the movement of the coach caused the passengers to sway like trees in a tempest. Then she bent and felt about the floorboards with her hands as her fellow passengers were doing, in an attempt to help the fellow immediately opposite her in his search for his dislodged spectacles.

46

They had been riding without a stop for quite some time, and by now had exhausted all their expressions of ill-usage. Really, Julia thought wearily, as she accepted a curt "Thankee" from the fellow to whom she handed the wire-rimmed spectacles, there can be few more foolish situations than finding oneself packed into a coach in a random pair, sitting facing two other complete strangers, and then being shaken vigorously every few moments for endless hours. If one then added the effects of a sultry early summer's day to the experience, Julia thought miserably, one could get the general impression of what one's fate might be in the afterlife if one were very wicked in this one.

She had been traveling for two full days now, and it seemed that even when the coach stopped to change horses, the scenery still swam before her eyes. The only comfort she could take from the experience was a mean one, for it was only her gratitude that she had the funds to sit within the coach, and not ride atop it as those less fortunate or more foolish, were doing. But yet, every jolting, bone-shaking mile brought her closer to London. So she sat back and closed her eyes, and felt the warm wind from the partially opened window upon her face, and tried to leave the coach, if not in her person, then at least in her mind.

Julia thought that despite her present discomfort, she had a great deal to be thankful for. She had not, after all, had to leave Mrs. Bryce before she had heard from her employment counselors in London. Two days after she had packed her bags, a letter had come summoning her to them. The letter had hinted of several suitable positions that had arisen, so Julia could at least save face when she presented it for her employer's inspection. It was a very little thing, to be sure, but on such small details, much pride may be spared. For instead of seeming to be fleeing, she was able to depart in a very dignified manner.

It had been a wrench to leave young Toby, but both Julia and her employer were able to comfort themselves secretly with the thought that children forget quickly. It may well be so, but still, though Julia was never to know it, Master Toby eventually grew to be a devil with the ladies, a source of great embarrassment to his family, and only settled down to respectability when he found a golden-haired, ice-eyed lady of his own to wed.

Julia's departure was also made more bearable by the fact that by the day she left, the mustard fields had left off their riotous celebration of spring and had gotten down to the serious business of growing. So she felt no tug at her heart when the coach trundled off out of the village, past now mundane acres of mere vegetable fields.

Still, she had been unable to leave without one last attempt at setting her record straight. After she had shaken hands with her former mistress, and Toby's distressed shieks at her departure had faded enough as his nurse bore him back shrieking to his nursery so that normal conversation could be heard, she had said, firmly facing the issue, "Ma'am, no word that the baron spoke of me was true. He was sadly deranged, you know."

But Mrs. Bryce had only stared at her as though she were the one who were unbalanced. She mustered up enough countenance to say stiffly, "Good-bye, Miss Hastings, I wish you well." And then she left before Julia could utter another traitorous word. She made it clear she felt that even if such a thing as insanity among the upper classes were possible, it was only another prerogative of the nobility. So most people would think, Julia had mused sadly as she stared at Mrs. Bryce's retreating back, and so she would be sure not to mention the incident to anyone else, lest by her own insistence on the matter she should convince her listeners that she were at fault.

Another jolt of the coach, this one accompanied by a rather piercing scream from one of the hapless topside passengers, interrupted Julia's reveries. Since the coach continued on its way and no body could be seen flying past the dusty windows, the general consensus of the inner passengers was that it had been caused by an understandable attack of nerves, and no great harm had been taken by anyone above. But now Julia could see that they had reached the outskirts of London itself, and now she firmly put aside her memories and concentrated on the future.

When the coach at last achieved the stage stop, Julia got down quickly and commandeered her luggage without a moment's pause. She had traveled this way before, and by now she well knew that a young female obviously traveling alone, arriving from the countryside, and moreover, not being met upon her arrival, was often in danger of being considered fair prey by many sorts of urban predators. So she ignored the helping hand offered by a well-dressed gentleman, turned her back upon the sweet-faced woman who offered her a tentative smile, and kept on walking to a line of hackney carriages when another rather dashing young female attempted to stop her by miscalling her, with every evidence of recognition and delight, "Mary, my dear Mary!"

She was sorry to be so hard, but if they were only well-meaning folk, they would understand, and if they were not, then she had saved herself a great deal of difficulty. Julia told the coachman the direction of Mrs. White's boarding house, and reflected that it was from her sojourns there that she had achieved such wisdom. Mrs. White ran a respectable facility, and there were always a few mature unemployed females in residence at her establishment. They had been the ones who had seen to Julia's education in matters to do with unprotected young women. These older, wiser females did not think it at all out of the way that Miss Hastings, although still in her extreme youth, should know all about the mistresses of houses of ill-repute, sporting ladies, and dissolute gentleman of London and their many and various means of luring innocents to their moral downfall.

If Julia had been a young debutante, she would have known nothing about the likes of the infamous Mother Carey and her chicks in their expensive bawdy house, nor would she have known of the human birds of paradise gentlemen of leisure selected for their adornment and then discarded through their tedium in much the same careless manner as they selected and discarded snuff boxes. But though all of Julia's tutors were respectable gentlewomen, and indeed many of them were the daughters of clergymen, not one of the elder women Julia had encountered at Mrs. White's had spared her shocking and cautionary tales of physical and moral danger. Indeed, after one look at Julia's face, hair, and form, many of them had considered her immediate enlightenment about such matters in the light of missionary work.

Mrs. White's house was a narrow gray townhouse which had once been in a fashionable section of town, but which now gathered its skirts nervously in from its iron railings as the surrounding neighborhood became decidedly more common. Julia accepted her traveling bags from her driver, stepped through a squealing throng of urchins at play, ignoring one cheeky lad's cry of "Ooo, pretty lady, 'ave you got a moment?'', and knocked upon the door.

In a few moments, Mrs. White appeared. She took one look at her visitor's tired face, and then she said, a bit sadly, "Ah yes, Miss Hastings. Do come in, I've your room ready, indeed I prepared it the moment I received your letter."

But as she led Julia to her spare and tidy room on the third floor, she thought, Poor lass, she's failed again. Yet Julia, seeing the flowered wallpaper, the neatly made bed, the pitcher and washstand all exactly as they had been before, felt not at all like a failure, but rather intensely grateful, for she had reached a refuge and she had a chance to start again.

Acting upon her guest's instructions, Mrs. White sent her maid-of-all-work to waken Miss Hastings just as the clock chimed seven. Although Julia could have afforded several days of leisure, she could not wait to secure a new position. It was not her purse she was concerned about, it was her spirit. She had discovered that the more time she took between posts, the less pleased she was when she secured one. Idle times were the ones in which she was most succeptible to bouts of self-pity and thus were the ones she sought to avoid the most diligently. So she donned her best severely cut black walking dress, brushed her hair until it gleamed like trapped sunlight in its plaited chains, and went down to breakfast. As soon as she had had her last morsel, she resolved that she would walk to the Misses Parkinsons' office, for she could see that it was a fine day.

But no sooner had she swallowed down the first of her eggs, when old Miss Constable, a pensioner who was living out her days at Mrs. White's and always took a dawn constitutional, came bursting into the dining room to banish all thoughts of plans or posts or interviews. "It is over!" the old woman gasped in a reedy voice as she brandished a newssheet, so breathless and disheveled that it was clear she had actually run back to the house. "See, see for yourselves! The Duke has won out! Napoleon is vanquished."

The excited ladies rose from their breakfast and gathered about Mrs. White, who, as proprietor, had won the right to read to them all from the broadsheet. Then all the ladies hugged each other and raised gallant toasts with their tea cups. For it was printed plain, Wellington had won the day at a place in Belgium called Waterloo, even as Julia had been journeying all unaware to London: on the eighteeth of June. Napoleon was routed, and must surely abdicate again.

There was nothing for it but that they must celebrate. Mrs. White gave her maid a half day off, and she then advised her ladies to get their wraps, for they would go out into the city to participate in the joyous day. In ordinary times, it would have seemed odd, the six assorted respectable gentlewomen strolling along the streets with no purpose in mind, exactly like fops on the strut. But this was no ordinary time.

The churchbells pealed wildly in every sector of the city as the news became generally known. All sorts of odd groups wandered the streets: clots of bakers, collections of school children with their masters, knots of common workers, all laughing and congratulating each other. But there was no actual dancing in the streets, and the most abandoned revelry that Julia experienced was toward the end of the afternoon when a wild young apprentice happened to spy her and swung about to catch her up and give her a sound kiss upon the lips before the shocked cries of her companions and the boisterous laughter of his fellows ended the encounter.

Mrs. White and her ladies were safely within their house again when evening came, for then, they speculated rightly, the more rowdy celebrations would be enacted by the lower classes. But as though they felt they must apologize to Julia, who was newly come to town, for the relatively mild reaction of the populace, they recounted tales of the previous year's extravaganzas when Napoleon had first been defeated. Then, they told her, there had been fireworks in all the parks, and public fairs, and balloon ascensions, and mechanical displays so marvelous and enthralling that they dreamed of them still.

"It is possible," Mrs. White said knowingly, "that we may never celebrate so wildly again, for victory was snatched from us too soon after all our jubilation. We may never again be so quick to embrace happiness."

Julia nodded wisely when she heard this, for it was an attitude which she could readily approve.

But there were some further festivities, for victory, impermanent or not, is sweet, and the city did not return to normal for several more days. Only then could Julia at last go to see the Misses Parkinson.

Miss Lavinia Parkinson eyed Julia thoughtfully after she had done writing out her cards of introduction.

"There," she said, handing them to her young applicant. "Dame Franklin only wants a biddable girl to companion her daughter, and the post wouldn't be for long, as they must have the chit popped off soon, since rumor has it their pockets are emptying quickly.. Lady Kirkland wants a companion, but don't get your hopes up, for she's a high stickler. Lady Cunningham wants a governess, but she is a foreigner and they are impossible to understand. I have no idea of what she's after, no one yet has pleased her. You may as well have a try at it, every other client I have has in the past days."

Julia agreed, took the cards, thanked Miss Lavinia prettily, and went to call upon her new prospects with high hopes. But if she had chanced to hear the conversation that ensued as soon as she left, her expectations would have fallen so low that she would have crept back to Mrs. White's and hidden underneath her bed.

For the younger Miss Parkinson fixed her sister with a curious stare and said, loudly (as there were no others within their offices just then), "I vow, Letty, the heat must have gotten you. Whatever can you be thinking of, sending that child off to either Franklin or Kirkland? They wouldn't have a beauty like that in their vicinity, much less their employ. Dame Franklin would be demented·if she hired on a companion who would outshine her pie-faced daughter, and Lady Kirkland fancies herself a Cleopatra. And to think that poor Miss Wittly and dear little old Miss Gowdy have excellent credentials and are in dire need of employment, and you never sent them there."

"Remind me, Fan," the elder Miss Parkinson said smugly, as she pushed out her chair and leaned over to scratch her leg, "what Miss Wittly and Miss Gowdy resemble."

"That's not to the point," her sister said crossly. "The dears can't help their looks."

"Neither can Miss Hastings," Lavinia Parkinson replied. "Not that they'll do her an ounce of good getting those posts."

"Then why send her?"

"Precisely because she's a stunner and Miss Wittly resembles a bullfrog and dear Miss Gowdy, a dried herring. After those fine lady employers get an eyefull of Miss Hastings, they'll be more appreciative of the virtues of our less comely clients. A beauty like Miss Hastings will strike terror into their hearts and they'll be bound to snap up our old trouts when we send them in after her."

"That's beastly of you, Letty, it is," Fanny Parkinson said, wincing to see the gusto with which her sister attended to her itching limb, although sympathizing, for Lord knew they never got a chance to unbend when the offices were full.

"The itch or the thought?" her sister replied unfeelingly.

It was afternoon when Julia approached the hotel where Lady Cunningham was in residence. Her interviews with Lady Kirkland and Dame Franklin hadn't taken long at all. But then, unsuccessful interviews seldom did.

Lady Cunningham saw her immediately after she had presented her card. The lady definitely appeared as foreign as Miss Parkinson had claimed her to be. But Julia could not determine her nationality. She conducted the interview as she lay upon a récamier in her dressing room, although she did not appear to be in any way in an invalidish condition. She was relatively young and very attractive in her white eyelet dressing gown. Her red-gold hair was artfully arranged, although obviously not altogether genuine, and her voice was clear and strong. But she seemed so anxious that Julia thought she might suffer more from nerves than any sort of bodily distress. Her accent was so heavy, however, and she spoke so rapidly, that Julia experienced some distress of her own. She had to spend most of her time trying to decipher the lady's meaning, rather than placing her nation of origin.

"You are, of courz, younker zan I vould like," the lady said at one point. "But zee children vould be hoppy az birtz wiz you." By the time Julia had reasoned that the children would be elated, rather than bouncing, the lady had gone on to explain the trip she was embarking upon. As near as Julia could make out without interrupting the lady every other word, her husband, Lord Cunningham, had been some sort of emissary at the Congress of Vienna, but Wellington's victory had changed everything for him, and he had been reassigned to Paris. Husband and wife had been separated for a long time, but now Napoleon's defeat had made her traveling to his side less dangerous and more feasible. The children were either a boy of seven and a girl of five or seven boys and five girls of indeterminate age.

Julia heaved a small sigh of relief when the matter was made clear by the lady's finally declaring, "Yez, I sink leedle Lucille and younk Villie shall be hoppy wiz you."

Julia dared not breathe lest her indrawn breath should be expelled too hard and make the lady aware of how thrilled she was to secure the position. It would not do for an employer to think her overeager. It was a sad fact of human nature that Julia had learned in difficult ways, that the more one seemed to be in need of kindness, the less one actually received.

"Then," Julia ventured to say, since she realized that her comprehension of the lady's speech was inexact, "I am to take it that I am being offered the position?"

"Of courz," Lady Cunningham said with some exasperation. Before Julia could think that she had aroused the lady's ire, she went on, "Eef you could see ze vimen I haff had to endure zis week! Old and fat vuns, skeeny and ugly vuns. Pah. Everyzing in a householt should be luffiy. Everyzing should be in harmony. Beautchiful furnishings, beautchiful peectures, beautchiful peeples," she rhapsodized.

Julia did not know whether to be flattered or annoyed that she had evidently been picked as a governess in much the same manner that a carpet or settee might be chosen. She remembered that the butler who had taken her card had been, in fact, quite handsome and dignified, but before she could begin to wonder what it might be like to work in a household where all the employees were chosen solely for their supposed bodily perfection, the lady went on,

"Zo! You vill begin zen?"

"Certainly, ma'am," Julia replied quickly.

"Goot," the lady sighed, lying back again. "Zen you must go and get your zings. Ve leaf in ze mornink."

"I shall be here early, so that there will be time to take your instructions as to the children before you leave," Julia said as she rose to her feet.

"Vot?" the lady cried, sitting bolt upright. "Teck my instructzions? No, no. Vot are you sinking uff? You are to kom wiz us. How could I leaf my darlinks behind? Zey haff not seen zere fazzer in years. You are to kome wiz us," she insisted, as Julia sank to her seat again.

"With you?" Julia asked faintly.

"Yez. To Pariz, of courz," the lady said, looking at Julia curiously, for the young woman's spirits seemed to have sunk as low as her voice.

"Oh no, ma'am," Julia said with honest sadness, "I did not understand that the position called for foreign travel. I'm sorry, but it is out of the question. No," she said, shaking her head mournfully as her briefest period of employment yet came to its end, "but it is quite out of the question."

The sun seemed to be rising from a different direction. But then, Julia thought, she had never seen the sun rising over the sea before, and so she stood at the boat's railing and watched the sunlight erase the puffy dark morning clouds and saw the outline of the coast of France come clear. In her excitement, Julia had been unable to even feign sleep and had stood guard through the night, waiting for the dawn.

Only a week previously, she had vowed that she would not be standing where she now was. She had been polite, but quite firm with the distracted Lady Cunningham. That lady had been unable to understand her reluctance to take such an exciting position, as had the Misses Parkinson when she had returned with the news. While Lady Cunningham had gone on in her rambling and garbled fashion about the excitement and adventure of such an opportunity, the Misses Parkinson had stressed the fact that the foreign lady had even upped her offering price. "For you've got her in a bind," Miss Lavinia had said gleefully. "She's dragged her feet on it and now she's in a pickle. She knows her husband don't want a foreign governess, for she's not bird-witted enough not to know that he don't want 'em to grow up talking as she does, and she's got to leave on the first fair tide."

Lady Cunningham had stayed Julia a full half hour in her attempts to convince her of the advantages of the position. But Julia had never doubted that the terms were generous. She had no quarrel with the salary as it was first offered, and in her extremity, Lady Cunningham had even raised that higher.

She became so anxious for Julia's acceptance that she had even hinted broadly of opportunities outside the position. For, she had said, looking slyly around her as though she didn't wish to be overheard, though they were quite alone, her hus-

band's house was sure to be overrun with rising young men of
the diplomatic corps, and she would see to it that Julia would
have sufficient time off to take advantage of the situation.
When that didn't seem to move her prospective governess, she
had spoken of all the other eligible young males that were
teeming through the streets of Paris in the aftermath of the war.
"Touzands uff younk, likely Hinglishers, and 'andsome younk
Roosians, Haustrians, and Prusszians," she had said dreamily,
implying that all that the forces of the occupation were looking
for in France was a suitable English wife.

But Julia had remained steadfast in her rejection of the post.
Or, at least, she had remained so until Miss Parkinson had left
off her professional air, hitched her chair close up to her client,
and said firmly, "Look here, Julia, I've got a dozen females
who would jump at this post. And I tell you honestly, I haven't
another opportunity for you. It ain't just your record, which is
spotty, my dear, sad to relate it, but there it is. It's that you're
too pretty, and too young, as well. Time will take care of all
those things, and this post will buy you time.

"I grant that Lady Cunningham seems a scatterbrain, but it
ain't her you'll be working with. And she's been more than
fair. If it's being stranded in the frog pond that's worrying you,
forget it. For she's offered to buy you a two-way ticket at the
start, so you won't feel obligated to stay on with her if you're
miserable, and you can't say fairer than that. You want a position, and she's offered you one. Now what's the impediment?"

Staring into Miss Parkinson's unblinking blue eyes, Julia
could not offer up one realistic objection. That was because she
suddenly understood that all of her reasons, although reasonable, were not realistic at all. How could she say that it was because she shrank from becoming an actual exile? She had left
her home, she had left her district, but she had not thought she
must put even further distance between herself and her past.

It wasn't leaving the country she feared, it was the fact that
once she faced up to the matter squarely, she must forever leave
off her self-deception as well. Being only a coach ride away
from her family had always enabled her to think of her absence
from home as only a respite, only a temporary condition that
could be righted at any time. She had always considered her decision to seek employment a stopgap measure. But now, con-
fronted with Miss Parkinson's waiting, watchful eyes, she

must at last concede that she had no real reason not to take this further step. In truth, she at last admitted, whether she was employed five or five hundred miles from her family made little difference. She had to live apart from them, and there really could never be any permanent homecoming for her.

Never, Miss Parkinson had thought, had there ever been a client who had accepted such a plum with such an air of heartbreaking tragedy. And while Miss Parkinson surprised herself by then proceeding to go on at length about the advantages of the position, so convincingly that she even found herself regretting that she had not been offered it, Julia sat quietly and attempted to accept her final truth. She looked about at the waiting applicants, anxious, homeless females of all ages and conditions earnestly seeking positions in other people's lives. She would be in this office many times again, she realized. For this was to be her life, and this was to be her future.

She did not have to leave for Paris in the morning, even Lady Cunningham had not really expected that, Miss Parkinson had said. "They always like to make impossible demands at the start, even the best of them," that astute female had confided, forgetting in her attempts to cheer Julia, that she ought not draw the lines between her wealthy patrons and her favored clients by calling the former "them," somewhat scornfully, as she always did when she was alone with her sister.

"That way, when you can't go along with them, as they know you can't, they think they have you beholden to them by their generosity. No matter," she had gone on briskly. "Lady Cunningham leaves tomorrow morning, as planned, with the children and their nurse. You're to take the packet when you can (and I really think a week's time is long enough to make her grateful when she sees you, yet short enough not to make her angry at a delay), and meet up with her at Quillack's Hotel in Calais."

Miss Parkinson had been quite right. A week's time was sufficient to all purposes. It was both long enough for Julia to make her regret her decision, and short enough to cause her to feel panic. She shopped for trinkets to send home along with her explanatory letter. She purchased some small things for her own wardrobe. She accepted congratulations on her success from Mrs. White, along with a great many stories about both the perils and the pleasures of foreign travels from the experienced ladies at the boarding house. Then, without hesitation she set out from London by day, reached Dover by night, and sailed on an advantageous tide an hour into a new day.

Now the sky brightened to a clear fresh morning and Julia left the rail to seek the privacy of her cabin. For she knew that an unaccompanied female must never seem to be loitering, for any reason. So when the packet was docked, and customs agents boarded it, Miss Julia Hastings appeared to be a calm, composed, purposeful young female, and even the French officials did no more than to rest their eyes upon her appreciatively when they thought she wasn't looking.

Though she was outwardly cool, it took every bit of her training not to show her excitement. Once she had accepted her fate, it was the resiliency of her character which made her admit the thrill she felt knowing that she was to travel in a foreign land. She had some French, from lessons taken with Lord Quincy's daughters, but now no syllable she heard from the streets struck sense to her ears. Perhaps it was because the information received from her eyes had taken precedence.

She stared at the citizens of Calais as the hired carriage took her to the hotel. There were peasants in their colorful garb, solid middle class citizens looking not too dissimilar from the stolid English burghers she had seen in Dover, and both French and English soldiers walked the same streets without rancor. In fact, she thought as the carriage drew up to the hotel, these citizens didn't seem to be a defeated people, they seemed happy and busy and perhaps only felt relief rather than resentment, now that Bonaparte's fate seemed finally settled.

Julia was pleased that the manager of the hotel spoke English, and she softly and clearly stated her name and the name of Lady Cunningham. At the mention of her new employer, the manager gave Julia a wide smile and a knowing look. In fact, she thought with annoyance as he grinned at her, this was the first time since she had arrived in France that she had been the recipient of the sort of look that the good women of Mrs. White's establishment had warned her against. So her back was very straight and her head very high when the manager showed her directly into a private salon, before he even attended to her luggage.

"Miss Julia Hastings to see Lady Cunningham," he announced with a flourish, and then, bowing, he retreated from the room, closing the door behind him.

The sole occupant of the room, a gentleman who had been seated gazing out the window, rose as she entered and turned to face her. He gazed upon her with great satisfaction before he finally spoke.

"Good afternoon, Miss Hastings," he said softly.

Julia stood very still. Then she could ask only, "Where is Lady Cunningham?"

"Why, she is here before you. Or, rather, as you will come to understand, I am she," replied Baron Stafford, with a twisted smile that had nothing to do with humor upon his lips. "You see," he added coldly, "it is as I told you. I, at least, honor my vows."

5 Only twice before in her life had Julia found herself totally incapable of coherent speech. The first time, she had been thrown from the top of a hay wagon during a friendly tussle with her sister, and when she had opened her eyes to see her father's anxious face looming above her as she lay upon the ground, the gift of speech seemed to have failed her. The second time had come years later, when she had entered her own house one windy October night with a strange gentleman standing rigidly at her side, and she had seen the amazed and aghast looks upon all of her family's faces. Then, she had not even had the presence of mind to introduce him, and had only heard him say, from far away, "Good evening. I am Sir Edwin Chester, and I've come to bring your daughter safely home to you."

Now she stood in the tastefully decorated private parlor of a hotel in a foreign land and gazed steadily at the gentleman before her, and it seemed that the sight of him had knocked the wind from her even as the fall from the wagon had, and the look upon his face frightened the wits from her, even as the shock upon the faces of her family had.

"Do sit down, Miss Hastings," the baron said in an offhand manner. "We have much to talk about."

But Julia would not be seated. She only stood and gripped her reticule firmly in her hands as though that were the only reality she could safely hold on to. Her first thought was to run, only it seemed that her knees were too weak to carry her to the door, much less to the street. And then when she remembered that those streets were unfamiliar ones and that she had no idea of whether she would be running to safety or to further danger, she merely remained standing, hoping inspiration for some sort of action would occur to her.

The baron looked at her oddly, then shrugged. He seated himself again, crossed his legs, and began speaking. "Then stand, if you will. The point is that I told you your services were required upon the Continent, and happily enough, it seemed that your services were for hire at the time they were needed. So I employed you."

Julia found herself sinking to a chair as he spoke, as though her watery limbs had made the decision her dazed mind could not. The baron only nodded approvingly at her action and then left off looking at her. He made a steeple with his long white fingers and seemed to study it as he spoke.

"I knew, of course, that the Misses Parkinson were your agents. The rest was simplicity itself. Well, I could hardly truss you up and carry you off from London in a closed coach, as in all the popular romances, could I?" he asked as he flashed Julia a brilliant smile, before he went on just as though she had given him a reply, "No. Of course, I could not. So I simply employed Lady Cunningham to employ you, and the thing was achieved in a far more correct and less athletic fashion.

"I don't know why you are so amazed, Miss Hastings," he added. "The only wonderment I find in it is that so many people accepted that ridiculous accent she adopted. For I told Lilli (your Lady Cunningham, Miss Hastings) that her accent wouldn't fool a child. I hired her on because she is indeed, truly, from France, and speaks in the most charming manner. But she insisted that most English persons are actually pleased when a foreigner mangles their language, since it confirms their secret belief that anyone not privileged to be born on English soil hasn't the wit to master it. In fact, she insisted that the more bizarre the speech, the more convincing she would be. If she had used only her own slight accent, she assured me, then she might well come under suspicion, but if she spoke some incomprehensible jumble, she would never be doubted for a moment.

"I am really most impressed by her astuteness," the baron commented expansively, "for I thought that Germanic-Slavic-French mélange she invented was the stuff of music halls. She is a far better actress than I gave her credit for. Now I wonder why it is that she only plays minor parts at the Sadler-Wells theater where she is usually employed."

As the baron sat quietly, apparently musing upon this theme, Julia found herself regaining her wits. Once her initial shock faded she found it replaced by a growing anger, a sense of injustice done which threatened to overcome her. But she reined in her emotions, reminding herself sternly that whatever else she might wish to do, she was in the unfortunate position of being alone with a mad person again.

She gazed at the gentleman as he relaxed in his chair. He was so neatly groomed, so very handsome with his pale skin and wide clear long-lashed eyes, that she found that she could understand his family's reluctance to confine him to some sort of custodial care. No matter how deranged he might be, his comportment gave little evidence of it. It could be that they cherished some unreasonable hopes for his recovery. Even if this were a misguided ambition, Julia found comfort in the very fact that his family had not placed him under restraint. If he were actually violent, she reasoned, no doubt he would not be running about loose.

So she pasted an artificial smile upon her lips, and then ventured to speak, softly and clearly, in much the same tones that she had often used with Toby when he had found an excellent hiding place when they played at Hide and Seek and then refused to disclose his whereabouts to her.

"Why it was a capital scheme, to be sure," she said slowly, "and there is no question that it did succeed. For here I am, and until the moment that I laid eyes upon you, my lord, I'll swear that I had no idea of your charade. It was all very well done," she concluded, giving him a reasonable facsimile of an approving smile.

The baron raised one dark, high, arched brow and looked at her very curiously as she continued.

"I concede that you have won. And very handsomely too. You were awfully clever. But now the game is up, and I find that I really must return home."

Julia forced herself to her feet and, discovering that her lower limbs still functioned, was able to give the gentleman a more realistic smile.

"It has been most interesting," she said sweetly, "and I confess that I have enjoyed the game as well, even if I did lose."

She planned to go on to enumerate the various ways in which she had found his scheme successful, and had begun a slow imperceptible movement to leave, when he rose from his chair and advanced purposely toward her. The sight of his cold and set features and the realization of his anger, as evinced by his tightly clenched hands, caused her words to catch in her throat.

He stood before her, not an arm's length away, and she realized that though his frame was slender, it was deceptively so. There did not seem to be padding in the firm wide shoulders of his tightly fitting blue jacket, and the set of his clenched teeth enabled her to clearly see the clean lines of musculature that ran from his jaw to his strong neck. Now, she felt real terror.

"You are either a fool, Miss Hastings, which I sincerely doubt, or you are laboring under some foolish misapprehension," the baron said, reaching out to take her chin in his hand and gaze directly into her eyes.

But now natural anger displaced all of Julia's carefully thought-out evasions. She slapped his hand away and cried, "Do not touch me!

"I do not like to be touched," Julia blurted, "and you are forever gripping my chin and looking at me this way and that, as though I were a noddy doll or some other sort of insensible object." Then, acutely aware of the flash of anger she had seen in his changeable eyes, she swallowed hard and went on in accents that she hoped did not sound so pitiful to his ears as they did to her own, "I'm sorry if I have angered you, I did not mean to do so, it is only that I have told you that you've won. I'll apologize as well, if that is what you wish. Only pray don't be angry with me. It's just that I'm not in the mood for any more games, my lord, and I should like to go home now. We'll play again another day, if you wish," she added, her voice now trembling as much as her knees were as he frowned down at her in silence.

"By God!" he exclaimed at last in an undervoice. "Do you think me mad?"

Since that was precisely the reaction she had least wished for him to have, Julia felt positively faint. When he saw her blanch, however, he looked as startled as she felt.

"Good lord," he said, reaching out to take her hands, and then dropping those two icy, shivering members as soon as he had gripped them. "You do."

There was such incredulity in his voice and such amazement in his face as he shook his head that Julia took heart. It did not seem as though he were about to go off in a blind rage immediately, so she had at least the space of a few heartbeats to quieten her breathing and order her thoughts.

"Miss Hastings," the baron said after he had taken an agitated turn about the room, "I assure you that I am in full possession of my senses. I realize," he added on a half laugh, which quite transformed his face, since she had never seen him honestly amused before, "that my assurances on the matter will have little weight for I don't believe that madmen generally *do* admit to their deficiency. I don't believe they even realize it," he continued, as though to himself, frowning once more at the direction of his thoughts, "but I promise you that no one has ever accused me of such. At least, not to my face. That's small consolation for you, isn't it?" he added wryly, before he smiled once again and said with finality, "I am not mad, Miss Hastings, and though like most men, I cannot prove that fact, I can at least reiterate it: I am, for all my sins, quite sane. Whatever gave you the notion that I was deranged?" he asked curiously.

"Why this whole episode," Julia replied, feeling as though she herself were unbalanced, trying to explain why she found the present situation she was in unusual, when the mere fact of it was incredible. Still, he now seemed so reasonable, there was the faintest hope that there had been some monstrous mistake made and discussion might right matters again.

"The fact that I am standing here now," Julia said bravely. "The fact that Lady Cunningham doesn't exist. The fact that you lured me to France, and wrote me those letters. None of it makes any sense, there's not a bit of it that is rational."

But now his air of sweet reason vanished again and he turned a face to her that was cold and implacable. Julia could not control the little gasp that escaped her lips, and at that, the baron seemed taken aback again. He made a sound of exasperation, and then sighed. "Sit down, Miss Hastings," he said in a neutral tone, "as far away as you wish, but close enough to hear me out."

Julia seated herself in a small gilt chair comfortably close to the closed door. The baron stood and looked down at her with a certain amount of calculation apparent in his gaze. Then he sighed again and said in very emotionless tones, "I told you the whole of it when we last met. But if you like, I'll go over it again. It is my ambition to reunite you with Robin. I know that you have cast him off twice before, you know that I am not precisely overjoyed at the thought of a match between you. But needs must when the devil drives. He is about to come into his honors. He will soon be the Marquess of Marlowe, if his father's doctors do not lie. And then he will be needed at home, to oversee his estates, to comfort his mama, to eventually establish his own family. As you were the one whose actions drove him abroad, and you are the one whose further rejection keeps him there, you are quite naturally the one to coax him back to England where he belongs. Now, I have promised to pay you very well for your efforts and even more if you manage to achieve these ends without actually tying the knot with him. Where is the madness in that?"

"But it's all of it mad," Julia cried, "for I told you before and shall tell you again: I have not heard from Robin for these past three years, nor do I wish to."

"I have letters from Robin stating all of this," the baron said wearily.

"And I tell you that it is madness, and none of it true," Julia said, tears of vexation starting in her eyes.

"Robin does not lie," the baron said flatly, with an air of impatience.

"Nor do I!" Julia insisted.

Her inquisitor cast one bright look at her, and then said, shaking his dark head, "No doubt it's a deep game you're playing. I cannot hope to fathom it, and since you are intent on keeping it to yourself, I shall not even try. But in any event, you are here. And you will cooperate, I believe, at least to the extent of confronting Robin. For you're a good enough business woman to realize that you haven't really any other choice.''

"Oh, but I do!" Julia stated flatly, for madman or sane man, it made little difference any longer, this was an interview she must end at once. "I have a return ticket. And I have funds enough to purchase another if you take it from me. And I have family that will purchase yet another if you take my funds. I think," she said with her head held as high as though she marched to the hangman's noose to the cheering of unseen crowds, "that you will have to murder me to prevent my leaving. And if you are truly not mad, you shall not," she went on as if reassuring herself aloud, "for if you are serious in your stated intentions, I cannot see how my demise will do you the least good.''

"And if you are, indeed, a young innocent wrongly accused," the baron said dryly, "I should like to hear you explain to all of your devoted family just how and why you eloped to France with the naughty Baron Stafford. For one word from me will cause Lilli Saverne to admit to her imposture as a lady and claim that she did it all for the both of us to advance the cause of *l'amour*. And as I shall not at all mind admitting that I fell prey to the same charms my poor deluded nephew did, how pleased your family will be with you, Miss Hastings, decamping with the nephew once, flying with the uncle a second time."

Nodding with satisfaction at the stunned reception his speech received, the baron went on lightly, "And if you are, as I suspect, playing a different game, only imagine how pleased the Misses Parkinson will be at your little prank. I don't know how you dressed the matter up last time, but I assure you, there will be no disguising it now. The recommendation I shall give you will certainly ensure your future employment, but only in a house of ill repute, I think. If you wished to impersonate a decent, hardworking young lady in order to achieve your ends, rather then openly joining the ranks of the fashionably impure, that is your own business. Or rather that was your own business. Now it is mine. And I will not allow the imposture any longer. So go, Miss Hastings. My instructions home will depart the moment you do."

He waved a dismissive hand to her and turned to face the window as though he were bored with the entire matter. Julia sat very still and attempted to order her thoughts. She could go home, of course. She could simply rise and leave in very dignified fashion and go home. Her family would believe her, they would never disbelieve her, she told herself fiercely. But if she could not live peacefully among them with the memory of her flight with Robin for them to help her bear, she knew she could never return to them with this new vile lie to contend with. If they lived upon some remote mountaintop, she could, but no, she realized with a sudden sick feeling, not in England, not anywhere in England, could they hope to surmount this shocking new addendum to her history.

And there was no question that her career, such as it was, as either governess or companion, would be abruptly terminated should such a tale gain currency. No, she had been quite right. It would not have served the baron's purposes to do her bodily mischief. Not when with one stroke of a pen he could quite coolly and competently murder all her expectations.

"Still here then?" the baron asked with sham surprise as he turned to face her again.

"You leave me no choice," Julia said in frustration. "It is too much to ask my family to live with. It would be enough to cost my father his position if I were to return to them with such a tale hanging over me. But I do not wish to go with you," she insisted, standing before him now, white-faced and dry-eyed, for it seemed that the matter had gone far beyond tears, "and I tell you again, you are misled. Robin wants nothing to do with me. I cannot say why he has written such letters, if he has indeed done so, but I tell you that it was all ended between us years ago. I have no sway with him. I cannot say that I even know him, for clearly, I did not know his mind then and if three years have changed me, why so they must have wrought some change in him as well."

She looked at the baron beseechingly, though it was not her intention to plead with him, but only to in some manner make him understand the enormity of his misapprehension. But she could not read his reaction.

His face was impassive and the expression in his eyes was hidden beneath his long lashes as he said coolly, "Let it be, Miss Hastings. I have no wish to indulge in idle speculation upon your motives at the time. I know only that we must attempt to undo what was done. Three years may well have changed you, but unfortunately, not outwardly. You are yet very comely. I had, I'll admit, cherished some hopes that you might have become blowsy or bloated, so as to make a true mockery of past illusions. There is nothing," he went on ruefully, ignoring her discomforture, "so deflating to a grand passion than to find that the object of one's youthful vision of exquisite unattainable beauty had become a good bit less spectacular and a great deal more easily obtainable. You would have suited my purposes better, my dear, had you allowed yourself to go to seed. But there are your purposes to consider as well, I suppose," he concluded in an offhand manner.

Julia did not reply for a moment, then she raised her head and said very carefully, in an attempt to match his coolness, "You leave me no option but to accompany you, but that does not mean that I have to listen to your unpleasant ruminations as well. And I shall not. Now please tell me where Robin is, when I am to speak with him, and when I can expect to return home. I assume that if I do as you say, I shall receive some blameless commendation from my false employer?" she added a bit more anxiously.

"Why yes," the baron said mildly, "of course you shall. *When* our business is concluded. But I find your other questions less easy to answer. You see, part of the difficulty lies in the fact that I do not know precisely where Robin is to be found just now."

As Julia gaped at him, he went on to say somewhat crossly. "All of Europe is in upheaval now, borders are being changed with the tides, places forbidden to the English are opened to them again. The expatriot set which took up residence in Greece during the war seem to be pouring into Italy and France. Robin was snugly ensconced on some little Greek island for months, but now I have some reports that he was seen in Brussels, and yet others state that he is on the move toward Paris. But no matter. That is where we had decided to go in any case," the baron said with finality.

"We?" Julia asked in confusion.

"Yes," he answered perfunctorily, "you and I, of course, and my valet."

"Just the three of us?" Julia asked, widening her eyes.

He observed her closely and then added negligently, "Oh yes, I see. Well, I imagine we can make room for an abigail for you as well. It should be a simple matter to obtain the services of one here.''

"I don't need a lady's maid," Julia said quickly, "for I never had one and don't need one now. But," she paused and then plunged on, "I certainly shall not countenance traveling with you without a chaperone. I am surprised that with all the care you've taken with your scheme, you didn't think of that.''

"A chaperone?" the baron asked in genuine surprise. Then his handsome face lit with real humor. "Here's a flight! A chaperone for you?" he asked again, before subsiding into peals of laughter. He was laughing much too hard to see the transformation that had come over his audience. Julia's cheeks showed twin spots of high color and her eyes lightened until they seemed to positively glow in her otherwise pale face.

She waited for him to be done with his amusement and then controlled her voice only by great effort.

"If you consider me as a candidate for wife to your nephew, I should think you would not wish there to be any gossip about me," she said simply.

"As to that," the baron replied, sobering, "I doubt you will meet many people who will wonder about you. I'm sorry, my dear, but this is to be no whirl of pleasure for you. I shall not run the risk of funding your merry adventures. I'd be several sorts of a fool if I brought you to balls and routs so that you might find a better protector and then loped off with some wealthy gent in tow. Oh no, my dear, you shall travel quite inconspicuously and I'll take care to see that there will be no one who will note or care to note your presence.

"Don't think hard of me," the baron went on, more kindly, "for it will all be to your own benefit. If it transpires that Robin is willing to forgive and forget, it will be better that no one knows that I brought you to his side. And again, if you wish to make the most of that glowing commendation from Lady Cunningham, it is wiser if no one notes you've been traveling about with me instead of her.''

Julia drew in her breath and then said, with all the courage she could muster, "You don't understand at all. It is that I cannot travel alone, with only a strange gentleman as escort.''

He looked at her in surprise. Then it seemed as though he drew himself up and addressed his next words to her as though he spoke from a great height.

"Can you be serious? Do you think I might be tempted to attempt your honor?" he asked icily.

She could only bow her head in confusion at the sneer in both his face and his words.

"Well then, Miss Hastings," he said, "content yourself. I should sooner think of coupling with a serpent than of having a try at you. One fool per family is quite enough, don't you think? I'll admit that you are very lovely, but I'm sorry, you are not in my style at all," he went on, "for I never cared for secondhand experiences."

He caught her hand quickly, before it struck his cheek, even before she knew she had swung it at him. She was so astounded that he could have anticipated an action that she had never taken in the whole of her life, that she scarcely took in his next utterance.

"Now, now," he said with a curious sort of elation, "I did say you were lovely, didn't I? No need to show your claws simply because I refuse your bed. You must become used to admiration from afar if you aspire to our family."

"I don't aspire to your family!" Julia shouted, struggling with him only to regain her hand, which he had taken in a firm and hurtful grip. "I never did."

"Oh, I believe you once did," he said though clenched teeth, drawing her so close by pulling upon her captive hand that she could see the knotted muscles in his lean jaw, "at least until you decided that Robin was nothing without his title and legacy. Only then did you decide against allying yourself with us. And what a difficult decision it must have been for you, coming so late, on what was to have been your very wedding night. Tell me," he said harshly, releasing her suddenly and flinging her away so that she stumbled before she stood, shaking, staring at him, "precisely how did you put it to him? For he never told us that. And I have often wondered. It must have been well said to have influenced him so. Did you say, 'Oh don't be a fool, Robin, what is love without money?' Or were you cruel, saying that only a plentitude of funds could make up for such a paucity of carnal expertise? Perhaps you were more discreet, saying only 'You are very young, Robin, I shall have you when you have grown in years, and annuities.' "

"I never refused him!" Julia cried out, in her extremity

speaking of that which she had vowed never to speak. "It was he who rejected me."

"Yes," breathed her antagonist, "of course. He carried you halfway across the kingdom with him and simply tossed you away."

"Yes," she said quietly.

"How very disappointing," the baron said coolly, although he was breathing raggedly and glaring at her as though she were a fiend incarnate, "I had expected a better story."

"It is true," Julia said, shaking her head as she attempted to discover some way to convince him of her honesty.

"And with no reason given?" he said relentlessly.

"He said he loved another," she said woodenly.

"Ah, the tale gets better. And you believed that?" he asked.

"No," she admitted softly.

"Then why do you imagine he deserted you, and left you all forlorn?" he asked in a travesty of sympathy, with the air of a man who is leading an idiot on.

"I do not know," Julia answered. For she had asked herself that question so many times that it now was as if she were speaking to herself again, as she had in so many of the long nights of her short life.

"Come, come. You can do better than that. You have no idea? You tell me young Lochinvar bore you off on his white horse and then abandoned you, and you have no answer for it? Come, Miss Hastings, I expect more of you. This is poor stuff indeed, coming from such an inventive young woman," he perservered.

But now Julia raised her head. Her white-gold hair had come loose from its pins in the violence of her encounter with the baron and now some of it spilled against her pale cheeks. Her eyes were wild and she spoke with violence. The shocks of the day, the incessant and callous questioning, the very helplessness of her situation now made her speak as she had never done before.

"I do not know," she cried, her voice so thin and shrill that it was unrecognizable to her own ears. "I never knew. Perhaps it is he who is the demented one in your vile family. Perhaps I disgusted him. Perhaps he hates those of my sex as much as you do and finds the same perverse pleasures in our pain as you do."

It was then that he struck her.

6 An enormous silence filled the small room. It was the sort of shocked, fearful silence which descends after an act of violence. The pale and wide-eyed young woman stood and held her hand against her cheek. The gentleman remained motionless as well, seemingly appalled and stricken as the young woman who faced him. He had not slapped her with much force, but her delicate skin immediately showed a red weal where the blow had fallen. For though she now turned her head from him, he could see that her delicately made hand was too small to hide the flaming stain of his anger.

Then the gentleman broke from his immobility. He held up his own shaking hand and examined it as though it were an alien thing.

"I have never done such a thing before," he said in wonderment, "never. Only a brute would strike a woman. Whatever the cause, no man can do such a thing and not feel shame. I can scarcely believe it of myself. I would never call such a man friend, yet now it transpires that I am such a man. There can be no excuse. Forgive me," he said earnestly, "for I had no right. It was not right to do, and I am deeply ashamed."

She looked at him and then lowered her own hand so that the

red mark upon her cheek was clearly visible. There was a small flicker of light in her eyes as she saw him wince.

"No," she said clearly, "I shall not."

"But I offer you my sincerest apologies," he said in bewilderment, "it ought never to have happened. Please understand that such deeds are repugnant to me."

"I understand that," Julia replied steadily, "but I do not accept your apology. For it was not given to me, sir. It was, instead, given solely to yourself. You are deeply shamed," she went on with cold mockery, *"you* cannot believe it of *your*self. *You* find such deeds repugnant to *your*self. That is no apology to me. Forgive yourself, then, if you can, but I cannot.

"But how can you even beg my pardon?" she asked, "when you do not know me? And what can that pardon be worth when you clearly hold me in such low esteem? I am only some insensate creature you have procured for your own purposes. If you could so readily deceive me, manipulate my future, and attempt to ruin my name, why should you stick at manhandling me? It is all of a piece," she concluded bitterly. "I see no incongruity in your actions, my lord."

He dropped his hand to his side and shrugged his shoulders in an inchoate gesture of futility. Now, for the first time since she had met him, the baron did not seem so implacable, such a relentless figure of authority. For without his armor of surety and cynicism, he seemed somehow both more youthful and more human. Julia decided to put what seemed to be a momentary lapse upon his part to the test.

"Lord Stafford . . . my lord," she said softly, "may I go home now?"

He hardly seemed to attend her words. But then he spoke.

"Ah," he sighed heavily, "I wish you could. But, no, no, you may not. I would wish," he said quietly, "that Robin had fixed his attention upon any other female as earnestly as you do. But he did not. And so, while I know I have begun what, believe me, I hope will be a very brief association, upon the wrong foot, I cannot end it as yet. No, you must stay. But for what it is worth, I promise you no further injury. Indeed," he said with a bit more of his former manner, as a skewed smile appeared on his lips, "you may have my word that if I forget myself so much again as to attempt you any harm, you may then leave immediately, at whatever time it may be, or wherever we may happen to be at that time. But more than that, I cannot give you.

"Now," he said more briskly, "I suggest you go to your own room. I will have you shown there, I believe it is a pleasant chamber. It's been a long journey for you, and I imagine that you will be pleased to have luncheon alone in your room and then get some deserved rest."

Before Julia could think he was exhibiting uncharacteristic kindness, he added, "I shall expect you at dinner, however. We will dine together at eight, as we have travel plans to discuss. I expect you precisely at eight, Miss Hastings. Your failure to be there will, of course, result in my notifying my agents in England to take certain actions, just as I stated before."

Julia nodded, and without speaking one other word, went to the door that he held open politely for her to pass through.

It was a bright, clear day and he had thought to accomplish many small chores before evening arrived. But Lord Nicholas Daventry, Baron Stafford, instead paced within a close, closed parlor on the ground floor of Quillack's Hotel and covered almost as many miles within those snug boundaries as he might have done if he had been out upon the busy streets of Calais.

He needed time to order his thoughts and he was unused to lengthy bouts of self-criticism. He was not known by any of his many friends or acquaintances for being given to intense, prolonged periods of introspection. Indeed, had any of them chanced to see him as he paced the narrow parlor, his actions and demeanor would have been as unrecognizable to them as they were to himself now. But then he had not, he admitted, been himself in any fashion since the onset of his acquaintance with Miss Hastings.

If she had been ceaselessly acting a part since they had met, he thought with a fierce frown, then so had he. But it was harder for him, he thought with displeasure, his face taking on an even deeper expression of gloom, for he was unused to such charades. Oh, he had, in his time, been required to simulate certain emotions and enthusiasms above the common; if one were to occasionally act as courier or gatherer of information in the services of one's country, then that was inevitable. But even his superiors never thought to ask him to perform more dire, clandestine deeds. For though it would come as a great shock to Miss Hastings, the Baron Stafford was popularly known as a pleasant, witty, and amiable fellow. Devious fellows like the Marquess of Bessacarr or the Viscount North would do for deeds requiring stealth, but Lord Stafford had such charming, easy ways it was generally agreed that he clearly had more of the makings of a diplomat than of a spy.

Before he had met Julia, the only time he had inspired terror in a feminine heart was when his observer thought he might not chance to notice her presence. If the sight of his physical person was the stuff of her nightmares, it was the heady stuff of rather more exciting dreams of the numerous other females who came within his orbit. And if he had behaved in a sarcastic, cold, and brutal manner toward Julia, then she at least had the signal honor of being the first female he had ever treated so.

For Nicholas Daventry had been surrounded by females since the moment of his birth, and he liked them very well. As an only son, arriving long after the birth of four daughters and shortly before the death of his father, his life had always seemed to be filled with caring women. Having all that constant, loving attention lavished upon him, plus the advantages of being heir to handsome looks and fortune, he might well have grown up to be the sort of self-satisfied fellow who expects devotion from women, rather than appreciating it.

It was only the happy fact that his mother remarried when he was four years of age, he often thought gratefully, and married a wise and patient man, that saved him from drowning in self-esteem. For his stepfather, a thoughtful man, had taught him to understand that love, unlike money, was more enjoyable if it was earned and returned and not simply taken and spent. It was his stepfather who had also gently prized him away from his adoring mother and sisters and arranged that he be educated at school, so that he might learn how to act in the company of men as well as women.

But there was one small, smug vanity that his wise stepfather did not think to save him from. For Nicholas came to young manhood secure in the belief that he knew womankind very well. He was firm in his absolute trust and faith in the essential goodness of their entire gender. It was a conviction that was to cost him dearly and change the course of his orderly life.

Had he disliked women or even felt superior to them as so many of his classmates did, then his stepfather would have no doubt corrected him in his fault. But the usually sagacious gentleman never thought to explain that it made little difference whether one judged any class of people innately superior or inferior to oneself, since such blanket judgments are always wrong. Young Nicholas respected and admired women, but in his indiscriminate affection for them he made the fatal error of forgetting that they were no better than his fellow men and were subject to the same human frailities.

And so, when at nineteen years of age, he met up with Miss Ivy Foster, he quite naturally made a complete fool of himself.

Ivy was an adorable madcap. From the moment he met her quite by chance while idling about town with some of his schoolmates, he was enraptured by her. However, he believed that he harbored few illusions about her. Since she agreed to walk out with him without a proper introduction, never permitted him to meet her parents, and never hesitated to meet him alone, he assumed she had no place in society and little care for its proprieties. In this, he was quite right.

And when their relationship went speedily from innocent diversions upon the streets of the town to far more worldly occupations upon the sheets of a rented bed, he assumed that she was a child of nature who gave freely when love was given. In this, he was absolutely wrong.

It was not that he was blinded by her charms, although he was decidedly enthralled by them. For at nineteen, he thought himself fairly sophisticated in that area. Before he had ever met her, his schoolmates had helpfully advised him as to how to supplement his formal education. Like so many other noble young gentleman, he had been taken on a few excursions to certain houses of a certain nature to learn some practical lessons in human biology. These private sessions had afforded him the opportunity to make a delicious discovery: that females were even more wondrous creatures than he had first realized. Not only could they provide a fellow with company and care, as he knew so well, but they had this other delightful ability to provide the most exquisite pleasure with their own physical persons.

But the joys one could experience during a night on the town in the company of several half-sprung young cronies, with an unknown female as partner, were as nothing when compared to that which one could achieve with a loved one. For young

Nicholas found that not only was there simple pleasure to be found in a lover's arms, there was the infinite pleasure of providing pleasure to a loved one as well. In very short order, Nicholas decided that he loved his merry little Ivy, and since he loved her, she must be his forever.

It was not guilt for his seduction of her that spurred his offer. Even though she was his junior by a year, he knew he was not the first to love her, and some small question remained in his mind as to who had initiated whose seduction in the first place. He was disappointed and regretted her lapse when he became aware of her previous loss of virtue, but he could not blame her in the least, not after he heard the tale she told. He quite understood how such an vulnerable girl could have been misled by an elderly, fatherly gentleman, as she had been, and he grieved for the betrayal of her innocence just as she did. No, it was not honor which prompted him, it was simply that he adored her.

He knew that she was exactly right for him. He needed her blithe spirits, just as she needed someone to protect and watch over her. Her buoyant temperament would please his mama, her sense of humor would tickle his sisters, and her black cherry eyes and midnight ringlets would enchant his steppapa. He believed that her low birth would be no impediment. His family could never be so top-lofty, he told her, and as they loved him, so they would allow him to wed where he loved.

So he was completely shattered when they not only did not condone his engagement to her, but demanded his immediate estrangement from her as well. He left her then, but only so that he could travel to his home to have it out with them. She refused to accompany him, and he could not blame her. He was sure, though, that once he had explained the matter in person, they would certainly understand. But though he explained, then raged, then importuned, then frankly demanded, they would not budge. He was too young, they said when he arrived. And he was too young, they maintained as he left them in insult.

At nineteen years of age, Lord Nicholas Daventry, Baron Stafford, left his school, renounced his loving family, moved into rented lodgings with his lover, and waited for his family to capitulate. Ivy would not wed him, she said sorrowfully, without their approval. That she would not do so without their generous allowance and with their stated threat of his being deprived of his future fortune as well was a possibility which never occurred to him.

Letters from his sisters did not change his mind. Advice from concerned friends did not move him. Lack of funds did not swerve him. He loved, as he did all else, with his whole heart. It was only when he arrived at their little flat one day to find Ivy humming as she packed, that his idyll came to an abrupt end. For, she explained simply, there was neither future nor profit in their association any longer. As he sat on their bed and dumbly watched her stow her belongings, she taught him the lesson his stepfather had neglected to deliver. And that was that females could be fully as deceitful, avaricious, and unprincipled as men were capable of being.

She could not waste her time, Ivy explained seriously. London could afford her greater opportunities to seek her fortune while the bloom of her youth was yet upon her. She did not blame him, she said handsomely, for there was no fault in it for either of them. Even her ideal, Harriet Wilson, she confided, that sage queen of the demireps, had at one time absolutely frittered away two entire years waiting for some young lover's family to come about, and only when she was convinced they never would did she at last quit the fruitless relationship. "For Nick," she said quite seriously as she snapped together her traveling case, "we can't be fools. What is love without money?"

It was a very thorough lesson, given by a gentle instructress. And it was an expensive one. Not so much in monetary terms, for though Ivy considered the amount of money given to her by his stepfather for her cooperation to be a princely sum, it was exceedingly little to pay to buy a young man's freedom from destruction. But if the cost were reckoned in terms of his loss of dignity, face, and confidence, then it was indeed a king's, rather than a mere baron's, ransom.

Nicholas Daventry returned to school, returned to the bosom of his family, and returned to his senses so much so that he could eventually even jest about his youthful folly. But he never did return to his previous self. He became a man: a gentleman in the best construction of the word, a credit to his name, a patriot, a sportsman, a staple of the ton, a staunch friend, and a devoted son. He remained a considerate lover. But he never loved again.

He had a reputation for being wise in the ways of women. His mistresses were always up to snuff, being either accredited society beauties whose husbands gave them leave to indulge in discreet affairs, or Cyprians of the highest rank and taste. But he always knew their price, and they always knew their place.

He planned to marry soon, for he was approaching his thirtieth year and wished to set up his nursery. He liked children very well. In fact, he had his eye upon the Incomparable of the Season, a certain Honorable Miss Merriman. But if this present business took him from her for too long, he knew she might well opt for George Ronan, Earl of Cowes, who was paying particular attentions, or an old acquaintance of his, Sir Reginald Beverly, who was paying particularly close inattentions. Still, if she were snapped up by either of them before he returned, he contented himself that there would be another Season, ruled by another equally suitable Incomparable. For he had learned his lesson well, and was careful of his reputation for being wise in the ways of women.

It was the present situation which caused him to prowl a parlor in Quillack's Hotel like a bear with an aching head, and not the thought of the Honorable Miss Merriman's inevitable nuptials. For it was clear to him that his young nephew Robin was caught in the same sort of a trap that he had been in, but that the poor lad had been allowed to remain in it for too long. He blamed himself for that.

Nicholas Daventry had returned from the fires of his disgrace tempered by strong feelings of responsibility and obligation to his family. Young Robin might be only his nephew, but he had always felt a bond of sympathy for the lad. Their circumstances were not too dissimilar. Robin had grown to adulthood in the close care of many women as well, for he had been a surprising late-life addition to his family and his two older brothers had been out of the house by the time he was out of his leading strings. Since his father was too old to be anything but bored by infants, and in any case was the sort of man who preferred the company of his older, more boisterous sons, Robin had returned his young uncle's attention with a gratifying amount of hero worship.

During their school days, Robin's upper-classman uncle was often pleased to confer honor upon him by returning his flattering adoration with flattering attention. And when his uncle was done with his famous adolescent misadventure, his nephew earned continuing favor by being sage enough or kind enough to never bring the matter up again.

But for all there was a link between "Old Nick" and "Robin Goodfellow," as they continued to call each other into adulthood, Old Nick had been looking the other way when Robin flew off with his lover, and that his uncle could not forgive himself for. He had fired off a letter immediately after he had heard the news from his distraught aunt, swiftly disengaging himself from the affair he had been pursuing that had preoccupied him so disastrously. Worse yet, he had foolishly thought the matter was done when the chit left Robin in the lurch. He had believed that a tour of the Continent was just the thing to clear his nephew's heart and head, and so encouraged it in yet another letter and then let the matter lie.

But Robin had been gone for three years and no letters, no messages, no wisdom anyone could put upon paper had changed his mind. His father could not rule him, as they had never been close and even when one son had succumbed to a fever and the other had fallen in the military, it was too late to pick up the threads of their relationship. His mama could only wail or nag at him. Only Old Nick could do some good, she insisted. What she left unsaid was the nagging fact that if Robin remained unwed, and then by some horrible chance came to his end while in that state of single blessedness, his uncle would be his heir. Heir to his fortune, and heir to his title.

His aunt's unspoken accusations did not move Nicholas and it was as well that she never uttered them. He might be a mere baron, but it was common knowledge that the Staffords never sought a title in their long history, not when, as it was commonly said, they had the blunt to buy a kingdom of their own if they wanted honors. But her spoken plaints had weight. For he did think he could influence his nephew. He had traveled to the Continent twice in fact, on various missions, and each time he had sought out Robin. And each time, he had been told, with a sad smile, "soon," soon he would return, just so soon as he felt he could face England and all of its unhappy memories again.

He would have gotten over the whole foolish affair long since, Nicholas thought savagely, pausing in his pacing to thump his fist impotently upon a wall, if she had only let him alone. But no, he thought, she did not. First, she told Robin she had reconsidered, and when his hopes were high, she changed her mind again. She kept him on a long lead: one that lasted three years and stretched across the channel. In one letter to his uncle Robin would jubilantly state that Julia would be his within the year, and then another would arrive a few months later saying she had had second thoughts again and he must wait upon her reply. Then, even as his father's condition worsened, Robin told his uncle he had received the devastating news that she had only been toying with him, for she was wed, and had been wed all the while.

The dark-haired gentleman looked down at his clenched fist and wondered again at the violence the wretched slut who called herself Miss Hastings caused him to feel. He could not understand her malice in the affair. If she had cast off Robin because he could not support her once his family had withdrawn their funds, why should she continue to torment him? It was to discover that that he had first set Bow Street upon her traces. When he found that it was another Miss Hastings, a Miss Harriet Hastings, that had been wed upon the sixteenth June, 1813, his fury had nearly overwhelmed him. When he was apprised of Miss Julia Hastings' history of employment, and realized that she was still on the catch for a wealthy mate, he decided to act.

She should have accepted his original offer, he thought, coming to rest at last upon the arm of the chair. But perhaps, he sighed, closing his eyes, she had her eye on a likely fool whom she thought might make an offer of marriage and did not wish to leave the country and ruin her chances. But there was no reason that he could fathom that would have made her continue to play at her game of innocence. Even Ivy had confessed all when she saw that the game was up. It was that air of outraged innocence, that aura of sweet blamelessness that set his teeth on edge and caused him to lose his temper and temperate thoughts.

No, it was not only that, he admitted. She was so beautiful, so cool and virginal with her demure dresses and her white spun-gold hair and clear light eyes and soft speech that at times she caused him to wonder if he were as mad as she had pretended she thought he was. He could understand why and how Robin had been so thoroughly gulled and how he could continue to be so totally grieved. For Nicholas had lied. Even knowing what she was, the thought of bedding her was irresistible.

But he would not even attempt her, Nicholas thought, opening his eyes to the advancing day and preparing to be done with his tumultuous, fruitless reasonings. Not only would it be a betrayal of Robin if he should lie with her, it would be a total loss of honor for himself. Nor would he ever strike her again. The sick and horrified feeling he had experienced when he realized what he had done, had caused him more pain than if he himself had been soundly beaten. And, he thought with grim amusement, so she *had* beaten him, the moment that he had touched her in anger.

Nicholas Daventry straightened and marshaled his thoughts. He would never get anywhere, he realized, if he continued to think of her as just another female, as she wished him to. If he were to carry out this mission successfully, he would have to think of her dispassionately, as he would any masculine enemy, and plan accordingly.

She was dangerous, he thought, because she was never honest, perhaps never even with herself. She had power, because she had such uncanny ability to act that she made a man doubt his own reason. In fact, he wondered why she had not sought a career upon the stage. And she had the ability to incite a man's desire. But he thought, pleased with how this new method of evaluating her cleared the matter, she clearly had weaknesses. In fact, on balance, she was remarkably unsuccessful. All her past actions showed that she obviously did not angle for a wealthy man's protection, but held out instead for an advantageous marriage. There was wisdom in that, he conceded, but still she had never succeeded since she was yet poor and unattached.

Once he thought of her in much the manner of a general assessing an opposing force, his future course of action became clear.

He would counter the danger she presented by making this venture as short as possible, and by avoiding her company whenever he could. He would touch her neither in anger or desire. And he would save his own soul whenever he was tempted by her by remembering that the lowest draggleskirt he could buy at the waterfront of this city this night would have more morals than she possessed.

Now the baron straightened. A smile played about his lips, his brow was smooth, and his eyes shone with amusement. He was himself again. He took out his pocketwatch and was amazed at the hour. He had a great deal to do, he thought as he strode to the door. He would hasten to take her to Robin. And then he would do all in his power to ensure that Robin fully understood the depth and scope of her vileness.

If he could not convince his gullible young nephew of her duplicity, the baron thought as he paused with his hand upon the door, he himself would pay any price, in coin or in kind, to see that the pair never wed. Nicholas Daventry did not make vows lightly, but now before he went out to see to arrangements for a trip to Paris, he gave his solemn oath to himself. He swore that Miss Julia Hastings would never be wife to his nephew. And if she tried, she would pay dearly.

Then, with the air of a man who has just accomplished a great deal, although he had only passed the morning in thought, he opened the door, bestowed a brilliant smile upon a passing maidservant and, squaring his shoulders with resolve, went out into the day.

Precisely at eight in the evening, Miss Hastings presented herself at the door to the private dining parlor. The baron rose to meet her and, acknowledging her punctuality, nodded to her as he showed her to her chair. Though he did not seem to examine her any more closely than he did the servant who brought them their repast, he took careful but oblique note of her appearance. It was both a little disappointing and a bit unnerving for him to discover that in her simple gray dress and beige shawl, she did not appear to be anything other than a very lovely, very sad young woman.

After all his morning's reflections, he had almost expected her to arrive swathed in red silk and done up to the nines, like the heartless temptress he envisioned her to be. He might even have been pleased to see her unkempt and hysterical with outrage, as the consummate actress he believed her to be. But instead she sat quietly, wrapped in her omnipresent shawl, and said nothing and ate sparingly.

When desserts were brought and they were left alone, he began to detail the journey which was to begin in the morning. Only then did he look her full in the face and see that she had attempted to cover the bruise upon her cheek with rice powder.

A shrewd bargainer might have let it appear to accuse him in all its blatancy. Still, in its concealment, the blemish became even more vivid to him. He had to think a moment before he silently congratulated her on her artful and correct decision that her attempt to ignore the incident would cause him to feel far worse about it than shrill or sullen accusation might. But this reasoning was too convoluted for even its author to follow for longer than the time it took for him to sip his demitasse.

She listened closely as he detailed the coach trip they must take first to Doullens to clear up some personal matter he must attend to, and from thence to Paris itself. She remained mute during his explanations. To prod her from her unsettling silence, he ventured to offer her a slice of a gateau that he found excellent.

"No, thank you," she said softly. "I find I have not much appetite."

"Do you think," he said smoothly, arching an eyebrow as he prepared for battle, "to make me feel guilty for your lack of appetite?"

"Oh no," she replied swiftly. "It is only that I am not too hungry tonight."

He sat and stared at her as she averted her eyes. He drummed his fingers upon the tabletop and then said so suddenly as to make her startle, "I am hardly a monster, you know. If you deal honestly with me, you will be honestly dealt with in return. This sulking pettishness does not endear you to me, you know."

"I don't wish to endear myself to you," she said, rising from her chair. "May I go to my room now?" Although this was said without a tremor in her voice, he could not help noticing the tears that had started in her eyes.

"Go then. Good night," he said abruptly, and found himself rising for courtesy's sake as she dropped her napkin upon the table and fled.

Nicholas Daventry remained at the table, scowling so fiercely that the servant who came to clear thought the elegant English gentleman must have possessed the nose of a Frenchman and detected the exact vintage that the hotel chose to serve those from across the channel. But the gentleman's thoughts were far from a vinous nature. He was, instead, remembering the manner in which his absent guest had involuntarily cringed when he rose so suddenly to his feet, before she realized that he was only correctly taking note of her departure. He was remembering the sorrow omnipresent in her eyes, and the way she had sat with her shoulders slightly raised, as though in some manner she had gathered herself up against assault and had no other means of protection.

The servant did not have to call the manager to offer up apologies for the inferior wine, as he thought he had to from the thunderously black look upon the English gentleman's face. The gentleman was only furious with himself. It was no one event of the evening that distressed him. It was the inescapable realization he had just come to this evening, that he had only wasted a great deal of his time and effort during the day. For not one of his fine resolves born of the morning had been able to survive its first night.

7 Julia woke to a new day with a new face staring down at her. She immediately scrambled to an upright position, caught the coverlets up to her chin, and asked in a voice squeaky with fright and early morning disuse, "Who are you?"

She had been roused from a dream of home and it had been so vivid that now in the moment of awakening she was not sure of where she was. A slight noise had blurred her dream and her eyes had opened to register the incredible fact that a being they had never gazed upon before was gazing back at them. It wasn't a very frightening face; in fact, Julia's sudden movement and apparent terror seemed to alarm it equally as much as she had been affrighted. Upon more careful reflection, Julia could see that it was a gentle feminine visage that regarded her. The woman appeared to be of middle age, and was small, with a compact form. She had a plain but intelligent face and chestnut hair with strands of gray interwoven in its neat braids.

"But I have only come to awaken you, mademoiselle," the woman said as she backed away.

Julia found herself vaguely remembering her circumstances, but when the woman added, "M'sieur le Baron, he told me that you must be woken, and dressed and ready to travel within the hour . . ." everything came back to her, and she sank back upon the pillows, her look of distress completely gone, being replaced immediately by an expression of sorrow.

"Ah yes," Julia sighed, as she ran a hand through her long and tousled hair, "then thank you."

Julia threw back the covers and was about to walk to the dressing table when the woman approached her bearing a laden silver tray.

"Please to rest yourself, mademoiselle," she said anxiously, "for I have taken the liberty to bring you some coffee and some fresh croissants, do you see, and some chocolate, too, if you like. If you wish to make use of the convenience, then I shall wait, but if not, I should be pleased to pour for you now."

There was such exaggerated concern in the woman's voice that Julia sat back promptly and said that she would be pleased to have some chocolate, thank you very much. For though she very much wished to visit the small adjoining chamber upon her awakening, the consternation upon the older woman's countenance was so acute that she felt it would have been cruel to deny her the immediate opportunity to pour the chocolate, arrange the napery, and smooth the coverlets, as she promptly commenced to do.

Julia thought that as soon as she had begun her breakfast, the older woman would have gone on her way, as it was a busy hotel and there must have been some other ladies awakening to find themselves in need of sustenance. But the woman only stood at a respectful distance and watched with deep concentration as Julia sipped at her chocolate. She was being observed so narrowly that Julia had the mad momentary thought that perhaps the baron had in some wise arranged to alter the innocuous beverage in some fashion to ensure her docility. It was excellent chocolate, and it was a bizarre fancy that undoubtedly had little basis in truth, yet, Julia decided as she regretfully put down her cup, she was not really very hungry. But it was becoming apparent that the nervous maidservant would not be gone until the breakfast was finished. Perhaps she had to make sure that none of the cutlery was stolen, Julia thought as she patted her lips with the napkin to signify that she was done.

But when she returned from the antechamber with her essential morning's ablutions done, the woman was still standing in the center of the room as though she had been awaiting Julia's return. Julia was unaccustomed to hotels, and unfamiliar with the ways of the Quality that normally patronized them. For all she knew, she thought uncomfortably as she sat at the dressing table and picked up her hair brush, it was she herself who was acting in a strange fashion, and not the maidservant. Then all at once it came to her that perhaps the poor woman was unable to leave until she was actually dismissed.

She searched for the right words as the maidservant's anxious eyes searched her face. "That is all," she said in a stilted fashion. "Thank you, but you may go now."

"But your hair!" the maidservant protested as she came forward and took the brush from Julia's fingers. "Please allow me!" she cried as she began to brush out the pale and tangled mass of it.

Her touch was gentle and beneath her fingers, Julia's hair began to resemble a glowing, gliding river of sunlight. As the determined maidservant drew up the golden tresses to arrange them, the recipient of her attentions hardly noticed that a fashion was being created for her that was far lovelier than any she herself had ever either envisioned or attempted. For Julia was not feeling so much privileged as beleaguered.

So when the maidservant had done, and stood back proudly so that Julia could see how cleverly her golden hair had been done à la Princesse, the nod and sigh of relief that the young woman offered was not in response to the artistry of her hairdressing, but rather to the fact that an idea had occurred to her. A pourboire, of course, Julia thought, smiling so broadly with relief that the maidservant smiled back at her. The poor woman expected some gratuity and had stayed on and would stay on performing all sorts of chores, until she received one. And she, like the untutored simpleton she was, had not realized it.

Julia rose from her chair and went to her traveling case. She rummaged about within it, taking care to conceal the actual location of her purse by positioning her body so that her precise actions could not be seen. The good women at Mrs. White's boarding house had instructed her so thoroughly that by the time she turned around with a few coins in her hand, she was sure that no eagle, much less maidservant, could have spied the location of her funds where they were sewn into a clever little side pocket of her traveling case.

"Thank you so very much," Julia said with some aplomb, now that she had the situation well in hand, as she offered the coins to the woman. She had expected some thanks, but no tears. Instead, the woman looked at the coins and backed away from them as though they were tainted, while her eyes filled with unshed tears.

"Ah non, mademoiselle," she said with evident despair. "Monsieur le Baron has already paid me handsomely. But what have I done wrong?"

It would have been difficult for an observer to guess who was more overset by the turn of events. It was not until Julia attempted to ease the maidservant's fears, and she in turn had tried to still Julia's anxieties, that both women were calm long enough for the matter to be made clear.

The baron had engaged her, the maidservant said, when she could control her trembling lips, to act as personal maid for the English lady for the duration of her stay in France. As she had been without work for a long time while war had cruelly ravaged her country, she was overjoyed to have found employment again. In fact, she ventured to say, the moment François (an old friend who was assistant to the night manager at the hotel) had heard of the position, he had sent word to her. She had been patiently standing in the hallway for hours, she explained simply, waiting for the dawn to arrive so that she could be prompt to serve her new lady when she arose. She had been in service to the noble Bonneuil family before the war, and had her English from her husband, who had been their children's tutor. And she assured Julia with an admixture of pride and a certain amount of trepidation, if only the young English lady would try her, she would find that Celeste Vitry was an admirable lady's maid.

Celeste began to nervously enumerate her many abilities, since the look upon the young English miss's face did not encourage her to think that her brief spoken résumé was suitable. When she had gotten to her skill with a needle, having just left off explaining her competence with a curling iron, Julia interrupted her gently.

"No no," Julia said quickly, "I do understand, Celeste, I assure you that I do. And there is little doubt in my mind of your excellence. But it is only that I do not require your services. I'm not actually a lady, you see. I myself work in the capacity of a servant when I am at home. I am a governess and a companion. It is only that I am traveling with the baron just now as . . ." But here Julia's invention failed her, for she could not say precisely what she was. She did not wish to make it public knowledge that she was employed by the baron. Nor did she wish her connection with Robin to be noised about. Neither did she want to explain the circumstances involving the absent Lady Cunningham. She knew precisely how deeply the waters of convention were closing over her head when Celeste grew very still.

"Ah, I see," she said a little sadly, "but then Mademoiselle, Monsieur le Baron would wish for you to do him proud, would he not? You are very lovely, but I can make you appear even more so, I promise you. He would never look at another when I was through dressing you, I assure you."

It was rather a relief for Julia to throw caution to the winds and tell Celeste the truth of her reason for being in France, but even so it took ten minutes for her to fully explain the matter. The maidservant was an excellent listener and when Julia was done, she shook her head sagely, as though she heard such tangled tales every day of the week. But there were many strange stories told in her country in these days, she assured Julia.

Then she artfully said three artless things which won her a new position. For first she told Julia that she was very glad to hear of her new mistress's virtue, since she had never worked for a "petite amie" before. Next, she explained that her own circumstances were such that she would have been forced to take whatever employment offered, whatever her own moral compunctions, for she had no husband since her man had marched off with the Emperor to Russia in 1811, and no employer since the noble Brouilles had been beggared by the new government. And then she told Julia quite simply that anything told to her in confidence would be as a thing dropped into a bottomless well. A fine lady's maid, Celeste said proudly, was expected to go to her grave with her lady's secrets upon her heart, and never upon her lips.

The baron looked at Julia's hair with approval when she met him belowstairs in the private dining room. He rose when she entered the room and did not seat himself again until she had taken her place at the table. But he did not say a word to her until he had cleared his breakfast plate, and noted that she had done with moving the food about on hers so that, at least, her place setting could be removed. Then, when there were no longer any servants in the room, he leaned back and addressed her.

"So you approve of Celeste?" he asked pleasantly enough.

"She is charming," Julia answered slowly. "I did tell you that I had no need of a personal maid. But as you have hired her," she added quickly, remembering that her maidservant had no other place to go should she lose this position, "it would not be fair to dismiss her now. I am only glad that she has had experience in her job, for I haven't the slightest notion of how to go on with her."

The baron only nodded and then asked idly, "She is old enough to suit her taste?"

Julia turned her large light eyes to him in puzzlement.

"I believe you requested an older woman to accompany you," he said a bit testily. "As chaperone," he reminded her, when she did not reply at once.

Julia rose from her chair and faced him.

"I am glad for her company, my lord, but I do not consider a lady's maid to be a chaperone. It was my reputation that I had a care for, and not my hair or my clothes."

He rose as well and gazed at her for a long moment before he spoke. When he did, his voice was so expressionless that she could not say if he were annoyed or amused with her.

"I wonder if anyone has ever taught you how to say a simple 'Thank you,' Miss Hastings? No matter," he went on. "We haven't the time to discuss your upbringing. We leave for Doullens now. I shall be riding alongside the carriage, and I don't know whether we will have a chance to speak alone before we get to Sir Sidney's pleasure palace. So I must tell you now, beware of everyone you meet at his home. He is a rackety sort of fellow, and has been living abroad for years, entertaining every Englishman that ventures across the channel in that rented chateau of his. His wife is a tart, his guests are disreputable, and he is not to be trusted. If there is anything you do not wish to be known, it follows that it is a thing that you would not wish him to know."

A shadow passed over the baron's stern face as he went on, "I must speak with him upon a matter of business. Unpleasant business," he added, "so be prepared to leave quickly, for he may not like what I have to say and we may depart at an odd hour. However, I will attempt to discover something of Robin's where-

abouts from some of his guests before I have that private word
with our host. In any event, Miss Hastings, I will take care to introduce you with a name that you have never heard before, and I
strongly advise you to remain in your rooms for the duration of
our visit. We shall say that you are victim to headaches.''

Julia looked down at her folded hands, and tried to conceal
her dismay at discovering she was to be mewed up as a prisoner
in her rooms for an indeterminate time, under a false name and
an assumed illness. The baron paused. Then he said in a more
gentle tone than he ordinarily used, ''Of course, if you wish to
become famous, or infamous, Miss Hastings, you are free to
come and go as you please at Sir Sidney's. I shall not chain you
up or ask my host to accommodate you in his dungeons. But if
as you say you feel the lack of a chaperone so acutely, I
strongly advise you to follow my advice.''

Looking at her downcast head and the shadow of her lashes
upon her cheek, he added rapidly before he went to the door,
''And if we stay for longer than I've planned, I'll see to it that
you get to take the air, at least. You won't dwindle to a skeleton
through my neglect. I assure you that it is privacy we are after,
Miss Hastings, and not punishment.''

Julia had dreaded the prospect of another long coach ride as
much as she had detested the entire journey she was now under-
taking, but as the miles slipped by, she discovered that travel in
the company of the baron was quite unlike anything she had
ever experienced before. She had ridden by coach many times
at home, and had taken both the mail and the stagecoach as she
traveled to her many different and far-flung places of employment. But now she appreciated the wide gulf that separated the
wealthy from the common man as she never had before.

For this coach that the baron had engaged for herself and Celeste was so well padded and well-sprung, that instead of a
lurching shock being registered at every fault in the road, there
was only a softly cushioned bounce felt by the passengers.
There were flasks of beverages available, a hamper filled with
light refreshments, and even a small vase with some wild flowers arranged in it pinned to the inner door. She and Celeste had
room and to spare to relax in, for the baron's valet rode in a second coach, and he himself rode on ahead, mounted on a fine
bay thoroughbred.

From time to time the baron would drop back to inspect the

coaches as they went down the road. As her maidservant dozed, Julia could watch her employer-captor-nemesis unobserved. He was all three of these things, she thought, as she watched him through her window, and perhaps even more as well. For she noticed that when he was not with her, and when he did not think himself observed by her, he became quite a different man than the one she had come to know and fear.

She had thought that there was little family resemblance between the baron and his lost nephew, Robin. Robin's hair had been long and tawny, where his uncle's was curled and dark. Robin's eyes were light brown, and his uncle's were that odd shade of hazel that imitates all colors. But the difference went further than that of superficial features. Although they both were slender, well muscled, and straight-limbed, she would have never thought them related. For Robin had been full of youth and laughter, full of grace and joy, and his uncle was stern, controlled, and stiff in his every angry gesture toward her.

But now as she observed the baron, unobserved, she could see that when he laughed at some jest that their coachman called down to him, he threw back his head and his haughty features could relax and his white-toothed smile was dazzling in its surprise. His eyes could sparkle with wit, not malice, his laughter could be infectious, not mocking. His slender body could be as graceful as his nephew Robin's when he was not pokered up with suppressed rage, his countenance could be light and open when he was not rigid with fury, he could be amazingly young and merry when he was not, she thought suddenly, with her.

But it made no difference whether he resembled Robin or not, Julia thought, for Robin had loved her, or at least, she had thought he had. And his uncle detested her, and that at least, was a fact that required little thought. She did not know why Robin had written those letters so full of lies, but she now could at last admit that he must have done so. For whatever else the Baron Stafford was, and he may have been a great many things, she no longer thought he was either a lunatic or an inveterate liar. He had the letters he claimed he did, of that she was convinced.

She had lain awake in the night, and thought of little else in the day, and now she believed such letters existed. She had been vilified because of them, she had been coerced into leaving her homeland because of them, she had even been offered violence because of them. But as the coach traveled on into the heart of France, she found she was as anxious to continue this journey as she had been loathe to begin it.

She had never wanted to see Robin again after that wild October night, but she knew that she must see him, she must face him, and demand to know why he had invented such monstrous stories about her. Not for his uncle's sake, although the fact that he treated her with such revulsion stung more now than when she had thought him simply deranged. She had to learn the truth for her own heart's ease.

Julia gazed out the window at the rolling fields of France, and only closed her eyes to rest when the baron rode by and chanced to glance at her.

It was nearing twilight when the coach rolled down the long drive to Sir Sidney's leased chateau. Julia might have shut her eyes for an instant to escape the baron's notice, but when the stir Celeste made as she gathered up possessions came to her ears, she realized that she had drifted off into the first easy sleep she had experienced since setting foot upon foreign soil.

The chateau was huge, and all Julia could take in was the startled impression that she was to spend the night in a castle, before the coach stopped and the footman raced to assist her from the carriage. Before she had a chance to wonder at how she was supposed to go on, the baron appeared at her side and took her arm, and Celeste took her place obediently in their wake. They walked the many stone steps to the huge oaken door, which swung open to meet them as smoothly as though they were taking part in a well-rehearsed ceremony. It seemed that everything was going according to some prearranged formula, and that she all unknowingly fell into the scheme of things without so much as a ripple.

When the short, stout, balding gentleman appeared and clapped the baron on the shoulder, shouting a jolly, "Hallo, why it's Stafford! Delightful to see you, m'boy," and his stunning lady-wife cooed her greetings, Julia did not have to breathe a word. She was introduced to the pair before she could take in her breath at the sight of the size of the vast entry hall.

"Miss Foster," the baron said calmly, "may I present Sir Sidney and his beautiful lady-wife?"

"Oh never so formal, Nicky," the statuesque red-haired

lady chided him, taking the baron's arm and disengaging him from Julia.

"We don't stand about on ceremony here, Miss Foster," the portly older gentleman said merrily. "Now, come, how can I call you Miss Foster, when I insist you call me Ollie as all my friends do?"

"I fear," the baron said at once, before Julia could begin to stammer out an answer, "that you will not be able to call her anything for a space, sir, for she has been suffering from a thunderous headache all day and I promised her some rest in a quiet bedroom immediately we arrived here."

"Suffers from the headache, and demands her own bed? Just like my little Gilly." Sir Sidney guffawed. "But I thought it was only the married ladies that protested so. Never say you've tied the knot, Nicholas old fellow?"

"Never say is quite correct," the baron drawled, as Sir Sidney's wife let out her indrawn breath in laughter, "but I should be pleased if Miss Foster could be shown to her room at once."

Even as the baron had done speaking, Celeste began to tug Julia toward the stairs, so she had only a fleeting glimpse of the crowd of well-dressed people who had come from the recesses of the great house to greet the baron and to try to catch a glimpse of the young woman he had brought with him. As she mounted the stair to follow a footman to her room, she had only the briefest view of the back of the baron's head as he lowered it to catch Lady Sidney's whispers to him as she linked her jeweled arm in his and led him away.

Julia's room was large and sumptuously furnished. Fat white and gold cupids cavorted across its vaulted ceiling and snuggled together on her bedposts. But as she had to remain in her room for the night, and for the next few days and nights as well, she came to be the most grateful for its cushioned windowseat. From there she could observe that the world continued to go on around her.

Sir Sidney came and went with a variety of lovely female guests, but Julia became accustomed to the sight of his flame-haired wife with the attentive figure of Nicholas Daventry in constant attendance upon her. She saw Lady Sidney and the baron ride out with the other guests in the early afternoon, she could observe them strolling through the rose gardens after luncheon, and in the night, she was able to crack the window open and hear their laughter above the music until almost dawn.

It seemed to Julia that her captor was well occupied upon this visit, but she only added that information onto her present store of resentment. She stayed in seclusion in compliance with his wishes. Her meals were brought to her room, along with various medicaments that their host thoughtfully provided for his unknown, ailing guest.

Celeste was very good company, but Julia was growing restive as another soft summer night came on and the music struck up once again. It was not that she wanted to dance, she told herself, it was just that she very much wanted to use her limbs. Even Celeste had been able to go for a walk in the afternoon, while she could only complete useless circuits of her room.

The evening was advanced and Julia was about to put on her nightshift, when a soft knock came upon her door. After Celeste had made certain that Julia had scrambled into bed with her coverlets up about her chin, she opened the door cautiously. The maidservent held whispered conversation and then, closing the door once again, came into the room with a wide grin upon her face.

"Ah, mademoiselle," she said happily, "you have not been forgotten."

"Don't tell me," Julia groaned. "This time they've sent up powdered newt or frog instead of hartshorn and warm milk for my headache. I think if I took all their remedies, I should never leave this place alive."

"No, no. This is a much better cure for your poor head. For I told Makepiece, M'sieur le Baron's valet, that if you lingered in your room any longer, you would in truth be ill. So he has spoken with the baron, and he brings you this message. There is a small garden he has discovered, very much in disuse, to the side of the house. You may go there tonight and breathe in some fresh air. Of course," Celeste warned as Julia positively leaped from her bed as though it were red-hot, "if anyone comes along, you must clutch your head," she pantomimed agony, "and return here at once."

With her maidservant to lead the way, Julia stole out into the halls of Sir Sidney's vast house and crept down the servant's stairs. She drew her beige shawl around herself tightly and paused at every noise. Their dinner done, the other guests were at cards or dancing, but still she dared not risk discovery. Finally, they achieved a back door. Celeste pushed it open with the flourish of a woman presenting the royal gardens of Versailles, instead of a simple deserted knot garden.

It was only the size of the bedroom she had just left. As it had no ceilings, the omnipresent cherubs that the Sidneys seemed to adore had to make do with sporting atop a bird bath. That, and a few thoroughly chastened rosebushes and a marble bench completed the decor of the forgotten garden. It was close to the house, but privacy was assured as it was ringed around with a hedge of boxwood. The spare, empty garden was like paradise to Julia.

After Celeste had left, Julia sat down on the stone bench and breathed in the rose-scented air and stared up at the moon as though she had been a prisoner in the Bastille for twenty years, rather than penned in a plush guest bedroom for two days. She could hear the faint, far-off music of a waltz, she could feel a slight, light summer night breeze stir her hair, and she felt at once elated and depressed to be abroad on such a night. It was a night made for adventure, but she wanted none. It was a night made for memories, but she dared not recall hers. It was a night made for lovers, and that she could never be.

So she sat and raised her face to the moon in much the same way that a pagan might make obeisance to the sun, as though she could draw warmth and sustenance from it, and she let the silvery light wash over her and tried to transcend the night. Then she scented something different on the night wind and heard a small sound too large for an animal to make, and she tensed.

"No need to be a Sarah Siddons, Miss Hastings," the baron's voice drawled, "for it is only your obedient servant. You can take your hand from your brow and drop that look of intense pain, unless the sight of me provokes it, of course. I only came by to see how you are faring."

She turned and saw him in the shadows. He was splendid in his evening clothes, and the white of his shirt and his eyes gleamed against their dark background in the bright moonlight.

"When can we leave?" she asked simply.

"Yesterday, I thought," he said, coming forward and standing before her. "Do you mind?" he asked, gesturing with a small cheroot that he held, its red tip a small glowing light in the darkness. "It's a filthy habit I picked up in my travels. But snuff, for all it's in fashion, makes me sneeze and I cannot see how the symptoms of illness can be a pleasure. Now this," he said, laughing as he traced a small incandescent circle with its red embers, "only makes me cough and gasp, and so is, of course, much more pleasant."

She could not see his face clearly, but he spoke so easily that she wondered if he were quite sober. As though he had over-heard her thoughts in the stillness of the night, he said lightly, "I've had a little claret, a dab of port, a taste of champagne, and a sip of cognac, but I assure you, I'm the clearest-headed fellow in the company. And that perhaps is why I've come out here. There is nothing so depressing as being the only sober member of a jolly troupe. I'd like to be gone fully as much as I expect you would, Miss Hastings," he said more seriously, "but my charming, convivial host has managed to elude me very nicely and I cannot go until I have had his ear in private. May I sit down?" he asked suddenly.

Julia nodded and must have murmured her assent, for he sat even as she moved away to make room for him, although there was already room and to spare for three persons on the bench beside her.

They sat quietly for a few moments and she could hear the orchestra beginning a sprightly country dance. "But Lord knows," he said, as though he had been speaking all the while, "I should like to leave this place."

"When can we go then?" Julia asked again.

"So soon as I can corner our clever host. He knows I have less than pleasant news for him, and like the king who slew the courier for bearing bad tidings, he confuses the messenger with the message." Though Julia said nothing, he went on just as though she had asked that which was in her mind, "Our de-lightful Sir Sidney, you see, has been living here for years. He has entertained hundreds of our countrymen and has a reputa-tion as a generous, immoral, but obliging host. The only prob-lem is that we have discovered that he has been obliging to the enemy as well. Now as he has birth, and some powerful family connections, it's been decided that the matter shall be resolved in an honorable, gentlemanly fashion. Oh no," he said in mock horror, "no summary execution, no internment in Newgate for this Jolly Ollie. No, he is simply to be told, on the *qui vivre*, that his presence is not welcome in England again. Never again, as a matter of fact. And I am the lucky chap who is to tell him."

There was nothing Julia could say. But she sensed that he needed someone to say something to him.

"How very difficult for you . . ." she began to say.

"How very nicely put," he said sweetly.

"I only meant," she said rapidly, "that it must be difficult for you to play at being a guest when you are, in effect, an enemy."

"I know," he said wearily, "I'm sorry. I should not have bitten your head off. It is just that it is a tiresome, unpleasant business. I am offered everything by my host, and more than that by my hostess, and all I want is to deliver my message and to be gone from here."

There was silence between them until Julia finally ventured to say cautiously, "She is very lovely."

"Then that *was* your bedroom window," he laughed. "You should take care not to stir the curtains when you spy on us. I take it you mean that you have observed the good lady of the manor and myself at our play. Ah yes, the fair Gilly," he sighed. "She has been in my constant company. I cannot ride, eat, dance, or walk without her beside me. I must peek under my bed each night like a frightened maiden to make sure she isn't there as well."

She wondered at his relationship with their beautiful redheaded hostess, but she did not dare to comment and chance his scorn. His mood was edgy, his temper uncertain, and she wondered again at just how much he had imbibed, however much he claimed he was the clearest-headed of the guests. They remained in the darkness without speaking, but Julia felt his gaze upon her, as though he willed her to conversation with him.

"Tell me," the baron said pleasantly enough, casting away his cheroot so that it made a fiery arc into the darkness, "did you take all of the medicines that our good host provided you?"

"No," Julia said in confusion. "You know I am not ill."

"Ah, but you were a good guest," he said, "for you didn't send them back and insult him, did you? No," he sighed, "the trick of being a good guest is to appear to enjoy everything that is offered, while discreetly refusing to use everything offered. But it is, as you say, difficult."

His face glowed dimly white as he turned toward her, and Julia was both gratified and a little alarmed by the odd mood of fellowship that had come upon him and by the strange way that he could anticipate her thoughts as though she spoke them aloud. As he gazed at her, she could not tell if he meant to offer her friendship, violence, or even ardor. She still did not know him. So she edged away just the merest bit and asked, "Is there anything I can do? To make it easier for you, that is to say."

In her gray gown, her white face surmounted by golden white hair, she was as plainly visible to him in the depth of the dark as was the radiant moon in the black sky above them. And it seemed to him that she shimmered and wavered in a nimbus of silvery light even as that inconstant planet did. He did not think he had drunk so much until he had come out into the night air. Then he found her in the empty garden, young, innocent seeming, looking like some lost fairy creature, her sad and beautiful face uplifted, yearning to the moon. Even knowing what she was, in that instant she seemed the only familiar person in that household of cheats. Then they had spoken and he had discovered the odd communion between them, the eerie way in which she seemed to understand so completely each thing he said this night. He took in a deep, shuddering breath of cool night air and forced himself to remember precisely who and what she really was, despite the effects of wine and moonlight. He had to stoke up his anger, she had disarmed him so, and all he could achieve was sarcasm. He laughed and said, "Anything that you can do to make it easier for me? You wish to ease me then? How delightful. Do you offer yourself to me to save me from my hostess? What a lucky fellow I am. What a choice of beds the night brings to me. One exquisite female wants me for her husband's sake, or for his fortune's sake, it is the same thing to her, I think. And the other offers herself, for what, I wonder?"

"Why?" Julia cried as she sprang to her feet, goaded beyond her limit of endurance, "why do you offer me friendship with one hand and snatch it away with the other?"

"But," he said, lowering his head and closing his eyes for a moment so that he could see things more clearly, "I never offered you anything. Or at least, I did not mean to do so."

He raised his head to find that he had been addressing the ether. For she was gone.

8

Sir Sidney bustled into the study, smiling even as he hurried to meet his guest.

"Don't get up, don't get up," he insisted as the other gentleman rose to his feet, "for I'll be joining you in a moment."

Then the stout Sir Sidney, his movements such a parody of stealth as to be amusing, made straight for the library shelves behind his desk. He extracted a set of heavy volumes, dark red leather tomes with ornate, incomprehensible titles in what might have been Greek picked out in gold leaf upon their spines. With a wink to his guest, Sir Sidney, as though with difficulty, carried the four volumes to his desk, puffing all the while at the exertion. With a negligent gesture of his podgy hand, he waved away the assistance offered.

"Heavy fellows, cost a fortune, but worth every guinea spent. My favorite works, the author's a fellow named Bacchus, perhaps you know him?" Sir Sidney asked, as he laid the books down upon the desk. With a practiced flourish, he began to open the uppermost one. As he did so, the entire stack of books fell open neatly in the middle to reveal that the book covers were false and that what lay within them was not pages, but

101

a cleverly designed box containing two decanters and a set of blown crystal glasses.

"Ha!" Sir Sidney said with satisfaction. "Now this, I think, is what a library is really for." He poured a brimming glass of amber liquid for his guest and handed it to him.

"I never was a bookish fellow," he commented as he took another glass for himself and settled back in his wide and comfortable chair behind the desk. "And here was this great library overflowing with books. And most of 'em in frog-talk at that, if they wasn't in Latin, which I never got a handle on, no matter how my schoolmasters thrashed me. So when I chanced upon these fine volumes, why I snapped 'em up. Now I sit in here half the day and have the reputation of a studious fellow, don't you know, and enjoy myself as well. And my dear sweet Gilly don't know the half of it, neither."

His guest very much doubted if his host's dear sweet Gilly ever cared to know even a quarter of it, but since for some reason, Sir Sidney seemed bent upon presenting himself as a devoted husband with an adoring, if overbearing wife, he said nothing. He was not here to shatter his host's illusions, if indeed he had any left. He was only here to deliver a message, and if Sir Sidney wished to play at some charade for his own pleasure, it made no matter to the eventual outcome of their discussion.

As though he had known what was to come, Sir Sidney had avoided him for three days, but now, at last, he was run to earth. The baron was then not surprised at his host's overly glib manner, or at the fact that he drank deep before he addressed his guest again.

"Out with it," Sir Sidney said then, placing his elbows upon his desktop, resting his many chins in his hands, and looking at his guest owlishly. "I swear, Nicholas; old chap, you've put me into a quake. You've been so single-minded these last days, all you keep parroting is that you wish private discourse with me. Whatever can it be?" he said, and then went on quickly before the baron could even draw in breath to speak, "I've thought of the most incredible things, y'know, m' boy," he said, slurring his words just a little, although his guest doubted that the jot of brandy he had drunk had been enough to cause it; Sir Sidney was known as a fellow with a hard head. "I think that I've been deliberately avoiding you these past days, that serious phiz of yours sent me into such disarray. I can't help but think that it's to do with m'lady fair. You've been with her every moment since you've arrived here, and don't think I haven't noticed it, too.''

Sir Sidney paused, and glowered at his guest. But Nicholas's face did not change. He sat at his ease, one leg casually thrown across the other, and returned his host's accusing stare with a bored look. This was a game he understood. But was the fool actually trying to frighten him off, make him so abashed at the discovery of his presumed adultry that he would slink away and let the matter be? If so, the baron thought ruefully, then Sir Sidney was not so clever as he had given him credit for being.

But now Sir Sidney's face softened, it became, in fact, almost clownish in its innocence as he went on to say, "I know she's a beauty and I know I don't deserve her. But if you've set your heart at her feet, I want you to know, m'boy, that I'll look t'other way. She may do as she wishes, so long as she stays here with me." He waggled his finger at the baron before he added, "Now, there's plain speaking, lad."

"It can hardly be plainer," drawled the baron, "but it also can hardly be more unnecessary. I don't pine for her, Ollie, and we haven't the sort of relationship that should give you either a moment's pause as to her constancy or the slightest upper hand over me."

Sir Sidney dropped his childish expression and looked genuinely shocked at that bit of information.

"You mustn't blame her for it. She is dazzling and no doubt obedient to your wishes," the baron sighed, "but I never mix business with pleasure."

"You wasn't so damned particular last time you visited!" Sir Sidney said venemously, all traces of good humor gone.

"I was not upon business then," the baron said coolly.

Sir Sidney rose and stepped out from behind his desk. He placed his hands behind his back and faced his visitor. He was no longer the charming host, or the offended husband, or the jolly fat man, the baron noted. He was now deadly serious, and very frightened.

"It's bad news then?" he asked.

"I'm afraid so," the baron said, not unkindly, as he too rose to his feet and set down his glass upon the desk. "All has been discovered, as they say in the old cliché, but rather than advising you to 'Fly, at once,' I am here to tell you that you may as well stay put. For you're not welcome back at home, sir, and

never shall be again. That's the sum of it. I'm sorry that you had
me on your hands for all this time for just this unhappy news. If
you had seen me at once, I should have been able to settle the matter immediately. But that is all there is to it. For what it's worth,
I'm sorry, Ollie," the baron said as he turned to go.

"Wait!" Sir Sidney cried. "Wait, Stafford. I must speak
with you."

The baron paused. It was this that he had disliked about the
assignment initially, this possibility that Sir Sidney would
plead with him for mercy. For he had no authority to change
anything. He only had the task of bringing the news. He attempted to explain this to his host, but Sir Sidney motioned to
him to sit again. He was so very visibly upset, that in all conscience the baron could do little else but agree.

"For God's sake, Stafford," Sir Sidney said, his face grown
very white and beads of moisture apparent upon it, "what am I
to do?"

"There's nothing to do," Nicholas said on a sigh. "It's been
decided. If I were you, I should consider myself lucky that there is
nothing else to it. Exile may not be comfortable, but it is, I understand, a great deal less uncomfortable than hanging."

"If you were me," Sir Sidney said, swinging about to address the baron with a glittering eye. "You cannot know what it
is to be me! Look at you. Look at me. My God, man, how can
you know what it is to be me?"

The baron made as if to speak, but Sir Sidney waved him to
silence with a trembling, flapping hand. "If I were you, then
no, I should not have done as I did. What would have been the
point of it? For it wasn't done for conviction's sake, Nicholas,
nor in malice. But I must have the blunt to keep this place running, to pay for servants, entertainments, luxuries. My estates
could not support my life-style. It wasn't even done for me. But
for her. Don't you see? It was all for her."

His guest felt supremely uncomfortable. Tears were coming to
Sir Sidney's eyes, the man clearly suffered. But still, knowing his
past history and knowing that such a man was many things, but
never only a sentimental fool, the baron said nothing and only
waited patiently for him to be done with his speech. It was to be a
plea for understanding, he knew. He did not have the power to
grant the fellow a reprieve, but at least he could hear him out.

"You're a man of the world, Stafford," Sir Sidney went on,

locking his gaze with his guest's, "but do you know what it is to love completely, even though you know it is folly? I adore her, even though I know she is unfaithful. But I allow her to be so, I even encourage it, all so that she will stay with me. I indulge her in everything. Yet, with all that I give her, I know very well that when my purse empties, she will leave me. And I cannot bear the thought of that. I don't like myself for it, but there it is. Do you know what it is to be unmanned by love?"

There must have been something, something quickly expressed and as quickly suppressed, in the baron's face that encouraged his host to go on.

"No, how could you know?" Sir Sidney said brokenly. "Only look at you. Females think themselves privileged to touch you. They dote on you: your form, your face, your voice, do you think I don't know? She was used to go on about your shoulders, for God's sake, Stafford. Do you know what it was like to give her a new emerald bracelet and hear her murmuring about your damned bloody shoulders?

"I am not so much older than you, Stafford," Sir Sidney said, drawing himself up with a curious sort of defenseless dignity, "though you wouldn't think it. Only five years your senior, in fact. Where is the fairness in that? I was born with this foolish, bandy-legged body. I was born with this insipid face. When I reached my third decade, I lost my hair and what was left of my form and then my honor, because of it. But it was not fair. Why should nature have made me plump and old before my time, and made you so wondrous desireable? Do not condemn me, Stafford. Oh no, not until you think on the inequality of mankind and the cruelty of chance. I must pay, and pay dearly, for love because of it. You are free to love where you wish because of it."

"This is nonsense and you know it," the baron said coldly. "Do you think that patriots are all models of manly beauty? And that traitors are all uncomely? What a simple world that would be. And do you think that having a pleasing aspect guarantees love and happiness? No, if these are actually your reasonings, they are false and inadequate. You had this home, located so neatly near the main routes to Paris, Brussels, and Vienna. You entertained your countrymen, you took their confidences as payment and then sold them for personal gain, whatever the spur. Shall we tell those poor lads maimed and murdered through information given that it was their lot to suffer because you lacked beauty in the eyes of your love? It's nonsense, Ollie. If you wish to believe it, then do. But be done with explaining it to me."

Nicholas shook his head in disbelief and then went on. "But I doubt you believe it yourself. Listen well, Ollie. I only delivered the message. I had no part in making the decision, nor can I alter it in any way."

"But you can," Sir Sidney said eagerly. "That's the point, you can. You're trusted, you're in at the top. Your word is as good as any man's. Better, actually. You could vouch for me, work for me, exonerate me completely. But," he said hastily, seeing the baron's expression, "I do not even ask that. Tell them you could not reach me. Tell them you had no chance for speech with me. Give me time, time to see how I can clear myself, for given time, I can.

"Give me time to gather the facts to convince them," Sir Sidney cried, grasping onto his guest's coat sleeve with his warm, moist hand. "You have some further business on the Continent, I know that. Forget me for a space, at least until you return home. Or tell them that you sought me out on the way home, rather than on the way going, and missed me, is that so very much to ask?"

"No," said the baron with finality, "it is not so very much, but it is far too much. I have given my word. I cannot break it. It is not and never was a matter of my personal choice, or my opinion or sympathy, in any wise. Believe me. I had a message to deliver. Merely that. It is out of my hands now. There can be nothing more upon my part."

"I warn you . . ." Sir Sidney cried out, his eyes wild with emotion, "I swear you will regret this."

The baron disengaged his arm from his host's grim clasp. He said only, "Do not beg me, and do not warn me. Can't you see?" He gestured impatiently. "It is over, it is done." Then he bowed politely and said coldly, "I thank you for your hospitality, Sir Sidney. I shall leave now. I do not think we shall meet again. Good day."

Sir Sidney stood alone in his study and trembled with rage. What he most feared, and had feared for years now, had come to pass. It could have been worse, he knew. Not only had he eluded the hangman's noose that might have awaited him, but there could have just as easily been a different sort of courier with an entirely different sort of message to deliver: a bland powder to place in his wine, or a keen knife to slip through his ribs. Yet, that might have been kinder for him.

For now that the war was over, he had no more information to sell. With no money coming in, he could never keep up life in his accustomed style for long. When that gaiety ended, he had always thought that he could at least return home. But now, he had not even that. He did not delude himself into thinking that she would remain with him for much longer than it took for his funds to run out. He would have no home, no wife, no future. But he was not the sort of man to give up easily.

He would work with the materials at hand, he thought, as he steadied himself and went to sit behind his desk again. He poured himself another libation and downed it rapidly. The Baron Stafford was not the man he would have chosen to work through, but a man must seize any opportunity when he fought for his life. And then again, he realized, he had always resented Stafford, just as he had said. The baron's being the chosen messenger had been a greater insult, perhaps they had known that. No matter, it would only mean that what he must do would not be so onerous a task. Oh no, Sir Sidney thought darkly, as he remembered his guest's departing words, you shall see me again, Stafford, and next time there will be a great deal more that you will offer to do upon your part. I shall see to it. And then, you will not thank me for my hospitality, or for anything, because you will discover that I am a man of my word as well.

"Brussels?" Julia asked.

"Brussels," the Baron Stafford replied flatly.

She had been sent the message to leave, even as she had sat down to luncheon in her room. It was fortunate that her possessions had never been unpacked in the first place, for she would not have had the time to fold up a handkerchief to carry away with her. Within moments of the notice given, footmen had collected her bags, Celeste had handed her her shawl, and she had gone down the stairs to the waiting carriage. Now, as they departed the drive and reached the main road, the baron spoke of their destination.

This time he rode within the carriage and his horse was led outside. He sat back and relaxed against the squabs and spoke to her for the first time since their strange meeting and parting the previous night. When he had come into the coach, she noted that his face bore the marks of strain. He was paler than usual and there was a grim set to his mouth. She thought that perhaps she had angered him in yet another way, but after a few moments she realized that he was distracted and did not seem to notice her at all. Only when they arrived at the main road, did he relax the set of his shoulders and seem to recollect his surroundings. He actually smiled at her before he spoke. But then he said, "Paris, then Brussels," and she left off searching his face for his reactions and only reacted to the news.

"But I thought only Paris," she said.

"We are equally distant from Brussels," he replied, "and I have heard that Robin was last seen there. If we cannot discover him in Paris, then we shall go to Brussels, of course. But I heard that he was on the move toward Paris. And toward Vienna, and Amsterdam and Egypt, and Constantinople as well, for all I know," he said gloomily.

He leaned his head back against the cushions and closed his eyes. "But," he said at length, "it is most likely that he is in Paris, for that information came from a fellow who is only usually three-parts drunk rather than four. And the Belgian location was given me by a fribble whom I would doubt if he told me that it was warm at the equator. No, we look for him in Paris, and only if he is not there, will we travel on."

Since Julia said nothing in reply, the baron eventually opened his eyes to observe her. She sat with her head lowered, her fingers raveling and unraveling a bit of fringe at the end of her shawl.

"You have a reason to dislike Brussels?" he inquired.

"I did not think I should have to go so far," she said sadly. Raising her head, she said earnestly, "It's foolishness itself, I know, but each of these places you name is the stuff of fantasy to me. They are names I read of in books or heard in my childhood and never thought to actually visit. When you say Brussels, you may as well say Constantinople or The Indies or indeed, the moon. The mere sound of those incredibly faraway places that I shall be forced to travel to sets me to quaking, and fills me with dread. I know it's nonsensical, but there it is. I am not a very adventuresome soul, I fear. I should have been just as happy to remain at home for the whole of my life."

She looked so sorrowful and sounded so forlorn that each of the two others in the coach reacted to her mood. Celeste made a little clucking sound and stopped herself just as she leaned forward to put her arms about her new mistress's slumping shoulders. She appeared so vulnerable, so pale and golden, so fragile a victim that the baron felt at one and the same time the desires to comfort her, to set her free, to forget his mission just to see her smile, and to shake her thoroughly until the truth spilled from her lovely, deceitful lips.

Instead, he gave himself a imperceptible shake and said, as laconically as if the subject was only of passing interest to him, "Indeed? How odd, then, that such a meek, timid soul should kick over all her traces and fly in the face of convention as you did. Perhaps age has mellowed you, my dear, for I do not think your history shows you to have always been so loathe to seek adventure."

She winced at his words, and turned her head aside so quickly that he felt as though he had delivered an actual physical blow to her again.

"I am sorry," he said in a muted voice. "It has been a difficult day for me, and I suspect I was only trying to make it so for everyone else."

He knocked on the window to secure the coachman's attention as he went on to say, "I believe I'll ride outside for a while to clear my head. I've had too much of Sir Sidney's hospitality and seem to have picked up some of the manners of his set during my visit. I need some fresh air to counteract it."

As the coach slowed so that he could disembark and mount his horse, he saw that Julia still sat with her head averted and her eyes downcast.

"We shall rest this night at a very pleasant inn," he said. When she did not reply, he said as his hand touched the door, preparatory to leaving, "It is quite famous for its cuisine."

She gave no response. As the door swung open, the baron then said in a rush, as though the words must be discharged from him in one breath, "I should be pleased if you would have dinner with me tonight." Then, as though he realized how foolish such a formal invitation sounded from its recipient's startled reaction to it, he smiled wryly and added, "You *do* have the option of refusing me you know, Miss Hastings. I insist you accompany me to Paris, but I invite you to my dinner table."

There was a silence as he paused, bent double, at the door to the coach awaiting her reply. The expression upon his cool visage was unreadable.

"Thank you," Julia said slowly, drawing herself up until she sat erect, "I should be pleased to join you."

But now, in the one unguarded moment before he swung out of the coach, the expression upon the aristocratic face was discernible. And it was clearly in that brief instant, wary.

"Thank you," he said unemotionally, and was gone.

The day was fine, and it was a relief for the baron to be away from his two companions, the enigmatic Miss Hastings and her new champion. He smiled to himself as he rode down the country road ahead of the two coaches. He had thought to hire on a maidservant for Miss Hastings' convenience and it appeared he had instead secured the services of a firm ally for her. For he thought it was entirely possible that no matter what risks he had taken in his life, he might never have been so near to death as he had been in that moment after he done with insulting Miss Hastings. Or at least, so he thought from his quick glimpse toward Celeste's livid face.

He had not meant to hurt the chit, but he had once more. If only she would drop this veil of propriety and be honest with him, it would make the rest of this increasingly difficult journey more bearable. His business for the crown was done. It hadn't been pleasant, not that he had any brief for Sir Sidney, but it was hard to be the instrument of any man's destruction. And now he had his own pressing, equally unpleasant business to see to.

He wished that he too could find an ally to be easy with as simply as Miss Hastings seemed to have done. But Makepiece, while a superior valet, was not a friend, nor a confidant, and would be appalled if his master so much as asked his opinion on any matter more personal than that of a neckcloth or a button.

At home, Nicholas thought, feeling for the moment a sudden longing for his native land that surpassed anything his reluctant traveling companion might have imagined he could feel, there were a great many people he could have discussed his problems with. There were his close friends and his family and his gray eminence, his stepfather. But in the general way of things, there was little need to ever so burden those he loved. For, the baron thought suddenly, so struck with the idea that he involuntarily pulled up on his mount's reins and came to a complete stand in the middle of the road, his life was a tranquil one and he had never needed a confessor or advisor. Or he had not at least since that boyhood affair with Ivy had run its course.

Before the lead coach could turn a corner to see the head of the expedition, the lofty Baron Stafford, sitting lost in thought, still as a statue in the park upon his horse, Nicholas kneed his mount forward again. *All I needed was a pigeon upon my shoulder and a sweeper at my feet to complete the picture,* he thought with some annoyance at his actions as he rode on. But the damnedest part of this journey he had undertaken was that he could think of no one, either at home or abroad, to whom he could have unburdened the whole of his heart upon the subject, so much as he wished that he could.

He had not told his revered stepfather the entire truth. Worst of all, he thought morosely, he had not even told it to himself, until now, until the thoughts became inescapable. For there had been rumors about Robin in London, and some of those were of such a nature as he would not repeat to anyone, not even himself.

He had ignored them. But then, there had also been that obscene caricature on display in the bookseller's shop window in Picadilly Circus, a full month before. The crowd outside the shop had been both amused and aroused to anger by the illustration of the wild set cavorting abroad while their country's security was menaced by her enemies. It had been well-done: the buxom lady labeled "Britannia," about to be sexually assaulted by the evil Napoleon, her cries for help unheard by the rolicking set of fashionables disporting at an orgy behind her. But Nicholas had not been amused. One of those gentleman depicted bore an uncanny resemblance to Robin. And he was shown in the vilest fashion, as the most debauched, or so at least his uncle thought. And so at least he told the shopkeeper when he bought up all the pictures, and so he claimed as he had his solicitors threaten suit against Mr. Rowlandson should he ever decide to reissue it with that same character in the background.

Burning the pictures did not end the matter, and he did not seriously think it would. He was wise enough to know that fire consumes only substance, and never essence. He had heard the tail ends of similar sorts of stories even at Sir Sidney's house party. Or, he wondered, had he only imagined that he had? But then they always seemed to abruptly trail off when he was noticed in the talebearer's vicinity.

Then there was this matter with Miss Hastings. He did not think himself so difficult in his judgment of human nature. It was true that Ivy had deceived him, but he had been a boy then, and had never been so misled again. From the first, he had to force himself to disbelieve Miss Hastings. Now, he dared not even call her Julia in his private thoughts, if he were to keep his distance measured and his rage alive. But lord, the baron thought restlessly, with all he knew, still she had all the trappings of an ill-used innocent.

If Robin were truthful, then she was a vicious and dangerous slut that should be shown no kindnesses. "If Robin were truthful!" The baron swore to himself at his own thought. There was the crux of the matter. Why should he disbelieve his own nephew? But her behavior forced him to doubt even the evidence of his own eyes. If by some mad chance she were telling the truth, then both he and his nephew had done her a terrible injustice. More unsettling was the fact that if she were telling the truth, Robin was not. And this led to conclusions so painful that the baron spurred his horse forward without realizing what he had done.

The great chestnut horse galloped down the road as though its rider were a fury. The truth, Nicholas Daventry almost cried aloud as he finally pulled the animal up, having raced so far afield that the dust from the coaches was no longer visible, however painful, he must have the truth. He was become as obsessive upon the subject of truth as those Greek philosophers that he had studied at school had been. But none of them, he thought with the characteristic sense of humor that always lurked beneath the surface of his personality and always saved him from despair, had ever sought to extract that rare commodity from the lips of a magnificently beautiful young female.

He would dine with Miss Hastings tonight. The offer had been made spontaneously, as an act of apology, but he would turn it to good use. As he could not shake her story by force or threat, he would befriend her and somehow, he would have the truth from her.

As he sat and quietened his mount and waited for the carriages to come into view again, he smiled slightly as the thought occurred to him that he was not trying something new at all. He was only experimenting with that theory which his own governess had taught him years before. He was going to attempt to catch a fly with honey. And if he could not, he thought, the smile upon his lips becoming not at all pleasant to see, he would capture it in the more common way—by crushing it.

9 Julia had the uneasy feeling that there was a hairline crack in the looking glass and that was why it seemed to show her the head of one person and the body of another. For Celeste had done wondrous things with her hair: Julia saw a mass of golden tendrils as she gazed into the glass, and the coiling, curling, sinuous hairstyle gave her face a classical romantic look that she had never associated with herself before. Somehow, the raised style also lightened her complexion and made her features appear more delicate. She conceded, as Celeste stood quietly and proudly behind her, that she had never been in better looks. But only from the neck up. Celeste was quite right about that as well.

Looking in the glass, first down at her drab mauve gown, and then up at that exquisitely coiffed head, Julia sighed and agreed with her maid. The juxtaposition *was* absurd. It was the visual merging of a countessa and a governess. But unlike her maid, Miss Hastings decided that it was the hairstyle that would have to change, and not the body. For she was a governess, or at least had been one, and she hoped would be one someday soon again. It would be far better to put her hair back the way it had been, she insisted, reaching for her hairbrush,

than for her to attempt to alter the rest of herself to suit her hair.
It wasn't Celeste's shriek of protest that stopped her from immediately flattening the creation and returning her tresses to
their normal state, it was the next words her maid uttered. For
they were undeniably true. It was simply too late to redo her
hair, or anything else. The baron had said dinner at eight, and it
only lacked a few minutes to that hour.

Julia had agreed to meet her captor and co-traveler for dinner, but only because at the moment of his invitation she had
felt a strange stirring of sympathy for him, he so clearly seemed
to wish to make amends. But now, as so often happens when
one rashly agrees to something that would normally be against
one's best judgment, she felt very anxious about the forthcoming evening. The baron's presence always presented her with
the twin emotions of fear and nervousness, and his attempt at
politeness tonight added uncertainty to those reactions. She
could only hope that the unexpected invitation might signal the
beginnings of a more civil attitude upon his part. And the best
way to foster that, she realized as she looked at her mismatched
appearance a last time in the glass, was certainly not to show up
late to dinner with him.

Celeste sighed unhappily as she handed Julia her shawl. She
had done her best with the coiffure, but the dress, although her
mistress claimed it was her best, was just as all her others were:
homemade, ill-fitting, and not at all the fashion. It was amazing that she insisted on dressing so badly, for so far as Celeste
could see, her new mistress had a form as perfect as her face.
But it was difficult to see very far. Miss Hastings had been
modest to a fault, even to the extent of snatching up towels to
hide behind if her maid entered her room after her bath. Perhaps, Celeste thought fatalistically, all English misses were so
prim. But to conceal one's body from one's own maid was a
rare thing indeed, especially as, from what her servant's practiced eye had been able to spy, Miss Hastings had a form as di-
vine as one could wish.

For although she was slender and as narrowly made as a
young boy, with fragile wrists and slight shoulders, her breasts
were high and shapely (when one could get a glimpse of their
form behind her omnipresent shawls), her waist was curved,
her legs long with trim ankles tapering up to firm calves, and
her derriere superb. The English, Celeste mused as she

straightened the room before she took herself off to her own dinner, were a very odd race. Indeed, she thought, if this was how their females normally went on, it was no wonder that their gentlemen traveled so extensively. The only wonder of it was in how they had managed to populate that small island of theirs in the first place.

The baron was in the private dining parlor before Julia arrived, and he rose to greet her as she entered. She thought the room charming. It was a small chamber with enough space only for the dining table and chairs and two other small chairs stationed near a wide, leaded-glass window which looked out over the inner central courtyard of the inn. Julia was so uneasy when she was first seated that she kept her gaze firmly fixed on that single view, as though there were something extraordinary to be seen there. But in fact it was a commonplace enough vista, with ancient blue paving stones in the center, some attempt at flowerbeds to the left, and a more successful functional kitchen garden far to the right. There were some tall trees at odd intervals, there was a bench or two, a rose trellis, and a well close by the kitchen garden. The stables were fortunately in the front, out of sight of the window. It was a pleasant scene to observe while one dined, but not, Julia had to admit to herself, so attractive as to occupy her attention as completely as it did.

The baron was in his own way a far more interesting sight, but she could hardly gape at him, so after one inclusive glance, she fell to studying her plate, and then the window again. He was dressed so properly for dinner that he made her feel a perfect drab. He wore a blue jacket with a velvet collar, a high white neckcloth, she had gotten a glimpse of a dark waistcoat and darker breeches when she arrived, and the single golden fob he wore keynoted the pristine perfection of his attire. His dark hair had been brushed forward, and he must have recently completed his toilette by washing and shaving, for his white skin seemed to glow and the faintest odor of lemon and bay rum emanated from him. In all, he was an attractive, handsome, perfectly correct dinner partner, and Julia wished she were anywhere on earth but at dinner with him.

"Yes," he said reflectively, "it is a remarkable view, I grant you, Miss Hastings. It quite took my breath away and I can readily understand how it has affected you. But I do think we ought to try to make conversation despite the magnificence of it."

Julia turned to him with a strong retort ready upon her lips, but the mischievous, *understanding* expression of wry amusement he wore, as though he expected her fury and was patiently awaiting it as a schoolboy waits deserved punishment, quite disarmed her.

"It is only," Julia said, relenting by speaking honestly of her helplessness, "that I didn't know quite what to say. That is, I don't often dine alone with gentlemen, unless you count those times with little Toby, of course. But since you don't seem inclined to throw custard at me, or weep if the waiter brings you snap beans, I don't know if I quite know how to go on this evening."

He laughed openly, as though delighted by her response, and seemingly as relieved to escape her bad graces as the toddler she was describing might have been.

"I don't know," he answered thoughtfully at last, "I might accept snap beans without a fuss, but I think that if they bring out some of that omnipresent ratatouille, I shall at least overset my water glass and feed it to the dog while they rearrange my place setting. Oh, pity, there is no dog in attendance. Now that is how you know you are in a French establishment," he said with a great deal of mock regret, "for any respectable English inn has a few dogs slouching about, looking sharp for a handout. I cannot imagine what little French boys do when they're served something nasty then, can you?"

Happy to be included in his unexpectedly high spirits this evening, Julia turned her sigh of relief into a little chuckle and said with as much spurious seriousness as he had used, "I don't think little French boys acknowledge that there is anything nasty to eat. After all," she said reasonably, "they do eat snails. And from an early age upward, I do believe," she concluded with such a look of censure upon her face that her host laughed once again.

They laughed often during that dinner. For when Julia realized what their first course was to be and then saw the look upon her host's face when he lifted the cover off the dish and held it out for her inspection, she was so overset by mirth that she had to request a glass of water before she could speak rationally.

THE ABANDONED BRIDE ❧ 117

"But do try one. Try to think of them merely as unknown creatures that just happen to be called escargots," her host implored. "Picture them to be a sort of a cross between crabs and kippers," he said brightly, and she had been unable to speak for some time again at the look of sweet reason he had given her along with his impossible request. Then she had made it impossible for him to drink his soup when she had, with great exactitude and an inspired bit of mime, described her encounters with members of that species which he had just devoured when she had been out early gardening after a rain.

By the time that they had been served chicken in a heavy wine sauce, they had done with their uproarious mirth and were merely chuckling weakly at each other, as people will do when they have laughed long and hard and wish to give their sides and cheek muscles a rest. Julia could not remember when she had had a better time, and only wished that she could completely forget who her host actually was.

But that was more than merely difficult. All the while that they had seemed so in concert, even while she had held her hand to her stomach to support her laughter, she had in some portion of her active mind remembered who he was, and in some portion of her wary heart observed him carefully. She was not the only one to do so.

The Emperor had so depleted the land of its able-bodied men that their waiter was, perforce, a waitress. The expression upon the proprietor's face had been one of hopeless helplessness when he had accompanied the girl to their private parlor. His establishment, his morose expression made manifestly clear, was used to better ton, abler servants, and higher standards. "C'est la vie" and "C'est la guerre": his language had all the right expressions for the situation, but their host's shrug as he left the girl Delphine to continue serving them was even more eloquent than speech could have been.

Julia knew the girl's name was Delphine by the way she had whispered that name hoarsely to the baron as she had served him his veal. She knew that Delphine was a very friendly girl by the way she smiled and smiled at the baron, even when he was clearly laughing together with his dinner guest. She was fairly certain that Delphine was a poor seamstress, for she seemed to have a badly fitting blouse, from the way it consistently slid off her shoulder whenever she waited on the baron.

And, Julia thought sourly when she had a moment to think alone while her host was sampling a new wine, the girl was either inordinantly proud of her chemise, or she had some secret message written for him alone on the inside of her frock, since she bent forward so frequently whenever she had a thing to give to the baron.

It hardly matters, Julia told herself when the baron gave the wench a pleasant smile as he put down his glass. If he confuses the sheen of grease upon her black tresses for the glow of health and if he finds the scent of garlic and overheated girl stimulating, it is scarcely my concern, she thought with a queer pang of virtue. But as their meal went on and their moods turned from high hilarity to more reflective speech, she was forced to conclude that in all honesty, he was no more than courteous and no less than kind, both to herself and to Delphine.

They discussed many subjects during that strange dinner, politics and poetry and all sorts of topics that a governess who possessed a questing mind and had had an empty hour or two to fill in the past could be expected to handle coherently. This was so obvious to Julia that she was amused by the frequent look of surprise that she often spied upon her host's face when she replied both sanely and knowledgeably about some subject he brought up. In turn, she was herself surprised not only at how little notice he took of the increasingly blatant movements of their waitress, but at how much attention such a staple of the ton had obviously paid to art and literature, when she assumed he had been occupied by far more worldly pastimes.

When the last plates had been cleared, and the last crumbs had been languourously swept from the tabletop, and one last, lingering, burning look had been tenderly offered by Delphine before she so reluctantly left them, the baron sat back and sighed.

"I shall never complain about lack of service in an inn again," he said, shaking his head. "I never knew that total attention could be far worse than meager attention."

"You ought to be flattered," Julia said lightly, although privately she was amazed at how he spoke to her as an equal and how readily she accepted that designation.

"Ought I?" he asked, giving her a bright and searching look before he answered just as lightly, "But there is no flattery in it, you see. There are so few healthy, mobile men left in this poor land, that the mere fact that I possess all my teeth, can walk unaided, and am above the age of fifteen and below the age of seventy makes me uncommonly attractive. Now were there a dozen hearty fellows within this inn tonight, and were Delphine to still accord me such outsize attentions, why then I would be delighted. But as it is, I fear it is the rarity of my appearance, rather than the glory of it, that inspires such admiration."

Julia smiled at his comment, but could think of no thing to add to it. If she were to deny what he said, she would seem to be just as doting as Delphine. If she were to agree, it would seem as though she were not a very grateful guest. Then remembering her status as guest and seeing that there was nothing left to eat or drink upon the table save for a bowl of fruit, even if she should be glutton enough to want more, she brought her napkin up from her lap, placed it upon the table, and began to rise.

"No, don't leave just yet. Please," he said.

"I did want to speak with you," he said as she sank back to her chair. "I had hoped that a pleasant dinner in a civilized atmosphere would help to erase some of the bad memories we share. We did start badly, Miss Hastings," he said quietly, his eyes direct and sincere and his entire body seemingly rigid and poised as though he were prepared to react to any sort of response from her, from mere verbal insult to wild physical attack.

At her nod of agreement, for there was no rebuttal she knew, of course they had started badly, he went on.

"I misjudged you," he said with utmost sincerity, as she searched his face for mockery and could find none, "and misled you, and misused you. Lord, I shouldn't blame you if you refused me the time of day. But I would like to make amends. And this evening was my poor way of beginning an attempt in that direction. Do you think we might go further?"

Julia looked down at her hands and drew in a deep breath. She could scarcely believe the words she was hearing. As he said no thing further, she looked up to find him watching her quietly, awaiting her answer. His gaze was fixed upon her face, his eyes were clear and free of any inward look of deceit, and even in the softened late light of a summer's evening, she could clearly see his expression was one of deep concern.

"Yes," she breathed, "that would be good. After all," she said in a rush, "it is not pleasant to be mistrusted, and I confess I have been careful of my speech in your presence, ever since you struck—" but here she left off speaking, for in truth, she still feared a sudden anger on his part and remembering the violence he had done her, suddenly wondered if bringing the subject up again would bring up his rage again.

His face grew very pale and he stood abruptly, seeming to loom over her. She gasped, wondering at how she could have been foolish enough to have been lulled by only a few kind words into endangering herself again.

But he only looked down at her, his hands closed into tight fists at his sides. Then he walked to the window and stared blindly out into the distance. "There is no way to undo what has been done," he said in a tight voice. "You have said you will not accept my apology, and indeed, I can now understand that, for I find that I cannot accept my own. I wonder," he said, his voice wavering a bit as he gazed toward her with a wrenched smile, "if you wouldn't mind picking up some instrument, that fireplace poker over in the corner for instance, or that candlestick upon the table perhaps, and giving me a sharp rap upon the head with it? For I don't know how else we can begin again with the score evened between us, and believe me, Miss Hastings, I very much wish to do that."

He looked so very unhappy that Julia rose from her chair and went to him where he stood by the window.

"I will forget it," she said softly, "if you will, and then we'll both be done with it. But if you really wish to make amends, then why not call off this wild hunt and let me go home?"

"You know," he said in a soft voice filled with regret, "I cannot, though believe me, I wish I could. But soon, soon the matter will be settled and you will be free to go anywhere you wish. In the meanwhile," he said, his voice and face brightening, "there is no need for you to suffer. I promised a fine fee for your compliance, and so you shall have it. I don't know where my head has been these past days. When we get to Paris tomorrow, I insist you take your Celeste and invade the finest couturiers. Buy bonnets, Miss Hastings, and frocks and slippers and gauderies and gauzies and thingamabobs for your hair and ribbons and bows. Buy trunkloads, my dear, I shall not begrudge you a groat for it. For I see how fine your hair looks, and how ill your garb befits you now. And please don't mind my saying so," he added quickly, "since such saying ensures an end to the problem. But within a day in Paris you can have frocks to match your face, have you all matching in fact, and all magnificent."

He beamed at her, he made as if to take her hands in his, and then drew back a step and raised his hands in denial as though she treatened him with some weapon. "Ah no," he said waggishly, "I remember, you do not care to be touched." But there, for the first time, Julia detected mockery in his voice and his eyes, and finding it, suddenly doubted all that had gone before.

"No," she said simply, "I don't want fine clothes and gauderies, my lord, and never did. For they'd be of little use to a governess. And I do wish to be a governess. Don't be fooled by Celeste's expertise, it is her hand you see in my appearance, and not my own wish."

"I see only you," he said, stepping closer, his hands still raised as a barrier between them, "and nothing of Celeste, or any other woman."

He said nothing further but looked at her so steadily that she could not pretend to be unaware of the question in his searching gaze. She hastily lowered her lashes over the secrets she knew must lie in her eyes, as though she feared he could read them there by the sheer force of his regard.

She sought a glib comment to end the unnerving silence, but when she opened her eyes again it was to discover him still looking at her. But now his eyes held such a sparkling, knowing look of amusement that she caught up her breath. Then smiling, still without a word, he reached out a hand and smoothed one wayward curl back from her forehead. No more than that. But as she felt his fingertips briefly, barely skim against her skin, she found herself realizing that she had far more to fear than his anger.

"Don't," she said, and he stopped immediately, but drew no further back. His gaze left her hair and brow, which still tingled from his imperceptible touch. They stood so close she could feel his warm breath and he could see the tiny blue traces of veins that lent an azure hue to the pink of her lowered eyelids.

"What happened between you that last night?" he asked softly, his breath stirring the light tendrils of hair at her brow.

She did not have to ask him which night, she would not pretend she did not understand. She knew the question very well, for she had asked herself the same on a thousand nights of her life since that night.

"I don't know," she said, to herself, to him, with the same pain that she always felt when she asked and answered that question.

And as they stood as close as lovers, she was not surprised when he asked, "Were you lovers?" although he was so near to her she could see that he seemed to be as startled at his own words as though someone else had spoken them.

"No," she said, shaking her head again and again in denial, closing her eyes so she could not see his look when the motion sent some strands of her scented flaxen hair sweeping lightly across his face, "no. Never. He never . . . we never . . . it was not that sort of love. No."

He stopped the sidewise motion of her head with one hand. Then he took his hand away, bent his own head, and kissed her lips lightly, as feather-lightly as her hair had touched him. Then he drew back and gazed at her curiously. And in a moment she found her lips beneath his again, and he kissed her longer, and more longingly, although he in no other way touched her. He stepped away then as she caught her breath and sought a thing to say to explain lightly why she had not torn away from him, why she had not resisted him, why she had lost track of everything but him in those odd moments.

But he only looked at her lips even as she gazed at his and then he said in wonderment, "No. You were not lovers. There's truth in that, at least," and he seemed as amazed as she was at his words. With an effort, he left off looking at her lips and asked again, "What happened that night? Now I understand even less."

"I don't know," she said. "I never knew." And because she wanted him to look at her with desire again instead of standing and staring at her as though she were some weird creature, and because she knew that in some wise, she was, and that even if she weren't she could not bear to be so close to him again, she said wildly, "And don't kiss me again. If you want that sort of thing, there is Delphine. And don't offer me friendship when you only want information. And don't make me trust you, when you know I cannot.''

Celeste Vitry was a woman of the world. She did not comment when Julia came rushing back to her room, wild-eyed and shaken. She did not say a word when she watched her mistress wash her face in the basin of warm water and then scrub it with a damp cloth and then wash it again with cold water, although she knew that to be unusual, not to mention being potentially ruinous to a fine complexion. And she had the grace to say nothing but good night when she left her mistress alone at last in her room.

Julia scarcely noted her maid's departure, she was so meshed in her own thoughts. She had thought the same things before, she had been over the same ground again and again, but the touch of his lips had not only brought it all back to her, it had added more. The leaping of her senses was new, although the pain of the memory was old. What had happened that night? She had not lied to him. She did not know.

He had never kissed her like that, Robin had never kissed her at all save for the chance dry peck upon the cheek, or the little warm salute upon the back of her hand, except for that once, the night they had parted. But then, she could not count that once, that had not been Robin at all. For it had never been that way between them before. In fact, she often was to think later, if he had covered her with kisses as he made his offer, she would have been too frightened to make any reply, instead of laughing as she had, and saying, "Oh Robin, me for your lady? Oh Robin, do not jest so.''

Even in the coach, on the long ride to the inn, they had done no more than hold hands, like the happy children they were. But she hadn't worried over it. She knew what gentlemen and their ladies must do when they were wed, for her mother had taken great pains to educate her girls early on. She told them she did not want them to end as a famous local girl in her own youth had: with a pair of twins at her breast and the vague notion that they had come to her because she had shared a peach with her lover, and somehow swallowed the pit.

No, Julia had known what to eventually expect. But it did not sound very comfortable or very easy, so she decided not to think about it until she had to do so. She nourished the vague hope that people often cherish about their own mortality: that in their case, what was inevitable might prove to be avoidable.

Then they got to the inn. And he had bade her rest and then change to her best gown for the ceremony, for his friend was coming to meet her and he wanted her in her highest looks for the grand occasion. He had left her alone in the room. And after a space she had begun to do as he asked. And then he had come back in again unexpectedly. And, Julia decided, rising from her bed, she did not wish to go over it again. A thousand times in one lifetime, she swore as she paced to her window, was quite enough.

She stared down at the same courtyard she had gazed at during her dinner with the baron. It was too bad, she thought, that they always came to blows or to words or to—and here she hedged even with herself for she did not wish to remember his kisses—or to physical contact of some sort, she temporized, for she had enjoyed his company. She had thought that such a fine-looking fellow would have had nothing on his mind but horses and wagers and fashions and gossip, as so many of London's leading gentlemen supposedly did. But he had a firm grasp of current events, he was lettered, and he could make such a merry jest that one could forget that one had to dine with a long spoon when one supped with the devil.

Julia stared out into the warm, blurred darkness of a summer's night. The moon was haze-covered but bright, and aided enough by midsummer's long twilight to yet show shape and shadow below. She could pick out the forms of the trellis of roses, and the well and the grape arbor. There were some other points she could not identify, but then she was not really trying, she was too busy trying not to think of where the baron was now. She had told him to seek out Delphine, and doubtless, he had done so. But the thought of Delphine and the baron enwrapped in that complex set of contortions she had been told of all those years before gave her an unexpected jolt of dismay. Worse, it made her remember how queer it had been to feel so completely enfolded and immersed in his regard even when all that he had done was simply to briefly touch her brow. And the memory of what had transpired after that set her to wondering at exactly how he would enact that heretofore unimaginable set of exercises, and how gracefully he might accomplish that which she had always thought to be essentially awkward.

She passed her hand over her face in an angry gesture, and tried to put such uncomfortable thoughts from her mind. For no matter how she envisioned the baron at that elaborate task, she could envision Delphine being ecstatic at his endeavors. But then, a lighted window near the kitchens drew her attention. As she was on the second floor she could see down into the window below very well, and was very unwell at what she saw. For it was Delphine. No doubt, she thought, it must be Delphine, those lush configurations could not be mistaken even at a distance. No one else surely had such a light blue blouse which would not stay anchored to her shoulders, or such a welter of long black hair to cover the absence of blouse upon those white shoulders. Delphine, Julia knew it could be no other, also stood at her window looking out into the courtyard this soft summer's night. Then a larger, darker, unrecognizable but plainly masculine shape appeared behind Delphine. A shape which sprouted a shadowy arm to circle Delphine's waist and draw her back from the window into her room again. And then the curtains swung closed.

It is what gentlemen do, Julia told herself as she stood by the window and sought to see behind closed curtains, and sought at the same time to drag herself away from the window. It must have been the ridiculous tear that splashed against her arm even as she leaned on the windowsill which called her attention to the movement of the rose trellis in the garden below. But it hadn't been part of the trellis at all, it had been, she saw now, as he stepped out of the shadows, the white of his neckcloth. And it hadn't been the last red glow of the roses she had seen as she watched Delphine, it had been the small red glow of his cigarillo. This she knew now as a certainty, as he looked up at her and she saw his pale face clear in the moonlight despite the blurring in her tear-drenched eyes, and she saw him bow, making a great circle with his cigarillo as he did so, making a deep and mocking bow to her there in the blameless moonlight.

10 The servant left the room with the last of the dinner's crumbs safely collected within the discarded napery he bore away. He had been so thorough in his cleaning that all he left behind him in the dining room was a deep and unbroken silence, and the two former diners, who sat and glowered at each other across the now empty table. It was the gentleman who spoke first, as the door nicked slowly closed upon the heels of the departing waiter.

"Three days, I believe," he said, as though he were replying to some question, although his companion at the table had not addressed anything but a singularly mistrustful look to him for some moments. "Yes, three days, I am sure of it. It was the very first night we arrived here in Paris. I asked you if your room was comfortable, I inquired as to whether the dinner had suited you, and then, just before I bade you a good night, I told you, no, I recall," the baron said with some show of discovery, "I *suggested*, I *strongly* suggested," he amended, "that you visit a dressmaker and have some new garments made. I believe I even suggested that since we were now in Paris you employ the services of Louis Hippolyte Leroy. As he was good enough for the Empress Josephine, I thought you might find him adequate. I left a purse upon the table to that purpose, I am sure of it,'' he said with a bit more force, ''for though I might forget a great many things, I always remember both promises and payments. It makes me a better landlord, and a better friend as well, I believe, for close accounting is important to both purposes. I'm not clutch-fisted, Miss Hastings, but neither am I quite blind. It is not the money I inquire about, it is the use it was put to. The purse is gone and so far as I can see, that garment you are wearing now, that grayish-brownish colored frock,'' he gestured toward her with a dismissive wave of his hand as he spoke, ''is the self-same one that you wore three days ago, or as near to it as to be its twin. I can see that it is not soiled, I am aware that it is fresh as a dew-washed daisy, but I am also acutely aware that it is not, I repeat, *not*, a new frock. And unless the French have gone mad with grief over losing the war, I doubt that they have begun to style such garments for foreign trade, so I take leave to doubt that it is one of the Parisian creations that you ordered and purchased as I requested you to do those three nights ago.''

The young woman looked unperturbed. Her expression did not change and she did not shrink back as the gentleman leaned forward with his chin upon his hand, his elbow upon the table, as he awaited his reply. Her pale face was composed, her chin was lifted, and her hands remained folded in her lap. It was well that they were, for that way the gentleman could not see how much they would have trembled had she not held them so closely together.

Her clear blue gaze met his regard evenly as she said softly, ''No, but I don't believe that you listened to my reply to your request, and if accounting is necessary to friendship, I believe that attention is even more of a requisite. Not that I require your friendship,'' she said hastily, dropping her gaze as she saw the fury gathering in the gentleman's face, ''but I did tell you that I didn't require any new gowns, and I did say that payment for them was unnecessary. But you left the coins there on the table just the same before you left, and I could not simply leave them there for the servants to gather up as some sort of superior gratuity. I took them, and I did use some of them,'' she said to his incredulous look, ''for I've been sightseeing with Celeste and I had no other French currency in hand. But I've been keeping strict accounts,'' she said rapidly as he began to speak.

But all she heard was a long sigh, and when she raised her eyes again, she saw that the baron was looking at her and shaking his head slowly, with no anger evident in his expression and only exasperation writ large upon his face.

"Miss Hastings," he said carefully, "you need new gowns. It is well that you have enjoyed yourself seeing the city, but I repeat, you can no longer do so attired as you are."

"But I do not," she said speaking just as precisely as he had done, "for I have no use for them at all. We've hired a boat, a little skiff really, that this fellow rows for us quite cheaply, Celeste and I, and we've seen the city by water. And we've seen the Bastille itself, and the Arc de Triomphe de l'Étoile that Napoleon commissioned, and the great cathedral of Notre Dame, and even climbed its stairs as far as we could go. We've been very circumspect and proper and we've stopped for luncheon at respectable cafés and I assure you, my mode of dress is unremarkable. Or at least, it is for my purposes. Although there are a great many fashionables here, my lord, I am not one of them, I don't go about with them, and so I don't need to be in the first stare of fashion. And when this incident is over with, I shall have no more use for fashion than I do now. I accept that I must be with you," she said, her voice becoming so soft that he had to strain to hear her even in the quiet room, "but I have no desire to call attention to myself."

"Yes," he said with such a world of agreement in his tone that she looked up sharply, "but for that very reason you ought to obey my wishes in the matter. Miss Hastings," he said seriously, his handsome, usually animate face still and solemn with the weight of his sincerity, "it was only because I wished to please you that I made my request, believe me. And so it is only yourself you harm by disregarding it. For it matters very little to me. My reputation will not be ruined, I assure you, if I am found to be traveling with a single young female. If anything, it would be enhanced in certain circles. It is very unfair, to be sure, but there it is.

"I should dislike to see you pent up in your rooms until we discover Robin, and I don't believe you run too great a risk in simply being seen with me. For though your countenance cannot be changed," he paused and added "fortunately" just to see her blush, and then went on, "if you should ever come across anyone who has spied you on our travels when you return to England, you can always easily persuade him that he is mistaken in your face. If, that is," he said sternly, "you are more discreet than you have been."

She looked at him in confusion as he said coolly, "In short, Miss Hastings, and I am surprised you haven't thought on it, this is a superior hotel, and the fact that I am traveling with a beautiful young female dressed like a lower servant gives rise to more gossip than if I am observed in the company of beautiful young lady who is up to the mark."

He paused and then went on with a hint of laughter in his voice at the outsized surprise with which she now regarded him, "Yes, absolutely. You are dressed most becomingly and properly for a governess or a companion. But as we don't have a child in tow nor am I precisely an individual who appears, on the surface at least, to be in need of the sort of chaste and proper companionship you insist you provide, it looks deucedly odd, my dear, when we appear in public together. Or when we dine together as we do now, or even when I meet and speak with you in the lobby of the hotel.

"I assure you," he said, laughing outright now at the look of confusion which had replaced the stubborn expression on her expressive face, "that if you were dressed à la mode, you would be exclaimed over, and indeed, yes, perhaps even inquired after. But as you are dressed now, you stand in some danger of becoming a sensation. A mysterious beauty is acceptable, my dear, and we can make up all sorts of false trails to go with your false name for them to sniff after. It's commonly done, you know. There are a great many errant wives and daughters upon the Continent, you see. But a stunning creature in rags in the company of a fellow like me? Now that's just the stuff of high scandal and low gossip that could cause a stench that might drift even across the channel."

Julia rose and stared at him with such a look of consternation that he said hastily, as he rose as well and came around the table toward her, "No, no, I didn't precisely mean rags, it was merely a figure of speech. I wasn't my intent to demean you, it's the way I speak. Damn. Miss Hastings, accept my apologies, I only meant that your mode of dress is very different from that which one might expect—"

"... Of an acquaintance of yours," she said quickly, finishing his sentence for him as he came to a stand before her. "I know, and I don't take it amiss. Why just look at you," she said on a desperate sounding sort of half-laugh. "One sleeve of that fine linen shirt is worth more than the whole of my plain stuff gown. And that waistcoat," she said, gesturing toward his new waistcoat, with its rich embroidery of gold and silver threads upon a background of deep scarlet, "is worth more than my entire wardrobe, I should guess."

"It is a bit much, isn't it?" the baron said ruefully, glancing down. "But then, it's French-made. I bought it at a shop where I had gone to inquire after Robin. I had to purchase something to make my visit there believable. If you think that it is lavish, though, you ought to see the jacket I had to order up in order to buy enough of the fellow's time. It's blue with a silver thread through it, and I don't know if I shall ever be able to wear it outside of a costume ball. But Monsieur LeMay is a famous tattle as well as a famous gentleman's clothier. The French are very good with female fashions, but they stand in the shadows of our good plain English tailors. This waistcoat is a bit gaudy, isn't it?" he asked suddenly, frowning down at himself so sourly and looking so dismayed that Julia felt very small and mean for having mentioned the price of his wardrobe. She sought to remedy matters by complimenting his waistcoat as lavishly as she could, but he scarcely heard as he had already left off regarding his vest and had proceeded to continue apologizing to her for his rash remark about her clothes. The babble of both their voices begging pardon reached each other's ears at the same moment and they left off speaking at the same time, looked at each other, and then began laughing together.

"You are right, I'll go to the dressmaker's," Julia said, even as she heard him say, "You're right, this vest goes into my deepest drawer." And then they both began to laugh again, and each time that they stopped, they would happen to get a glimpse of each other's face, and then they would be set off again. It was a long time till they both were still enough for long enough to let their mirth be done.

"I'm sorry—" Julia began again, but he interrupted her by saying simply, earnestly, "Be done with sorry, Julia. And so shall I. There's too much to be sorry for, and we can never go forward if we continue to go back to 'sorry.' "

She said nothing in reply but only stared at him as much for the novelty of hearing him speak her Christian name, as for the shock of hearing him so honest with her. He did not seem to notice either his slip of the tongue or his intended utterance, as he went on, "There's simply too much bad ground we'd have to go over if we persist in going back to apologize. And we've gone too far to go back in actuality, for it won't be long before we've achieved what we've set out to do. Or," he said with a strangely self-conscious and wry smile, "what *I've* set out to do, at any rate. Robin's not far from us, of that I'm sure. We might as well try to get along in amity until he shows up. For even if that is to be tomorrow, it's still a long way home again. Peace then, Julia?"

She might have made a comment about his useage of her name without her permission, she was to think later. She might have at the very least simpered a bit before she answered, to let him know she was aware and amused at the liberty he took. She might have even been justified in light of all that he had done to her and with her, in calling her proper term of address to his attention and turning her back upon him and his proffered hand of friendship. But she looked at his still face and into his watchful, hopeful eyes and instead, she simply put out her hand for him to swallow up in his, and said, "Yes, truce, then. Let us have a truce."

They stood in calm silence for a moment, as he continued to hold her hand in his. And then she remembered her position and his, and slipped her hand away from his light clasp as she said, not with triumph but with a note of wonderment, "Then you do understand that I will return to England just as soon as you have gotten to see Robin? You do see," she said, turning from him, unable to meet his eyes for fear that she was saying too much and that she was sundering their newly made pact of peace, but unable to stop herself since her need to be fully understood was so strong, "that I want nothing more than to go home, and that there is nothing between Robin and myself any longer?"

She held her breath unknowingly, until she heard herself expel it after he said, "Yes, I do see."

Then she dared say nothing further, feeling that it would be unwise to ask more than that concession from him. But he went on, in a more ironical voice then he had used previously, "But then, I'm not known to be remarkably acute when it comes to pretty ladies, so you must not expect too much of me. God knows, I do not. But still, for what it is worth, let us say that there are certain elements to your story which do have the ring of truth. Isn't that wonderful?'' He laughed. "For if you have told the truth, I am nothing but a kidnapper and a beast, and here I stand saying magnanimously that there may be something in what you say. It's a bad situation all around, isn't it, Julia?'' he asked suddenly, seriously.

She turned back to see a look of bitter confusion upon his face. He seemed young and lost, at once both vulnerable and in need of some sort of reassurance. So she quickly said, before she could be craven enough to think better of it, "Is it bad enough to make you change your mind about my staying on, my lord? What I mean is, since you see you may have made some error in judgment, perhaps there is the possibility of my returning to England now? At once? I didn't really expect so,'' she sighed, as she saw his expression harden again, "but you cannot blame me for asking when I saw the opportunity.''

She silently railed at herself for her rashness as he stood and regarded her without emotion or speech. Then she asked as she forced a smile, in an attempt to take the curse off the moment, "But whatever did happen to permit you even the shadow of doubt as to my honesty?''

She hoped that her question and her smile might lighten his mood again, for however she felt about her enforced stay in France, there was no question that it was more than bearable when he choose to be a pleasant companion, and there was no sense at all in her alienating him.

She had not angered him, but her attempt to win free of him had altered his mood and he was again in voice and in expression the man she had known before: amused, worldly, and cynical.

"Ah,'' he said at last, matching her tone for levity, though he observed her through wide and grave eyes, "but that is simple enough. The sort of female that I had envisioned you to be would have ordered up a few trunkfuls of clothes by now, and by this evening would certainly have been attempting to wheedle her first bracelet from me, to match her new outfit. And then too,'' he added, with something in his expression that she could not read, it was not quite humor, but then it was not altogether serious either, "there is the rather incredible fact that you were not Robin's lover to contend with as well."

She was stung again by the observation that had perversely annoyed when he had originally made it, after he had first kissed her. But then she had been too amazed to protest. Now she was too foolish not to. Instead of using his words to her advantage, she thought later, as she ought to have done, since he was showing so much self-doubt this night, she went on to challenge him again by crying, idiotically even to her own ears, "How can you know that?"

But now the expression he wore was too clear not to read and she stepped back a pace as a lazy, sensual smile spread across his lips.

"My dear Miss Hastings," he said happily, "as I have said, my judgment in the matter of young females is sadly amiss, but there are some things I would have to be three weeks dead not to know. Unless you earn your livelihood as some of the poor drabs in the lower sort of brothels in the Rookeries do, as a professional virgin, I suspect you know nothing of the arts of love. Now, those poor creatures are sold and resold as untouched goods, and they are quite good, I understand, at the imposture. Of course, they are starveling things, so thin as to be almost genderless, but then, they have to pass for children. I don't understand why virgins are never thought to be voluptuous," he mused, the growing glint in his eye showing that he was peripherally aware and profoundly amused by her horrified reaction to his words, "as though leanness were intimately associated with virtue and poundage implied promiscuity, but such is the case. Although I have often found the truth to be the reverse. I don't even understand why there should be such a thriving market for their strange talents either, for I myself find little erotic in the prospect of profound ignorance. But then again, there are some fellows who would only feel successful dealing with someone who is in no position to make comparisons, I suppose.

"And then," he went on as though to himself, although clearly he was vastly pleased with how wide her eyes had grown, "there are some old fools who firmly believe that commerce with a virgin cures the pox. It doesn't, you know," he said off-handly. "It only stands to reason that all that it will

produce is another poor soul with the pox. But I suppose they
are desperate. Miss Hastings, I suggest you either breathe in
quickly, or else breathe out at once, you are becoming the most
alarming shade of blue,'' he volunteered, diverting from his
topic.

''Des-picable!'' Julia breathed, only realizing as she said it
that he was right, the word was far more sibilant than she had
intended, and it seemed to hiss out of her as her pent-up breath
was released with its utterance.

They stood facing each other in the empty dining room. His
face was impassive, but one of his thin dark eyebrows was up-
raised as if in a query as she stared at him in outrage. Though
the room was silent, the hiss of her breath seemed to still hang
in the air between them. And then, incredibly, she found that
she had emitted a tiny giggle. She stifled the sound at once, but
then she saw the merciless amusement in his eye. She began to
giggle again, and then she started to laugh aloud, and so did he,
and soon they both were laughing uproariously together again.
It did not seem that she could catch her breath to stop when he
caught her up in his hands, his face suddenly alive and intent
and filled with a terrible urgency, as he shook her the once and
cried, ''Julia! This is insane, this communion between us. I
don't understand it, but don't hinder it any longer. Don't play
with me any longer. Be honest and let's resolve the matter between us now. Why did you leave Robin? What happened that
night between you? Only tell me and I swear that I will try to
understand.''

But as the laughter died in her throat, she realized that as
she had never understood, so he could not be expected to
either. Still she said in a rush, her words tumbling out as her
wild laugher had done, ''I told you. Nothing happened that
night. He came and told me that he could not wed me. He
sent me home with his friend. That is all that happened.
That's the jest. Can you see it? Won't you laugh at it with
me?'' she cried, before she wrenched away from him and
ran to her room.

Julia had composed herself entirely by the time she judged it
time to sleep. She had dismissed Celeste. She could hear no
more noise in the corridors of the hotel. She had managed to
thrust the matter of her confrontation and sudden departure
from the baron from her immediate consciousness since she

had returned to her room. But now she was alone, and not only could she no longer avoid thinking of him, she could not even escape the inevitable confrontation with herself.

It was very late and she lay upon her bed and closed her eyes and felt boneless with weariness. But she knew from experience that it was the kind of exhaustion that had nothing to do with being physically spent, and so she knew that sleep would not come easily. So she lay back in her bed in the darkened hotel room and let her eyes drift open to stare at the dim shapes upon the ceiling, and knew that they would not close of their own accord this night until she had gone through it all, all over again.

She had tried to tell him the truth, she had wanted to do so. But at the last she had remembered that despite the bond of communion that seemed to have grown between them, and no matter how frequent their mutual laughter, she was still, after all, his captive, and he was still, in a sense, her jailer. Yet she had not lied to him. She had only, she thought, smiling grimly to herself in the shadows, omitted telling him a part of it. Still, she had never told anyone the whole of it, so why should she think that it would be easy to confide in him? To have told him would have been to have trusted him entirely, and she was not sure she could ever do that with one of his gender again. Certainly, she thought self-righteously there in the dark, excusing her cowardice, she did not owe the truth to a man who was her warder. But however true that observation might be, it made her feel no better.

Nothing would really make her feel better, she knew that. But if she were to go over it again, she thought, as she always thought, as a person who has mislaid something and reviews their actions in the hopes that they can remember the one insignificant detail that will bring it all back to them again thinks, then, why then she might at least buy sleep. And there was always the remote hope that this time would be the time that she might at last actually understand it.

He had said, for she remembered exactly, even after three years, "Go rest, little one. I'm off to tell the landlord to whistle us up a vicar. And order us up a wedding feast, as well. And we'll begin it all as soon as Edwin gets here—you will adore Edwin, sweet, he is adorable . . ." and here he paused for her giggle, and then went on, "After you rest, get into your best dress, for we want to remember this day always, and I don't want you thinking twenty years hence, 'I ought to have worn my blue.' . . . Lord no, don't wear blue! What am I saying? What an ill omen. Wear rose. Yes, a petal-soft rose color. For happiness. And it suits you, and I want Edwin to envy me from the bottom of his heart. And then I'll come for you and we'll be wed. Love,'' he had said caressingly, smiling to himself as he touched her cheek before leaving her, as though he liked the sound of the word, for he had never called her so before. Then he had left her and gone down to see to the ordering up of their wedding.

She had laid down to rest obediently, for she had been an obedient child, although she hadn't felt a bit tired, only excited beyond belief. And then when she felt enough time had surely passed, she had gotten up from the bed and picked through all the dresses Mama had packed in the case, looking for a rose-colored one. Mama had sewn a lovely cream-colored frock for her to be wed in, for it suited her long golden hair so well, she had said, but Robin had specified rose. So she searched until she found a pink muslin dress, never so fine as the cream-colored silk, but almost the color he wanted, and what he wanted was right.

Then, because she had wasted so much time looking for the right dress, and dithering over whether it was close enough to the ellusive petal color he had specified, she realized that it had grown late. The wind was howling outside, the fire in the bedroom's grate had died down, and even the water in the washbasin that the maid had brought when she had lit the fire had grown from steaming hot to only tepid. But Julia was a good, cleanly girl, so she stripped to her waist and washed herself thoroughly before she put on the frock that was to be her wedding dress. She even had a vial of lavendar water and she thought she would dab some behind her ears or perhaps, daringly, between her breasts, so that she would be scented as well as washed for her wedding.

As she toweled herself dry, she thought that it might have been nice to have had her mother or a sister there to see to her and to wish her well, but Robin had explained that it was not possible to have them present without involving them in possible blame from his family. She shuddered a bit when she thought of his family, but then remembering that Robin had said that all would be well when they were wed, she sighed, and thinking of him, she was so occupied that she did not hear him when he tapped at the door. And the force of the wind outside prevented her from hearing him when he opened the door and asked her leave to come into the room again.

She only became aware of him when he caught her around the waist from behind and hugged her to himself. Her start of alarm subsided to a contented sigh as she felt the long clean length of him against her back, and she heard his voice from right beneath her left ear as he dropped his mouth to the entrance of her ear to whisper, "Dreaming? But it isn't even night yet, little one. I'm keeping you up far past your bedtime, am I not, child? But the storm is fierce and the roads are bad because of it. So the vicar is late, and dear, adorable Edwin is tardy as well."

He had been drinking something potent, she could scent it on his breath along with the sharp strong scent of cinnamon and clove. But it was a comfortable scent, like that of baking day at home, so she only stretched herself in a happy sigh against him and she felt his arms tighten about her waist.

"Let's have a look at you, child," he whispered on a husky laugh, and he spun her around to face him, even as she remembered that she was not yet completely dressed. She had been holding a towel in front of herself when he had come in, for she had stripped to her waist and her rose dress still lay upon the bed in readiness for her. But when he turned her around, in that one instant, in that one moment of decision that she was to relive a hundred times for every heartbeat of it, she dropped the towel thinking, "Why not? He is to be my husband."

Or was it pride in her young body, she was later to often wonder? Or was it an unknowing act of lust? Had it been only a prelude to a jest? Or was it only the action of a very young girl, very much in what she thought was love with her future husband? She herself would never precisely recall her own reasons, and had things transpired differently she might never have had to try to fathom them at all. But as she spun around to face him, she dropped the towel and dropped her gaze to the ground as she did so. So she could not read his face when he saw her. That was to bother her very much a thousand times later. It was to plague her like an itch along the inside of a bone, where one could never reach it. For she had no idea of what his first reaction had been. The first moment she had any idea something was amiss was when she heard his voice, low and somewhat shaken, saying, "Ah, then. Then you are really not so much the child after all, are you, Julia?"

She had looked down at herself. Fool! her later self was to cry, so many times later, reviewing the scene, why did you not look up into his face instead? You would have time enough to spare to gaze at yourself in the years to come. But as it was, she had glanced downward and all she had seen was her own two rose-tipped breasts, clear in the light of the room. Then she had looked to him, to see him staring at her breasts as well, with a look of . . . what, she was never to ascertain. For she only saw that look upon his face for a fleeting moment and it was neither lust, nor shock, nor revulsion, nor desire, but all those things and something else as well.

Then he had pulled her close and kissed her very savagely and frightened her very badly. Because that kiss was not her gentle Robin, and that rough embrace was never his, and neither was his face familiar in the moment after he was done with the kiss and had thrust her away. But when she had caught up the towel again, and held it to cover herself and taken in a deep breath and dared to stare at him at last, then it was Robin's gentle face that she saw again. But his words could not have been his.

For that was when he told her of the other that he loved, and of how it would never be fair to wed her when he really loved another. And she had never believed him, and still did not.

So nothing happened that night between us, my lord baron, she whispered to herself there in the dark, I told you nothing but the truth. I merely omitted a few details. But as they made no sense, it makes no matter.

Since she had begun it, Julia knew she must end it or never find sleep this night. So she passed the next few hours as she always did when that scene came back to her with that much clarity. She wondered again if it was something about her body which had revulsed him, perhaps it had been her breasts—their form, or shape, or size. Then she wondered if it had been something more intangible, sufficiently repellent but so discreet that she could never discover it for herself; a thing she lacked the courage to ever ask another being about: such as a scent, an odor, or a miasma that clung to her. Or perhaps it had been her wanton action or her kiss that had tipped the scales. Perhaps it had made him think she was loose and unprincipled, well used to doing such wild and abandoned things. Or perhaps it had been something he found disgusting in her very kiss itself.

And so Julia whiled away the small hours of the night as she so often did, wondering at what it was in herself that was so repugnant, or what it had been in her actions that had been so intolerable. She never doubted that she was at fault in some manner for what had happened. For she had never been, for all her youth, a fool. And she knew that Robin, ah Robin, he had loved her well—until that moment. That one decisive moment when something in herself, or of herself, had banished him forever.

11 The frail elderly gentleman selected his breakfast with great care from the array of shining chafing dishes left out upon the long buffet table in the dining room. It was a pleasant morning, the early summer sunlight shone in through the long glass windows to illuminate the room, and there seemed to be little reason for the gentleman's rather pained expression as he paused over the broiled mushrooms, kidneys, and eggs. But then, with an exhalation that was only the merest suggestion of a sigh, he walked past the chafing dish, and with finicky precision, took instead a simple golden roll and laid it alongside the plain dish of porridge and solitary brown egg mounted upon a silver cup that he had already chosen for his breakfast.

A footman bore his choice of breakfast to the long damasked table. There, in solitary state, although the table clearly had room and to spare for a dozen other diners and their companions as well beside him, the gentleman sat down in silence to his light breakfast. He had consumed his gruel with placid disinterest and had begun tapping upon his egg in rather aimless fashion, as though he had little interest in actually decapitating

140

it, when the door to the room swung open suddenly to admit his host, come in to breakfast with him.

"Vicar!" cried Sir Sidney to the older gentleman as though he had not seen him in a year, when in fact, they had parted company not eight hours before. "My dear fellow, how glad I am that you're a early riser too. I hate to breakfast alone. But I see you've hardly anything left upon your plate. Come, come, have a bit more to sustain you for the day. Try the kippers, they're excellent, I have 'em brought in 'cross the channel fresh every day, you know, since so many of our guests are homesick for 'em. But you're a worldly fellow, have a bite of these cutlets, the cream sauce is superb, the Frenchies are a wonder with sauces, you know. Or these kidneys, marvelous, I swear it. At the very least, dear friend," Sir Sidney said heartily, as he piled his own plate higher with each of the treats as he enumerated them, and noticed his guest's delicately bilious expression as the plate became more laden, "join me in another pot of tea. That is, if there's room enough for us both in there," he concluded, laughing as though he had capped his sentence with a play on words that was both new and original.

Sir Sidney bore his own plate to the table, shooing away the attentive footman by telling him both loudly and abruptly to clear out as his services weren't required and that he'd call for him when he was done with his meal.

"Fellow's been working for me for years, I dare say," he grumbled to his guest as he settled down in a chair opposite to him, "but he still don't understand a word I say unless I shout at him. Damned foreigners expect you to learn their bloody language instead of the other way around. Or at least," he said darkly, pointing an egg-bearing fork at the vicar, "so they'd have you believe, but I never knew a servant didn't learn his master's language in a trice, so's he could learn what was going forth about him. Take this lot of Frenchies, they might know what you were talking about chapter and verse, but just try to get 'em to admit to it."

The other gentleman did not reply immediately, but waited instead until the footman had actually left the room and closed the door carefully behind him. Then all he did was smile politely and resume his attack upon his egg, as he murmured "Doubtless," to his host.

"You're not eating enough to keep a flea alive," Sir Sidney

protested, with his mouth so full that his cheeks bulged and his words were muffled. "Have more, Vicar, there's plenty enough to go around."

"It's not the amplitude that concerns me, it is my own fortitude. That is to say, it's my digestion, not my discretion, that's at fault, my dear," the vicar explained. "I'm sure that there's enough," he went on, setting down his spoon after only a mouthful of egg, and dabbing at his pale and thin lips with a spotless napkin, "for I think that I may be the only houseguest left here with you, Ollie."

"No, you're out there," his host answered more clearly, having swallowed most of his food and washed it down with a gulp of steaming tea, "because old Duchess FitzAllen and her young cicisbeo are still here, as are Kirkland and Dabney and their opera dancers, and the two Charter brothers, and oh yes, Lord Lambert and Count Voronov as well."

"They left at first light, Ollie," the vicar said quietly.

"Rats leaving a sinking ship," Sir Sidney said savagely, putting down his cutlery suddenly and leaving off the affect of hearty, jolly host just as abruptly. His heavily jowled face grew a sneer to replace his habitual smile as he went on to say angrily, "Well, they're the sort that sails only with a fair current, but they've ruined it for themselves in future, for they'll not be welcome back here when the tide turns again."

"I had understood," said the vicar softly, giving his plate an imperceptible push away from himself even as he gave his chair a slight nudge away from the table, "that it was more in the nature of a tidal wave than a tide actually, Ollie dear."

"Well, you understood wrongly," Sir Sidney replied quickly, "for it's only a temporary misunderstanding that I'll soon set to rights. It's all grist for the rumor mill and nothing more. After all, Vicar," he said ingratiatingly, with a shadow of his former smile, "you have known me forever, you've stayed on here with me as my guest for time out of mind, can you actually see me as a traitor?"

"Actually," the vicar said in his usual whispery voice, "yes, Ollie dear. But don't feel you must make explanation to me," he said quickly, raising one thin, veined hand to silence his host's next expected words, "for it's quite unnecessary, I assure you. I'm the paltriest of fellows, as you well know. My only value in life now lies in the fact that I am an entertaining guest. There's no need for you to make apology or, indeed, to even take note of such a fribble as myself. You've had me on here as guest, time out of mind, it's true, old dear. But I don't feel too guilty about it, for after all, I did earn my way. Why, I entertained your guests royally, Ollie, you can't deny that. I always knew the latest gossip and passed it along without stint. And when I heard, by the by, in the course of discovering the latest on-dit, what was being said of my own host, I never batted an eyelash, for it isn't fit for me to judge you, Ollie. But I was awaiting you this morning, my dear. For I'm sorry to inform you that I am one of those rodents too—I'm leaving today as well. Well, after all," he said with a thin smile, "there's scarcely a need for a jester is there, when the court is no longer in session."

Sir Sidney stayed very still, and then he began to laugh. He laughed long and loudly and then, noting that his napkin was both egg- and sauce-covered, he wiped his eyes upon the back of his sleeve and let out one last and gusty chuckle. Then he said without a trace of humor remaining in his voice, "Always admired your crust, Vicar. You could murder a man, step over him, and hand the dripping dagger to someone and ask for new cutlery since your own knife was dirtied. I liked that about you, Vicar, I did indeed. Even the way you adopted that name, 'Vicar,' when you grew old, when everyone knew that the Baron Watchtower had always been an absolute rakeshame who could only qualify as a clergyman to the devil himself."

The thin, ascetic gentleman bowed his head graciously, with a gentle smile, as though he was receiving a great compliment, as his host went on with a sort of grim, relentless delight in his voice now, "The tales of your youthful adventures are legend, Vicar. They say that you bedded everything that walked the earth, just for the novelty of it, in your day. And that the further jest was that you did so for love or for money, for lust or for a lark, with the highborn and the low, from whatever class, situation, gender, or even species, I don't doubt, that you happened to fancy at the moment, or so I heard. I even heard that you only live here upon the Continent because your name's so ripe that your family wants no part of you at home at all."

"Now gossip is not your métier, Ollie, you really ought to leave it to us professionals," the vicar chided in the dry accents of an aged headmaster. Then he added conversationally, "All the rest is true, but you have that last the wrong way around, for I choose to stay abroad myself. After all, what have I in common with the usual run of English nobility of my own age? Can you just see me, Ollie my dear, in some gentleman's club on St. James Street, with all the other old fellows boring on about their army experiences or adventures in Society as they sip their cordials and comment on the news nostalgically, while I think back on my adventures in a thousand bedchambers as I eye the footmen reminiscently? No, it would never do, would it? Not while I have an excellent nephew to whom I can leave the twin chores of breeding and burnishing up the family name. No Ollie, my exile here is entirely my own choice. I am a professional guest by personal inclination as well. I know that it comes as a surprise, but as it happens, I've a great deal of blunt. It's only the fact that I choose to leave it all to my charming nephew that makes me such a sponge who lives upon the good graces of hosts such as yourself. It appears," he said with an expression of bemused wonder, "that I possess a conscience after all, for I find that I wish to leave my tediously conventional young relative a great deal more than merely the title itself."

"Then if I'm still willing to foot the bill for your services, why are you leaving?" Sir Sidney said abruptly.

Something flickered for an instant in the older man's gentle countenance, but then was gone, leaving the aged face as grave and calm as it was before his host had spoken.

"Ah well, Ollie," the vicar said regretfully, "it is a paradox, you see. Precisely because I have to be universally pleasing and acceptable everywhere, I must take care where I am accepted."

"Meaning," his host said in an ugly, threatening voice, "that I am no longer acceptable?"

The vicar made no reply, but with an ironic smile, only spread his two thin hands out to either side of his body in a gesture of total helplessness.

"Damn it, it's all lies!" Sir Sidney shouted, banging his hand down upon the heavy wooden tabletop so hard that the plates and teacups danced.

"As you say," the vicar replied imperturbably.

"Vicar," Sir Sidney said suddenly, "you can do me a service before you leave."

As his guest looked up warily from the spreading stain of tea upon the tablecloth that he had been observing, Sir Sidney heaved a bitter chuckle before he went on to say, "Aye, you've convinced me further protests of innocence will be disregarded. But as a man of the world, you know as well as I do that if I manage to retrieve my good name, all will be forgiven, so I hardly need to blather on about it now, before I've got the facts in hand. But there's a thing you can do for me to achieve those ends, for all our old time's sake."

The vicar regarded his host with a stilled and watchful expression as Sir Sidney said harshly, "You needn't look at me like that, vicar, I'm not about to ask you to commit murder. It's only gossip I'm after. It's a little thing that I've had to make big because of your own decision to leave. It's the sort of thing I'd have asked you over a hand of cards, by the way, if I had my choice."

"Ah well, then," the vicar asked in his usual amused accents, "then out with it, Ollie, if it's who's been sleeping in my bed, I'm sure to know."

"Not precisely," Sir Sidney said, leaning in closer to his guest. "His bedtime habits don't interest me much, unless they're spectacular. I'd like to know what you know of Lord Nicholas Daventry, Baron Stafford."

"Ah," said the vicar.

She looked uncommonly well in her new frock, Nicholas thought. And so he told her, before she left to go on another shopping expedition that he had ordered, or, he thought ruefully, on another sightseeing expedition as she preferred. For though she had colored up nicely at his compliment, and seemed to be all acquiescence as he told her to go ahead and purchase some more finery for herself, even as he did so he had the distinct notion that she had passed some sort of unspoken orders to her maidservant. She might yet, he thought with real amusement, dash into some shop and hurriedly buy a pair of gloves so as to comply with the letter of his command, and then pass the remainder of the day goggling at works of art in some museum to comply with the spirit of her own desires.

He smiled to himself at the thought of her possible furtive activity. Then realizing that he often smiled when he thought of her, he frowned. For she was a beauty, and a fellow ought to be moved to more explicable passions when he refined upon such a magnificent female face and form. Yet though there was no doubt that she could spur the expected emotions when he encountered her, it was not unusual to find that it was laughter which she provoked in him as often as it was lust. And laughter was a powerful aphrodisiac. At least, he discovered much to his own discomfort that it was apparently so in his own case.

He ought, at the very least, to mistrust her. At the very most, with Robin's damning letters as his guide, he should detest her. But he had spent much time in her company during their journey to Paris and had dined with her each evening since. And as time went on, he found to his dismay that he enjoyed her company enormously. He appreciated her looks and enjoyed her conversation. But he discovered himself pondering too often about the question of her innocence, and musing far too long on the eventual outcome to their journeying.

It was not simply because she was a joy to look upon. There were, he had found, a great many deliciously lovely females in the world. Her hair might be likened to sun on spun gold, but what of it? He had seen, as well as run his fingers appreciatively through, tresses that could be compared to moonlight, starlight, and candlelight on a variety of poetic substances. Her eyes were clear and light blue and ringed with lustrous lashes. But he had gazed into orbs clear and green, and bright and brown, and shining and black, in fact, female eyes of a whole spectrum of dazzling colors had returned his interested stares with interest. And if now that she had worn her new gowns he could see her form was both straight and curving, slender and full, ripe and boyish all at once in that splendidly contradictive way of well-turned womanflesh, why then he had held and admired many such forms, many sweet times. He was, after all, and always had been, a connoisseur of her sex.

But never had he met a female who had all her virtues at once. And who was able, as well, to always make him laugh, and to always know why he laughed, and who would laugh herself with him at the delight of it.

He wanted her. That was plain, and that was regrettable. If she were the witch Robin had painted her, then he would turn from her forever and she would pay dearly for her dual deception. But if she had been honest, and even then Robin did not want her, and she did not want him, as she had said . . . Lord Nicholas Daventry, Baron Stafford, realizing the direction that his thoughts were leading him, attempted to cut them off ruthlessly. His plans for a future mistress, he told himself sharply, were more than merely premature, they would be stillborn if he did not pay attention to the immediate task before him. He tried to concentrate instead solely upon the direction in which his feet were presently leading him. For the Baron Stafford was on his way to yet another appointment with yet another social lion who might know where his errant nephew might be.

There should be no difficulty in finding traces of Robin's trail, Nicholas thought irritably, wondering at his singular lack of success as yet, for there was little doubt that he was in the best of positions for locating any soul on the face of the civilized planet from where he was right now. All of the focus of Europe, and all of its famed, were here in Paris at present. Wellington was here, Metternich was here, the King of Prussia, the Emperor of the Russias, the great of all the Continent were here in the beating heart of Paris, now that Napoleon himself was not. And while that would-be king of the world rode the seas aboard the English ship *Bellerophon* and gazed out over English waters to his closed and clouded future, Nicholas mused that perhaps Bonaparte, like any lesser cuckold, still dreamed of this, his beloved city even as she gave warm welcome to other men who loved her well.

For despite the fact that he had only been in Paris for a little over a week, the baron had already been to balls and galas and gambling hells and restaurants and operas, where he had seen the famous and their familiars disporting themselves. He had gone to all the festivities in a singularly unfestive frame of mind. It was never pleasure he sought, only information. But he was so skilled in amiability that there was no one who guessed at his mission as he went from waltz party to card party, from state dinner to intimate supper, from soiree to orgy, always amused and amusing, ever obliging, but always detached and watchful. He had heard a thousand rumors, but had acted on none, for they were all merely rumors and he sought confirmation.

Now he walked the streets of the notorious Palais Royal district and he nodded to several acquaintances remembered from

London as he strode past houses and cafés that offered diverse amusement, There were a great many Englishmen here now, along with members of all the allied armies, and men of all nations could buy pastimes here. But the baron had no interest in any diversion that was for sale, he never had. He did not flatter himself that he received more invitations than other fellows from the smiling females who stood about in front of their shops, for he knew it was not his trim form which enticed them, but the expensive cut of his clothes upon it, and not his handsome face which they longed for him to lay on their pillows, but his equally handsome purse.

But for all the certainty in his hard-won wisdom he would have been greatly surprised to learn that many of the businesswomen he passed and smiled his regrets at would have been pleased in his case to have made a donation, rather than a sale. His first mistress had left him a legacy of caution, which he knew of. But she had also robbed him of his vanity, a theft that he had never discovered and which ironically was perhaps her greatest parting gift to him. It was that very lack of conceit which, unknown to himself, enhanced the carefully schooled charm he had been practicing since he had set sail from England. It had always made him remarkably successful, and this time it had been no different. Yet though a great many people had wanted to tell him his nephew's whereabouts, and a great many had told him all sorts of stories about Robin, as he now walked through the streets of Paris he was dishearteningly aware that he was no closer to his nephew or the truth about him than he had been in his townhouse in London.

Nicholas paused for a moment to puzzle out a signpost above him. The original name seemed to have been scratched out a long time in the past, probably during the days of the Revolution, or so he guessed, so it must have been a saint's or a king's name that had been written there. A new name had obviously been given the street during the Emperor's reign, but now that the wheel of fortune had turned once again, yet another name had been hastily scrawled atop that last one. As he attempted to puzzle out the latest designation for this street, which in itself embodied the history of a turbulent generation, he felt a hand placed lightly upon his sleeve.

"It is now 'La Rue du Roi,'" a well-bred English voice said

pleasantly, "but if you were looking for 'La Rue de l'Empereur,' Nick, it is also that."

"Vicar! Good lord, sir, what brings you here?" Nicholas said in surprise, although more than surprise caused his usually cool white countenance to take on a warm and suffused darker glow.

"Don't rate yourself, Nick," the vicar said in amused tones, although a gratified and understanding smile appeared upon his thin lips. "It's quite natural to call me Vicar, all my friends as well as my enemies do. I know you take particular care not to do so to spare my feelings, but rest easy, my lad, I choose the name, after all. It is a parody, of course. It may signify all sorts of wicked things to the world, to be sure, but as I embrace it, as well as the whole of my naughty history, I remove the sting and the stigma from it. Or so at least I think I do. No matter. What brings me here, Nick? Why I have a friend here."

"Then sir," Nicholas said quickly, "I shouldn't like to take you from him, but if I could have a few words with you? There's a café a bit further up the street," he added in a hopeful tone.

"No, not the café, for my poor lights and liver and whatever else abides within this wretched frame of mine won't take another glass of good red wine, and it should pain me, lad, to watch others imbibing what I cannot. But we could walk on a space together, I think. And you needn't worry about taking me from my friend, Nick, for you are he," the vicar said, smiling as he took the baron's arm, as if for support, as they continued along the street.

They seemed almost of a height, although they were actually of very disparate size. The vicar had been an extremely tall man in his youth, but it appeared that his age had diminished him so that he stood even a little less tall than the baron, and his slight frame increased his appearance of almost translucent frailty. Yet Nicholas noted that even as the elder man seemed to lean upon his arm, he bore no additional weight upon that limb and though the older gentleman gave every impression of fragility, there was nothing but strength apparent in his hand's clasp. The vicar, the baron thought again, was never to be taken at face value, nor should he ever be underestimated, as it seemed he so often wished to be.

"I wanted a few words with you, Nick," the vicar said as

they strolled along the famous avenues, "but I wanted it to appear to be of little import and less note, so it is best that we just chat as we stroll on. I have just come from Sir Oliver Sidney's establishment, where, as you know, I have been a guest forever. The fellow's in the bucket, Nick, but that you know as well, for I believe you put him there yourself not a week past. No, no, please don't insult me and yourself by denying it, I know what I know. And if you wish to know more, you will please allow me to know better. There's no treason in saying nothing, is there lad?"

Wise to the vicar's ways, Nicholas remained silent and felt the old man's approval in a slight pressure being made upon his arm.

"Good, good," the vicar said happily. "Now Nick, I left our Ollie in a somewhat precarious position. He's lost his friends, his source of funds, and most likely his lovely lady as well, or at least he is bound to do so, perhaps even by the time we finish speaking. For she's not, alas, the picture of constancy. Now Ollie has hopes to recover all. Unfortunately, he most likely means to go about it using the same methods that lost him all."

The vicar delivered himself of a little sigh signifying profound regret, and then they both paused to acknowledge the salute of a rackety duke of their acquaintance. The vicar resumed speaking as the fellow passed, as though there had been no interruption at all, "And unhappily enough, Ollie seems to bear you some personal ill will. So, of course, before I left, as a sort of final payment for battening on his good offices for all these years, he asked me to tell him everything I knew about you." And here the vicar paused.

But Nicholas kept on walking. He refused to miss a step and so said smoothly, merely the one word, "And?"

"*Very* good," the vicar said. "Well, I told him all, of course."

It took all of the baron's control to continue walking as though nothing important had been said, and even more self-restraint than he knew he possessed to keep from flinging the vicar's thin hand from his arm as he would throw off a venomous spider.

"I told him," the vicar said obliviously, "about your liason with Lady Davies, and your brief and secret connection with

Gwen Lindsay, and your patronage of Mary Flowers, Julia Johnson, Lucille LaPoire, and that little filly from Madame Felice's stables. I'm sorry, my boy, but I also told him about your fling with that shocking Turner woman.''

Nicholas felt the tension leave his shoulders and he found he could draw in his breath more easily. There hadn't been a word about his errands for the crown, nor a syllable about his present search, only common gossip about common indiscretions. The vicar turned toward him slightly and gave him a smile that showed all of his small white teeth. Doubtless, the baron thought, the older man had felt the tension ease in his body as well. Perhaps that was why the old fox had held his arm so closely in the first place, so as to better gauge his involuntary reactions. It never would do to underestimate the vicar, he thought again.

"Yet," the vicar went on musingly, "with all I divulged to him, Ollie was nonetheless unhappy with the information. And I don't think it was that he was disappointed, as sad to relate, I always am, at your unswerving devotion to the female gender." Seeing from a sly, sidewise glance that his comment had not fazed his young companion in the least, the vicar laughed softly and went on, "Not a quake to be felt. No, lad, that is why I never do underestimate you either. So he asked me about your companion on the trip, this mysterious Miss Foster, the poor girl with the aching head who never showed her nose outside her rooms save for that one night you met her in that little garden.''

But at that, the baron was taken aback for a moment, which caused the vicar to give him a sharp look before he said easily, "But I told him she was Nobody.

"In short, lad," the vicar said, as he slowed their pace by hanging back a bit, "Ollie was after something to hold over you. But though it shames me to tell it, I could not come up with a thing to his purposes.''

At this, the vicar paused for long enough for the baron to understand that he might at last speak.

"And this inability to produce something suffcent to my ruin was due, I take it, to the exemplary life I lead?'' he asked quietly.

"No, Nick," the vicar said softly, "no man who breathes is immune to some scandal, past or present. Or at least, no one

I've ever encountered in my interesting lifetime. Rake or prelate, I've never met a saint. But your sins are, on balance, not very grave ones, never the stuff of easy blackmail, at any rate. I hear a great many things, lad, but I tell only a fraction of what I hear, and that always to a purpose. I know the identity of your sometime employers and I find I quite agree with their decision about Ollie. He was a very good host, and in his fashion a fair enough friend, but I always took care with what I told him. I suffered, you see, from the absurd notion that whatever I said to him ended up being translated into another language somewhere along the line.

"I have been and done a great many things, Nick," the vicar said softly, "but what Ollie forgets is that whatever I have been, I have always been an Englishman.

"And it is for that reason that I tell you, Nick," the vicar said with some urgency at last, "to find Robin. For he is not so impervious to scandal as you, and Ollie is seeking him, too. No, I said nothing of him, I did not have to. Ollie has ears as well. But our Sir Sidney is desperate, and he is not without resources. You may be able to escape any net that Ollie casts, but I tell you, the same is not the case with your nephew. Find young Robin before Ollie does, Nick, and before he is actually become the new marquess."

"And as to his whereabouts?" the baron asked.

"That," the vicar said sadly, "I cannot say with any accuracy. I believe him to be on his way to Paris. But then again, he may be tarrying in Belguim. I am sorry to be so unhelpful, I would enlighten you if I could. But even I have limits." He smiled before he went on to say, "I can only urge you to make all haste to discover him."

But now the baron fixed the older man with a steady stare and asked with great sincerity, "What is the truth about Robin, sir? Since you urge me to discover him quickly, I cannot help but think you know it as well as he himself does. And if you wish to aid me in any way, you know I would be forever in your debt if you could disclose the facts of his disappearance and his continued exile to me."

"There are some things, believe it or not, that are not mine to tell," the vicar said somberly. "Some tales which loyalty to my friends or honor due my country prevent me from divulging, so much," he said with a twisted smile, "as I might love to have you in my debt, my boy."

"But have you not just said that I am your friend?" Nicholas asked reasonably.

"Ah," the vicar replied in almost a whisper, "forgive me, Nick, but you see, there are friends, and then there are friends of the heart. I really can say little more."

"Forgive me, sir," the baron said after they had walked on in complete silence for a while, "but though I know it will be damned difficult to remedy now in either case, I think I would almost prefer that it was your honor rather than your loyalty which prevented you."

"Yes," the vicar replied, "of course."

The older gentleman left off his conversation to look hard at the street for an instant, although anyone not so close to him as his companion might have thought that it was only that he had gotten a mote of dust in his eye and had to pause to blink it away. And then he took the baron's hand and clasped it hard and shook it firmly and said loudly, "My dear fellow, it was delightful. We must meet again sometime. Dinner, perhaps? Please don't hesitate to call at my hotel."

But as he bent close he said, softly, rapidly, and only for the baron's ear, "Be quick about it, Nick, and be wary. But find him soon. Before Ollie does."

He proceeded to make a deep bow as full of flourishes as a trumpet fanfare. Then, as swiftly and silently as he had appeared, he was gone, leaving the baron alone and feeling even more lost than he had been before.

12

She would not have chosen yellow. But then, Julia thought, that was only one of the many reasons why she was not a world-famed couturiere, demanding and receiving outsize fees for outrageously stylish frocks such as the one she wore now. For yellow or no, even she had to concede that the garment she had just put on was the latest kick, the highest cry, and the last recorded syllable of fashion. But, Julia thought, in very much the manner of the former governess Miss Hastings, fashion being as it was, it was more likely that somewhere in this very city there was now another garment, created not five minutes ago, that was even more in fashion. In fact, she thought, there was every possibility that by the time she left her room, went down the stairs, and reached the hotel's private dining room where the baron awaited her, her frock might be hopelessly passé. It was such a diverting thought that she wore the smallest smile, only a suggestion of little uplifted upper lip, to go with her new gown as she went in to her dinner.

And so when Nicholas rose to his feet as she entered the room, he wore a matching smile as he thought and said, "Enchanting."

"Thank you," Julia said, and to cover her embarrassment at

how hard he stared at her, she looked downward, plucked at a fold of her dress, and said quickly, "But such a bright yellow! And I was brought up to understand that a fair-haired lady never wore yellow. It was Clarice, my youngest sister, who has the darkest brown curls, who was the one to wear such hues. Betty and Dorothea and I never dared. We made do with light pastels, while poor Harriet, being red-headed—since Mama is fair and Papa is dark, and I understand that such combination of parents often produce red-headed persons—had the most difficult time of us all in selecting materials for her dresses."

When she looked up, Julia was surprised to see the baron regarding her with a wide grin that could only be called fond.

"Incredible," he said, "how the unflappable Miss Hastings can be reduced to babbling by only one word. But only if that word is complimentary."

Julia did not know precisely how to reply to him, or what to say that might dispel that irresistible and alarmingly bright and admiring look that he turned to her. It was very difficult to speak to him when he gazed at her in that manner, as though he was seeing only her, as she really was, and as he seemingly wanted her to be.

He looked at her so keenly that she involuntarily began to draw her shawl around herself as was her habit, only remembering at the last that Monsieur LeRoy had threatened murder if she dared to wear her shawl with his creation, and suicide if she insisted he design one to replace it. So she drew herself up instead. She attempted to forget the insubstantial nature of the material of her frock and remain calm beneath his intent regard as well.

"No wonder the fellow has survived so many regimes," the baron said, tapping his quizzing glass upon his hand and walking around Julia as she stood immobile for his inspection. "He's famous for insisting that the garment should reflect the 'freedom and natural shape' of the form, but I never appreciated how right he was till this moment."

Now, of course, Julia could say nothing, but something in her aspect, perhaps her encrimsoned cheek or her downcast eye, caused him to take pity on her confusion and he said in a lighter tone, "And it isn't just 'yellow,' as if the fellow had given you a banana skin to wear, but yellow and black, my dear, a most dramatic combination. You look as refreshing and welcome as one of those great swallowtail butterflies my stepfather is fond of collecting. Those borders there on the hem and sleeves, that black Greek key design, and those few flourishes and ruffles he's added for interest, the way that fold is caught up in a little theatrical swag to the side of the skirt for example, I am impressed. No wonder the chap was so successful here he had our ladies killing for so much as a copy of his designs, even as their husbands and brothers were fighting to the death with his countrymen.

"Now don't sneer, Miss Hastings," he said with real amusement as he caught the startled look she gave him. "I'm not thinking of going into the designing line myself, nor do I spend my idle hours perusing the *Belle Assembly* to catch up on the latest female fashions. Nor do I pass so much of my time gaping at the ladies, either, or at least," he said thoughtfully, "I don't pass my time gaping at their *clothes*, at any rate. No. But I did grow up in a household almost exclusively made up of women. And since my stepfather taught me that it is only common courtesy to learn that which is close to the hearts of those closest to one's heart, I perforce acquired a great deal of information about the arts and craft of feminine fashion. And while styles may change, the touch of a master's hand does not, and that gown, Julia, would be lovely in any time, or any age. But fashion's a peculiar art in that it always needs a fair accomplice. By itself it's interesting, upon the wrong subject it's appalling, but with a beautiful model to display it, it transcends mere function and becomes art. In that gown you make me wish I were an artist, Julia."

Julia did not know how in the world to respond to such a fulsome compliment. But she was weary of simply being rendered speechless each time he poured the butter bucket over her, and was moreover beginning to entertain dark doubts as to the sincerity of his praise since he seemed to be very well aware and amused at how it always made her mute. So she took her seat at the table with as much aplomb as she could muster and said as coolly as she was able before she shook out her napkin to lay it in her lap, "Thank you so much, my lord. But I was not aware that you were raised in a household composed only of women. I thought you and Robin had grown up together."

It had been her problem with handling his praise that had made her, unthinking, mention Robin. For she realized even as she uttered his name that she had never brought him up in conversation of her own accord before. But now she had, and it seemed both natural and a relief to discuss him as casually as she might any other person from her past. There was the additional gratification of seeing her companion's slight start of surprise before he seated himself opposite her and answered.

"Ah no," he replied. "We only saw each other on occasions of state, or when my mama had a bit of information too weighty or incendiary for a mere letter to hold. His home wasn't far enough from ours for an overnight stay to be necessary unless a storm blew up while we were there, but then again, he didn't live close enough for daily contact either. No, a visit to his home was a whole-day affair, no matter how you looked at it. Then, too, Robin is so much my junior that I seldom spent much time with him even when I visited, as I didn't actually meet him until I had almost left my youth and he had only just begun his."

"But how can that be when you are only four years his senior, or so I believe I heard you say?" Julia asked, wondering whether her mathematics or her ears were at fault.

"That's true," he answered, pausing with his glass of wine halfway to his lips, "but four years make a great difference in one's extreme youth. And a passable one later. Remember that he was only a boy when he met you, Julia, and I was already an older, wiser man."

It might have been the unspoken accusation that she thought she heard, or it might have been the merest suggestion of censure in his tone, but Julia answered more hotly than she would have liked, "I did not think that a man of two and twenty was considered a mere boy, my lord. Perhaps standards are very different for the different sexes, but still there is little doubt that a female of that age would have already been considered a responsible adult, if not even a bit long in the tooth. In fact, three years have passed from the time I first encountered Robin, and as I am twenty years of age at this moment, I am still not reached that age that he was then. And yet I have not been considered so young that it prevented me from being employed and all on my own and entrusted with the heavy responsibility of others' children to boot for all those years, as you well know."

She frowned as she finished speaking, for what had begun as annoyance at his across-the-board vindication of Robin be-

cause of his supposed youthfulness had ended sounding a bit
meaching and plaintive. Whatever else he thought, she did not
want him thinking she was angling for his pity. But when she
looked at him, it was not pity that she saw in his expression, it
was rather a look of profound surprise. He sat with his glass untouched, slowly lowering it to the tabletop again, and seemed
very much struck with what she had just said.

"You were, then, only seventeen when you ran off with
Robin?" he asked slowly, as though he asked the question of
himself. And in truth, he scarcely heard her affirmative reply
he was so occupied with arguing with himself. For he thought,
why, what of it? as he remembered that Ivy was only eighteen
when he had become involved with her. But the difference between Ivy's eighteen and this chit's twenty was so profound as
to be immeasurable. He tried to steel himself against Julia
again by remembering how badly he had fared when he had attempted to judge Ivy. But as they were discussing age, he had
been, after all, only nineteen then and if he hadn't learned anything of human nature in a decade's time, then he supposed he
never would. He couldn't even concentrate on that revelation,
he was still so amazed that Robin had been all of two and
twenty when he had met up with Julia. At that same age, Nicholas thought, whatever his youthful sins, he himself had become a man. Why, then, had he been so convinced for all these
years that Robin had been a beardless boy when he had gotten
entangled with what he had envisioned as a heartless female?

"I've always thought of him as much younger than myself,"
Nicholas said wonderingly, speaking aloud when he had
thought he was speaking to himself, and then not caring that he
did so. "It's odd, but there are some people, usually ones that
you have known forever, that you always attribute one age to
and never correct, even in the light of truth. We all laugh because Mama continually refers to her youngest cousin as a babe,
though that lady has grandchildren of her own now. And I, and
Robin—I'm guilty of the same thing, I suppose. And I expect it's
because his mama cosseted him overmuch and kept him in ringlets
in the nursery so long and always cautioned me, who she saw as
an older, rougher chap, to look after him. I suppose it's because he
always looked up to me, and called me Uncle even at school, till I
threatened to beat him to death if he did so again, and even then I
became 'Old' Nick to his Robin 'Goodfellow.'

"It's possible too," Nicholas went on, now looking to Julia, "that I liked having a young male relative think me a more mature and worldly fellow, and so I kept him forever young in my thoughts. You see, before I came upon the scene, there were two boys born to my poor mama who did not survive their infancy. So when after four daughters I arrived, even though I proceeded to thrive, I was fussed over so much by all my lady relatives that I must have found it a blessed relief to have Robin think me so all-wise, capable, and masculine.

"Whatever the reason, it is shocking that I never envisioned him so close to my own age. Lord, so he will be five and twenty now! I say it," he said, shaking his head and raising the glass of wine at last to drain it, "but I really don't believe it."

"I don't believe that we ever see that which we don't want to," Julia said, "and I imagine that I'll always keep my baby sister Clarice childish in my thoughts, even when she's a crone. If I ever see her as middle-aged, why then that would mean I would be ancient, and I don't think I could bear that. No, really," she said, glad to hear him laugh, and pleased to see him relax, "I am that vain, at least. But if you were an only boy in your family, why were you not also as coddled as you say that Robin was?"

When he did not reply at once, but only gave her a measuring look, she stammered, "That is to say, Robin never really discussed you at all, you know, save for saying that he had a sage old uncle, 'Old Nick,' that understood everything. And that I should like you very well, as you should no doubt, he said, get on with me as my looks were quite in your style." Then, feeling that she had said quite enough in error and far too much in her attempt to remedy matters, she fell silent.

She wondered if she had gone too far, if she had overestimated the intimacy of the moment and made a social gaffe. Because he dined alone with her and seemed to enjoy her company, and forgot himself so much at times as to speak to her from the heart, did not mean that he trusted her enough to discuss his family with her. A great many things might be easily conversed about in polite society, and a great many more in impolite society, if she could judge by some of the shocking things he had said to her in the past when he believed the very worst of her. But though they might have lately had lively conversations on a great many topics ranging from literature to politics, a man's family, she knew, especially a nobleman's family, was considered sacrosanct. Especially, she reminded herself, in the presence of one's social inferiors. Her face clouded up as she picked up a fork to pick at her salmon mousse, and she silently vowed to discuss nothing more intimate from now on than her opinion of the soup, when he spoke, cutting across her thoughts.

"I might have grown as spoiled as week-old milk, had it not been for my stepfather."

As the dinner went on and the waiter bore in dish after dish of culinary magnificence that the hotel's famous chef had labored over, Julia ate them without tasting, though she savored the tales the baron told her of his childhood well enough. When the desserts came, Julia became aware that she was uncommonly full, almost too stuffed to partake of her favorite petits fours. Then she realized that she had eaten far too much, all the while not knowing that she had done so. For it appeared that in the same manner that she had so often aided Nurse and gotten Toby to devour his hated vegetables by telling such exciting tales that he had opened and closed his mouth without being aware of it as she popped them in, so the baron had gotten her to finish off her own dinner. When he eyed her untouched dessert plate, she told him this, and he laughed so long and hard that she was sure his demitasse would grow cold.

"Then it's only fair that you turn the tables, and get me to polish off this array of desserts," he said at last, indicating the plates of cakes, pastries, sweetmeats, nuts, and fruits. "Come, Nanny, and tell me about young Clarice for a start, the dark-and curly-haired one who must remain forever in the schoolroom so as to preserve your vaulting vanity."

She protested, laughing, as she told him that it would scarcely be an act of friendship to get him to eat up that lot. But as it turned out, she needn't have worried. For when she had done with her narrative, although equally as much time had passed as had during his recitation, and though she had his undivided attention throughout, he had scarcely touched a bite to eat. Though it seemed he enjoyed the stories about her young siblings and her mother and her father and his haughty employer fully as much as she had enjoyed hearing of his sisters and aunts and mother and wise stepfather, his face grew grave and still as she ended up her tales. His stories had been reminiscenses of his youth, embroidered with humor and finished off with a precis of how each of his family was faring at present. But of necessity her stories, while fully detailed and filled with loving and amused remembrance, ended quite differently. For she was an exile, and there was no way that any part of her history could conclude without that fact, without that blot.

She tried to gloss over it, she attempted to pass it by, but it was like an ugly wound upon a seamless surface.

"And now, Julia," he said at length, "what are your plans? After this episode, I mean to say. For you shall have earned a fair purse for your part in it," he added gruffly, as though he disliked bringing up the mercenary aspect of their relationship once more.

She was glad at least that he had not again mentioned the possibility of her accepting any offer Robin might make. But she was glad in the way that a woman freezing to death is glad at least that it is not snowing.

"The money," she said quietly, "will be an insurance for my future, I suppose. Or perhaps in time it will be used to buy more lavish gifts than one would expect a woman of my station to endow. I may yet become a great favorite of all my future nieces and nephews. But I shall return to work when I return to England. There is really no other course for me."

"Julia," he said in as quiet a tone, "what of marriage then?"

"What of marriage then?" she laughed. "Come, sir, what respectable fellow would have me?" But before he could reply, she added almost prosaically, "And I don't want them. No, no, quite honestly, I assure you, marriage is not for me."

He remained silent for a moment, as she bent her head and seemed to pluck at a loose thread upon the napkin on her lap. In the light of the many candles which depended from the overhead chandelier, her hair glowed antique gold and her long lashes left soft shadows beneath her downcast eyes. In the glow from the four guttering candles in their silver holders upon the table, her cheeks were flushed and her lips soft and secretive.

"There are other occupations, you know," he said in a voice as low as shadows, as soft as the light which surrounded them, "some never so onerous as companioning or governessing." The sibilance of his words were as a sigh, or did he sigh, she wondered, as he went on to say, "Occupations that are a pleasure, where one's love is given for pleasure and it is the pleasure of one's lover to pay well for it."

She looked up then, and met his questioning look. His eyes seemed the elusive gray of smoke tonight and their surround was clear and white in the soft light. His handsome face was still, as though he scarcely breathed as he awaited her reply.

"Are you being so kind as to offer me a 'slip upon the shoulder'?" she asked as coolly as if she were asking the time of day of him.

"It's a rather antiquated expression," he said on a little smile, as he absently plucked up a bit of candlewax and smoothed it between his fingers, "but yes."

"After all you have thought of me?" she said with some wonder.

"Well, there it is," he replied. "After all I *had* thought of you."

"I ought to be honored," she said. "I ought to be pleased, at least, that you no longer abhor me."

"It ought to have been offered more romantically," he said. "It ought to have been better done. There shouldn't be this table between us, for example, and as you have recently confessed to having overeaten, I ought to have waited at least until you were recovered from the meal. But suddenly I found that I couldn't wait for the right setting. Although," he said as he lay aside the bit of candle and put both hands upon the table as though he were about to rise up, "I find that now I do regret that I didn't wait till I had you in my arms."

"Oh, I wouldn't," she said calmly, "for then I would have to slap you as well as tell you no. And physical violence does not come as easily to me as it does to some persons I know. But I would have no difficulty, at least, in telling you no. Definitely no," she continued as she rose from her seat without fuss and placed her napkin upon the table. "Absolutely no," she said as she walked to the door. "Decidedly no," she said as she curtsied low. "And positively no," she said as she opened the door.

"Not for love, nor for money," she declared, holding her head high. "And not only because, as they say in another antiquated expression, 'I am not that sort of girl.' But thank you for the dinner, my lord," she said, and inclining her head as would a queen, she nodded to him and left him. And she would have felt much better about it, even though she already found herself hard put to hold back her tears until she got to her room, if she had not then heard the sound of his enthusiastic applause following her all the way up the stairs.

There were still a great many sights of Paris that had thus far been deprived of Miss Hastings' eager stare, but as they had managed without her regard for a few hundred years they would have to wait a little while longer. The young woman's thoughts this morning were upon England, not France. It wasn't only because of patriotism or homesickness, though she was presently experiencing both phenomena. It was primarily because of the flashes of lightning which were illuminating the paper she was writing upon and the gusts of rain which followed upon the heels of the claps of thunder she heard this summer's morning.

When she had awakened, the August morning was as dim as the night she had just passed. She had only managed to fall asleep toward morning, and as she at last closed her eyes she had been far too preoccupied to take much note of the fact that it was rising to a more sullen greasy sort of grayish-green dawn than is normal. But soon after she had risen and summoned Celeste so that she might dress and plan her day and attempt to forget her night, she had been advised against any daylight excursions. For as Celeste had said, casting a knowing glance through the windows, rain might be the least of the weather woes such a morning sky betokened.

But she refused to stay caged-up in her room. That, she thought rebelliously, would be a cowardly act. In a bit more vengeful spirit, she decided that it would be conceding her opponent a victory that in truth only the weather had won. So, after breakfasting, she made inquiries of the manager of the hotel and was shown to a snug little combination waiting room-writing room-library on the main floor that had been arranged for the comfort of hotel patrons.

It was very charming, to be sure, but there was little question that her own room would have been far more comfortable. For though she had an elegant little gold-inlaid writing desk to work at, she was not alone in the room. There were a few gentleman reading newspapers, and a few ladies waiting for the rain to let up. It was not that Julia had grown antisocial, even if she had, her fellow travelers quite correctly paid her little attention. But the windows had been shut tight against the weather. And one of the gentlemen smoked a particularly noxious cigar which beclouded the warm and airless room, and a few of the ladies seemed to have embarked upon a war of the senses with their lavishly applied competing perfumery. Yet Julia sat stoically and composed her letter, and would not have left her station even if the gentlemen had taken to pouring scent over themselves and the ladies had lit up their own little cigars. It was almost lunchtime and she had not seen the baron. But should he appear, she reasoned, he should not have the satisfaction of seeing her pent-up in her rooms in embarrassed confusion after his outrageous offer.

Although her pen kept up an even, flowing pace, it was not an easy letter for Julia to write, and not only because the closeness of the room made breathing increasingly difficult. There were a great many facts in the letter, but very little personal truth. For Papa, William, and Harry, she wrote of exactly how many stone steps there were in the great cathedral of Notre Dame; for Mama and the girls, she expanded upon the current fashions she had seen here in Paris. But for everyone, there was only the little line about what a fine position she had, and a tiny, writhing, embarrassed little squiggle she managed to pin down at the very bottom of the letter as though she had run out of room, when she had, in fact, run out of courage, about how charming Lady Cunningham and the children were. Perhaps someday, some great time later, the truth could be let out. But even then it could never be in a letter, she realized, as she concluded the missive with her love and a relieved sigh.

She hadn't even had time to wonder if she ought to begin another letter to take up the time until luncheon when she heard a voice that had become intimately familiar to her through both hearing it in actuality and remembering every syllable it had ever uttered, say pleasantly, "Ah, and here she is. Good morning, Miss Hastings. Did you pass a good night? I do hope so. I have been looking everywhere for you, my dear. Allow me to present Lady Preston. Miss Julia Hastings, Lady Mary Preston."

Julia looked up from her letter to see the baron standing with a slight, rather washed-out looking female of indeterminate years in a frock that was in much the same condition as its wearer. But the lady wore a rather anxious expression as well as her unfashionable dress as she put out a thin hand and spoke a hesitant "How do you do?" in one of the most weary little voices Julia had ever heard.

Julia spoke her proper greeting but didn't have the slightest idea of what to say next. She had deliberately not been introduced to anyone for the whole of the journey so far, and she had believed that as they had begun, so they would continue. She hadn't the vaguest notion as to why the baron stood there, smiling down at the two indecisive females with the most pleased, contented expression upon his face.

"I know," he said presently, when the continued silence between the two women began to draw some attention to themselves from the others in the room, "that you two will get on beautifully together. My dear Lady Preston, I shall take Miss Hastings in to luncheon today. You must have some unpacking to do, so why don't you go along to your rooms and have some rest and then some luncheon there for today at least?"

"Oh yes. Thank you. I shall, and thank you," Lady Preston said, bobbing and curtsying to them both before she backed away and gratefully took herself off and left them alone.

Julia fixed the baron with the most speaking stare as he smiled down at her and then motioned her to take a seat beside him near a large bow window which overlooked the streaming street.

"I should have liked a smoke as well," he complained, seemingly unaware of the pressing questions she was about to ask as he settled himself, crossed his legs, and cleared some moisture from the pane to have a look outside, "but the other fellow has done it for me, and all I have to do is to breathe in to get the benefits. But I didn't know you cared for tobacco, so I was rather surprised to find you in this room. And the other scents in here! That can never be just you, can it Julia?

"No," he answered himself, "for you usually bear the faintest scent of young and green things, and it is decidedly overripe in here at present. Don't get exercised, your skin's so fair I can see your blood begin to boil. Her name is Lady Mary Preston, and she is definitely a lady. She has everything but funds at present, and finds herself in dire need of employment so that she can work her way home. She is a widow, she is of pure and good repute, she is of a certain age, and she is hired on as your chaperone. Now why are you gaping at me like that? She's the most unexceptional, cleanliest, pleasantest one that I could find on a moment's notice. If you wanted royalty, you ought to have specified it."

"I don't understand . . ." was all that Julia could say, dazedly.

"I may have to be off to Brussels soon, it may just be that our Robin's nesting there at present. I thought I might travel fastest, just as the saying goes, alone. And so while you are here, as well as for the meanwhile, I thought you might need company, and," and here his voice grew softer, "respectable chaperonage, just as you requested."

But Julia had been thinking hard as he spoke. And as soon as she came to a deduction, it came to her lips.

"Because I turned you down!" she cried out as quickly as a cat pouncing upon a piece of string, but unfortunately so loudly as well that the only female present who had not already been eyeing her companion, now turned an interested gaze upon them.

"Because when I did, I finally convinced you of my— honesty," Julia said happily, her triumph barely contained, lowered her voice to a fierce whisper.

"It was because of my own reasons," he contradicted gently. "I dislike shattering your illusions, but I am not such a coxcomb that I believe any female who rejects my attentions must be a virginal one. Sometimes it is simply a question of their bad taste."

"Oh," Julia said simply, regretting her outburst profoundly. She was glad to be able to turn her head to the window as though she were looking out at the coaches splashing through the streets. And so she completely missed his uncontrollable fleeting smile.

"Well, I did wonder," she said in an attempt to be as casual as he, "why you asked, since you said that you never understood the attraction to be found in ignorance."

"So I did," the baron said idly. "But then, you presuppose that I believed you."

"I see," she said, reddening up.

"And," he commented casually, "even if I did believe in your chastity, you forget that ignorance, like the bliss it is supposed to provide, is a very transitory state. It is a condition which can be corrected very simply, Julia." Then, before she could think of whether it was better to be very angry, flattered, or amused at what he had said, he went on.

"Just as I told your lady chaperone, Julia, it is time for luncheon. Will you come in with me?"

"Yes, my lord," she said absently.

"Now that you have a chaperone, it would be nice to hear you say 'Yes, Nicholas,' " he said, rising and taking her hand as he assisted her to her feet.

"Oh," Julia said.

"But not 'Nick,' " he continued, as he put her hand on his sleeve and held it there lightly by covering it with his own. "It's far too short. Now 'Nicholas' lasts an age, and takes up a good bit more of your time."

She stopped in her tracks and looked up full into his face and spoke the truth as best she knew it from her heart.

"This is not at all fair," she complained softly. "You have gotten me altogether off balance."

"Yes," he said, smiling, "I know."

That night, a great many persons thought of Lord Nicholas Daventry, Baron Stafford, before they gave themselves up to sleep. Julia Hastings did, of course, for she still could not fathom what had brought about his new attitude toward her, if it were a new attitude, and wondered if it would last, and if she wanted it to do so, and if she could bear it if it did not.

Celeste Vitry included the baron in her evening prayer, for she had a good position that paid well, with undemanding duties, and she was a devout and grateful woman.

Lady Mary Preston folded her thin hands together and said a prayer at her bedside as well, and it did include the Baron Stafford, but then it was only proper to give thanks for one's employer, and Lady Preston was always proper, even with her Lord.

Sir Oliver Sidney, tossing sleeplessly upon a lumpy mattress in a pension on the high road to Belgium, thought of Baron Stafford, and the thought prevented sleep, and the thought contained some prayers that no just god would hear.

And Nicholas Daventry smiled in his sleep because he dreamed of young and green things, and in his dreams, believed in them again.

13 Since her arrival in Paris, Julia had taken great pains to arrange matters so that she might see the city each day. She had known that since a great many things might transpire, she might never come this way again. So she had been determined not to miss a moment of her opportunity to explore the great city. It wasn't only enlightenment she sought, she had discovered that a busy mind and a pair of weary feet made brooding upon her wretched situation more difficult. Now, with the arrival of Lady Preston, Julia was making the acquaintance of a totally different city: Paris by night. And she discovered both to her delight and dismay, that it was making her forget her situation very well indeed. So well, in fact, that there were times that she found herself actually enjoying it to the point where she wished it would never end.

A boat ride around the daylight city with Celeste may have been educational, a coach ride through the moonlit streets with the baron was breathtaking. Walking through hushed cathedrals gazing at stained glass windows with Celeste had been extremely interesting, strolling through the gardens of the Tivoli by the Rue de Clichy exclaiming over fireworks with Nicholas was enthralling. Viewing famous landmarks each afternoon had been illuminating to be sure, but to see them picked out by starlight at Nicholas's side each night was dazzling. And where she had to purchase several little guidebooks to pore over as she had toured with Celeste, she now need refer to no other source of information than the lips of her noble escort.

Though Nicholas scoffed at any idea of himself as a learned man, claiming only that he had picked up a great deal of knowledge from his previous travels, still Julia was not so gullible as to believe that one could acquire such a thorough classical education from mere voyaging. If it were so, she had argued, then every gentleman who ventured abroad should return a prodigy of learning. And that, she told him reasonably, would have made the Vikings, for example, such mannered, lettered fellows that they would have commenced to set up universities wherever they went, instead of pulling down villages. When Nicholas could speak again, he allowed as how she might be right, and that his education might well have been a little helpful to him. But he was so entertained by her notion of enlightened Norsemen that he went about for the remainder of the evening postulating about the courses that might be offered at the College of Eric the Red, until she was weak with laughter and lightheaded with happiness. And that, she now told herself sternly, would never do.

She was becoming, she argued to herself this languorous summer evening as Celeste lovingly labored over the arrangement of her hair, very much like a prisoner who forms such a strong attachment to his jailer that he is fearful of the day of his release. For no matter how she dressed the matter up, she thought as Celeste selected a new ice-blue frock with silvery sleeves for her to put on, she was still a captive, no matter how pleasant her captivity may recently have been made. A bird cage may be ornate, it might be furnished with charming swings and perches, its little occupant might be pleased with daily treats, but nonetheless, Julia thought as she slipped into her dress and inspected herself in the mirror, a bird in a cage ought never to forget that its cage existed. And, Julia thought sadly as Celeste went to see if there was anything Lady Preston required before she accompanied Julia to dinner, she herself ought never to forget that it was only birds that had never known freedom that were capable of surviving in captivity.

With all that Nicholas had given her of late—her new clothes, her maid, her chaperone, and, not the least, his own full attention and constant company—he had taken much away from her as well. For she realized that now, not only was she bereft of her freedom of choice and action, but of her fine rage and the sense of injustice which had sustained her through it all. If she should come to love her state so much that she thought nothing of her condition, then she was in fact, little better than if she had accepted Nicholas's shocking offer. No, Julia thought unhappily, perhaps she was become even worse, for at least a female in such a position had few illusions and could feel that she earned her way.

It was true that she was where she was at present so that she might at last face Robin and have the truth from him for herself as well as for his uncle. But in the last days there had been little talk of Robin. There had been instead only general conversation and laughter and the continuing discovery of a mounting sense of mutuality between herself and Nicholas. Yet she also realized that if the baron had once hurt her physically when he had not actually known her, he now had the potential of inflicting far more pain without lifting so much as a finger against her. Now he need only to speak a word to cruelly wound her. And that one word would be "good-bye." Because against all judgment, against all intentions, against all good sense, Julia had grown to care for him deeply.

Curiously, it was only once Nicholas had gotten her an acceptable chaperone so that her reputation might be preserved that her heart had been utterly lost. For when she had dined with him and spoken with him and dueled verbally with him before Lady Preston had come upon the scene, there had always been that element of fear in their relationship that had enabled her to keep her distance. She had never let down her guard. Or at least, she thought, remembering those moments when his words or his eyes or as that once, his lips had lulled her entirely, she had never let it down for too long. She had been able to remind herself constantly that not only was he a man and therefore always suspect, but a vital, intelligent male at that, thus doubly dangerous. Most damningly, he was also Robin's uncle and primarily concerned with his nephew's welfare, as he himself had admitted. But then Lady Preston had arrived and bringing with her the illusion of safety, she had all unwittingly brought about the downfall of Julia's defenses as well.

Julia had been enabled to accompany Nicholas everywhere once Lady Preston was in tow. Lady Cunningham might not exist, but Lady Preston decidedly did. And she was irreproachable. Knowing that her name and person stood in no immediate danger with that good woman at her side, Julia had allowed herself to enjoy the baron's company entirely. And only now, days later, had she come to understand that once the shadow of fear had been removed, her ability to love, which she had been sure had been blighted forever, had burgeoned, as all dormant but living seeds will do when exposed to the light.

But such an attachment was useless from so many points of view that Julia could scarcely finish enumerating them to herself each night as she counted them instead of sheep until sleep overtook her and saved her from total despair. He was a nobleman, she was a commoner. And not only a commoner, but one who had totally ruined her reputation by running off in an abandoned manner with a gentleman. Not only a gentleman either, but one who was Nicholas's nephew and who for some reason had told his uncle how perfidious and cruel she was. And not only did Nicholas believe his nephew, but so much so that he had deceived her, abused her, entrapped her, and now paid her to confront his nephew.

Part of the baron's plan of entrapment, she was sure, was to offer her a position as his mistress. Another part of it was to woo her so completely with his wit and warmth that she had not room in her heart or head for anything but him.

There was a certain dreadful justice, Julia thought, as she paced her sumptuous hotel room and waited for her chaperone to accompany her to an evening out with her employer and tormentor, in the fact that she could not become his mistress even if she wanted to. Just as there had been some insurmountable obstacle to her marriage, so there would surely be the same one should she decide to embark upon her ruination. There was a certain moral comfort in this, Julia thought, reaching for a gauzey silvery whisper of a shawl, but it was such a cold one that she drew the shawl about her as though it were common, comforting flannel that could take the sudden chill from her limbs and heart.

Still, it was a shocking thing to suddenly acknowledge, even if only to herself, this tempting terrible little thought that she would even consider becoming any man's mistress. Although he was not just any man, not with those eyes, and that smile, and that wicked sense of humor, he was nevertheless undoubtedly, almost blatantly, a member of that gender she had forsworn. But lately this nagging, incessant, and insistent little thought was never too far from her: that such employment might be the very answer, the only answer, at least for her.

Because it seemed that she did not want to part from him. It wasn't that she feared that she would forget him, it was rather that she worried that she might not have enough to remember of him. She discovered she wanted something more of love to recall when she grew old than just the folly of one innocent, abortive evening when she was seventeen. The mean little voice often whispered that as she would always bear the marks of shame in the world's eyes anyway, wouldn't it be far better to have for keepsake the memory of a breathing lover that she had once held to her own beating heart, rather than only the sad, sterile remembrance of a love that was conceived only in imagination and that had died at birth?

When the argument became too persuasive, Julia would be glad of the unknown handicap which prevented her from any such wild, immoral flights as she entertained in her fancies. But then she had to laugh at herself. For if she did not know the world very well, having neither been in it or about it for too long, she knew herself very well, having been forced to bear her own company for so long. She knew the truth was that if she had no such restriction upon her, she would very likely have had to invent one. Her upbringing had been conventional and the real world she lived in, when she was not with the baron, was a censorious one.

She knew very well that a woman who choose to flaunt society and live with a gentleman without benefit of churchly sanction, was a woman who placed herself forever outside society's blessings and protection. And when he was bored with her, and gentlemen always became bored with their mistresses, why then, she would have no recourse but to seek another such as he. And there was no other such as he, not upon the face of this wide world, and that she knew as well as she knew her own name.

And so Julia was very glad that she was honest enough to admit that she was temperamentally and morally unfit to ever become the baron's mistress. And she was, of course, glad that she did not have to rely on that weak argument alone to withstand him, since she also possessed that unexpected, unfathomable impediment to love with any man. Being so glad of so many things, it was curious that when she turned to greet Lady Preston, she had tears in her eyes, unless, of course, they were tears of happiness at her situation.

"My dear Miss Hastings," Lady Preston said in her soft little voice, "you look quite beautifully," and she gave Julia such a pleased and sweet smile to go with her words that they were lifted out of the commonplace and became instead, a very real compliment.

But so it was with Lady Preston, Julia thought as she returned the smile and the compliment. The lady's looks had improved even as her fortunes had. The securing of a paid position had had a cosmetic effect that went beyond the new frocks she now wore. Her cheeks had color, her eyes were clear, and her spine seemed straighter. But it was not only her looks which were pleasing. For the lady was in every good construction of the word, a lady. When she was alone with Julia, she never presumed to ask too much, nor did she err by noticing too little. When she accompanied Julia and Nicholas on their rounds of restaurants or touring sites, she never imposed her personality or her sanctions upon them. But then she never had to, as Julia was always aware of her quiet personality, and Nicholas never forgot her presence.

Most importantly, persons of the baron's class, seeing him dining in public with a lovely young female, might be moved to inquire as to her name, and being refused it, might be inclined to inquire further. Hearing that the other lady at the table was Lady Mary Preston, they would lose interest, knowing that with such a female present, there would be little scandal broth to stir. If it were a romance, they would reason, they would soon read the announcement of it in *The Times*. And if it were not, then the chit were some relation surely, for any other sort of connection would be impossible to imagine with such a paragon to give it countenance. The lady's impecunious late husband may have forced her to seek employment, but her name was known. And her name was solid.

"And you look radiant as well," Julia said, finishing up her compliments. But it was true. The lady looked unusually well tonight. Her thin cheeks were flushed, her eyes were bright, and she bore an air of almost febrile excitement. Julia might have even inquired as to her health if she had not surmised that the lady's condition was only due to her enthusiasm for their destination this night. For last night she had ventured to say that she.had not been to the Opera in years, and was quite looking forward to it. Since Lady Preston's every word and action was usually measured, Julia took that statement as excitation bordering on hysteria.

But the baron would not have noticed if Lady Preston were so elevated that she walked three inches above the carpet when he came to Julia's rooms to call for them. He only gave the lady the most cursory of glances as he bowed to her, bade her good evening, and told her rather mechanically how well she looked, while all the while his gaze kept sliding back to Julia. When he could at last turn to her, he said at once, "Silver and blue tonight, eh? You make me rue my cowardice, Julia. For we might have been well matched, you and I. That expensive blue jacket arrived today. You know, the one I told you of, the frenchified one with the silver threads. And although Makepiece has been crooning over it since it was delivered as though it were his newborn babe, I reckon it so overwhelming that I haven't allowed him to take it out of its papers. So I hope you won't mind the company of a fellow togged out with all the color and dash of the financial sheets, for I'm only all black and white to your silver and blond and blue. You look like a moonbeam, Julia."

He gave her a little grin with the compliment that made her feel as though it was the sun and not the moon that had come out in the midst of the night, and to cool her cheeks and her spirits, she began to ask him questions about the Opera. He took each of their arms and, still wearing a small smile for Julia's continuing inability to cope with his compliments, took the ladies to dinner.

Julia often told herself that night life was not her style, and that it was just as well that a governess-companion could not experience firsthand those pleasures she had often heard her employers and their friends speaking of, such as dances and routs and supper parties and balls. She had gone to a waltz party as·well as several evening soirees with the Honorable

Miss Carstairs when she had been that young female's companion. It was true that she had always sat, as was correct, on the sidelines with others of her order, behind the dowagers and the infirm. But she had been able to see a great deal of what was going on over their heads and through the spaces between their seated forms, and she hadn't been much impressed nor very regretful of her lot in life, save for some few moments when the music at the waltz party had threatened to lift her from her seat and carry her to her feet. But the one thing she had always secretly coveted was the ability to attend the Opera or the theater. And so from the moment she entered the Opera, until the moment she found herself seated in a box high in its rafters, she believed that she felt dizzy because she did not draw or expel one breath the whole while from the sheer weight of her awe.

The theater itself was gorgeous. She had never understood the true impact of the word until she had seen the gold and gilt and rococco carvings and plush of the interior of the building, and now she found that even that word did not do justice to the sight. Once within, there was such a gabble of voices as to make the Bible stories she had read of the tower of Babel seem insignificant. Not only was everyone talking at full volume, but as there were gentlemen and officers present from every victorious army, there was every language and accent imaginable competing loudly for attention.

The gentlemen outnumbered the ladies, but those females present were attired in no less magnificent fashion than the theater they ornamented. They might be in France, but here there were no sabots, nor any high white bonnets on fresh-faced females as there had been in Calais. No, here there was gold cloth and scarlet silk and silver gauze, and all seemingly in too short a supply to adequately cover the ladies that had chosen them as dress materials. Despite Celeste's and Lady Preston's assurances, Julia had felt that her own gown showed perhaps a jot too much white skin above the swell of her breasts, but now it seemed that she was wrapped to her ears in comparison to the others of her gender.

The atmosphere was warm and airless, a hundred perfumes hung in the still atmosphere even as a thousand less palatable odors did. The bright flare of the footlights and the glitter from the patrons themselves assaulted the eye even as the din confused the ears, but Julia was enthralled. She gaped at the thea-

ter, she shamelessly stared below her at the coxcombs and the
dandies and soldiers and then she looked up in wonder at the
statesmen, heroes, and generals in adjoining boxes. Then she
could marvel no more at them, for the lights dimmed, the noise
abated, and the music struck up.

It was as she thrilled to the expertise of the dancers and their
stirring ballet representing the allied victory at Waterloo, that
she became aware of the others in the box with her again. She
felt a firm but gentle touch upon her arm and heard the baron
say, quite close to her ear, "I'm sorry, my dear, but she is quite
right. We must go. And now, at once."

Julia was far too grown-up and self-contained to sulk or
pout, but as the coach bore them back to the hotel she devoutly
wished that she were Toby's age once more so that she could
just fling herself down upon the cushions and have a good
howling cry. They had left the theater quietly and furtively
while the music had continued playing. Julia had looked at the
stage to the last, until she risked tripping in the dark, so she
could have just one last glimpse of the ballet as it went on.
Then it had been easy enough to commandeer a carriage from
the line outside the Opera, since none of the drivers expected
such early departures. It seemed to Julia that she had been allowed just a glimpse of something exciting and enthralling beyond imagination and then had been unceremoniously snatched
away from it, like a child who had been discovering hiding
upon the stairs observing a brilliant grown-up party past her
bedtime.

She said not a word of this, but her face must have spoken
her thoughts eloquently, for when they were snugly ensconced
in the hotel's small salon sipping at their coffee in their comfortable armchairs, like proper old pensioneers, she thought
glumly, the baron spoke. Lady Preston was seated at a distance
from them, perusing a magazine, so he need not have lowered
his voice to such an intimate register, but he did, nonetheless,
to ensure their privacy.

"She was right, Julia. It's unfortunate, but true, and I'm a
fool for not having thought it. But you wanted propriety, my
sweet, so you mustn't complain when it puts a crimp in your
style. You were far too busy ogling the soldiers to notice, but
she turned ashen and I thought she was going to pitch over
headfirst into the pit. 'My lord,' she cried, and I don't know if

she meant me or someone rather higher, 'we are the only respectable females in this entire company!' " The baron smiled
as he mimicked the lady in a passable horrified falsetto.

But then he went on reflectively, "It's true, you know. All
the genteel ladies were at home lamenting either the loss of
their empire or their emperor, I imagine. That lot we saw were
the sort that can be counted on to cavort with the victors in any
land, in any century. Still, there are some highborn ladies who
might have sat it out when they realized their error and written
it off as a lark. But 'a proper chaperone,' you said, and 'a
proper chaperone' you received. Want to change your mind,
Julia?'' he asked suddenly, dropping his voice lower, to a
husky timbre that sent as many shivers up her spine as his
words did.

"We could then go to all the theaters, and all the balls, and
all the places I haven't dared to ask you to accompany me to,
and oh, what fun you should have, Julia, what joy we should
both have. We wouldn't have to go home for ages, and when
we did, ah Julia, there would be no end of delights ahead of
us."

He was looking at her with such earnest entreaty that Lady
Preston, glancing over toward them, permitted herself a small
smile at how animated the pair's discussion had grown. There
was something entirely ludicrous, Julia had time to think as she
looked to see her chaperone's reaction to the words she could
not have heard, in receiving an invitation to a life of mortal sin
while one's very dignified chaperone sat and dumbly nodded
her blissful approval to it. Thus, she wore a faint and foolish
smile herself in reaction to his words, rather than the horrified
scowl she ought to have treated him to. But all she said
was, "And Robin?"

It was brief, but her reply was as effective as a spirited
speech might have been, for he fell silent for a moment. She
felt a peculiar pang as she saw how his long lashes closed to lie
outlined like dusky fringes upon his high cheekbones. His face
appeared strangely gentle when the quick comprehension in his
eyes was thus shuttered and shaded. She was still staring bemused at his newly vulnerable aspect, when his eyes snapped
open and she found herself caught and looking deep into his
aware, alert regard.

"Julia," he said immediately, "you know I never intended

you for him. From the first, I believed it to be a mistake. Although I may have altered my opinion about a great many other things, in that, at least, I have not changed my mind. Come Julia, Lady Preston is a charming companion, but this respectability is a cumbersome thing, is it not? Give over, love, do,'' he said, a smile quirking the corner of his lips. ''Stay with me. I'll accept that you have principles, but 'love the sinner if not the sin,' '' He laughed low in his throat as he added, ''Yes, I'll quote scripture for my own purposes, just as the good book says, as well as for yours. For it's what you want, you know. It's right for you, you know.''

''I cannot,'' she said, as though the words were wrenched from her, ''I could not.'' And then with a smile that attempted to match his own, though she could not see if he smiled back now, as her gaze was fixed upon her own lap, she said gently, so as not to give offense, ''And it's no loss, you know. For I could not, even if I could.''

Her reply was a puzzle, so he had to take as answer that which he had not heard. She had not said ''I will not,'' or ''I should not,'' or even ''How could you?'' Instead of becoming irate, or insulted, or aghast, as she previously had done, she seemed genuinely sorry for what she, not he, had said. So Nicholas took her by the hand and urged her to stand with him and then he walked her to Lady Preston.

''My dear lady,'' Nicholas said sweetly, ''it's grown extremely warm in here, and Julia and I should like to stroll in the cool of the evening before retiring.''

''Ah. Of course. And so it is. I will just take my shawl against the threat of sudden breezes, which are not all the thing for the constitution,'' Lady Preston said as she gathered up her reticule and shawl, ''and I shall have a seat outside as well. What a good idea.''

How odd, Julia thought as the three of them stepped out of the salon and then down the hall to the back door that led to a cobblestone-paved courtyard garden area. How strange, she thought as Lady Preston nodded with satisfaction and took a seat on a bench beneath a sheltering tree. For Lady Preston merely said, as she seated herself in the dark as comfortably as if she were in a drawing room, ''I should suggest you avoid notice, but at least I shall be here should you need me.''

Julia's feeling of wrongness, the sense of something sadly

askew, increased as she paced quietly by Nicholas's side and he led her deeper into the darkened garden. But then she thought, Of course! It is he who pays her wages, and I, after all, really have no champion at all. It came to Julia all at once, like some blinding revelation, so complete and unexpected that she paused in her tracks. She is a lady, of that there is no question. Yet she never was here to ensure my reputation, but only to swear to it.

Nicholas spoke quietly and Julia started. Was he inside her head again, she wondered, could he see through her eyes as well as into them? For he said as though he had been privy to her innermost thoughts, "It's not only you, Julia, nor is it only your chaperone and her circumstances. Society knows that a female may be ringed around with armed guardians and yet be unchaste. We've grown past the days of bolting up our women as we did our castle doors. A chaperone is employed to lend respectability, but everyone knows that respectablity can't be lent, it must be kept. Now," he said in warm and friendly accents as they stood quietly in the shadows, "allow me to illustrate the point."

Without any fuss, as though it were the most natural thing in the world, he gathered her up in his arms and bent his head and kissed her. At first she only offered no resistance. And then, to her shock and his delight, she followed his lead and offered a great deal more to him than lack of objections. After long and languorous moments, he raised his head again and she lay stunned against his chest.

Then he murmured, with traces of suppressed, luxurious triumph in his voice, "Now, what is this of 'cannot' or 'could not' when I speak of love, when I speak of a future for you and me?"

With effort, Julia straightened herself and drew apart from him. She sought to find her normal voice and composure and only when sure that she could speak coherently, she replied, " 'Cannot,' 'will not,' you refine too much upon my every word," she said with a shaky laugh. "So I'll try to say it plainly and be done. I won't be your mistress, Nicholas, because I am Julia Hastings, and she is not the sort of girl to become anyone's mistress, even though she is the abandoned sort of female who will tell you straightaway that if she could be anyone's, she would be yours. But wait," she said, knowing he was about to speak and wanting to get it all out in a rush for fear that her lower lip, which had begun to quiver, would impede what she had to say, what she knew she ought to say, "there's more."

She drew in a deep breath and then said, closing her eyes so that she could see the shape of her thoughts and not his face, "I will not because of things that you would consider foolish, like conscience and morality. But if it makes you feel any better, I cannot as well. You see, I couldn't even if I were the graceless wanton you think I am. I just wouldn't be satisfactory. You can ask Robin," she said at last, unable to say another thing as her voice broke on the "Robin" at the end.

She fought to get her countenance under control, and had almost successfully commanded her chin to cease trembling and her lip to steady itself, when he undid her. He didn't say a word, but only took her in his arms again and held her very close. Only that. Then, of course, she had no choice at all left. She wept.

When she had steadied herself at last, or at least become still enough to begin to feel ashamed of her outburst, and aware of his arms about her, he spoke.

"Julia," he whispered into her ear in the quiet of the night, "you must tell me. It cannot be that shameful a thing. It can never be that ugly or that hideous to me if it concerns you. What happened that night, what occurred between you and Robin? I cannot know you, indeed you forbid my knowing you by continually evading the truth of it. Is it fair to condemn me for hurting or misjudging you when you keep this important a thing to yourself? You arrange it so that I am fated to lose whatever I do. It simply is not fair to me. Tell me, Julia. Here and now. Please, Julia."

"But I have never—" she began, but he cut her off by saying softly, "I know, and that is why you must."

So there, in the midnight garden of a hotel in Paris, Julia lay her head upon the Baron Stafford's breast, and with the steady beat of his heart against her ear, comforted like a homeless puppy with a ticking clock in its basket, she softly spoke of the events of the night that was to have been her wedding night.

But for all that it had changed her life, for all that it had so constantly shaped her every action since, it was overall a very brief tale. And when she was done, Julia stood silent, resting against Nicholas, still feeling his hand absently stroking her hair, as he had all the while that she spoke. But then she began to feel a little foolish, a bit childish, as people always do when their worst despair has abated and they become aware that they are still being comforted.

"I must find Robin," he said at length, as though he did not know he spoke aloud, for then he dropped his mouth to her ear and whispered for her to hear, "I must find Robin. There is some misunderstanding in this. The fault is not in you, Julia. I could swear to it, but only Robin can attest to it. I must find him." The he put her away from him, but only an arm's length away, and he still held her by both shoulders as he looked down into her face and spoke.

"It is what I set out to do, but you, you wicked creature, you made me falter in my determination. I tarried because I enjoyed your company so much I was loathe to part from you, or so I told myself. Now I think it was rather that I didn't wish to force the final confrontation. Perhaps I wished to delay the moment of truth. So I lingered, little Circe, and you did indeed change me into a swine. For after a while I never gave a thought to ending the matter. I was so very busy thinking up ways and means to get you into my bed.

"Now I shall leave for Brussels in the morning. And I shall ask you, Julia—mind, I said 'ask' you—to remain here to wait for me. I shall, if I can, bring Robin back with me, and then we shall have the whole thing out in the air at last. It is time, and past it, to end this matter."

"And then?" Julia asked.

"Why then, you shall be free. That is to say that you are free as of now, but then there will be no further constraints upon you," he said, still holding her by her shoulders and unconsciously tightening his hands upon her even as he said "free." So the next question came to her quite naturally.

"And your offer?" she asked softly, seeing the answer in his face even in the darkness before he spoke. The bright white of his eyes was obscured for an instant as he closed his lids as though in pain.

"Forget it, Julia," he said heavily, and then in an attempt at humor, he said as he let her shoulders go, "At least, I hope you do. Lord! What a family we are for making you offers. I should not blame you if you never wished to clap eyes upon any of us again. But please," he said at once, as though his own words had alarmed him, "tell me. Even though I repeat, you are free, will you at least stay here and wait for me? I think it to your advantage to, Julia, for it is only Robin who can explain that night to you, and answer all of the questions that may enable you to live your life more fully and freely in future."

When she did not answer at once, he asked again, "Julia, will you wait here for me? At the very least you must allow me to see you safely home from this adventure."

He spoke of safety and he spoke of freedom, Julia thought as she stood chilled in the warm night air. And he did not know that she never felt safe from him while he breathed upon the earth, although she never felt safer than when she was with him. And as for freedom, she thought sadly, he had only removed her from her cage. But it hardly mattered now, since like a wily falconer, he had trained her with soft words and rewards to come to his hand whenever he put out his finger.

"I shall wait," Julia said.

14

Everywhere that he went, they wondered at why he had not yet met up with his friend. At first, he had been amused, and then by slow degree as he had ridden from villa to village, from city to countryside, he had grown annoyed, then vexed, and then decidedly angry.

"But, old man," Lord Blake had said in Lille, as he poured another glass of port for his unexpected overnight guest, "you only missed him by inches, I'd swear it, for no sooner did his dust die down than you appeared. Not that I'm not delighted to see you, old man, for I am, you're like a spot of England. Tell me, how are things at home?"

"Good heavens, Nick, you would have met in the doorway had he stopped to tie his shoe!" John Taylor had said in Ghent. "Not two days past!" the Hawkinses in their ornate rented house in Bruges had marveled. "He was here yesterday, and you arrive today. Now who's chasing whom?" Cyril Hampton, Duke of Austell, had murmured thoughtfully as he settled back in his armchair in his hotel in Brussels to interview his guest.

He had been traveling for two weeks now, and everywhere, every weary mile he progressed, he heard of how odd it was that he had so narrowly missed encountering his good friend Sir

Oliver Sidney. But nowhere did he hear a word that could lead him to Robin, and nowhere, he heard, was Sir Sidney able to find out about his nephew's whereabouts either. "I say," Lord Beddoes had murmured, "Why don't you two fellows link up? Save yourselves a deal of trouble, you know." "I would love to," the baron had managed to say through his tightly clenched teeth. And so he would, he thought, although he did not think it would save Sir Sidney a whit of trouble if he did so.

This night he lay in his bed in a fine hotel in the heart of Brussels and knew that Ollie rested somewhere in the same city. But he did not believe that Robin did, no, in fact he was almost sure now that Robin did not. For he had one advantage over Ollie, and that was that once he had known Robin, and his nephew's essential self would not have changed, no matter how time and tide had shaped his life. If Robin knew he was seeking him, nothing would keep him away. So he would make a few more searching inquiries for his nephew to be completely certain that word of his quest was known everywhere, and then he would gladly be out of this city and this country. He would leave the barren field for Ollie to winnow. Let him come up with a handful of dust for his efforts, Nicholas thought as he laced his hands behind his head and stared up at the ceiling, to match the lungfuls of dust that I have gotten as I unwittingly followed behind him on every step of my search.

But he was weary of this place, he thought as he settled himself into bed in preparation for his now expected nightly bout of sleeplessness. And if a fellow could weary of such a beautiful city, then there must certainly be something amiss with him. And, of course, Nicholas thought wryly, there was.

For he hadn't known such sleeplessness existed before he had met her. He hadn't ever found exotic foreign cities a bore nor itched to be quit of them. Even in the days of his disappointment and turmoil over Ivy's defection, he had been able to comfort himself with available females, if only for the mundane expediency of getting past the lonely midnight hours easefully into a new day. But now nothing brought him solace but the thought of her, even as the thought of her brought him only the desire to be back with her again. And that desire kept him as constant to her as though she had been at his side as a spectral presence gravely watching his every action for every interminable moment that they had been apart.

Grave considerations indeed, Nicholas thought as he frowned to himself and found his feather pillow grown as comfortable as a tombstone. He smiled at his own play on words and thought that she would have liked it, for her lively sense of humor was perhaps the best thing about her. That was, he corrected himself, if one forgot her sympathetic nature, her inquiring mind and high spirit and beautiful face and exquisite figure and delicious lips, and he rose from his bed and went to look out the window to see if there were any lights to see still lit at this small hour of the night.

Bedeviled as well as besotted, he thought as he stared out into the blind night. For when he thought of those soft and yielding lips, he remembered how untutored they were and how he had delighted in teaching her how to return his kiss in the way to please both herself and him. But remembering her innocence, his desire turned to despair again. Then he recalled her brief story, and that transmuted his desire to sorrow, his ardor to shame.

Instead of seeking her out in her pathetic exile in the countryside and offering her payment to confront Robin again, Nicholas thought as he lay his head upon his arm upon a dark windowpane, he should have sought her out to beg her pardon and pay her well to forget the whole affair. But then he might never have gotten to know her, he thought, and that would have been a loss as great as the one he risked in losing her now. And he would lose her, he thought wretchedly, unless he had both skill and luck within the next few weeks.

It was the confused telling of her tale that had made all his suspicions comprehensible to him at last. It was her inability to understand that which now was increasingly and shatteringly clear to him, which even as much as her kiss had confirmed his belief in her essential innocence. He must find Robin, he thought with such an overwhelming sense of urgency that he was tempted to rush from his room out into the moonlit streets seeking some sign of his nephew. He himself could explain a great deal to Julia, but only Robin could completely lift the burden of her disgrace so that she might believe in herself again.

It was amusing, he supposed wearily, that this search, which he had begun so that Julia might persuade Robin to return home, was only continuing now so that he might persuade Julia to come home with him. He still had obligations to his family and he would attempt to fulfill those, but no more than that.

Thoughts of his nephew made him heart-sore so it was as well, he rationalized sadly, that he was so totally preoccupied with Julia. Then too, Robin was, after all, just as his stepfather had said, a man now, and able to make his own decisions.

As for himself, his decision had been made before he had even become fully aware of it. He had wanted her in his bed even when he had believed the worst of her. Then he had wanted her companionship, even as he mistrusted her. Now he wanted her in any way in which she choose to come to him. But he knew she must come to him, and as his wife, if he were ever to know peace.

This was an altogether new experience for him. With all his wide experience of women and the various pleasures they offered, and for all her ignorance of his sex, in many ways she made him feel, strangely enough, almost virginal in his emotions. For he found himself in the odd position of pursuing a female for the usual purposes, only to discover that he eventually valued her so much as a person that her womanhood became almost an incidental gift. He had always loved women, yet he knew that this was the first time that he had ever loved *a* woman completely. He had been his mama's and sisters' adored child, just as Ivy, he saw now, had been his adorable, amusing infant. Other women had been plush cornucopias of goodness, satisfying but replaceable. Julia Hastings was unique. She was the only person he wished to share his life with.

But had she spoken of impediments? He laughed to himself as he left the empty window to pace his room. What she perceived as hindrances to her future were only illusions, shadows thrown against the wall by ignorance and fear, which could be banished in a moment by exposing them to the full light of truth. Robin could do that for her, and then she would be free to choose whatever course she would. But once she was able to build her new life, how could she choose himself as life's-mate, he wondered, after all that he had done and been to her? Deceiver, kidnapper, seducer, and blackmailer, oh yes, Nicholas thought with a weary sardonicism, she has every cause to love and respect me.

That she had kissed him and confided in him was as nothing, he thought bitterly. That she desired him was no credit to him, for she was just as she had claimed, very ignorant of such emotions and very unused to the ways of men. And that she trusted him now was the opposite credit to him, for she was, just as she had often denied, still so very young, and as was pitifully apparent to him, so very alone.

She had been right about him at the outset, Nicholas thought despairingly, for he was certainly mad. How else could he possibly entertain any notion of her forgiving him or wanting him as husband after she had gotten her self-respect back again? And he knew it would be more than wrong, it would be dishonorable to press his suit while she was still confused or still dependent upon him. He could only wait upon matters, attempt to bring her Robin as embodiment of the truth, make restitution, beg her forgiveness, and in the fullness of time, hope to receive it and more.

Nicholas lay down and closed his eyes, now only hoping that when he opened them again it would be to the sunlight of another day, so that he could be up and off about his business once more. But he opened them a second later to see the same shifting shadows of bleak night. For in that moment of half-sleep he had seen Julia's face, remembering it as it had been in that moment after he had struck her, and then it struck at his heart with as much force as a blow, that he could never hope to make restitution, that he could never hope to honorably have her.

When a dull, damp morning dawned at last, Nicholas was out of his bed, washed, and dressed for his journey with his traveling case in hand even before the lowest scullery maid in the hotel had lit the morning kitchen fires. Even if he had brought Makepiece with him, he could not have been gone from his room faster. So it was that he found himself with enough time, after he had settled his bill with a yawning clerk, to sit down to a breakfast before he mounted up and rode back across the trail he had just taken. He sipped his coffee and thought of England, even as he buttered his bread and knew he must return to Paris. For there was where Robin was bound for, or so he believed, or so he hoped.

It was as he left the dining room and crossed the wide lobby on his way to the stables to see to his mount and begin his journey that he heard his name being called. He turned to see the young clerk that he had dealt with in the early hours coming out from behind the desk and hurrying over to him.

"Ah, my lord," the young man said as he came abreast of the baron, his face a study of an admixture of embarrassment and deference, "please to forgive me. It was such a stupid mistake, but my superior would discharge me if he discovered it. It is the policy of the Hotel LeReinne to ascertain from each departing guest their future destination. In case of postals to be forwarded, or inquiries, do you see? In these unsettled times," the young man went on apologetically in his carefully enunciated English, "the authorities wish to know such things of foreign visitors. Do you understand, my lord?"

Nicholas only remained silent for a moment. He saw very well, and permitted himself a genuinely pleasant, placating smile as he looked down at the perspiring and anxious clerk.

"Of course," he replied smoothly. "But it would be difficult to give you my exact destination, as I shall be continuing to travel about the region. Still, if there are any messages for me, I will collect them if they are forwarded to me in care of the Hotel Alphen in Amsterdam."

"Amsterdam," the young clerk nodded.

"Yes," said the baron and began to leave, but then checked and, turning about, said so suddenly as to make the little clerk's shoulder's leap, "but this is to be considered confidential, and only for receipt of my messages." And smiling to reassure the young man, he reached into his pocket and, withdrawing a coin whose color and denomination made the young man's eyebrows rise even as his shoulders just had done, gave it to him along with a huge wink.

"Just so, my lord," the clerk said, pocketing the sum before bowing low to his departing guest.

A few moments later, in a darkened corner of the lobby, the clerk received another English coin to keep its compatriot company.

"Amsterdam," the clerk whispered upon receipt of this sum.

"Amsterdam, ah!" Sir Sidney said, and turned upon his heel before the fellow could complete his bow.

Lord Nicholas Daventry, Baron Stafford, mounted his horse and with broad unconcern headed to the north, as he whistled to himself. But he smiled to himself as well as he calculated how many more streets he must ride before he could safely turn his mount and gallop back to the west where his ambitions lay and his heart remained.

* * *

"I think," Julia said very carefully, "that it is becoming increasingly foolish to remain here."

"I agree that it may seem so," her companion said calmly, "however, the baron did leave explicit instructions and those were, I believe, to the effect that we wait upon his return before taking any further action."

As this was undeniably true, but also undeniably flat, Julia made no reply. She only gazed over at Lady Preston and watched that good woman as she sat and read through her fashion magazine. They sat in the hotel's small salon, for their bedrooms had become overly familiar with prolonged use, and there was nowhere else that they could agree upon to go. Julia had rejected any idea of further sightseeing, as she had said rather testily that she had seen everything of interest by this time, and her feet and her eyes were weary. But the truth was, she sighed to herself, that even a peek behind the heavenly gates would bore her at this point. It seemed she had lost the ability to concentrate. Her book lay open in her lap to the same page that it had been opened to an hour past. It seemed, she thought sadly, that no book, no sight, no sound could interest her, unless it was the sight of a certain face, or the sound of a certain footfall.

But she had waited as she had promised she would, for more than two weeks. Now it appeared that awake or asleep some part of her was always listening for his return, so that she could not fully appreciate anything else around her. Not that there was much else to enjoy, she reminded herself. As she had gotten a proper chaperone, Celeste had gratefully taken up the duties she was most familiar with, that of a lady's maid, and so did not keep her company beyond tending to her hair, person, and apparel. And though Lady Preston was charming, and always in readiness to accompany her charge anywhere, she was, Julia thought sourly, as distant as an Alp, and almost as warm as one. She smiled to herself as she thought that Nicholas might enjoy that simile, but then frowned again as she wondered if she would ever get the chance to tell it to him.

She was almost ready to leave for home. Alone if need be, alone most probably. Her chaperone would doubtless wish to wait for her wages, as would her lady's maid. This was, after all, Celeste's homeland. But it was becoming apparent that she herself was no longer needed. She sighed as she thought it, so heavily that Lady Preston looked up for a moment. At that, Julia took up her book and dabbed at her eye as though it were some passage she had been reading that had so affected her. What there might be to cause such sorrow in a tour book devoted to Paris, Julia could not imagine, but her action seemed to suit Lady Preston and she went back to pursuing her fashion plates.

For a certainty Lady Preston would opt for waiting for Nicholas's return, Julia decided, for each week that she waited her purse grew larger. Julia no longer deceived herself about the lady's intentions, and so she no longer felt under any obligation to the older woman and had no compunctions about taking her own course of action as she saw fit. But she couldn't determine what that course should be.

Certain facts were irrefutable. Nicholas had gone, and he had asked her to wait for him. But he had not come back, and there was always the possibility that he would not. The gentlemen of his family, Julia thought, as she had thought for several long sleepless nights now, were famous for changing their minds.

He had asked her to be his mistress, and then against all probability, there in the darkened garden, after she had unburdened herself to him, she had known that she would do whatever he asked of her. And then, of course, he had withdrawn his offer.

When she had been seventeen, she thought now, dropping her unread book back to her lap and staring at the pattern of tiny green and gold cabbage roses and buds upon the wall, she had believed that Robin had broken her heart. But now she knew that he had not, he had only caused her to hide it away. It was his uncle who had unearthed it despite all her caution, and finding it still intact, it was he who would complete its destruction. If she had thought that what she had felt for Robin was love, then she had learned better, and it was his uncle who had taught her. For young Robin, there had been admiration, laughter, and a sense of flattered importance that such a grown-up, accomplished fellow could want her. For Nicholas, there was also laughter and admiration but then, for him, there was everything else as well, including this miserable feeling that nothing in life was worth a thing unless he was with her.

Yet it appeared that just as Robin had abandoned her on a windy October night when she was miles from home, after a proposal of marriage, so Nicholas would leave her here in this hotel after his offer of carte blanche, for history had a love of balance. And then, too, Julia thought, just as Nicholas himself had said, she had a singular lack of luck with his family. These thoughts gave rise to such agitation that she found herself rising from her chair, as though their sheer turbulence had swept her to her feet.

"I . . . I find I have the headache," Julia temporized, as she saw Lady Preston gazing questioningly up at her. "You need not accompany me, my lady, for I'm only going up to my room to lie down for a while until it passes," she explained, knowing only as she voiced it that this was in part exactly what she wished to do. At least, she wanted to be completely alone so that she could make plans without fearing that evidences of her plotting would show upon her face.

Her decision came to her all at once even as Lady Preston gazed mildly upon her. Though she had wrestled with the problem night after empty night, dreary day after increasingly joyless day, now suddenly, it all came clear. She must be gone from this place at once. If he had deserted her, she would be better off leaving before the time spent waiting for him became advanced enough to become embarrassing and made her a figure of ridicule or pity. She had had quite enough experience of that in the past. Then again, if he planned to return, then she decidedly should be gone when he got back, for whatever she might wish to do when she was with him, she knew very well that she must never be his mistress. With him or without him, she must accept that there would be pain. She must eventually lose him, and better now than when she made either a complete fool or a slattern of herself.

"Yes," she said distractedly, now thinking only of what she would and would not include within her portmanteau so that she would not weep over her decision, "I think I shall lie down."

"He will be back, you know," Lady Preston said as she turned a page, as calmly and coolly as though she were commenting upon the satin bonnet she saw pictured there. "He loves you very much. I have seldom seen such devotion. Celeste has even remarked upon it, and she is *French*, so you can see how impressive his condition is, for he is usually the most discreet gentleman. The baron has a great reputation for tact, you know."

Julia could only stare at Lady Preston, as that lady essayed a smile, so real and so full of sweetly wistful reminisence that for a moment her thin face was unrecognizable.

"But go and lie down, my dear," Lady Preston said, "for although that cannot help, I cannot see how it can harm you." And then she turned her attention back to her magazine and resuming her normal expression, appeared to become quite engrossed in the depiction of a cerise evening cloak.

Julia left her chaperone without another word. Now was definitely not the time to dwell upon the discovery that the lady had a human heart, now was not the time to allow anything to shake her newfound resolve. So she kept her mind as uncluttered as possible as she approached her room, and tried to think only of what she ought to leave behind her, and what she ought to write in her farewell note.

She would have time enough to pack and to write a farewell novel, Julia thought when she entered her room and glanced at the ormolu clock upon her mantelpiece, for Celeste had her day off to visit old friends, and Lady Preston told time by her meals. She could be counted upon to leave her charge in solitary state until the dinner hour, and it was now only a few moments past teatime.

Julia found that her packing took only moments. She had decided to leave all the garments that the baron had purchased for her, save for the inexpensive pale pink one she already had on, and was surprised to discover that she had only four of her own frocks to place in her portmanteau. Celeste had given two drab stuff schoolroom gowns away, and had consigned another two rather ancient styles to the sewing basket. For all she knew, Julia thought mournfully, looking at the pitiful contents of her traveling case, her blue and gray cotton and her mauve muslin that her Mama had stitched might now be part and parcel of some quilt that the frugal Celeste had stitched up for the deserving poor.

And that was why she paused in her escape, she told herself. And that was why she opened the wardrobe door and took out the ice-blue and silver gown that was her favorite and held it up to herself so that she might have a last look at it in the looking glass. It was so favored because it was the one she had worn to the Opera with Nicholas, the one he had admired and the one he had held in his arms that night in the garden when he had made and rescinded his incredible offer. That was why she considered taking it away with her for the space of a moment. She rationalized that it was, after all, part of her wages, before she began to argue with herself, warning herself that taking the one dress would signal her desire to remain and would then surely be the beginning of taking all the subsequent wages of sin.

She stood before the gilded looking glass, with the silver and blue frock held up before her pink morning dress, her golden hair arranged about her flushed face in the softly curling tendrils that Celeste so dearly loved, and she stared at the woman she had become in the few weeks since she had left her native land. This fashionable female, this elegant, grown-up, yearning lady could never be herself, she thought dazedly. Indeed, she was now entirely unrecognizable to herself. No longer was it only her stylishly coiffed head that seemed unfamiliar. She was still unused to seeing her own white shoulders rising from her frocks, as well as the fashionable but shocking expanse at the top of her high breasts that was constantly on view, accentuated by every new gown. Perhaps that is why she did not startle too badly when a low voice intruded upon her thoughts.

"Hello, Julia," he said, leaning against the door which he had closed softly behind him.

And without hesitation, without even much surprise, as though everything she now saw reflected before her in the gilded mirror were equally unbelievable and so equally acceptable, she spoke, as she lowered the blue gown and slowly turned fully around to face him at last.

"Hello, Robin," she said.

He had not changed much, she thought. He stood with a faintly amused smile upon his lips, and lounged against the door as she stared at him. He was still slender and beautifully dressed, his tawny hair was still arranged in a "wind-swept" fashion, his face was still alert and handsome in that faintly mocking way. He was unmarked and only some trace of shadows beneath his clear amber eyes showed any passage of time. But then, she thought, it has only been three years, after all, nothing much can have changed since I last saw him, except perhaps my entire life.

"I prefer the rose gown, but then, as you may remember, I always did have a partiality for that color," he commented.

Then, as he continued to return her appraising stare, he said more softly, "You have changed, completely. You have grown up and fulfilled your promise. You've grown lovelier, as I though you might."

"Thank you," she said calmly, as though there were nothing fantastic in the conversation, as though it were all a dream, and for all she knew, she thought, it might well be. With her sense of unreality to guide her, she was as candid as a child who walked in her dreams might be.

"Why are you here?" she asked solemnly. "It was Nicholas who searched for you, and now is gone in pursuit of you. He isn't back, is he?" she asked suddenly, all her interest awakened at once at the thought. She felt both fear and delight at the prospect of the baron's return, and her spirits fell when Robin answered, with a small smile.

"No. I haven't found him. At least I haven't looked for him yet. First I only wanted to assure myself that what I heard was true. And incredibly, it is. You are actually here. You see, Julia," he said, coming forward into the room to stand before her, "when the vicar in his usual uncanny fashion learned and then told me that you were traveling with Old Nick and looking for me, I was frankly staggered. I had thought you happily wed at home, Julia," he said in almost a chiding manner, "or at least wed. Perhaps even with a little Julia or two at your knee. I sent a friend to inquire after you years ago and he saw the banns posted at your local church. A Miss Hastings to wed a Mr. Southwood. Whatever happened, my dear?" he asked gently.

She gazed at him without affront and said without rancor, "It was my sister's name he saw, Robin, for I never wed."

"What, did all the fellows in Surrey go stone-blind?" he asked lightly.

But reality began to intrude upon Julia, as time passed and he did not disappear in a vapor, or fade away into the ether. For the first time she began to realize that it was Robin himself who actually stood before her and that she could speak with him as an equal at last, or at least, since their stations would always differ, then as an adult to another reasoning adult. If the past three years had brought her anything, it was this gloss of maturity. Seeing him again now after being out in the world, and after being outcast in the world, was as if to see him for the first time. She saw then a pleasant, attractive young man, and nothing more; nothing godlike, nothing exceptional, nothing to make her heart race, certainly nothing to make her uneasy or fearful. As the girl that had loved him three years ago was vanished, so it seemed that her awe of him had gone completely as well.

"Robin," she said seriously, as though she were reading a moral tale to a very young boy, "it would have been better if they had all gone stone-deaf. It was not what they saw that offended them, it was what they heard of me. The day that I ran off with you I was reckoned an adventuress. Had I wed you, I might even have been admired for my effrontery, they would have called me your 'spirited' or 'dashing' lady. When I returned alone, I was called far more, and far less, and named something other than your 'lady.' I never married, Robin, but then, I never wanted to again, so you must not fret, at least, about that."

But then realizing that this last was untrue, or at least had been patently untrue for some weeks now, she fell silent for a moment to collect her thoughts. Robin looked down at his boots and she thought she detected a faint flush along his lean cheek.

"Then I fail to understand, Julia," Robin said, "why you have come all the way to France to discover me again."

"She didn't want to, you know," Nicholas said, from the doorway.

"Nicholas!" Julia cried gladly, and she took a few steps toward him before she recalled herself. He stood at the entrance to her room and his sober face gladdened for a moment at her spontaneous greeting. He seemed drawn and pale, he was covered with the dust of the road, but he was undeniably there. Julia stood staring at him and then said, in wonderment, "You've come back."

"Well of course I have, Julia." He smiled wearily as he entered the room and put out his hand to take Robin's. "Hello, Robin, I've looked for you over the face of the entire Continent, but I didn't think to find you here in Julia's boudoir, lad."

"Nick, we must talk," Robin said seriously.

"Why certainly," his uncle replied on a sigh. "Why else do you think we have come?"

15 When Julia had been very young, she had once strayed directly into the path of Lord Quincy and a hunting party he had organized. She had seen his great gray horse bearing down upon her and it hadn't seemed either real or important. But after her father had swept her out of the way, and after the riding party had stopped to comment upon her narrow escape and offer her father congratulations for his quick-wittedness, and long after Lord Quincy had done with praising himself for the excellent horsemanship that had prevented him from running the both of them down, Julia had found that her legs would not work. They simply would not function. And her father had to lift her and carry her, trembling, all the way home.

Now, in an elegant bedroom in a hotel in Paris, Julia discovered herself experiencing the same phenomenon. Nicholas must have seen her distress, or known of it in the uncanny way that he always anticipated her, for before her numbed legs could betray her he had left Robin's side and assisted her to a chair. Now she sat and looked at the two gentlemen who had come into her bedroom and she heard their voices and watched their faces, and tried to assimilate the reality of them.

196

Neither had taken a seat. They stood before her, Robin leaning back against a wall near the window, since it seemed, as she began to remember now, that he always liked to drape himself over any available surface, and Nicholas relaxed as if at his ease with one hand resting on a chair's back as they spoke. Julia could not pay attention to their words at first. Just as she had noticed only the fact that Squire Quincy had a smudge of dirt near his nose on that long-ago morning, now she could only marvel at how bizarre it was simply that they stood and chatted in her bedroom. This room had been the scene of so many dreams and fancies of and about the two of them. Its delicate gold and rose-pink furnishings, seemed a particularly unreal setting for the two vital men who stood within it in actuality now.

Now as she watched them with wondering, wandering belief, she could see that there was little physical family likeness between them. Nicholas had the advantage of a few inches over Robin, although Robin's frame was so slender that he appeared taller than he was. Both were pale, but Robin was all autumnal in his russet hair and eye coloring and Nicholas was more vivid with his white skin, dark, curling hair, and wide gray-green eyes. Both were slender, both well made, both had that clean and deceptively narrow length of limb that belied their tensile strength. But overall, their resemblance was one that was discreet rather than apparent.

Then, even as she sat dumbly and gazed at them, their voices began to intrude upon her recovering mind.

"Yes, I passed through Waterloo," Nicholas said easily, "and it was an eerie feeling to see the blackened grasses and the blasted rye fields. But it was a faster route than the Tubize road because of the rains."

"But Nick, old fellow, the road was merely muddy, not impassable, and I made very good time once I reached Mons," Robin replied.

"What?" Julia cried, for it began to seem as though she had lost her wits completely rather than having simply misplaced them. "What?" she went on in rising accents. "We meet after all this time and travail and you discuss the *roads?*"

At that, they left off speaking and turned toward her. They looked at her incredulous face and then at each other and then, in their matching laughter, at last Julia could see their matching heritage clearly.

"So you are returned to us," Nicholas said, as his mirth subsided. Yet he continued to gaze at her with a slight smile as he explained, "But Julia, it was only right to wait for you to join us. And then, we are English gentlemen, you know. I imagine that even on Judgment Day, when the deserving dead arise from their graves to meet their maker and go to their just rewards, there will be a group of Englishmen standing about making idle chat about the weather as they wait for their Lord to shine His countenance upon them. It just isn't the thing to immediately plunge into the crux of the matter, you know. But as usual, you are right. There are other things to discuss than roads. How do you propose we start, Robin?" he said then in a serious voice, all hint of his humor vanished and only his concern showing in his face.

Robin seemed unfazed as he answered lightly, "I might inquire as to why you rode down the wind to see me, and spread the alert through the length and breadth of the civilized world that our meeting must be at once."

"And I would tell you that I have word of your father," the baron said softly.

"Ah, and is he passed from this mortal coil then?" Robin asked, tilting his head to one side.

"No, not when I left England, but by now it is entirely possible that he has. And if not now, then soon enough, barring a miracle that I do not think even Prinny's favorite leeches capable of pulling off," Nicholas said, watching his nephew closely.

"But there is nothing new in that, Nick," Robin said carefully, looking down as though he found his waistcoat of surpassing interest.

Julia watched the two men and dared not breathe a word. There was that in their attitude, although their voices were mild and their reaction subdued, which reminded her of cats circling each other before they attacked. They were so occupied with each other that she believed they had forgotten her entirely.

"And if he is gone, then I shall be king of the cats. Shall I then contrive to leap to my feet in joy and vanish up the chimney to begin my reign? Isn't that how it was done in that old folktale, Nick?" Robin asked as he became engrossed in an embroidered fleur-de-lis upon his waistcoat. "But," he went on thoughtfully, "I should be nothing so high as that, I would only be a marquess of the British. So I think I'll pass up the chance to rise up the chimney. I won't go home, Nick," he said abruptly, and looked up quickly to watch his uncle's reaction.

"But not because of Julia," Nicholas said quietly.

"No," Robin said as softly, not even glancing at Julia as she sat up sharply upon hearing her name mentioned. "No, not because of Julia, as you most likely have already discovered."

"But you see," Nicholas said patiently as he shifted his weight and leaned both hands heavily upon the chair, "I had to insult her, deceive her, threaten her, do her physical injury, and abduct her to learn that. Would it not have been simpler, Robin, to have simply told me the truth originally?"

"But I didn't want you to know, you see," Robin replied in so low a voice that Julia had to strain to hear him. "And I assumed I'd be safe enough because I supposed her to be wed, you see. Conveniently wed, conveniently obscure, convenient for my purposes." But then he looked up at Julia and with a brighter eye and clearer voice, he said, "I thought you only a ghost of my past, but what an unquiet spirit you turned out to be! I am sorry, child," he said in something of his old manner, although Julia detected more bravado than naturalness in his voice, "I had no idea that dear old civilized Nicholas would turn pirate in his efforts to lure me home. That was your intention, wasn't it, *Uncle,*" he asked with a trace of anger as he turned to the baron.

"You must come home," Nicholas answered calmly. "You'll have the title, and the responsibilities and the land to see to. You said that Julia was the impediment, so I attempted to remove her from your path by throwing her into your path. The poor lady almost got trampled by our mechanations. She deserves far more. I think, Robin, that at the very least, she deserves the truth from you."

But at the word *truth,* a subtle change came over Robin. His face grew paler, and he closed his eyes for a moment. When he spoke again it was with an effort.

"Then I am to suppose that you surmise the truth?" he said with the ghost of a smile. "I doubt it, Uncle, I really do. A great many credible things may have occurred to you, but I doubt if the truth is among them."

Now Nicholas looked steadily at his nephew and said in a measured, emotionless voice, "Robin, I am not a fool. I have heard Julia's story and she is not a liar, poor lady, although I believed her one long after I ought not to have, because I did not wish to come to a natural conclusion about you. Then, too, I have had speech with the vicar."

Robin stirred visibly at the mention of the vicar's name, but his uncle only noted that and went on, "No, the vicar is circumspect at all times, as you know. But still, matters began to become clearer. And as you must know as well, there is the bothersome fact that Sir Ollie Sidney is on your traces. It is my forced cooperation in a difficult matter that he is after. But he would not be so hot upon your heels if he did not think there was profit in it for him. And there is only profit for him when someone has made a slip. I suspect it is your money he is after as well as my compliance. He would threaten to destroy the family name, you know."

"What's in a name?" Robin laughed, but his laughter was weak and he seemed to be thinking furiously.

The room grew very still and Julia grew very confused. There was something that had been said, or had almost been said, that she knew she ought to understand. But she could not, so she only sat quietly and hoped that they would forget her and go on with their conversation and give her the key to what hovered at the edges of her consciousness.

Then her patience was rewarded in a manner that made her wish that she had not wished for a revelation. For then Robin broke from his immobility. He abandoned his position by the wall and paced a few steps. Then he swung back to his uncle and looked at him with such distress that Julia felt her heart constrict, for even though she knew his age, he seemed nothing more than a badly frightened boy again.

"I didn't want you to know," he said despairingly. "That was the sum and substance of it. I knew I could fob the others off in a thousand ways, but your opinion was always so important to me. So long as it was safely secret from you, Nick, I could bear it. I told you that farrago about Julia's deception so that you wouldn't press me to return. Because of your history, I thought you'd believe it, and I believed her comfortably wed and out of it. But I never meant to endanger you in any fashion, and I know that Ollie, for all he looks a buffoon, is a dangerous man. And I never wished to hurt Julia. In fact," he said on a bark of a laugh, "I believed that by abandoning her, I was saving her from hurt. I was being noble that night, Julia," he said as he looked to her imploringly. "Forgive me, I meant it for the best, you know."

"The point is," Nicholas said as he too looked at Julia, "that she doesn't know. And you must tell her, Robin. In all honor, you must. You see," he went on as his nephew gazed at Julia disbelievingly, "she thinks it was some deformity or monstrous aberration in herself that repulsed you."

As Robin continued to gaze wordlessly at Julia, Nicholas walked to her side and placed his hand on the back of her chair. "Yes," he said sadly, "and so she believes to this day. True, Julia?"

But Julia understood nothing of the sorrow in his voice, nor of the horror in Robin's eyes, she only leaned forward and, holding her hands tightly in her lap, grasped at that one question, the one that had never left her waking mind for very long for three long years.

"Why did you leave then, Robin?" was all that she could say.

"Ah Julia," Robin said at last on a long sigh that seemed to come from the depths of his soul.

Then he took in his breath, and with it he seemed to take back in some of his natural presence and jauntiness. He seemed to relax. He half sat, half perched upon an inlaid table's edge, in the casual way that he so often had in the past, as though it were too much trouble to settle down in a chair like an old or average person. He ran his hand once through his hair, enhancing its contours even as he did so, as it had obviously been styled to accommodate his characteristic habit. Then he blew out his cheeks in a sigh again and then, looking at Julia and his uncle, he at last spoke.

"I never meant any of this, you know. But the bard, of course, was right. I wove a very tangled web in my efforts to deceive. Or you might say, it was because I did not wish to deceive that I did so. No, Nick, don't fidget, I'm coming to it. Julia," Robin said, looking at her straightly, "I was going to use you very badly. It was all to your benefit that I did not. There was nothing wrong with you, child. Never. Not for a moment. And I did like you very well, and you were as ex-

tremely pretty then as you are extravagantly lovely now, and
there was no defect in you in heart, mind, or person. But you
see, I could never love you, not in the way you ought to have
been loved. And it was never your fault, child, for you see, the
simple truth is that I could never love any female in that way.

"You didn't know, Nick," Robin continued, now rising
again and restlessly pacing as he avoided his uncle's eye, although his uncle never took his eyes from him. "Well, how
could you? I kept it very close after I discovered it myself.
Which is not to say that I didn't fight it with good British fortitude, for I did. To no avail. Even though I could achieve that
which I was supposed to with a professional female, there was
more alcohol than delight in it, and alcohol, you know, makes
me foully ill when I take it in excess. Which, it transpired, I
had to do in order to do what I was expected to. Oblique
enough to save Julia's sensibilities, Nick?" he asked, looking
up from the carpet he had been studying and, unexpectedly,
grinning at his uncle.

"Perhaps it would be better if you were a bit more transparent," Nicholas said with a trace of temper as he saw Julia
frowning slightly in her efforts to comprehend all that Robin
had so lightly said.

"She shall have the truth, but no pictures," Robin replied
caustically, and then he went on at once, "You see, my dear, I
found that I preferred the intimate company, shall we say, of
my own gender to that of yours."

He waited a moment as Julia's eyes widened in comprehension, and then, nodding, he went on, "I found a number of like
spirits, of course, at school and, when I got out, in London. We
flocked together, as the saying goes. Oh dear," he interrrupted
himself to sigh ruefully, "why is it that our deepest shames and
fears can so easily be contained in platitudes? Never mind,
Nicholas, I'll go on. So we commenced to have a fine time together, my friends and I. We were discreet, we were cautious,
and we were fools to be so complacent, it turns out.

"For someone brought a friend to one of our revels. And
though he looked deceptively mature, the lad turned out to be
shockingly young. What he did at our soiree preyed upon his
mind and so he confessed all to his father. Who, as it happened,
turned out to be no less than an honored duke, and who had, to
our misfortune, the ear of the Prince. We had to fly, of course.

But I did not want to, you see." Robin sighed, shaking his tousled head.

"So I came to Surrey," he said with artificial brightness, "to rusticate and escape the scandal. Then I hit upon a capital scheme for concealing my preferential way of life. I chose the youngest, prettiest, sweetest, most naive child that I could to take to wife. One lovely enough for my Uncle Nick to admire, for it was upon his expert taste that I based my criteria," he said with a brilliant sidewise smile, before he went on to add, "and one with no connections. Oh sorry, Julia, I meant to say no social connections. So that even if she eventually discovered me, she could do nothing about it.

"But I was not a monster, Julia," Robin said quickly, "for after all, if I had been discreet, you might never have known. And there was a great deal that I could give you: a kind of love, a great deal of gold, and a title. And even, I thought, with luck and enough rum, an heir."

Robin's embarrassed laugh dwindled into silence. Julia sat with her head bowed, and Nicholas stood quietly at her side. Neither man spoke, they knew it was Julia's moment alone.

"Robin," she finally whispered, her eyes large and very frightened at what she must now ask, "what changed your mind, then?"

"That towel, love," Robin sighed with a twisted smile, "or rather, the lack of it. For want of a nail the horse was lost . . ." he recited, before his smile faded and he went on. "For want of a towel a wife was lost. Because you see, child, in that moment I realized that you weren't a child but a warm and loving and dismayingly complete woman. I knew then that to be able to return your kiss in a way I ought to have quite naturally done, I would have had to go back down to the taproom for quite a few more hours. I knew that it was never fair to you, or to me. You were simply too young and too sweet to do that to, Julia. I liked you very well, so I left you. I honestly thought you'd soon forget me and marry some local fellow before the year closed out.

"Then I left for the Continent with my good friend Sir Edwin Chester, who is an older, wiser, worthy gentleman whatever his unfortunate tastes, even you cannot say nay to that, Nicholas. He brought Julia home swiftly and safely when my heart and head failed me that night. Then we came here. And here I shall stay," he declared with challenge in his tone, "for here I am myself, and I am, according to my own lights, happy."

Julia shook her head in disbelief, perversely seeking a hole in the fabric of his story. It was a strange narrative, but there was no part of it which gave her so much difficulty as that which freed her of all fault for that night. It was as though she had grown so accustomed to believing in the invisible flaw within herself that she refused to accept the daring notion of her blamelessness.

"But Robin," she persisted, "if it were only that, then why didn't you tell me?"

There was a profound silence after she spoke, and though she awaited his reply, Robin only looked at her oddly. But then, unexpectedly, Nicholas bent close to her and spoke gently, "He did not dare, I imagine. Even though he thought highly of you, he didn't dare put his life in your hands. You see, Robin's way of life can be a way of death in our country. It is a capital offense, Julia, punishable by hanging."

"Oh, I doubt they'd actually stretch my neck, Nick." Robin laughed bitterly. "Noblesse oblige and all that, you know. My title would buy me exile rather than the topping cheat. But unless I passed my life in a tissue of lies that would make this situation appear to be only a matter of a few fibs, I would be told, man to gentleman, to leave my country forever. It does not take much, you know. Just before I left home, you'll recall, there was the celebrated case of that waiter accused by his busboy. Only accused, mind you, but nonetheless it only took five minutes for a jury of his peers to vote him out of this life.

"There are ways around it," Robin said knowingly. "Oh yes, there are. I could be like Sir Bailey up in Yorkshire, who spends his life as a recluse, never passing through the very gates of his estates lest he succumb to temptation again and ruin his name. Or even better, like Lord Crowell, who parades his wife in the highest reaches of the ton. But she is a trull who holds his title dearer than her honor and presents him with bastard babes every year to carry that prized title onward. I would not do that, Nick," Robin said fervently. "It would be far better that one of your blood take my name after I am gone, than one from a nameless litter spawned by some opportunist. . . ."

He paused, collected himself, and then said soberly, "The

vicar is no fool, you know. I could do worse than to follow his lead."

They stayed in silence, then, the two gentlemen and the lady, in the opulent rented bedroom. Each was immersed in his own thoughts to the point that no one of them noted the quiet grown profound enough to make the mantel clock's tiny, tinny chime resound like that of Bow Bells in the hushed room. But when Julia looked up and out into the world again at that intrusion, she found that Nicholas was watching her closely.

"Do you understand now?" he asked simply, placing his hand upon her shoulder.

"Yes," she said, facing him squarely and answering as honestly as she was able. "As much, that is to say, as I can, I think."

"And do you forgive me, child?" Robin asked with concern.

The warm weight of the baron's hand upon her shoulder seemed to give Julia's body warmth, and she drew confidence from the way he continued to stand at her side. The two men who had shaped her life so strangely in the past few years waited for her reply, and even as she drew in her breath to answer she knew that for all of them far more than the next few years was dependent upon what she next said.

"I am not a child, Robin," she replied thoughtfully, "but I was one when you knew me, and yes, it would have been disastrous had we wed then. So, instead of blaming you, I suppose I must thank you. No, Nicholas, don't look at me that way," she protested with a little laugh as she read his face, "I am no saint, and although I am relieved beyond words to know that I'm not a freakish thing in any wise either, I'm human enough to wish Robin at Jericho for these years of doubt I suffered."

She shook her head in a sorrowful negative and added, "I can't undo the past so it's useless to say what might have been had you not come into my life, Robin." And then, with a small, sweet smile she added, "But I can't forgive you either."

Robin hesitated, and then, smiling sweetly himself, merely shrugged his shoulders in a gesture of helplessness, and Julia could feel Nicholas's hand grow heavy upon her even as she went on to say in the same thoughtful tones, "For there is nothing for me to forgive, you see. Nothing. Yes, you ought not to have offered for me, knowing what you did, and you ought not,

I suppose, to be what you are. But then, none of us have been precisely what we should have been, have we? I ought not to have been such a ninny as to agree to marry you without knowing you, and Papa ought not to have given his consent so quickly, for I would not have made a move without it. And Nicholas should never have believed the worst of me without proof, or forced me to leave England to come to the last place on earth that I wished to be. So if you come right down to it," she said reasonably, "I ought not to be here right now."

Nicholas removed his hand from her shoulder as she shook out her skirts and rose from the chair so that she might cease to look up at both men and face Robin directly.

"But I am here, so let's make an end to it now. I would wish that it all had happened to some other person. But at least it's over. Or, at least for me it is. And for whatever it's worth," she smiled as she put out her hand, "I wish you well in future, Robin, I truly do."

Robin took her hand, but even as he had it in his clasp, he turned a bright look toward his uncle.

"And you, Nick?" he asked quickly. "Do you? Ah, might as well ask for the moon, I suppose. Julia forgives that which she cannot fully comprehend. She's not a gentleman and hasn't been to the best schools and clubs, thank God. Still, if I cannot condone it fully myself, why then, how can I expect it of you? *C'est la vie.* Only don't despise me too much if you can help it, and keep it between us, if you will. I should rather Mama believed no girl good enough for me than the reverse. I don't mind being the family skeleton, but pray don't rattle my bones too much."

He bowed to Julia, and then straightened his shoulders.

"Well," he breathed with an air of great decision, "I believe I'll be going along now. Don't fret about Ollie, Uncle, for I'll have a word with him myself. I'll simply tell him that he's too late, you've discovered all and are in such a rage that you've already vowed to spill it to the family. He can't sell secrecy he don't possess, so if he broaches the subject to you, just agree to the tale. I don't think," he added, giving his motionless, grave-visaged uncle a measuring look, "that you'll have to simulate too much rage, at that."

"No," his uncle agreed grimly.

Then as Robin grew white about the mouth and turned

blindly to the door, Nicholas cleared his throat and added in a clearer voice, "No, it's an unworkable scheme, dear boy. If he'd believe me to be so enraged, why then he'd believe me willing to pay anything for his silence before the world. Now wouldn't it be far better if we both faced him? Say, as two gentlemen who might choose to live extremely different lives, but who have a fondness for each other through memory as well as blood that transcends present circumstances. Such gentlemen can have no secrets from each other, and never would, for they would know that their friendship could withstand anything but deceit. He can't sell a secret that doesn't exist. I don't know about you, Robin, but certainly I think I would not have to simulate enthusiasm for your company. And if he asks you, I hope you would agree with me."

Robin stopped in his tracks, and then, smiling as tremulously and as suspiciously broadly as his uncle, advanced upon the baron. The two men positively slapped their hands together before they gripped them hard and grinned at each other. And Julia, seeing it all through a sudden blurry mist, made a liar of herself. For as she stood and watched them repeatedly and wordlessly shaking hands, she was supremely happy to be there at that moment. And she would not have been anywhere else in the world, for the world, even though she was undeniably there against her will, on her own, and very far from home.

The afternoon late summer sun shone down broadly upon the diners at the outdoor café near the banks of the Seine. It was such a bright day that many of the gentry taking refreshment there had to squint their eyes to see their dishes of ice properly, although their ladies were more fortunate, having their parasols to shield them from the full glare.

So it was that one gentleman had his eyes screwed up tightly as he attempted to watch a playful quartet of persons at another table. It was hard to ascertain whether he was affected by the glare or brought to the brink of either laughter or tears by their apparent outsized merriment. For he soon had to bring his handkerchief into use, if only to clear his eyes so that he might better see the gentleman who joined him at his table.

"Oh, hello there, Ollie, my friend," the vicar said pleasantly as he pulled out a spindly chair, dusted it with his own handkerchief, and then dropped gracefully into place, even though he had not been invited to do so. "How good to find you here in the city of light. Now who was it told me you were in Amsterdam?" he mused. "No matter, for clearly, you're here now. How goes it with you, then?" the older gentleman asked, all solicitude, as though he were speaking to a man in his sick bed rather than in a fashionable café in the heart of Paris.

"Is there anything you don't know, blast you?" the heavy-set gentleman answered angrily, although he never took his eyes off the other table.

"I sincerely hope not!" the thin old gentleman replied with a great show of horror. He smiled, and although he did no more than signal to the waiter and order up a cup of tea, he seemed to be enjoying himself hugely. "A charming sight, is it not?" he sighed at length when his companion did not speak. He gestured toward the four persons at the table at the far end of the café, the four who were laughing and talking together, the four that his host could not tear his gaze from.

"And such a singularly unusual circumstance," he said confidentially, dropping his voice, "for there sits Lord Nicholas Daventry, Baron Stafford—why he's the same chap you were asking me about, Ollie, when last I saw you! Well, here's a bit of gossip for you then, for there he sits with his young nephew, Robin Marlowe, Earl of Shepton, and Lady Mary Preston and some young filly she's looking after. But the singular thing, Ollie," the vicar whispered although still grinning terribly, looking rather like an ancient turtle in his glee, "is that it's rumored that young Robin has a rather queer kick in his gait, and yet his family don't give a rap, so long as he's discreet enough about it to stay on the Continent. Now I don't know what this modern world is coming to, Ollie, I vow I do not."

But at that, his companion slammed his fist upon the table and rose. He gave the other table one last fulminating look and then turned to the older gentleman, who was gazing at him blandly.

"Damn you, Vicar," Sir Sidney shouted wrathfully, and then, shoulders slumping, he slouched out into the street and disappeared into the afternoon crowds.

"Oh dear," the vicar chuckled to himself, "and he's left me with the bill to settle, of course. But it was worth the price," he whispered to himself as he fished for a coin from his vest pocket, "for value received."

Then the old gentleman made his way to the table his erstwhile host had been observing. He made a courtly bow which brought a smile of gratification from Lady Preston, and then he declined the baron's offer that he join them.

"I only came, dear friends," he said, standing by their table so wreathed in smiles as to be a bit frightening, like a dessicated Father Christmas, "to tell you of the departure of another acquaintance. Sir Oliver Sidney, it appears, has no further business here, and I imagine, we'll see no more of him. Pity, that," he remarked in a singularly unsorrowful fashion. "But the pity is," he said with some real emotion and a more wistful smile, "that I imagine that means you will soon be gone from here as well, my dears."

Lady Preston nodded in affirmation, and the young earl grew a wistful expression as he acknowledged the truth of the statement. But at those innocuous words, the vicar noticed, Miss Hastings' lovely face immediately went the color of the damask tablecloth, and she bit her lip and dropped her gaze to her lap. And the Baron Stafford, who had carried state secrets through a roomful of assassins without so much as batting his long eyelashes, grew suddenly so still he seemed to be carved from alabaster.

"Yes," the baron breathed at last, "now we may take passage home on the next fair wind. Yes, at last it is over."

16

They stood on the quay and waited for their turn to board the packet. Had they arrived earlier, they would have been among the first to embark, for they were traveling in first class style and they were clearly members of that class which always took precedence. But there had been minor delays in starting out and then major farewells to be done with. Now it had been decided for both prudence and the sake of appearance to wait until the last soul and shipment had been taken on board before they went on the ship themselves to begin their journey home.

It was a warm and muggy August morning, and the miasmas of the sea were supplemented by the stench of the flotsam and debris that wharfside slips always seemed to collect. Julia attempted to breathe shallowly to escape the aroma which greeted her whenever the vague, inconstant breeze shifted slightly to shore. She looked longingly out to the wider sea beyond the ship. There the waters seemed clear and open and of an entirely different constitution than the oily, dank stuff which sullenly lapped at the dockside beneath her feet. She tried as hard not to look down as she did not to breathe in deeply. For now and again the thick waters below the boards where she stood showed hints of prodigies as they floated by, things she would rather not define, as they were either long deceased, or soon to spring to unnatural new forms of life.

She could, she knew, have stayed within the more cleanly atmosphere of the parlor of the waterside inn, where both Celeste and Lady Preston now comfortably awaited their summons to leave. Both women were making the return journey with her. Lady Preston was on her way home after all her weary journeys and unexpectedly, Celeste had taken passage as well. The maidservant's practicality had outweighed the call of nationality. She had heard that French maids were in demand in England, she told her present mistress, and if a lady were foolish enough to pay for a mere accent, why then she thought she should be twice as foolish not to provide one for a price. But Julia had decided to forego the company of both women just now. She could have time with them once she was at sea. She had two more personal good-byes to make this morning, and she needed both privacy and solitude in which to compose herself. One farewell would be difficult enough, for it would be to a person, but the other, much harder leavetaking would be to a dream.

Even as she stood apart and brooded alone, Robin and Nicholas were making their last good-byes only a few paces away from her. She had thought that there was not much further that they could have found to say to each other, as she knew that they had stayed up late the previous night, talking and settling accounts together. But then, she sighed, so too had she stayed up most of the night, talking and attempting to settle matters with herself, and yet here she was this morning, still unresolved, with even more thinking yet to do.

She was going home at last. If her reputation was not cleared in the matter of her elopement with Robin, then at least some of her personal shame was absolved. It seemed that she had been only a fool, not a freak of nature. And it appeared that no further damage would be done either to her name or her honor by this recent sojourn abroad with his uncle. But it was neither her conscience nor her reputation which troubled her now, it was her heart. If she had found her self-esteem again on this journey, she had paid for it dearly. For even if the incredible thing that Robin had stated were true and there was no thing wrong with her at all, no bar to normal love and life, how could it matter when she was about to be parted from the one man it would ever matter for?

But part from him she would, Julia vowed, with a sudden firming of her resolve. She did not need Lady Preston to tell her what was proper. Standing here on the dock, with a breeze from home in her hair, it was as though she was already there in truth, and a certain sense of reality settled over her. Foreign travel disordered the brain, it made one wander in one's wits as well as in one's itinerary, she thought. She realized, as more worldly travelers had done for centuries before her, that often things that one thought or did upon alien soil were things that were alien to one's true nature. No, she sadly acknowledged to herself, Julia Hastings, for all her sins, could not be, and could not wish to be except in her deepest midnight fancies, the fancy-piece of any gentleman.

That did not mean that she could not regret her nature. For she perceived a truth that no explanation could erase—that her essential nature was as much of an impediment to her longings as the phantom flaw that Robin had banished had been. The only man that she had ever desired as a man desired her only as his mistress. Yet even though she knew it was her only chance at happiness, she could not oblige him. Her conscience simply would not permit it. She was, she thought on a sigh, either a true puritan or a deluded prig. But that was what she was, she thought, straightening her shoulders and giving one last little mournful snuffle. And if she changed herself beyond recognition to achieve a desire, why then, she reasoned, she would be like one of Cinderella's stepsisters, slicing off a toe or two to fit a slipper that was never meant to be worn by her.

Having reached that conclusion, Julia felt far better. It was true that the sun seemed to have dropped from the sky, the waters that seethed beneath the wharf seemed to have become inky black, and she felt as though she were waiting for deaf Charon to ferry her across the Styx rather than bluff Captain Aherne to take her home to England, but at least she saw her way clear. Oh yes, she thought, she saw a clear and empty and long road to the end of a lonely life ahead of her.

The two gentlemen finally left off talking and Nicholas gave Robin a clap upon the back, even as they shook hands warmly. Robin spoke a brief, low word to Nicholas, and then he alone came to where Julia was standing and waiting.

"Time for a good-bye, Julia," Robin said gently. "I'll come no closer to home than this dockside this time. What is there for me in England save for regret and threat and fear of a misstep? But still, I've promised Nick that one day I shall visit again. He's agreed to mind the shop as best he can for me, and I'll direct the rest in letters home. It's to be a devastating Italian widow that I've lost my heart to this time, by the by," he grinned. "Which ought to suit Mama to perfection, for she had a dancing master in her youth that was a grand infatuation. Her papa of course forbade the match, so to salve her feelings of loss she is fond of going on at length about how perfidious his entire race is known to be. She'll understand my continued absence well enough, I think.

"And after that," he said, "there shall be an Austrian countess, then an impoverished French lady, and then an avaricious Spanish courtesan, I believe. I shall see to it that I loose my foolish heart to a legion of unworthy ladies over the next decade, so that I may be understood in my continuing absence."

"Oh Robin," Julia said, forgetting her own sorrow at the sadness she saw reflected in his face, "I am so sorry."

"Oh don't be," he said with surprise, looking closely at her, "for I'm happy enough in my life, Julia. I've Edwin and the vicar and my other friends. I've made the best decision for myself, don't fret for me," he continued smiling at her brightly.

"Blue," he said suddenly, with reproof, "blue, Julia? When you know how I prefer you in pink?"

She was confused until she realized that he was smiling again and looking at her frock, which was a light azure with a darker blue overskirt.

"But it is not me you're dressing for now, is it?" he asked, and then went on in a low voice before she could reply, "Yes. I did you a very good turn that night. I may sometimes regret all that I have given up, but then, I can never regret all that I have brought about. Julia," he said abruptly, bending to kiss her cheek and whispering rapidly, "be a good girl now, and take care of yourself, and make forgiving a habit, and you will be a very happy girl—ah, you are right—woman. Good-bye, love."

Then, releasing her hands that he had caught up in his, he bowed and turned back to Nicholas, who had stood watching them.

"I won't wait for the sails to go up and wave until you're a dot in the distance, that sort of farewell is maudlin. Good-bye, Old Nick," he said, putting his hand upon his uncle's shoulder.

"Good-bye, Robin Goodfellow," the baron said, putting his hand over his nephew's.

Then Robin gave them both a brilliant smile that went no further than his lips, and he clapped his hands together, bowed, and turned away. He was gone and out of sight even before the echo of his handclap had faded in their ears.

When the last sight of Robin hurrying down the wharf had vanished, Nicholas turned and looked at Julia. He was frowning as he reached into his jacket's inner pocket.

"Blast," he muttered, "this jacket may be everything that causes Makepiece's heart to flutter, but it's damned inconvenient just the same. Comfort's been sacrificed for line, and I glitter in the sunlight as though I were all in spangles. Yes, I am wearing it today, or else the fellow would have driven me mad. I decided that if I had to put the thing on, it might as well be while I was still on foreign soil. I don't know when I shall return, and there is every possibility that I'll be lucky enough to be too stout and gouty to fit into it when I next visit these shores."

As he continued to take papers from his inner pocket, Julia noticed that he was indeed looking even more elegant this morning than usual. The jacket that he complained of was a trifle excessive in its cloth and cut, having a rich and shining silver thread prominent among the blue ones, and it fit his trim form as though it had been put on with an artist's brush rather than a valet's assistance. But although it may have been a trifle dandyish for its wearer's taste's, Julia thought it so dashing that she could only nod her head in reply to him.

"Ah, here it is," he sighed at last. And then, looking at Julia very soberly, he gave her two envelopes. "This one," he said as he handed her the first, which had her name upon it in spidery handwriting, "is a glowing reference from my friend, the ficticious Lady Cunningham. Lady Preston, my friends, and my family will all swear to her existence. It could probably net you employment with the Queen, it's such a high recommendation. No, actually, I'll go so far as to say that if royalty were a position filled by merit, it would *make* you Queen. It's really very impressive," he said more seriously.

Then he handed her the second envelope and said hurriedly, "That is a bank check for your wages. It's a goodly sum, but never enough, I know. There is no way I can pay you to recompense you for the discomfort, fear, and brutishness of your experiences, but at least the money is a substantial sum."

As he stood and gazed down at her with a worried, anxious frown, she found her wits enough to protest as she handed the envelope back to him, "But there's no need to pay me for what transpired. It's as I told Robin, there can be no blame attached to him for what occurred."

He smiled wryly before he said softly, "No, Julia, you have it the wrong way around. It is the wages for your experiences at my hands that you are being paid for."

"Ah," she said, and was all she could say. Because to refuse his money would be to declare her feelings for him, and to accept it was to accept the truth she had struggled against all night and all morning: that she had been in his employ, and that her only chance for a future with him would be to continue in his employ.

Without attempting to open them to so much as to glance at their contents, she sought to fold the thick envelopes double so that she could stuff them into her reticule, and her struggles to do so fortunately kept her from raising her eyes to his as she murmured, "Thank you, so kind."

"Then you are satisfied? We are even at last?" he asked, as she managed to pull the strings of her purse tightly about the edges of the envelopes.

"Yes, yes," she replied, wondering distractedly if she ought to make her good-byes to him now. She would board the boat soon and then she might not see him again until they landed. Even then she would speedily hire a coach to take her home and so this might be the last chance for private speech with him.

But again, it was as though he were privy to her thoughts, for he said gruffly, somewhat angrily, "I may not have a chance for private speech with you again for some time. No doubt your loyal chaperone and maidservant will close about you like bramble bushes did around the sleeping beauty when we are aboard ship. Then, when we arrive no doubt you'll be all haste to be home. And then I'll have to manufacture a thousand excuses to get to your home and visit with you, and I'll have to endure suspicious looks from your family, or make ridiculous excuses for my presence to your new employers. It's not easy for a gentleman to seek out the companionship of a governess or a companion, without he looks like a bounder, or she, like an adventuress," he complained.

"So, as they're having a bit of trouble lading that pianoforte, or whatever it is in that crate they're unsuccessfully trying to drag aboard ship," he said, glancing rapidly over his shoulder to the packet, where a team of sweating sailors were attempting to haul a huge packing case over the edge of the deck, "I'll speak now as I find the time to do so. But I warn you, Julia, I will not forever hold my peace after that. I intend to make convincing you of my earnest my life's ambition. I seize the moment now, but I promise I'll continue to badger you—Lord," he breathed in exasperation, "if I cannot even make a proposal to you without hectoring you again, how can I ever expect you to believe in my good intentions?"

"Oh no!" Julia cried out at once, raising one hand to her lips in her distress. "Pray, oh pray do not make me that offer again! For I'd like to part from you with good feeling and—"

"Julia," he said, cutting off her speech by taking her shoulders in his hands and looking at her keenly, "you don't understand. I do not make the same offer. You would be a dreadful mistress, believe me. Yes," he said with a smile at last warming his features, "you would. Don't even consider it as an occupation for a moment. You haven't an ounce of guile, you'd never flatter, much less cuddle, when you didn't feel like it, and you'd go up like a skyrocket if a fellow so much as looked at another female. No, a chap would be demented to want you as his mistress. But he'd have to be certifiable, or at least as mad as you thought me when we first met, if he didn't want you for his wife. And I do, Julia, I do."

"But you can't," she said, knowing even as she said so, that he did, for that bond of commonality they shared could not be so right in everything else and so wrong only in this. But she dared not believe, because she had been so disastrously wrong when she had believed in love and in a loved one's promises before. So she thought of all the reasonable reasons against their union, and as she thought them she spoke them as though they were some incantation she chanted to ward off disappointment and deceit again.

"I am a commoner without a penny piece," she protested, closing her eyes against the hope she saw in his and shaking her head vigorously in denial with every word she uttered until slips of her golden hair blew free about her face, "and I have no reputation as well as no birth. I am known to have run off with your nephew in the past. And I have worked for my livelihood, and I am past the first blush of youth, and what would people say?"

"And I am leagues in love with you," he replied, holding her shoulders tightly, as though he feared she would run from him, "and well you know it. As to the rest, everyone would congratulate me for winning such a bride, and pity Robin for falling out with you. As I do. Poor lad, perhaps I pity him even more for that than for anything else of his condition. And I would never marry for money, and none would expect it of me," he went on, never taking his eyes from her, more serious than she could ever recall him being.

"And my family would approve, perhaps it is yours you ought worry about, for they might never trust one of my class again. In fact, my stepfather would be pleased beyond words," he said, his lips now curling upward at the thought. "He's a great believer in breeding humans as one would cattle, and would be thrilled at my bringing new blood into the family to ensure vigor and improve our unsteady line. As for your age, you are but a babe, and as for your working, it was an honorable alternative to your living on pity. Julia," he said imploringly, "these all are as nothing, you know. I list them only to placate you. The answer should come from how you feel about me. Julia, do you care for me, as I do for you?"

He had been sensitive enough to her hard-learned caution that he did not demand she declare her love. She had only to agree with him. But habits of years cannot be unlearned in an hour, even with love as their tutor. Julia looked into his clear, knowing eyes and found that she could not at that moment, for her life, utter the truth: that he was her life.

He saw her indecision, her inability to respond at once. He began to speak again, but thought better of it, and with one swift motion, he pulled her to himself and kissed her long and hard.

The sailors aboard the packet almost lost their difficult cargo overboard as they spied the elegant gentleman and the beautiful blond lady on the edge of the dock lost in a fervent embrace beneath their very eyes. The French seamen were enchanted and declared the couple their countrymen, on the basis of the gentleman's garb and the lady's evident cooperation. Some of the English hearties protested that while the lady might be French, the gentleman's decisive, no-nonsense manner marked him as one of theirs, and wagers were being laid on the matter before the couple parted.

But the pair were oblivious to all but each other, and when Nicholas drew back from Julia, he said on a shaken breath, "You do love me, I'd swear it. We are companion spirits. Can you not say it, Julia? Can you accept me and say that you will have me?"

Julia rested within his clasp and watched those lips that could say and do so many delicious things to her. And then, as though she wanted to be on record as having voiced every last objection before she embraced happiness as completely as she had embraced him, she said shyly, "Are you absolutely sure, Nicholas? Have you forgotten all the things you've done and said to me?"

She hadn't considered her exact words, or even paid much attention to them. After all these weeks of doubt, she had only wished for the felicity of being asked just once more, to be fully certain of his meaning before she gave her answer. So she was surprised when he drew back from her, a look of bitter wrath crossing over his face.

"So you still do not entirely trust me?" he asked bleakly. "It is because of how I treated you when we first met. You said then that you would never forgive that blow, and now I see it has indeed come back to haunt us. I had feared as much. When we are ninety-odd, Julia, and you grow cross with me, shall you still fling that blow back in my face as I delivered it to yours? Lord," he said shaking his head sadly, "I wish there were some way to even the score so that the thing were as dead and gone as the tangle of lies which begot it. I would wish us to begin our life together with a clean slate. Is there no way that I can erase that insult from your heart and mind?"

A moment before, his angry reaction to her question had caused Julia to fear that her greed for reassurance had ruined her future. But now she saw that his guilt might do the same. And now, suddenly, she saw how easily joy could still be snatched from her grasp. Then she knew that she was done with trusting the outcome of her life to the vagaries of fate, and that if she were to win happiness, she must seize it in her own hands. So she thought quickly even as she continued to lean her head against his shoulder, her two hands limp against his chest.

"Ah no, Nicholas," she whispered at last, "I do not forget it. How can I when you cannot? But I shall not let it come between us. I promise. You will not need to erase it from my mind or my heart, my love."

At her words, his eyes widened and then he gazed searchingly into her uplifted face. What he saw there, the radiant mixture of love and yearning and laughter, and something else, something delightful and roguish in her smile that he could not define, caused him to take in his breath with wonder.

Which was just as well in view of what happened next.

For in a moment the spellbound sailors saw the expensively styled gentleman plummet backward into the murky waters. What they had not seen was the beautiful lady's two white and dovelike hands straighten themselves against the gentleman's broad chest and deliver him a capable push when he was off guard, strong enough to topple him over the brink.

The sailors lowered ropes and grappling hooks immediately to save the gentleman, for no one of them wished to plunge into the bilge-encrusted waters unless they must. Then they noted that though he stayed afloat he seemed to be coughing and spluttering a great deal. A few brave seamen had resigned themselves to plunging into the noisome waters to assist him when they realized that he was not drowning so much as whooping with laughter.

When he had been safely pulled to the dock by ropes, and a servant who was clearly his valet had snatched a blanket from a surprised carriage horse to toss about his drenched shoulders, he continued to stagger with laughter. And then, when the sodden gentleman went up to the beautiful lady and laid his streaming arms about her shoulders and she did not even pull away despite the ruination of her fashionable gown, the English sailors fell to collecting their debts. For it was clear, the French sailors sighed, that no one of their countrywomen would allow such treatment to a frock of such high fashion, and certainly, no one of their men would lack so much savoir faire as to come, dripping and spluttering, to his love. The two were English, they concluded, and in the saying of their own tongue, drunk as a pair of lords.

"Wretch," the baron breathed at last, when he could, gazing into Julia's apprehensive eyes. "But thank you. Now, indeed, we are even. *Now* will you have me?"

"Now," sighed Julia with content, snuggling close into his reeking, streaming clasp, "yes."

October 1815

17 The wind outside the bedroom window was throwing itself against the panes with such force as to cause them to rattle in their casements. Makepiece sniffed. It wasn't just the cold of the October day which made him deliver himself of such an ill-bred sound, although the chill of this autumn was enough to creep into any man's bones. It was instead the thoughts of the increasingly difficult position he found himself in.

He could understand, not condone necessarily, but understand, he thought, for he was a fair-minded man, that a gentleman might not wish to take his valet with him on his honeymoon. So he hadn't said a word on that head when he had been left behind at Greenbriar House after his master had been married last month. But now that the Baron Stafford had returned he had been ordered to remove all of his master's clothes and personal possessions from his own chamber and install them in the Queen Anne bedroom. For his master was, incredibly enough, going to share his bedroom quarters with his new bride!

It wasn't done, Makepiece thought morosely. It was not at all the thing. It would be remarked upon by any visiting gentleman's gentleman. But he continued to pack the remainder of his master's clothes even as he rued his actions. For all in all, the baron was a fair employer and a pleasure to dress, since a valet's efforts could not go unremarked when displayed upon such a fine figure of a man. And then, too, there was the lady Julia's maidservant to consider. Celeste was a level-headed female and it would be difficult to continue an increasingly interesting relationship if he were to leave the baron's employ.

Makepiece had been as full of sighs as a fireside bellows since he had begun his chores, but when he chanced to take a certain object from his master's chest of drawers, he recoiled as though he had uncovered a cobra. So when the baron came into his one-time quarters to find a cape that had not yet been transferred to his new rooms, he saw his valet standing holding an object over a waste basket, an expression of deepest sorrow upon his face.

What ails the fellow now? the baron wondered. He knew his man had been very miffed at having been left behind for the past month. But he refused to explain to his valet that he had been delighted beyond words to discover that a fellow didn't need clothes on his honeymoon, even at a fashionable spa. Or at least not when he was fortunate enough to be wedded to an adored and adoring, increasingly abandoned bride. Still, he had to say something to Makepiece now at any rate, since the fellow looked as though his heart were breaking.

"Whatever have you got there?" the baron asked quickly, snatching up his cape from out of his wardrobe and tossing it over his arm.

"It is, though it is horrible to contemplate, my lord, none other than Monsieur LeMay's exquisite jacket. Though you would not know it now. I have washed it, I have ironed it, I have scented it with herbs, I have done all but beat it upon the rocks," Makepiece said on a rising note of distress, "but it is unsalvageable. It is ruined, my lord. It reeks of the sea and less seemly things. Its fabric is dulled, its shape is forgotten. It is worth nothing now," the valet said with something very much like a muted sob, as he dropped the parcel into the trash.

"Ah no," the baron said quickly as he bent to retrieve the limp bundle. "It is worth a great deal to me, at least. Don't toss it out, Makepiece. Rather, parcel it up well so it doesn't make the place redolent of fish, and label it and store it in the attic somewhere.''

A blast against the windows that set the shutters to shuddering made the baron start and reminded him of the oncoming storm again. Suddenly he was all haste to be gone to rejoin his waiting wife. For they had decided to ride out to greet the storm, and race their horses with the winds until the rains came. But still he delayed a moment more. He stood holding the ruined jacket and thought of the festivities they would have after their wild ride, the warming, the comforting, and then the lying easily snug within their bed while the wind raged without. This stormy October night, he vowed, with a smile playing about his lips, would be the one she would remember long after details of the other had been forgotten.

Makepiece's incredulous stare recalled him to the present and the baron tossed the bundle to his man.

"Yes. Wrap it and tag it," he said merrily, "so that I can always have it as a reminder of a debt paid. With interest." He laughed before he turned and left his wondering servant to do his bidding.

Then he made his way quickly downstairs, for the wind was rising and he had been absent from his bride for a full five minutes, and he could not let her feel neglected. Or even half so lonely as he did now, without her at his side.